THE TURNING SEASON

Ace Books by Sharon Shinn

THE SHAPE OF DESIRE
STILL LIFE WITH SHAPE-SHIFTER
THE TURNING SEASON

TROUBLED WATERS
ROYAL AIRS

MYSTIC AND RIDER
THE THIRTEENTH HOUSE
DARK MOON DEFENDER
READER AND RAELYNX
FORTUNE AND FATE

ARCHANGEL
JOVAH'S ANGEL
THE ALLELUIA FILES
ANGELICA
ANGEL-SEEKER

WRAPT IN CRYSTAL
THE SHAPE-CHANGER'S WIFE
HEART OF GOLD
SUMMERS AT CASTLE AUBURN
JENNA STARBORN
QUATRAIN

Viking / Firebird Books by Sharon Shinn

THE SAFE-KEEPER'S SECRET
THE TRUTH-TELLER'S TALE
THE DREAM-MAKER'S MAGIC
GENERAL WINSTON'S DAUGHTER
GATEWAY

THE TURNING SEASON

SHARON SHINN

ACE BOOKS, NEW YORK

THE BERKLEY PUBLISHING GROUP
Published by the Penguin Group
Penguin Group (USA) LLC
375 Hudson Street, New York, New York 10014

USA • Canada • UK • Ireland • Australia • New Zealand • India • South Africa • China

penguin.com

A Penguin Random House Company

This book is an original publication of The Berkley Publishing Group.

Library of Congress Cataloging-in-Publication Data

Shinn, Sharon.
The turning season / by Sharon Shinn. — First edition.
pages cm. — (A shifting circle novel)
ISBN 978-0-425-26169-9 (hardback)
1. Shapeshifting—Fiction. 2. Fantasy fiction. I. Title.
PS3569.H499T87 2014
813'.54—dc23
2014016673

FIRST EDITION: November 2014

PRINTED IN THE UNITED STATES OF AMERICA

10 9 8 7 6 5 4 3 2 1

Cover illustration © Jonathan Barkat; fur background © Mikhail Klyoshev /
Shutterstock; flower pattern © Iryna Omelchak / Shutterstock.
Cover design by Judith Lagerman.
Interior text design by Laura K. Corless.

For Kay and Sue
Because if shape-shifters really do exist,
I'm certain you're sheltering some at Homeland right now.

CHAPTER ONE

I'm at the supermarket in town, trying to decide between two brands of apple juice, when the first fiery pains go ripping up my back. I panic. I almost drop one of the bottles in my haste to get it back on the shelf, and I simply abandon my half-full cart in the aisle. By the time I push my way past dawdling shoppers, make it to the parking lot, and stumble into my Jeep, the pains have gone from intermittent to continuous, and the visual migraine has kicked in. It's as if something has taken a bite out of my right eye's field of vision, leaving behind a circle of serrated tooth marks. Within five minutes, that circle will uncoil into a straight line of marching *V*s and begin pulsing with gray and orange shadows.

Fuck! I think as I try to start the car, my hands so shaky that I almost don't have the strength to turn the key. *This isn't supposed to happen for at least another week!*

Normally I have about an hour between the first tendrils of pain and the onset of transformation, but the timing is off, so who knows what else might be affected? I'm in broad daylight on the busiest street in Quinville on a Wednesday afternoon. Oh God, if I change here, everyone in the world will see me . . .

I finally get the motor to catch and I screech out of the parking lot and onto Highway 159 as fast as I can, cutting off some poor old woman in a beat-up sedan who's trying to turn left into the grocery store. I'm calculating in my head. Quinville makes a modest clump of civilization along both sides of 159, but within five miles, the road will shake off the urban clutter as it heads back into open Illinois farmland. Say ten minutes to get clear of the worst of the traffic. Another twenty minutes till I reach the County Road W turnoff. If I can make it that far, I can just pull off the road, cut the engine, and wait for disaster to strike. Thirty minutes. Surely my body can hold on that long.

I'm stuck behind three cars at the longest light in town; otherwise, I would have been tempted to run it when it turned red. The back spasms have morphed into a slow, steady thrum, not unbearable, but the migraine is starting to build; I lean my skull against the headrest and let terror and pain fight for dominance. I squint against the sunlight and the flashing visual cues, wishing I had my sunglasses with me. Keeping my left hand on the wheel, I fish in my purse till I find my cell phone. The light changes to green just as I open my list of contacts, so I hurriedly push the first name that comes up.

It happens to be Celeste's, and of course she doesn't answer. "Listen, it's Karadel. I'm heading home, and I'm about to *change*. Don't know how far I'll get. I'm going to need someone to come get me. I'm going to call everybody, so whoever gets there first . . ."

Traffic is slow enough to allow me to call and leave messages with Bonnie and Aurelia as well, but then we clear the last light and cars start moving at the speed limit. I'm too rattled to try to drive and talk at the same time, plus the pulsing lights of the migraine aura are making it hard for me to see the road. I toss the phone onto the passenger's seat, clench both hands on the wheel, and concentrate on driving.

For about three miles outside of Quinville, Highway 159 maintains two lanes in each direction, divided by a sad strip of prairie grass and flowering weeds, but soon enough it will slim down to two lanes separated only by a double yellow line. Every driver's goal is to get ahead of the slowest-moving vehicles before those lanes converge. Theoretically, you can pass cars at a dozen spots in the next thirty miles, but practically speaking, those opportunities are few because the oncoming traffic rarely lets up long enough for you to take the chance.

Like the red Camaro ahead of me and the black Escalade behind me, I'm in the inside lane going as fast as road conditions will permit, just praying that no one swerves into my path or comes to a sudden stop, because I'm in no condition to make defensive-driving maneuvers. I'm barely alert enough to recognize that I'm running out of road. The Camaro guns its motor and zips ahead of a rusted-out old Ford pickup, but I don't react quickly enough, and the truck eases over in front of me at a maddeningly leisurely pace. I brake so hard that the Escalade looms menacingly in my rearview mirror, but nobody hits anybody, and we all continue down the road at a greatly reduced rate of speed.

The near-miss has dumped adrenaline into my veins. Great—now my heart is pounding as well as my head, and my hands feel rubbery on the wheel. I've lost much of my peripheral vision, but darkness hasn't started encroaching on my eyesight yet. How much time left now? Fifteen minutes? Twenty?

Not nearly enough time to get to my house.

I shift my grip, take a deep breath, and stare so fiercely at the road ahead of me that my eyes would start burning if they weren't already hot. Maybe five minutes to the turnoff. I can make it that far. I have to. The pickup has slowed to something like forty miles an hour, but that might be a good thing; I can sort of keep things together at this speed. To my left, an unbroken line of family cars, 18-wheelers, motorcycles, and SUVs whooshes past. The driver of the Escalade is riding impatiently close to my bumper, and I know he'll take the first chance he sees to pass both me and the pickup. But even if the oncoming traffic were to thin down to nothing, leaving a straight and empty stretch of road bordered by cornfields on either side, I wouldn't make the same attempt. I don't think I have the hand-eye coordination. I don't think I have the judgment. I'm not sure I could make it back on the road.

Then suddenly—finally—like the mile marker to heaven, I see the green sign for the cutoff to W. I don't even bother with the turn signal, just peel off from 159 with a faint whine of tires. There's hardly ever any traffic on W, which leads only to a few isolated homesteads like mine and huge tracts of undeveloped land offering a pretty equal mix of grass and trees. Of course, the isolation of the route is a mixed blessing on most days. The road is well behind on necessary maintenance, and the asphalt is an obstacle course of potholes, cracks, and failed repairs. I've increased my speed as much as I can without running the risk of hurtling off the road, but every bump and fissure jars me against the seat belt and slams my head nauseatingly against my spine.

Nausea—that's usually the last symptom. Five minutes or less by now. The September day is chilly, maybe fifty degrees, but I hit the controls so the four automatic windows roll all the way down. The only thing worse than transforming in a public place in the middle of the day would be transforming in a locked car with all the windows up. No way to get out. I try not to think about what will happen if I change into something too big to crawl out the window. That hasn't happened for a while now—years, really. Even a deer, even a wolf, would be able to squeeze through a car's rolled-down window, wouldn't it? I've never been a bear or a giraffe—a moose only a couple of times—and the elephant—well, that's never happened again—

My stomach clenches and I slap my hand across my mouth. I don't actually throw up, but I can feel the bile at the back of my throat. *Almost time, almost time.* I'd love to get another mile down the road, but the trade-off isn't worth it. The blackness has started to build up at the corner of my vision, little lights are dancing through the pulsating *V*s of the visual migraine, and I'm in so much physical pain that it's hard to tell what's slamming up from my backbone and what's jackhammering down from my skull. *Stop gambling,* I tell myself, and wrench the Jeep to the shoulder. It's really just a little strip of crumbling asphalt that drops into a low ditch of prickly weeds, but even a semi ought to be able to get past my vehicle without smashing it to pieces.

I leave everything in the front seat—my phone, my purse, my clothes—and exit through the passenger-side door. Immediately, I feel better. No matter what happens next, at least I won't be trapped. At least I'll be able to go crashing off into the undergrowth and look for some kind of cover until one of my friends comes to find me.

I'm crouching barefoot on the side of the road, but the pain drives me all the way to my knees. I can feel the dry knife-edges of the weed leaves slicing at my bare toes and ankles; I can feel the broken stone of the asphalt digging into my calves. But I scarcely notice. The migraine has enveloped my whole body. It is cracking my skull in two, it is pummeling my stomach, and I am bent over so far that my nose rests between my knees. If I move a fraction of an inch in any direction, everything on my inside will spill out, in vomit, in blood, in viscous leaking fluids of mucus, saliva, and brains . . .

One more powerful compression, as if a giant hand is squashing me from above with such force that I grunt involuntarily. And then it's all over.

The pressure, the pain, the nausea. Gone, evaporated. I feel light, almost weightless. I feel lithe and strong and absolutely *right*. My body has once again survived a violent passage and rebirth and delivered me to a shape that calls to it as seductively as its own.

For a moment, I just revel in the bliss of well-being, then I take a moment to determine what I am. I extend my left arm, to find it covered with fluffy marmalade fur; I've unsheathed five impressively sharp claws, and a slinky tail wraps around from behind. A cat then—housecat, probably. I don't feel large enough to be one of the bigger wild felines. I bunch myself up against the right front tire, but my arched back doesn't even clear the wheel well.

Good. A cat is the best I can hope for. Mobile, self-sufficient, commonplace. I could fend for myself for weeks if I had to, make my way to my property under my own power, and never raise the slightest bit of curiosity from any passersby I might encounter.

I wonder if this transformation is purely random or if my serums are actually taking effect. I have been trying—with limited success—to guide my body in the choices it makes, to channel it into more socially acceptable creatures when the imperative to change takes it over. I have, in fact, been injecting a specialized concoction for the past few weeks, hoping to become this very animal. Perhaps this is proof that I've been successful—to a point. Perhaps the early transformation came about because of that very concoction. Perhaps I have staved off one side effect only to incur another.

Worries for another day.

As always, once I enter animal state, I find it difficult to focus on the everyday, ordinary concerns that usually preoccupy my mind. I'm still *me*, I have my own memories and my same powers of reasoning, but all the familiar obsessions seem distant and unimportant. New imperatives claim my attention—usually, depending on the shape I've taken, revolving around finding food and finding safety. I'm easily distracted by scents, sounds, movements on the periphery. I'm much more focused on the challenges of the immediate present.

Which, I have to confess, is sometimes a relief, considering how much my human brain usually frets over the unsolvable troubles of the future. Sometimes descending into the wild is like a brief vacation from my chaotic and all-too-demanding existence.

But right now I can't afford to give in to the cat's impulse to go stalking through the high grass toward the promising rustle of bird wings. I can't go chasing after butterflies and bees. I'm still far from home, and someone should be on the way to get me. I need to be here and relatively alert whenever that someone arrives.

I face the car, bunch my muscles, and make a smooth leap through the open window on the passenger's side. I'd forgotten about the purse and phone and clothes I'd left on the seat, so I skid through them in a sloppy landing, then hop over the gear shift to the driver's side. The afternoon sunlight has painted a golden square on the fabric, and both the warmth and the color are inviting. I pat at the cloth with my left paw, find it suitable, then drop down into a contented curl, wrapping my tail around my head. A nap is the best way to pass the hours, stay out of trouble, and conserve my strength, all at the same time. I feel my narrow jaws open in a gigantic yawn, then I resettle my face against my paws. I am instantly in a light, untroubled sleep from which I know I can wake at a moment's notice.

Cats really do have the best lives. If I could choose, this is the shape I would always take.

No. If I could choose, I would always stay human.

I'm not paying close attention, but I think it's about a half hour before I hear the sound of a car that doesn't just zoom past, but actually slows down then rumbles to a stop as it pulls over right in front of me on the shoulder. I instantly come awake and scramble up, setting my paws on the top of the steering wheel so I can peer out the windshield. Shapes and colors are weird, distorted, so I have to concentrate to pull out human memories to compare against the images I'm seeing now. But I recognize the battered old station wagon even before the door swings open and the driver steps out.

Bonnie. My luck is in. By far the most reliable of my friends, she has not only shown up to rescue me, she has no doubt phoned everyone else in our circle to let them know their services aren't required—hell, she probably picked up groceries, paid my electricity bill, and arranged to have Highway W resurfaced while she was at it.

She doesn't spot me right at first, so as soon as she slams her door, she stands beside the car for a moment, hands on her hips, and looks around, as if wondering where I've gotten to. She's probably six feet tall, 140 pounds if she's just finished a big meal, angular, knobby, impatient, brilliant, and totally unaffected by anyone else's opinion. Her short, curly black hair is showing a few singular strands of gray, one of the few clues to the fact that she's just over sixty. Her eyes are dark brown and even when she's laughing, her expression is fierce. If she were a shape-shifter, which she's not, she'd be a bird of prey, I've always thought. Hawk. Falcon. Eagle. Something you wouldn't mess with. Something that rarely, if ever, failed.

I drop to all fours, gather my muscles, and leap through the open window to the street. The motion catches her attention and she sees me. Relief crosses her spare features as I trot over.

"Karadel. Thank heavens," she says, bending down to pick me up. In human shape, I don't often seek out casual physical contact, but this particular body craves affection. I like how she cradles me against her thin chest; I respond with a low purr of contentment. She takes a moment to pet my head and scratch my chin, but Bonnie's not one for lingering on niceties, especially when there's work to be done.

"Let's get you home," she says, opening her car door.

I prepare to jump inside, but my claws catch on Bonnie's arms to halt my forward motion when I realize there's somebody in the passenger's seat. Alonzo looks over with his usual deadly serious expression.

"Hey, Karadel," he says.

I squirm in Bonnie's grip, trying to get a look at her face, and attempt to express my opinion. *What's going on?* It comes out, of course, as a musical burble. I could as easily be asking for dinner.

"I know, I know, he's fourteen years old," she says. She has known shape-shifters for most of her life and never seems ill at ease conversing with them in animal form. "But you know he knows how to drive. He can go on first in the Jeep and we'll come along behind him. If he has any trouble, well, we'll just pull over and leave the Jeep on the side of the road."

Of course I know Alonzo can drive. I taught him myself—in my Jeep, as a matter of fact—but we stayed mostly on my property and were never this close to a well-traveled road. It's true I've never seen cops on W, but they're constantly patrolling 159, and that's entirely too close. Bad enough that Alonzo's too young to get a license; he's also African-American, and most of the cops in this district are white.

When I try to get this point across to Bonnie, she just shrugs. "She's worried that you can't handle it," she says to Alonzo.

He nods. "I'll be careful. Keys in the car?"

"That would be my guess."

He climbs out of the station wagon, unfolding his lanky body with care. He's taller and skinnier than Bonnie, growing taller and skinnier every day, though I know she and Aurelia feed him enough calories to turn him into a linebacker. But it's not just adolescent awkwardness that makes him move so stiffly. He was an abused child, a shape-shifter whose father feared and hated him, and I'm not sure we'll ever know the extent of the damage done to him. Bonnie says his torso and limbs carry dozens of scars, though she hasn't seen a physical reason for the precise way he moves and holds his body. But I've never seen him loosen up, even for a minute. Never seen him dance with abandon or run with joy. I don't know if he can.

I give up trying to argue and make myself comfortable on the seat still warm from Alonzo's body. It's a matter of moments before Alonzo starts the Jeep and edges it past the station wagon and Bonnie takes off after him. In this shape, I can't accurately judge speed or distance if I'm not moving under my own power, but it seems to me that we're traveling pretty sedately. If we don't, in fact, encounter any police, we are home free, because Alonzo is the most careful driver on the planet.

Bonnie talks for the duration of the trip. "I don't know how long you won't be human, but I thought I'd leave Alonzo with you for the next few days," she says. "He can do the chores and feed the animals and call me if you need anything." She glances over at me. "We've taken him out of school for the semester—thought we'd try homeschooling for a year and see if that goes any better," she adds. "He does have a couple of friends, and they've been coming over in the evenings but the classes just weren't—they weren't—I don't think Quinville Middle School is the right place for him."

Bonnie and Aurelia have been taking care of Alonzo for the past two years, ever since Ryan rescued him and brought him to us. They're the perfect foster parents. Bonnie's a retired teacher and Aurelia's a lawyer, and they've fostered kids off and on for the past ten years, so they both know the system. Oh, it might seem like a black kid from an urban neighborhood wouldn't find the best home with two whiter-than-white lesbians in a rural setting, but I can say this for certain: When he came into our lives, he wouldn't speak. He was afraid to touch anything. He only ate when no one else was looking. He slept on the floor for the first three months, seeming to believe that climbing into the bed made up in the room set aside for him would result in punishments too dire to describe. And now he eats and sleeps like a normal kid, and he answers direct questions, and once in a while he ducks his head and smiles.

And when he changes shapes into a deer or a badger or a coyote, no one chains him to a pole in the basement and beats him on the head with a metal pipe.

So, yeah. I think he's where he belongs.

"I left a message with Ryan and actually spoke to Celeste before I found you," Bonnie goes on. "Celeste says she can come out over the weekend, so maybe I'll come get Alonzo then and she can take over." She glances at me again. "Am I wrong, or is this not your usual time to shift?"

Mrrrr, I answer.

"Right. Well. You can tell me later," she says. "But I'm under the impression that your cycles have been a little out of whack lately. And if that's the case, you might start thinking about more permanent solutions to your situation."

Right, I want to say in sarcastic echo. If I had the faintest idea how to come up with a permanent solution to "my situation," I'd have implemented it long before now.

But I know she's not referring to my random and unpredictable shifts into alternate shapes. She merely means that someone who's caring for close to thirty animals on a remote property needs to display a certain level of responsibility—needs to make sure that if she's not going to be available to put out food and clean out cages every single day, someone else will be around to do the necessary chores.

There's a lot of irony here. I've always been the most responsible person I know. I have *never* shirked a task. I have *never* let my own dreams and desires interfere with the duties I knew I had to assume. I've never even allowed myself to entertain too many dreams and desires. Mine will be a short life, but a rich one, built around a guiding imperative: to care for a distinct group of wild and exotic creatures who have no one to defend them but me.

It is only on days like this, in shapes like this one, when the buried feral instincts briefly come to the fore, that the traitorous thoughts even have the power to rise to the surface of my mind.

What if? I think on days like this. *What if I could just run away?*

It's still bright afternoon when we arrive at my property. Alonzo, with utmost care, turns from W onto the rutted gravel of my drive. The Jeep doesn't even jounce along the track as it usually does under my impatient heel. All of us climb out, and Bonnie and Alonzo turn toward the barns and cages. There's not much I can do to help them, so I just head for the porch of the rambling old farmhouse and hop up on the wooden bench set under the overhang. I sit there, tail curled around my front feet, and take a moment to glance over the property.

From this vantage point, I can only see part of the compound, which consists of about ten buildings clustered together in a relatively cleared and cultivated area, and another fifty acres of land that has been left entirely wild. The house, the barns, the toolshed, and a couple of trailers—housing for visiting shape-shifters—were already here when I arrived eight years ago. At the time, the place was a veterinary office run by a woman named Janet Kassebaum, who specialized in shape-shifters. I inherited her practice when she left. In the past five years, I've made some changes: adding corrals, fencing in dog runs, turning one of the barns into a sort of animal dorm. I needed to have places to keep all the creatures I was collecting, the injured birds, the lame dogs, the tortured cats. Sometimes I heal them and let them go. When they're too badly hurt, I heal them and give them homes for life.

It takes Bonnie and Alonzo about an hour to feed and water the animals, and by then it's coming on toward sunset. Bonnie ushers Alonzo into the house to make sure I have human food supplies on hand as well, before she pushes back out through the door to tell me good-bye.

"He says he'll be fine out here on his own for a couple of days, but I'll call in the morning, of course, to make sure everything's all right," she tells me. "As soon as you're human again, give me a call, and we can talk over a few things."

I don't answer, of course, and she sighs. "Known shape-shifters for more than forty years and I still forget that they can't *talk* to me," she says. She comes close enough to scratch the top of my head with her short, blunt fingernails. "Catch you later." Five minutes later, she's gone, her car lights sending a brief searching arc of illumination across the barns and trailers and clumps of grass as she makes a U-turn and drives away.

I hear Alonzo rummaging in the kitchen, then I catch the beep of the microwave. I wonder what he's found in the freezer that appeals to him. I'm not a particularly inventive cook, but I like to make batches of chili and stew and soup and freeze them against the erratic onslaught of company. There are weeks at a time when I'm the only human for five miles. Then there are weeks when I have five or six other people staying on the property. I like to be prepared to feed them, at least till they've had a chance to lay in their own groceries.

The door creaks and Alonzo steps outside to join me on the bench. It's chilly, but that never bothers Alonzo; he likes being outdoors in all kinds of weather. He's balancing two plates and has stuck a can of soda under his left arm. One plate holds a steaming pile of chili con queso so thick it doesn't need a bowl. The other features a small mound of canned tuna and a slowly melting scoop of vanilla ice cream.

The chili's for Alonzo. The tuna and ice cream are for me. I don't care much for fish when I'm in human form, but this shape loves it—and Alonzo, being Alonzo, remembered that.

Ice cream I love in about ninety out of a hundred of my incarnations.

The thoughtfulness makes me wish I could put my arms around Alonzo and give him a big hug, but instead I rise to my feet and prance around on the bench to show how excited I am about the prospect of a meal. He sits down, placing my plate on the bench where I can easily reach it and resting his own on his knees, then pops the top of his soda. We settle in to eat in companionable and satisfied silence. He must be as hungry as I am, because we're done in about ten minutes, and—being Alonzo—he straightaway takes the dishes in to wash them.

When he comes back outside, he's already got his iPod in his hand and his earbuds in place; unlike Bonnie, he's not going to attempt to make conversation. But he sits next to me again, which for Alonzo is a striking overture of friendship, and he gives my head a cursory pat. I feel my mouth stretch in a huge feline yawn, exposing all my wickedly sharp teeth, and I lick the last trace of ice cream from my whiskers. I'm tired again, and I curl up in a ball beside Alonzo, close enough so my back rests against his thigh. He lays a gentle hand along my rib cage and I hear him laugh out loud when I begin to purr.

I think, for this short period of time, anyway, Alonzo is actually happy. All in all, the day that started so disastrously has brought with it its own extraordinary gifts. Not at all what I expected.

CHAPTER TWO

The next two days pass harmoniously enough, with Alonzo taking Bonnie's phone calls every morning and evening, spending a couple of hours a day caring for the animals, and the rest of the time playing video games or reading. He's not a natural reader, but Bonnie has insisted he finish a book a month and she's told me he's found a few authors that he actually admits to liking. Most of them appear to be horror and science fiction writers, both of which she regards with deep suspicion, but she'd never renege now. My guess is that he'd rather watch television or surf the Internet, but I get crappy reception out here and my selection of DVDs has never held much interest for him in the past. But he makes do. God knows he wouldn't complain. And he still seems—if not actually happy—content. Which for Alonzo might be the best that it gets.

There's obviously not much for me to do, but I spend part of each day prowling through the various animal shelters, making sure all is well. None of the avian species like it when I pace past their cages;

the songbirds flutter and chirrup, and the birds of prey bridle and fidget. The hawk with the broken wing watches me with unnerving intensity, and I'm just as glad there's a wire crate between us. I've never actually *seen* a hawk kill or carry off a cat, but I've been assured it's possible, and this particular one looks like he's ready to make the attempt, broken wing and all.

None of the birds react this strongly when the barn cats stalk through the aviary, eyeing them with longing and calculation. Maybe the birds know the cages keep them safe, but I really don't think that's it. I think they can tell there's something different about me—something wrong—I'm a danger that they can't identify, so they can't assess it. I'm not quite cat and I'm not quite human. Not quite prey meat, not quite rival. Something to fear and revile.

It's even worse in the kennels, where the dogs start barking as soon as I nose through the door. In fact, the three beagle puppies, eight weeks old by now, will not shut up the whole time I'm in the barn. Two of them whine and paw at the gate that holds them in their little enclosure; the third usually stands with his feet on the top of the fencing and barks without ceasing. The short, sharp, indignant sounds are designed to express outrage, raise the alarm, and let me know in no uncertain terms that he is *not* afraid of me. My plan is to give all three of them away, and soon, but I wouldn't mind if this little guy found a permanent home with me. He's got tons of personality and boundless energy, and he's wriggled his way into my heart.

The only two dogs that never raise a ruckus while I'm visiting the kennels are Scottie, my ancient setter, and Daniel, who's currently a Doberman but is human about half the time. Daniel spends most of his days lying on his side on a blanket in one of the unlocked enclosures, and he barely looks up whenever I pass. He's not very social in either of his forms and he's happiest when everyone leaves him alone. Scottie usually greets me with a faint whuff and comes over to inspect me. He touches my small nose with his big wet one, wagging his tail just enough to show he's friendly. He was freaked out the first few times he encountered me in an alternate state, but over the past eight years, he's gotten used to my transformations. Now it seems as if he recognizes me no matter what shape I've taken.

I can't express how comforting I find that to be.

Most of the rest of the animals—the rabbits, the raccoon, even the turtle—don't seem to notice or care when I stroll by. Either they're less sensitive or more miserable; sometimes it's hard to guess. In any case, they all appear to be in good shape, and I assume they will be fine under Alonzo's careful attention.

I never know how much time I'll spend in animal shape, but it's usually not more than four or five days. So surely it won't be long before I am myself again, before we can all go back to normal.

If I've remembered my calendar correctly, it's Saturday morning when Celeste arrives, taking the turn onto the gravel driveway way too fast and coming to a halt with a noisy jerk. When she climbs out of the SUV, she's loaded down with burdens—a laptop carrier, a suitcase, and a couple of bags of groceries. She looks like she's run away from home or has arrived at the kind of summer camp where you need to feed yourself. At any rate, it's clear she's poised to stay for a while.

Alonzo has just let the dogs into their fenced corral, but the minute he locks the gate, he ambles over to greet her. He's actually smiling; if he was capable of it, he'd be beaming. But his voice is reserved, even a little cool, when he says, "Hey, Celeste."

"Zo! My man!" she exclaims, slinging her laptop bag farther back over her shoulder so she can free one arm to hug him. "So you drew the short straw, huh? You were the one who had to come babysit Karadel and all her critters."

"I don't mind. I like it here."

She looks around comprehensively, taking in the buildings (some of them a little weatherworn, I admit), the tangled acreage (prairie grass and a few scrubby trees), and the general air of isolation and solitude. She doesn't have to say the words aloud to make it plain this is the last place she'd want to be stuck for any length of time.

If ever someone was made for a sophisticated urban environment, it's Celeste. She's got a thin model's body, and she wears the most outrageous ensembles with the negligent ease of someone who knows she looks fabulous no matter what she has on. She doesn't step out of the house without full makeup, brightly polished nails, and the perfect belt for her ensemble.

Plus, she's gorgeous. Her astonishingly diverse racial heritage has bequeathed her an exquisite face—high-sloped cheekbones, tilted black eyes, full lips, and a smattering of freckles across her café au lait skin. Her dark hair has a tighter curl than Bonnie's and she wears it longer, so when it's not pulled back in a ponytail it makes a Medusa-like swirl of shadow around her face. The physical grace notes were gifts from a broad international ancestry. Although some of her antecedents are a little murky, she knows that she has at least one forebear who was Japanese, one who was Nigerian, one who was Scots-Irish, and one who was Sioux.

And one who was a shape-shifter. Can't forget that.

She's my best friend, but sometimes when I'm around her I feel gauche and dull and excruciatingly ordinary. My mother used to read me a bedtime story about Country Mouse and City Mouse, and I have long ago repeated it to Celeste. She's the pampered, pretty city girl; I'm the dogged, homespun country girl. It doesn't matter that, in the book, Country Mouse learns that there's no point in envying someone else's lifestyle. Everyone wants to be City Mouse. Everyone wants to be Celeste.

She finishes her inspection of the property and heaves an exaggerated sigh. "Well, it could be worse, I suppose," she says. "It could be *snowing*."

Alonzo takes the grocery bags and the suitcase and leads Celeste inside. She thoughtfully holds the door open so I can trot in behind them. The front door leads directly into the kitchen, a big warm room paneled in honey wood and hung with copper pans and dried herbs. Janet was responsible for the original decorating, but I've added a few touches of my own. More flowerpots in the windows, filled with cheery blooms. New curtains with motifs of fruit and blossoms. A new set of ceramic dishes in bright reds and deep ochres. In human form, I crave color; even in the animal shapes that don't register hue, I like to look at the varying shapes and textures. They remind the person inside that she will be back one day to take possession of these objects again.

"I didn't know what kinds of scraps you'd been subsisting on since you came out here, so I brought a bunch of goodies," Celeste tells Alonzo as she begins pulling groceries out of the bag. She knows perfectly well about the two freezers full of Tupperware containers, but it turns out she hasn't exactly been shopping for staples. So what we have here are chocolate donuts, gooey butter cake, chocolate-covered raisins, five different kinds of chips, three kinds of cheese dip, and a bottle of premixed margaritas.

"You can't have any of the booze," she tells him. "But the rest of it's all yours if you want it. Oh! And I have a cooler in the car. I picked up some barbecue on the edge of town. We can have that for dinner."

"What kind of barbecue?" he says. Testing her.

She swats him on the head. Love tap. "Chicken for me, pork for you. Did you think I'd *forget*?"

He ducks his head and doesn't answer that. But he's smiling. "I'll go get it. Anything else in the car?"

"Uh—*yeah*. What do *you* think?"

"Movies?"

"About twelve of them! I didn't know what you'd seen so I checked out, like, half the new releases."

"Cool," he says. "I haven't seen hardly anything."

I hear Bonnie's voice in my head. *He'll sit and watch cable all day, movie after movie, but he doesn't like to go to the theater. At first I thought he just didn't want to go with* us, *and then I thought maybe his friends don't like movies. But then I figured it out. It's dark. He feels trapped. It triggers all his irrational fears. So we let him rent whatever he wants.*

"I haven't seen anything, either," she says. "Work work work. That's all I do. This is like a vacation." She glances expressively around the kitchen. "Well, the kind of vacation where you go to a dude ranch for the summer and you have to clean out the horse stalls and bale hay or whatever. *That* kind of vacation. Still. It will make a change."

Celeste is a freelance writer and editor with a couple of big clients she can work for remotely. She's said more than once she doesn't know how shape-shifters ever held down jobs before the advent of the Internet, because being a contract employee who works from home means never having to come face-to-face with your boss or your customers. Of course, her own particular brand of transformation is the best—she can change at will, and she's always the same animal, a slim bobcat with a golden pelt and unnervingly huge eyes. It would hardly be like having a disability at all to be able to control it so completely. It would almost seem like being normal.

"I fed the dogs this morning, but there's a lot more to do," Alonzo tells her. "But I can handle it. You don't have to help."

She gives him an incredulous look. "*I* am the adult here! *You* are the child! *You* are the one who is helping *me*!"

This actually makes him laugh. "Yeah. You keep telling yourself that," he says and slouches out the door.

Celeste is Alonzo's favorite person in the world. I'm even more grateful on his behalf than my own that she had the time to come out here this weekend.

The two of them largely ignore me for the rest of the day as they do grinding physical labor around the property. Despite her princess appearance, Celeste is a hard worker; give her a task, no matter how distasteful, and she'll get it done. Now that there are two of them, they can finish the chores that require four hands, spend a little more quality time with the dogs, and make sure everything is as tidy as a backwoods zoo can be.

Celeste also takes a couple of hours to listen to my voice mail and call back the four or five pet owners who've phoned to make appointments for their animals. I don't have that much retail business anymore—once Janet left, I tried to gently encourage the majority of her clients to switch to one of the vets in town, "So much closer to you in case there's an emergency." But there are always people who are too stubborn to make a change—or who develop unreasonable animosities toward certain medical professionals—or who come to the unshakable conclusion that you *need* their attention, their money, their business, that you are living out here all by yourself and you must surely be lonely, broke, and desperate. Those are the clients who still come to me, and they've long ago learned to adjust to my erratic schedule, though they don't have a clue why I am sometimes available and sometimes not.

"Hi, yes, this is Celeste Saint-Simon, I'm calling on behalf of Dr. Baylor, you left a message? She's not available right now, but her calendar will open up by next Wednesday if you'd like to make an appointment."

So many lies in those simple sentences. First of all, I'm not *Dr.* Baylor. My wildly unpredictable shape-changing patterns made it impossible for me to attend school beyond eighth grade, so I studied with my father and on my own, and I got my GED before I was seventeen. I've taken a few online university courses, but naturally I wasn't able to attend college or vet school; everything I know about animal medicine I learned from Janet before she retired.

Well, before she died—though I allow people to think she's still alive. Over the years, I've paid the fees to renew both Janet's vet license and the clinic's facility license so I can continue to buy medical supplies and write prescriptions in her name. I've even attended the North American Veterinary Conference as Janet Kassebaum so I could rack up continuing education credits. My clients don't know this, of course; I let them believe I've acquired my degree and passed my boards. It's just been easier to let them think I'm qualified for the position I've gradually assumed.

And, really, I think I know as much about animals as any vet in Quinville. Hell, I've *been* half of those animals at one time or another, which I think gives me peculiar insights into what might be wrong and how it feels. I can't always fix the animals, but I've never failed to make a diagnosis. That's the *real* reason some of my customers won't go anywhere else.

The other lie in Celeste's statement isn't so much a falsehood as a guess. She *thinks* I'll be back to human state by Monday or Tuesday, but she doesn't know for sure. And lately I wouldn't want to be placing any bets on what my body will do next. But I appreciate Celeste's efforts all the same.

By sundown, she and Alonzo both look tired but a little pleased with themselves, having accomplished everything they set out to do for the day. He flips through her DVD selections, now and then grunting in satisfaction, while she heats up the take-out barbecue, tosses a salad, and opens three bags of chips.

"I know you don't want to eat the salad, but that's the price you pay for all the rest of this great stuff, so no complaining," she tells him when he eyes his plate with disfavor. I think it is a measure of how far Alonzo's come that he would, even with just an expression, indicate he might not be happy about a food option.

"If I eat the salad, how many donuts can I have?"

"Three."

"All right."

She hasn't forgotten me, either; I have my own plate of barbecue, potato salad, and chipotle cheese dip. They make several trips between the kitchen and the living room, where tray tables are set up in front of the overstuffed sofa and the DVD player has already been cued up, and finally all of our food has been transferred to the viewing area.

"This is the life," Celeste says, sinking back against the cushion with a tortilla chip in one hand and a margarita in the other. "Hit play." She takes a sip and sighs with satisfaction. "Here we go."

Over the next forty-eight hours, Celeste and Alonzo watch about ten movies and eat about a hundred pounds of food. Okay, I'm exaggerating, but she *does* drive into town Sunday evening to load up on more junk, and comes back with three pizzas and a bucket of fried chicken. I don't know why she isn't fat. Well, certainly this weekend she's been working off the calories, but I think she eats like this all the time, and I don't think she hits the gym more than once or twice a week. It's a mystery.

Alonzo, of course, could stand to gain a little weight, so I don't think two days of abysmally bad nutrition will hurt him. Though I also don't think the few apples and salads Celeste requires him to eat will really negate the fat, salt, cholesterol, and *crap* he's put in his body under her supervision.

Monday afternoon I wake up from a catnap to find myself human, lying on my side on a tufted rug on the living room floor. I'm naked. I'm also cold and a little stiff, but mostly I'm really, *really* happy to be back in my own body. I jump up, grab a decorative blanket to wrap around myself in case I run into Alonzo, and hurry to the kitchen to grab a bagel, because transformation always leaves me ravenous. Then I head to my bedroom, which takes up about a third of the second story. I've made the big space more manageable by dividing it into zones. A smallish section is a sitting area composed of two chairs and a small table. A larger section holds the bed, an armoire, and a couple of dressers. There are so many windows that the room is filled with light if the sun is anywhere to be seen, and the view is open and calming—acres of uncultivated land dotted with trees and waving with tall prairie grasses.

Used to be the room Janet shared with Cooper, her boyfriend. After they died, it was a year before I could bring myself to move into it. But it's such a comfortable, welcoming place that I couldn't let it go to waste. In this room, I never feel trapped or suffocated. I don't feel like my options have narrowed down so much that there's only one place in the world I can live and be safe. Or, I still feel that way, but I don't mind so much.

My feline alter ego was a pretty finicky creature, but I still feel a need to rinse off the residue of my last incarnation, so I take a shower and wash my hair, reveling in the feel of hot water on my bare skin. Once I step out of the shower into the steaming bathroom, I apply extra moisturizer, scented body cream, just a few touches of makeup. Human luxuries. I don't bother trying to style my shoulder-length hair, which is a dense, heavy brown that takes three hours to dry on its own; I just pull it back into a ponytail. A red sweater, black jeans, tennis shoes, and I am once again my familiar human self.

I hunt down Celeste and Alonzo and find them playing a game of horse at the battered old basketball hoop. It's stuck in the ground in front of what used to be a patio and is now a broken and crumbled slab of concrete; clumps of grass and weeds have pushed up between the cracks, and they cause the ball to take odd hops when it bounces against them.

At first, neither one sees me, and I watch them take a few shots. From what I can tell, both players are stuck at *O*, and it's not because either is politely holding back so the other person won't feel bad about missing a bucket. Even when she's facing off against a teenager, Celeste has a competitive streak, and Alonzo can't bring himself to deliberately miss a shot. He's a decent basketball player, and one of the few group activities he'll participate in is a pickup game in his neighborhood. He's good enough that the other players always welcome him—good enough that I think he'd get better with a little coaching. But Bonnie says he won't try out for the school team. Too much pressure, maybe. Too much time naked in the locker room, where other kids might see his scars.

Alonzo sinks a basket from the top of the key—well, the back edge of the concrete—and Celeste misses the same shot. "Shit," she says. "*H-O-R* for me."

"Go, Alonzo!" I call, and they both look my way. Alonzo lifts a hand in a casual wave, while Celeste pushes back some stray hair and gives me a quick appraisal.

"Well, look what the cat dragged in—literally," she says, and then laughs.

"Gee, thanks. Just the sort of positive reinforcement I need," I reply.

"I think you look pretty good," Alonzo says.

By this time I've crossed the patio and I'm close enough to give him a hug, which he endures more than enjoys. "Thank *you*, more sincerely," I say. "You've been a lifesaver these past few days! I *really* appreciate it."

Celeste dribbles the ball a couple of times, then bounces it over to Alonzo, who catches it one-handed. "Hey, I've been mucking around in dirt and dog poop for the past three days, too."

"Yes, but you're not as nice about it."

She grins. "This *is* me being nice."

"So did I miss anything important?"

"Daniel changed and left Sunday night," Alonzo says. "One of the puppies got out, but we found him after a couple of hours."

"You have two customers coming out Wednesday afternoon, one on Thursday morning," Celeste adds. "I wrote everything down in your appointment book. Oh, and I put all the bills in a stack on your desk. I would have paid them but I couldn't find your checkbook."

"Yeah, plus I couldn't tell you how much money I have in my bank account anyway, so just as well," I say. "Okay, great. Thanks again. Are you guys gonna stay for dinner?"

"I will," Celeste says. "But Bonnie called this morning and says she wants to come back for Alonzo tonight. She misses him."

Alonzo drops his head and concentrates on bouncing the ball between his feet, but I think he's smiling.

"I'll call her. Maybe she can stay for dinner, too, before she takes him back." I give Celeste a stern look. "A *healthy* dinner, for a change."

"What?" she says. "Don't we look healthy?"

I roll my eyes. "I'm gonna go check on the animals. See you back at the house."

I head toward the barns. Behind me I hear the satisfying sound of the ball rattling through the hoop. Alonzo has scored again.

I'm halfway across the open area between the patio and the kennels when Scottie bounds up to me, his whole body quivering with excitement. "Hey, boy," I say, dropping to my knees to wrap my arms around his neck and let him lick my face. "Did you miss me? Here I am. Yeah, boy. Good to see you, too."

He accompanies me on my rounds, where I cause much less excitement in my human state. The hawk with the broken wing has made steady progress; I might be releasing him within the week. The injured raccoon is gnawing at the cage and looks determined enough to eat his way through it. Fine, he can go, then. I put on a padded vest and heavy gloves, carry him out of the barn and to the edge of the property, and let him go. He takes a few steps into the thick grass, pauses to look back at me, and then runs off as fast as his little feet will take him.

Be careful, I want to call after him. *Stay out of trouble. Come back if you need anything.* But I don't, even though no one is listening.

It's close to five before I'm back in the house and remember I'm supposed to call Bonnie. I cradle the phone between my ear and my shoulder as I move through the kitchen, checking supplies, pulling out ingredients. Bonnie would love to come for dinner, but Aurelia is working late. "Anything I can bring?" she asks.

"Looks like I'm out of milk. Oh, and some fresh tomatoes would be good. You would not believe the *junk* Celeste has been feeding Alonzo."

"As long as he's eating, I don't mind."

"You'd mind if you saw the menu."

My own meal is much healthier—chicken and rice, a salad, fruit, rolls, raspberry sorbet, though I know Alonzo will have another donut for dessert instead. I find myself humming as I mix ingredients and slice strawberries and set the table. The initial disorientation I always feel upon changing states has evaporated, and I feel good. I feel healthy. I have friends around me and meaningful work ahead of me.

At times like this I'm able to convince myself that my life is just like everyone else's.

A s expected, the meal is convivial. Bonnie never drinks if she's going to get behind a wheel in the next twelve hours, but Celeste and I each have margaritas, and we're all in pretty mellow moods. Well, for Bonnie, *mellow* means leaning against the chairback instead of sitting bolt upright, and smiling instead of frowning when someone uses a four-letter word.

Over dessert—which, for Celeste, consists of sorbet sprinkled with the crumpled bits of half a chocolate donut—Celeste points her spoon in Bonnie's direction. "Here's something I always forget to ask you. You're like this legendary 'friend to shape-shifters,' but how did that happen? There aren't that many humans who just suddenly learn about us and want to help us out."

Bonnie's eyes rest on Alonzo as she clearly tries to figure out how much detail to give. "My first girlfriend was a shape-shifter," she says. "Met her in high school." Her spare features soften as she smiles at a memory. "Beautiful girl. Wilder than *you*." She nods in Celeste's direction.

"How'd you find out she was a shape-shifter?" I ask.

"And was it before or after you were dating?" Celeste adds.

Again, Bonnie's gaze is on Alonzo. I think this would be a much more revealing conversation if he wasn't at the table. He appears to be oblivious as he focuses on a chocolate donut and the last of the vanilla ice cream, but my guess is he's as curious as anyone else.

"We were in a chemistry class together our junior year. We were doing some experiment—I can't even remember what—mixing together a couple of compounds that created this noxious gas. Our teacher insisted it was harmless," she says in an aside, her stern face still show-ing disapproval, "but a couple of people started coughing and one of the boys opened the windows. Derinda was coughing harder than anyone and all of a sudden she jumped out of her chair and said she was going to throw up. Ran out of the room."

Bonnie lays her spoon aside. "After a few moments, I asked the teacher if I could see if she was all right, but he was so busy trying to wave the fumes out the window that he didn't answer, so I just went after her. Found her in the girls' bathroom, crouching in one of the stalls. She kept saying, 'Don't come in here, don't come in here,' but she sounded really scared. I asked if she wanted me to get the nurse and she said no, and then she started crying. And then she said, 'Don't let anyone else come in.' Of course—school bathroom—there was no lock on the outside door, but I'd brought my backpack with me, and I had a notebook in it. So I made an 'out of order' sign and stuck it to the front of the door with a wad of gum. And then I came back in and said, 'Okay, I think it's safe.'"

She pauses for a moment. Her wide, dark eyes are a little unfocused as she gazes back at that old memory. I do the math; this must have happened more than forty years ago.

"But she wasn't there. On the floor of the stall was a pile of clothes and this—this creature. An otter, though at the time, I wasn't sure what it was. All I knew was that Derinda wasn't there, and this ani-mal was, and that Derinda had to be the animal. I couldn't think what to do or what to say. I just stood there staring at her as she came walking out on these—she had the most delicate little feet. I can still hear the sound her claws made on the tile floor of that bathroom. She came mincing out from under the door and then looked up at me.

"I'm sure she was afraid. She told me later that she'd never changed in front of anyone before. She had no idea what I'd do—call the teacher, call the cops, put her in the trash can and take her to the principal's office. But she knew her fate was in my hands. So she came out and she looked up at me, and she waited for what I'd do next."

"What *did* you do?" Celeste asks.

"I got down on the floor and I said, 'I don't know what to do to keep you safe. Should I put you outside? Will something eat you if I do that? Should I take you home?' Well, of course, she couldn't answer. She started running between me and the window, back and forth. I said, 'You want me to put you outside?' and then she came to a stop. I took that as a yes." Bonnie shrugs. "So I picked her up, careful as I could, and hid her under my jacket. I picked up her clothes, too, and folded them as small as I could. Then I snuck out of the building, and put her down under some trees. And she ran off. I hid her clothes under a bush, then I went back to class. Told the teacher she'd gone home sick."

Bonnie takes a deep breath. "Two days later she was back in class. Didn't say anything to me right then, but we walked home together when school was over. And she told me that she was a shape-shifter, and described what her life was like, and said she'd never known anyone outside her family that she could trust. We started dating, and we were together three years." She stops abruptly. I can tell Celeste is dying to ask the obvious question: *Why did you break up?* But even Celeste can sometimes tell where the boundaries are.

I'm surprised when it's Alonzo who speaks up. "Did you love her as much as you love Aurelia?"

I tense up, wondering how Bonnie will answer. A couple of months ago, he'd asked me if I loved Ryan, and I didn't know what to say. *Sometimes yes, sometimes no. It's complicated.* I think Alonzo's experiences with love are so limited that he's still trying to figure it out.

Well, I suppose all of us are still trying to figure it out.

Bonnie gives him her full attention, not seeming at all alarmed by the necessity of answering the query. "I loved her as much as I knew how, considering I was only seventeen when we met. I don't think I understood back then how generous you have to be when you love someone else. I don't think I got all of it right."

He pushes the donut crumbs around on his plate. "What if you were still dating her, you know, when you met Aurelia? Who would you pick?"

She still doesn't seem alarmed, though I think this question is even worse. She leans back deeper into her chair and seems to consider. "What a very interesting dilemma. If I'd still been with Derinda . . . I don't think I'm the kind of woman who leaves one person for another, so I doubt that would have happened. But Aurelia and I would have been very good friends, I think. We would have been special people in each other's lives. I would always be happy the universe had thrown her in my path."

That seems to satisfy him; he nods and reaches for another donut. Bonnie straightens in her chair and becomes her usual brisk, no-nonsense self. "That's the last donut for you, young man. In fact, eat it while you gather up your things. It's time we were going home."

She offers to help me do the dishes while Alonzo stuffs his dirty laundry in his gym bag, but I wave her off. "I'll make Celeste help," I say. "She hasn't worked hard enough the past three days."

Bonnie and Alonzo are gone within fifteen minutes, and I start clearing the table. Celeste pours herself another margarita and stays seated at the table. "I don't feel like helping," she informs me.

I grin. "That's fine. You've done enough. In fact, you've been uncharacteristically wonderful."

She snorts. "Comma, *bitch*."

Dirty dishes in my hands, I turn back to her, laughing. "What? I didn't say that."

"Yeah, but I can hear it in your voice, so you may as well just say it out loud."

I scrape food into the trash and load the dishwasher. "Well, *bitch*, I really appreciated you dropping everything and coming here to hang out in the boonies with me and Zo. I'm sure you had to give up dozens of social engagements and dates with hot guys, and I thank you from the bottom of my heart."

"Hot guys have been in short supply lately," she says. "But there's a new bar that opened up in the Square. Supposed to be a lot of fun. So if you want to make it up to me, let's go out Friday night."

I wrinkle my nose in distaste, but I nod anyway. I'm always ill at ease in bars. I don't know how to talk to strangers, I don't like loud music and flashing lights, and I'm afraid to drink too much because I have a long, winding drive home. But sometimes I think if I spend one more solitary weekend alone on the property, I'll turn into a stooped and demented old crone before I've even hit thirty.

The Square is a section of Quinville that contains about eight bars and five restaurants across a few adjacent blocks. It boasts the only nightlife to speak of in the whole town, so I've been there dozens of times. I think Celeste goes almost every week. She'll meet a guy in one venue or another, date him for a few months, then move on. It can be pretty humorous sometimes—we might encounter three of her ex-boyfriends in the same night. She's still on relatively good terms with most of them, but one night this drunk guy came up to our table and started shouting and waving his arms and threatening to cut her up. The bar owner called the cops and had him hauled off.

There's usually *some* kind of excitement when Celeste's around.

"Sounds like fun," I say. I snap shut the dishwasher door and return to the table to sit down. There's enough left in the bottle for me to pour myself half a margarita.

"We could invite Ryan," she says.

I hesitate a little too long before I say, "Sure."

She leans her elbows on the table and gives me a piercing stare. "So what's up with you two, anyway?"

I shake my head and give her a wide-eyed expression. "Nothing."

"Yeah, right."

"You know. I'm serious and he's not. I want to stay here and take care of the property and all the animals, and he wants to travel around the country. I'm too responsible. Or he's too irresponsible. We don't suit each other."

"Yeah, but he's crazy about you."

"You think so? Maybe."

She makes a throaty sound of irritation. "And I always thought *you* were crazy about *him*."

I sip my margarita. I have spent so much time trying to figure out how I feel about Ryan, and I still can't put the emotions into words. "He fascinates me. I feel drawn to him. I feel connected to him. He— when he shows up at my door, I feel this little kick of excitement. Even now. But he's—" I shake my head. "I'm always in this state of high alert when I'm with him. I never know what's going to happen next. I can never fully relax."

She tosses back the rest of the liquid in her glass. "So? He's never boring. That's not a bad thing." She grins. "Especially for a very dull girl like yourself."

"Bitch," I say obligingly.

She leans forward again. "But I suppose the real question is: Do you love him or don't you?"

"I'm not sure that is the question," I say slowly. "I think it's: Do I trust him or don't I?"

"You don't trust him? *Ryan?* What, you think he'd cheat on you? Steal your money?"

Suddenly I'm irritated. "If you think he's so perfect, why don't *you* go out with him?"

34

She grins. "We'd claw each other's eyes out within a week. We're too much alike."

"I don't think you're alike at all."

That surprises her. In fact, it's sort of an article of faith between Ryan and Celeste that they're twins separated at birth. They tend to like the same music, the same movies, the same politics, the same people. Sometimes they'll call each other up to ask the stupidest questions. *What time did you wake up this morning?* Or *If you could either learn to fly or learn to become invisible, which would you choose?* They crow in delight when their answers match.

"What's different about us?" she demands.

I salute her with my glass, now almost empty. "*You* I'd trust with my life."

Celeste spends the night, but only because I take away her car keys. "Friends don't let friends loose on Highway W after too many drinks," I tell her. She's only slightly annoyed and not even remotely surprised.

She's gone in the morning before I get up, but that's all right. I have plenty to do. Animals to care for, bills to pay, e-mails to answer.

One of the e-mails is from Nina Kassebaum, Janet's mother, who still doesn't know her daughter is dead. It's hard to explain why I've kept up this deception for so many years. The two of them weren't close—Janet left home when she was eighteen and never laid eyes on either parent again. She told me the only reason she answered her mother's letters was because she didn't have the energy to be cruel enough to ignore them. They never talked about important things—I'm not sure her mother even knew about Cooper, Janet's shape-shifter lover, and she certainly didn't know that creatures such as shape-shifters existed. They would trade observations about the weather, and Janet would tell her about some of the human clients she'd met and the more interesting ailments their pets had contracted. Her mother would respond with similarly bland news and anecdotes.

It was obvious to me that, even if Janet didn't care about these meaningless exchanges, her mother was desperate to keep this faint connection between them alive. Janet never went into much detail about the abuses that went on when she was still under her parents' roof, but I gathered there had been a fair amount of violence and invective. She just walked away, but her mother couldn't let her go. It gave Nina the slimmest, sparest thread of comfort to believe Janet didn't hate her, Janet was happy, Janet had not been destroyed by her mother's choices.

I can't take that comfort away by telling her Janet is dead.

And, I'll be honest here, I get a certain amount of satisfaction from the connection as well. My own mother died when I was a little girl, my father when I was in my early twenties. Shape-shifters tend to live short lives, because the stresses on their bodies just take too great a toll. I miss both of my parents. I miss having someone in my life who loves me simply because I exist—not because I'm funny or charming or smart or beautiful or gifted or kind. Just because I am. And despite what Janet thought, I believe her mother loved her for that very reason.

So I continue to write to Nina, and she writes back, and both of us, in a very small way, rejoice.

Today I don't have much news to share. I type up a recipe Bonnie gave me last week, tell her that Alonzo has been here for a few days to help out, though of course I'm not specific about why I needed him. She's become interested in Alonzo, I don't know why; she asks after him when I don't mention him in our infrequent letters. I wonder sometimes if she had been a foster child herself, though I can't ask her because it seems like the sort of thing I ought to know. She even requested a photo of him once, which I duly sent. I had to remember at the last minute to send one of Alonzo by himself, not one that showed him standing next to me.

I conclude:

Well, that's about it for now. Tons of work still to get done before I can call it a day. There's never any "time off" when you have animals to take care of.

TTYL.

I sign the e-mail with her daughter's name and hit send.

I do have work to do, but I'm not going back to the barns and kennels. I'm heading to the tiny laboratory Janet set up in the smallest room of the house. She's the one who started experimenting with various serums and concoctions, trying to find the right combinations of chemicals that would prevent or slow down Cooper's transformations from a man to a wolf. She never found the magic potion she was looking for, but she did make some extraordinary discoveries—that changed her life—that changed mine. For three years, I worked alongside her in that little lab, trying to figure out what cues my body sent that triggered my transformations, trying to figure out how to redirect them or block them altogether.

Janet's theory was that shifters carry the complete genomes of all the animals they transform into, as well as the usual human components. Those who only turn into one kind of animal have somehow managed to switch off all the other genomes, probably through some kind of methylase enzyme complex. She also believed that shifters who only change at infrequent intervals possess a particular kind of RNA retrotransposon that actually alters their DNA. She'd learned all the scientific jargon at vet school; I didn't always understand the words, but I'd learned how to carry out the necessary experiments nonetheless.

I've had some promising results. For the past three months I've been inoculating myself with enzymes isolated from a shape-shifter named Isabel who always turns into a yellow tabby—though I don't know if I took cat shape last week because of those doses or because of some random imperative in my bones.

Last year, my goal was to cut down on the frequency of my transformations, so I used genetic material donated by Baxter, a shape-shifter who changes once a month or less. That experiment had actually been a wild success from my point of view—for the past nine months, I've only changed shapes about once every four weeks, a schedule so steady and so reliable that I actually *had* come to rely on it. I had started to think that I could live something approximating a normal life if I was human three-quarters of the time and could always plan around my transmogrifications.

Apparently not.

I've been reluctant to combine serums—start injecting myself with Isabel's enzymes while still influenced by Baxter's retrotransposons. But maybe that's what I have to do if I want to design my own personal schedule and type of transformation. Maybe I have to play Dr. Frankenstein and stitch together my idea of the perfect shape-shifter, gathering components from various donors until I have the entire creature expertly assembled.

I already know what that bizarre hybrid would look like. She would have the enviable ability of a shape-shifter named Lanita, who can take whatever form she likes. If she couldn't have Celeste's gift for transforming at will, she would have the ability to stave off transformation for up to a week if circumstances dictated. She would be blessed with the knowledge that her time in animal incarnation would last no longer than a day.

But no shape-shifter I've ever met has the skill I really want. The ability to stay human forever.

You'd think that, instead of experimenting with the DNA of shifters, I would start doctoring myself with vials of human blood, but that's the very last trial I would undergo. Shape-shifters learned the hard way that we can't tolerate infusions from our genetic cousins, most likely because their blood can't handle all those extra genomes. Occasionally, a human-to-shifter transfusion proceeds without trauma, but other times it results in catastrophic consequences—delirium, madness, death. There are terrible stories of shape-shifters who are critically injured in car crashes or workplace accidents; ambulance drivers rush them, unconscious and bleeding out, to the nearest hospital, where the ER personnel try to save their lives with blood transfusions.

Most of the time, they would have been better off if they'd been left to die at the scene of the disaster. Most of the time, they die anyway, but not before they've gone on some kind of rampage—small and personal, or big and terrifying. A few years ago, a shape-shifter over in Missouri got a blood transfusion and ended up crazed, warped, and guilty of murdering five people.

So I'm wary of injecting myself with human blood, even in a small, measured amount.

Lately I've been thinking about making a shape-shifter cocktail, controlling for time, controlling for species. I figure it might be time to up the ante, assume a little more risk. There's no easy or foolproof way to tell if such a cocktail will work, since test-tube experiments don't yield much information and I refuse to experiment on one of the animals under my care. The only way to really know is to try the formula on myself. Since I want to become a cat on a reassuringly predictable schedule, I mix up a potion that includes equal parts of Isabel and Baxter, and I fill a syringe with the result.

And then I hesitate.

Every time I rest the tip of the needle against my arm, before I break the skin, I ask myself if the possible costs are worth the potential gains.

Delirium, madness, death. Versus the chance at a more normal life.

Every time, I have plunged the syringe into the muscle. Every time, I have said the answer is *yes*.

CHAPTER THREE

The instant I arrive at Celeste's place Friday evening, she says, "Oh no, you're not wearing *that*."

I look down at my clothes—a cute purple sweater, low rise jeans, flat shoes with bronze accents. "What's wrong with my outfit?"

She doesn't answer, just shakes her head and pushes me through her cluttered apartment toward the tiny bedroom. Throwing open the closet door, she reveals a wildly disorganized riot of fabrics and accessories, and contemplates for a moment. "Let's see—where's that spangly red shirt?"

"I don't see how you think I can fit into anything you own," I say. We're close to the same height, but I must outweigh her by thirty pounds. She's flat-chested enough to be able to wear spaghetti straps and short, form-fitting bodice tops that let her belly button (and navel ring) peek out. I don't go anywhere without an underwire bra that offers "maximum coverage."

"Yeah, yeah, but this top is all stretchy—it looks good on anyone.

Here it is." She pulls it out of the closet and hands it over. "Man, if I had tits like yours, I would always be wearing scooped necklines and bending over like crazy."

We're way past needing any modesty between us, so I peel off the sweater and pull on the red shirt, and holy God, it clings to me like a second skin. "*Celeste.* I look like I'm naked. I can't go out in public like this."

"Well, you can and you will. You look great. Here, now you need brighter lipstick. And you want something for your hair? I have feathers."

"I am *not* putting feathers in my hair!"

Celeste, of course, *is* wearing feathers, long streaming blue ones, clipped just behind her ear, so they spill out like a bright surprise from the chaos of her unbound curls. Her only other accessory is a gold necklace hung with a jingling collection of gems and charms. She looks great, of course, but part of it is that ingrained confidence, the conviction that she can carry off any style. I don't have that self-assurance. Whenever I try to dress up for a night out—fancy clothes and extra makeup—I always figure I look like a little girl trying to wear her big sister's wardrobe.

"Well, a sparkly little clip, then. Come on. We're going to a bar, not a prison. You should look like you expect to have a good time."

In the end, of course, I agree to the faux-red-jewel barrette as well as the stretchy top, though I insist on a filmy patterned scarf that I can throw around my shoulders if I feel too exposed.

"You look cute," Celeste decides, and off we go.

It's about a ten-minute drive to the Square, then a ten-minute hunt for street parking, and by this time, it's dark. Celeste is practically skipping as we cruise up the street, passing two other bars and a restaurant as we aim for the new place. It's got an old-fashioned neon sign out front featuring the word ARABESQUE above a martini glass and a woman's bright red mouth puckered for a kiss.

"Wow. Arabesque. Gotta be the first time anyone in Quinville ever said the word," I observe.

"Don't be snarky," Celeste says. "Though, I have to admit, the first time I heard someone pronounce it, she called it Ara-bes-kyoo. Took me forever to figure out what she meant."

I'm still giggling as we arrive at the door, where there are two guys sitting on tall stools taking cover money and stamping hands with special ink. Apparently Celeste knows one of them—young, long-haired, with the kind of dreamy looks you see in models on romance books—because she exclaims, "Marcus!" and instantly starts flirting. Using one hand to dig for my wallet, I hold out my other hand to the second attendant so he can stamp it.

"Have to see your ID first," he says. "Sorry."

I look up at him, laughing again. "Really? No, I'm flattered."

He laughs back. He has a round baby face that looks made for smiling and big dark eyes filled with bright curiosity. He's seated, so it's hard to tell, but I'd guess he's six-one or six-two, kind of bulky, a big guy who probably has to work at it to stay in shape now that he's edging out of his twenties. Probably doubles as the bouncer, since the slimmer, prettier Marcus doesn't look like he has the body strength to throw someone out into the street.

"We're supposed to card anyone who's under thirty," he says.

"Okay, so now I'm not as flattered," I say, handing over a five dollar bill and my license.

He takes them both but doesn't look at either. He's tilted his head to one side, assessing me. "I'd say—twenty-five," he estimates.

"Dead on the money," I admit. "Do you guess height and weight, too?"

He's grinning again. "No. I don't want people looking at *me* and saying, 'I bet that porker weighs four hundred pounds.'"

"Surely it's more like two twenty," I say before I can stop myself.

He looks impressed. "Pretty close."

"I work with animals. I've gotten used to guessing weight just by looking. Well, I can do it with live creatures. I can't look at a *car* and know how much it weighs."

"What kind of work do you do with animals?"

I glance at Celeste, but she's deep in conversation with Marcus, and no one has lined up behind us, so there's no reason to stop talking to the bouncer. "I'm a vet." *Sort of.*

"Here in Quinville? I've been looking for a place to take my dog."

"Well, I'm kind of on the fringes of Quinville. Off W a ways. What kind of dog?"

"Black lab. Her name's Jezebel."

"What's wrong with her?"

"Maybe only that she's ten years old."

I nod sympathetically. "Yeah. You know, ten years—that's a long time for a big dog. So she's slowing down? Anything else?"

He nods. The round face looks briefly sad. "She limps a little, like her back leg hurts. Maybe she has arthritis."

"Maybe. Or a torn ACL."

"Like football players get?"

"Pretty much."

"Would you be willing to take a look at her?" he asks.

"Sure, but there are plenty of places here in town. I mean—where've you taken her before? I assume you *have* kept her rabies shots up to date?"

"Yeah, but I just moved to Quinville about a year ago, and I didn't like the first vet we tried. He was kind of—" The bouncer shrugs. "He made me wonder why he wanted to be a vet, to tell you the truth. Didn't seem to like animals much."

"You do wonder sometimes why people choose their professions," I agree. Out of the corner of my eye, I see Celeste rest a hand on Marcus's shoulder. It looks like a good-bye gesture, so I assume she's about concluded her conversation. "I guess you better stamp my hand so I can go in," I say.

"Gotta double-check first," the bouncer replies, flicking on a little flashlight so he can study my license. "Looks like you're of legal age— Karadel? That's your name? Wow, never heard that one before."

"My grandmothers were named Karen and Adele, so it's not quite as exotic as it sounds at first," I reply.

"I like it. It's pretty. I'm just Joe."

"Nice to meet you, Joe," I say, and hold my hand out. He carefully inks the back with a stamp that features a bold A in the center of some swirly vines. "Will this glow in the dark?"

He grins. "I don't know. I never bothered trying it on myself."

Celeste is beside me, nudging me toward the door. "Enough chatting. Let's go in and get a drink."

Absurdly, I give Joe a little wave as we walk off, and he waves back. Celeste leans close enough to whisper in my ear. "See? That red shirt is magic. He liked your boobs."

"And here I thought it was my sparkling personality."

"Boobs *always* make a personality more sparkling."

The interior of Arabesque is a pretty standard urban bar scene—dark walls, dark flooring, dramatic lighting, but not enough of it, a lot of tables clustered together along the walls and in the middle of the room. There's a serving bar on one wall and a low stage in back, with a sizable dance floor right in front of it. The band is still setting up, which means we can actually hear ourselves speak, at least for the moment.

"A couple of my friends are meeting us here, I figured that was okay," Celeste tells me as she pauses to let her eyes adjust so she can look around.

"Gee, kind of late to tell me if it *wasn't* okay."

"Comma, bitch," she adds.

I laugh. "But, sure, I don't mind. *Tus amigos son mis amigos.*"

That's not really true. I've met a bunch of Celeste's friends and found them all fairly shallow and interchangeable—pretty, empty-headed twentysomethings who share apartments and hold meaningless jobs and spend most of their time talking about the drinking they're going to do on the weekend. Seriously, I once had the most excruciating conversation with a girl named Tiffie who literally could not think of anything to ask me except where I liked to party. When I apologetically replied that I didn't get a chance to party very often, she said, "But which do you like better? Black Market or Galaxy? The mixed drinks are better at Galaxy, I think, but they have better music at Black Market." I had no reply for this, so I just started asking her stupid questions: *Who's your favorite band? Do you ever get a chance to go to St. Louis or Springfield? What bars do you go to?* I had never felt so old in my life.

I don't see Tiffie at the table where Celeste eventually steers me, though the three girls sitting there could be her spiritual sisters. They're all slim and blond, dressed like Celeste in strappy little tops that look too small for them and cropped jeans that hug their boyish hips. They greet both of us happily and I give everyone the broadest smile I can summon, since I don't want to spoil anyone's mood, but I'm already sorry I'm here. I don't know these people, I don't like these people, I have nothing in common with these people, and

I am a dead bore. I'd rather be back on the property mucking out dog cages.

"What do you want to drink?" one of the girls asks. "We just ordered another pitcher and a couple more glasses."

"Beer is good for now," Celeste says, and I nod. I don't plan to drink enough for it to make a difference.

"So how are you doing, girlfriend?" one of the other blondes asks Celeste. "We missed you Saturday night!"

Saturday night. When she was out at my place, watching DVDs with Alonzo, and never once complaining about what she might be missing back in town. Celeste doesn't even glance at me to see my contrite expression.

"Doing great. Ready to start *dancing*," she says enthusiastically. "Anyone here we know?"

The blondes start reeling off names of the men they've spotted so far, one of whom I recognize as Celeste's most recent ex, then the waitress arrives with a foamy pitcher of beer and some fresh glasses.

"Let me get this one," I say, because I feel like I should contribute *something* to the evening and I don't figure I'll be drinking much from later pitchers. I ask the waitress, "Could we have, like, pretzels or chips, too?"

"Sure," she says. "Be right back."

But she hasn't returned yet when the band members hit their first noisy chords and suddenly we're assaulted by a wall of music. One of the blondes starts dancing in her chair, shimmying her shoulders and moving her hips, but I don't recognize the song. Celeste leans over to shout something in the ear of one of her other friends, and I take a long, long pull on my beer.

It's going to be an endless night.

I know the second number, though, CeeLo Green's "Fuck You," and Celeste turns to me in delight. It's our current favorite song, the one we play for each other when we're feeling down, so we both jump up and sashay to the dance floor. This early in the night, not many people are dancing and most of them are women, but the upbeat rhythm of the song shoves any thought of embarrassment right out of my head.

I don't know what it is about music. I can be in the most forbidding, curmudgeonly of moods; I can be feeling withdrawn, awkward, socially inept, despairing of ever connecting with another human being. And then a certain song starts playing and I just toss aside all inhibitions and go boogying across the floor. I don't care if I look stupid, I don't care what people think about me. I just dance.

One of Celeste's old boyfriends told me that he'd learned a long time ago that the women who were the most outrageous dancers tended to be the most inventive in bed. I think he was hitting on me; I was never sure. At any rate, he was still dating Celeste, so I didn't follow up. I always wondered if he'd have still believed his theory if we'd ever been lovers.

"Fuck You" is followed by a few other upbeat tunes, so I start to feel fairly happy, even when the blondes join us. Some guy I've never seen before snakes through the people on the dance floor to tap Celeste on the shoulder. She spins around, cries out in delight, and gives him a hug, then the two of them immediately start dancing at each other in a highly suggestive fashion. I grin and push my hair out of my face. When this song ends, I wave at the others and wind my way back to our table to finish my beer.

Oh, but someone's sitting at the table, watching my approach. Ryan. I feel my heart give a traitorous leap; I feel my blood, briefly, turn to glitter in my veins. But I manage to mold my expression into one of muted pleasure, the look you might wear any time you unexpectedly encountered an old friend with whom you shared a long but casual history.

He stands up at my approach so he can give me a chaste kiss on the forehead, but I feel his lips burn against my skin. I manage to be smiling when he straightens up and grins down at me. Ryan is slim but muscular, with a runner's build. No matter what he wears, even a T-shirt and jeans, he manages to produce an air of relaxed elegance. His sandy brown hair is streaked with sun. It's straight and cut short except for the strands that fall into his eyes with a boyish charm. He looks like he should be modeling yachting attire for a J.Crew catalog, except he's not quite pretty enough. His skin's a little rough, his nose has been broken, his front teeth are slightly crooked. And there's an expression deep in his blue eyes that makes you think, if he wanted to, he could beat up all the other sailors on the boat and pitch them overboard without a moment's remorse.

There's just enough of a break between songs for us to exchange a snatch of conversation.

"Celeste told me you guys were going to be here tonight," he says. "I thought I'd come say hi."

"You look good," I say.

"You look really sexy," he replies. "I have to think Celeste picked out your clothes."

"Asshole," I say in a pleasant voice, and we both laugh.

"Those were two different statements," he clarifies. "You look sexy *and* I think Celeste picked out your clothes. You'd look sexy in a tracksuit."

"So how've you been?" I ask.

"Good. Traveling a little. Just got back from Denver a couple days ago."

"What's in Denver?"

Before he can answer, the band launches into another song. Ryan smiles and spreads his hands apologetically, and I nod and shrug. He points to the pitcher and raises his eyebrows. *Can I have some?* I don't see a clean glass on the table, so I pour more beer into my own glass and hand it over. He drinks the whole thing straight down, then leans over to shout in my ear.

"I'm going to get another one! You want anything?"

"Can I just have some ice water?" I shout back.

He rolls his eyes, but nods, unsurprised. While he fights his way through the crowd toward the bar, I munch on the pretzels the waitress left on the table. They're stale.

Ryan returns a few minutes later, trailed by our waitress, whose tray is loaded down with another pitcher of beer, two glasses of water, and a plate that holds a burger and fries. Ryan puts his lips to my ear and says, "Wanna split it? I'm hungry, but not that hungry."

"I'm *starving*," I exclaim. "Thank you!"

We share the food, nudge each other a few times to point out people we think look particularly ridiculous on the dance floor, and trade a few other unimportant observations the next two times there's a break in the music. I'm trying to decide if this is the most uncomfortable half hour of my life when Celeste and the blondes return to the table. Celeste throws her arms around Ryan and gives him a big kiss, which he enthusiastically returns.

"Denver International Airport," she demands. "What gate did you fly out of?"

He squints, trying to remember. "B22."

"So did I!" she cries. "Last time I was there! But they changed it at the last minute from B11, so I practically had to *run* down the terminal."

"That's exactly what happened to me!"

"Oh my God, you two are *almost the same person*!" I say.

Ryan grins and Celeste mouths the word "bitch" at me. One of the other women says, "It *is* spooky how much they're alike."

He turns to her with a warm smile. "Hey, Rain," he says, or at least I think that's what he says. Rain? Her name is *Rain*? That's worse than Karadel. "You look good."

She giggles. "So do you."

The band plunges into some weird techno piece with a throbbing beat, and Ryan holds his arm out to Rain, a questioning look on his face. She nods and they head to the dance floor, where they instantly begin energetic gyrations. It might be my imagination that the other two blondes wear envious expressions as they watch them go.

Celeste's attention has been caught by something else. She pokes one of her friends and nods at a table a few yards away. I can read her lips as she asks, *Who's that?* But I can't hear what the girl shouts to her over the pulse of the music. I follow Celeste's gaze to see who looks so interesting.

He's pretty easy to pick out. He's a long, lean guy resting his long, lean body against the table, his back to it, his elbows on the edge. He's wearing jeans and a black T-shirt, cowboy boots, and a leather belt with a big buckle in the shape of a longhorn bull. His hair is as black as Alonzo's, but straight, a little shaggy, and his face has that fallen-angel beauty that instantly lets you know he's trouble. You can almost see the sad little clattering shells of broken hearts trailing behind him and curled around his ankles in a forlorn heap.

Just the type Celeste likes.

There are two others at the table with him, people I vaguely recognize. One's a local guy, kind of a troublemaker. He owns a junkyard off of 159 on the opposite side of town, and he's always being cited for some kind of property-law infraction. He's not as handsome as the stranger, but they look enough alike that I guess they might be brothers. The woman at the table, I think, is the junker's wife. She's dressed in a black shirt that's as low-cut and clingy as mine, she's wearing a lot of makeup, and she doesn't look happy to be here. I can sympathize.

From Celeste's expression, I think she's trying to figure out a way to introduce herself to the new guy, but it's a little too early in the evening for her to simply walk up and ask him to dance. I wouldn't bet against that happening within the hour, though. Right now, she just watches him for a few meditative moments while she sips at her beer. Then she sets the glass on the table and heads to the dance floor, the other blondes in her wake.

I finish up the French fries, watch the dancers, drink the last of my water, and wish I was at home by myself with my dog and my DVDs. When the next song is equally loud and has an even heavier beat, I stand up and head toward the door for some cool air and a break from the sensory overload. No one who knows me will be surprised that I have briefly left the scene.

I step outside and take a deep breath. The scents of asphalt, diesel fuel, and back-alley trash clog the air, but I still perk up a little just at the contrast. Why did I let Celeste talk me into this? If we had brought *my* car to the Square, I could just drive home now. Surely Ryan or Rain or perhaps the handsome stranger would take Celeste home. Surely there is no reason for me to spend another minute in this place, in this town. In fact, at the moment I can't think of a reason I'd ever need to come into the city of Quinville again.

"Hey," says a man's voice behind me, and I spin around, electrified with a moment of terror. The bulky shadow moves into the light and I recognize Joe the bouncer.

"Sorry, didn't mean to scare you," he says.

I give a shaky laugh and pat my throat. "I didn't mean to over-react. I just didn't realize you were here."

"Till the place closes," he says. "Two A.M."

"God, I hope I'm gone long before that." My voice is glum. I wouldn't be surprised if Celeste plans to stay till every light in the Square goes out.

"You're not having a good time?" he asks.

"I'm not much of a party girl," I confess. "I don't really like bars. I only came here tonight because—well—I mean, you have to get out of the house *sometime*."

He nods, like that's a reasonable statement. "I like bars, but the dark, smoky, quiet kinds. You know, where you sit and have a beer and talk to someone. Maybe play darts or watch the ball game."

"So if you don't like places like Arabesque, why are you working here?"

He shrugs and perches on the edge of his high stool. I have the distinct feeling he sits so he doesn't seem like such a large and men-acing presence, which makes me warm to him even more. Although, of course, he might just be tired.

"Needed a job and this was a job I could do," he says.

I lean against the brick wall of the building, which still holds heat from the day's unexpectedly high temperatures. Now Joe and I are face-to-face and both of us are in enough light that we can see each other's expressions. "I wouldn't think being a bouncer at a dance club would pay enough to cover the rent," I say.

"No," he acknowledges. "I do some other part-time stuff. A buddy of mine runs a trucking company, so I drive some routes when he needs help. Over the summer I worked a few hours on the night shift at Home Depot."

It all sounds kind of aimless, not to say shiftless, but he strikes me as a generally more solid type. "You ever give any thought to a more permanent kind of job?" I ask.

He grins. "Well, yeah. All the time. I just haven't figured it out yet."

I laugh. "What did you do before you moved to Quinville?"

"I was a cop up in Joliet."

That widens my eyes because that certainly seems like a nice, upstanding sort of career. "Why'd you quit?" I have a terrible thought. "Or—" *Get fired.* "Never mind."

"They didn't kick me out, if that's what you're thinking."

"Sorry."

"I liked being a cop. Maybe I was a little too idealistic at the beginning, but I thought we were doing some good. I liked going to the high schools, talking to the kids. I didn't like being the first one on the scene at car accidents and murder scenes, but I figured that was part of the job."

Clearly there's a major "but" coming. I wait.

He shrugs again. "My partner shot and killed a guy. He was shooting at us, it was self-defense, my partner was cleared of wrongdoing and back on the job right away. But I—" Joe shakes his head. "I realized I couldn't do it. I couldn't take aim with my gun and kill a human being. And when you're a cop, you have to be prepared to take a life. So I turned in my badge."

The story makes me like him even more. I'm all in favor of less killing, but there doesn't seem to be a way to say that that doesn't sound hokey. "And why'd you leave Joliet for Quinville?"

"Well, there wasn't a reason to stay in Joliet anymore," he replies. The way he says it makes me think something besides the job had gone sour. A relationship, maybe. "And my buddy said I could drive for him till I figured out what else to do, so Quinville seemed as good a place as any."

"And has it been?"

His round face creases into an expression of equivocation. "I guess it could be," he says. "But so far I kind of feel like I'm just marking time."

I can understand that. I'm familiar with the sensation of being poised on the edge of tomorrow, always anticipating the big event that will give shape and meaning to the following days. "Yeah, but you know what they say. Life is what happens while you're waiting for life to happen."

He wrinkles his nose in dissent. "I always thought that was kind of dumb."

I laugh. "Well, my *point* is, you shouldn't waste too much time, or it will all be gone before you've accomplished anything."

"Thanks for the cheerful thought."

"Yeah, you can see why I'm not exactly the type of person to be hanging out at bars frittering my time away."

"So what about you?" he asks. "What brought you to Quinville? Or were you born here?"

The true story would pop the eyes right out of his head, but I can tell a well-honed variant. "Nope, I grew up in Barrington. Kind of a ritzy suburb outside of Chicago. My dad was an art dealer and he was always going to little small-town art gallery openings, trying to find the next, I don't know, Thomas Hart Benton or John Singer Sargent. And a few years ago, he went to a gallery in Champaign and met an artist named Cooper Blair, and he *loved* his stuff. So my dad started repping him, and our families became friends. Cooper lived with Janet, who ran a veterinary clinic off of Highway W. I used to spend summers working with her, and then I took classes, and then I took over the business when Janet decided to retire." I shake my head, as if I'm still surprised by the vagaries of life. "I mean, I never would have thought I'd be happy living out in the middle of *nowhere*, but I find the life suits me."

"You don't miss the big city?"

"Well, Barrington's pretty far out from downtown Chicago. It's not like I was down at the Loop every night, anyway."

"Do you go back much? Visit your family?"

"My parents are both dead."

His face instantly changes. "Aw, I'm sorry to hear that. That must be tough."

I nod and don't answer. Because of course it's tough. I still miss my father every day; he was such a large, powerful presence in my life. Smart and forceful and utterly determined. Once he set his sights on something, he invariably achieved it. He's the one who convinced Janet to open the clinic here—he picked out the property, he paid for it, he helped furnish it. He believed that our small circle of shape-shifting friends needed a haven, a place where they could come for rest and healing, and he was going to see that place built if he had to put it together with his own hands.

Well. He really thought *I* needed a refuge. I was in my hormone-fueled teens then, and taking on bigger and wilder shapes every few days, and he was deeply afraid for me. Barrington isn't downtown Chicago, that's true, but it's a highly developed urban setting, and it's hard to hide an elephant on your back lawn. He was happy enough to found a clinic for the shape-shifting community at large, but he would not rest until he built a place where I could live in safety. I think the first time I ever saw him relax was the day Janet officially opened her doors to clients.

"So, no brothers or sisters, either?" Joe is asking.

I shake my head. "No. I have a couple of cousins, but they don't live in Barrington anymore. So I haven't been back to Chicago in—maybe five years? Wow, long time." I focus on him. "How about you? Family in Joliet?"

He nods. "Couple of brothers, both married, both have kids. My dad's dead, my mom's remarried, everybody seems pretty happy."

I resettle myself against the brick, trying to get more comfortable. "Sometimes that makes it harder," I remark. "When everyone else seems to be doing great, and you're the only one who's still trying to figure it out."

That makes him grin. "Yeah, and my younger brother was always the screwup. I was always the one who got it right the first time. But now I'm just—" Joe spreads his hands to indicate his incomplete life. "And he's got the great job and the great kids."

"Great wife?" I ask.

The grin grows wider. "Nah, she's a ballbuster. But *he* seems to like her, so I guess that's all that matters."

"So you go up for birthdays, holidays, that sort of thing?"

"Yeah, or football games or whatever. We're tight."

I'm trying to think of a polite way to ask if he's made any friends in Quinville—because, if he's lived here a year and he *hasn't*, he's a pretty lost soul—when the music changes from some mournful Coldplay number to the grinding rev-up of "Footloose." I almost squeal.

"I *love* this song," I say. He's a total stranger and I'm standing outside on the sidewalk, but I can't keep my feet still. I'm practically dancing in front of the bouncer in the doorway of Arabesque.

But he doesn't think I'm a dork, or if he does, he's one, too, because he's raised his hands and is making syncopated gestures along with the chorus. He's grinning broadly and mouthing the words along with the band. I've actually started singing, though I'm keeping my voice low, but I've shoved myself wholly away from the wall and now I'm starting to act out the lyrics and shake my ass a little more. He pushes up from the stool and gets his feet and shoulders into it, and pretty soon there's no way to pretend we're *not* dancing together, right here in front of the club. Celeste would die if she saw me, but I'm having too much fun to stop.

The song comes to its abrupt crescendoing conclusion and we both freeze in exaggerated poses, then burst out laughing. "Hey, that was fun," he says. "Sitting out here, I never get to dance."

"You like to dance? Most guys hate it."

"I always think I don't till the music starts."

"That's how *I* feel!" *We're twins,* I think, *just like Ryan and Celeste.*

We both have our heads cocked toward the door, half hoping the band members will play another beat-driven tune, but it seems "Footloose" is how they ended their set. We can hear the distorted sound of the lead singer promising to be back in a few minutes, and then a Beyonce song starts issuing from the speakers inside. Joe makes a face.

"*This* isn't my kind of music."

Before I can answer, the door opens and people start streaming out into the night. Most of them are smokers, their cigarettes between their lips before they're even out of the building. Quinville passed a no-smoking ordinance a couple years ago, and people are still complaining, but it doesn't seem to have hurt business here in the Square.

A few of them are couples who have come outside to argue or make out. Celeste and the good-looking stranger are among them, already holding hands. She passes so close to me I could touch her on the cheek, but either she doesn't see me or she pretends she doesn't. They slip around the corner of the building where the smell of trash might be stronger but the shadows are deeper. I'm thinking maybe I can convince Ryan to give me a ride to my car so I can go home now; it's looking like Celeste might appreciate having me out of the way come closing time.

"I guess I should go back in," I say to Joe. "My friends might be wondering where I am."

He nods. "If you wanted, you could give me your address," he says, his voice so offhand he's clearly making an effort to keep it that way. "In case I have time to bring Jezebel out to see you."

"Sure," I say, smiling to show I'd welcome a visit from him—and his dog. "Take 159 to W, go right on W, and stay on that about eight miles. There's an abandoned red barn on the left side of the road and a stone wall on the right side. I'm right past the stone wall."

He's not writing it down but he's nodding at each landmark like he's committing it to memory. "Oh, hey, I think I've been down that way a few times to go hunting," he says.

I can't stop my expression of horror. "Hunting? You shoot things? You won't kill a person but you'll take a gun and kill an *animal*?"

He looks both chagrined and a little defensive. "Bowhunting. Not guns. And I don't hunt anything I can't eat. And if we don't thin the deer population, it gets out of control—"

"Since we've killed off so many of their natural predators," I rattle off. "I know. But *still*."

He heaves a sigh. "So I guess you don't eat meat. Maybe you're a vegan."

Now I'm the one who looks defensive. "I eat meat. Sometimes."

"And you don't think that's hypocritical? That you'll eat meat if someone *else* has done the killing?"

"It's kind of like you and the cop thing," I answer. "I know someone has to do it, but I don't want it to be me."

"Well, don't hold it against me," he says.

I don't know you well enough to care is one option for a reply. But I don't say it and, anyway, it's not quite true. I mean, I don't know him, but I like him well enough to think it would be nice to care. "Give me a little time to get over the shock."

"You probably do stuff that I'd think was gross, too," he says hopefully.

Now I laugh. "Yeah, like neutering dogs and cats and looking up their butts with scopes."

"Ew! Yuck! That is totally gross," he responds. "But *I* don't hold it against *you*."

"It's not the same thing! I'm saving lives and you're taking them."

"I'd be saving lives if everyone was starving and the only food they had was the meat I brought home."

This makes me laugh. "I get the feeling you're the kind of guy who can argue all day about something," I say. "Am I right?"

"Kind of. I told you. Brothers. You can't ever give in, man. You can't ever admit you're wrong."

I want to say *Sounds exhausting*, but before I can get the words out, there's a terrific clatter from the back alley. Metal trash cans rattle and clang together, and then comes the high, unnerving sound of a man's voice raised in sharp pain. I jerk around to stare in that direction, as do all the people loosely gathered in front of the club. Joe's on his feet, his hand going to his belt. *He carries a gun?* I think a little numbly, but no, it turns out he's holding something that looks like a two-way radio. The expression on his amiable face is suddenly alert and focused, and he's gathered his big body from relaxed to ready in the space of a heartbeat.

"Stay here," he says, a command that's loud enough to include everyone in the immediate vicinity, and then he takes off in a cautious run for the alley. He's staying close to the building, as if hoping its bulk and shadows will protect him from violence, and I have a weird, fake-memory flashback of seeing him approach another crime scene in just such a grim and careful fashion. Dressed as a cop. Weapon in his hand. Death around the corner.

There's another noise explosion, more metal trash cans being kicked or battered, and then a shape staggers out from behind the building. It's just one guy, but he looks off, somehow, like he's drunk or disoriented. One hand is pressed to his cheek, one to his chest, and the only way to describe his gait is *reeling*. As Joe steps up to intercept him, I recognize him as the junker's good-looking brother.

Where's Celeste?

CHAPTER FOUR

Despite Joe's command, I step closer to the alley, trying to figure out what's happened. For a moment, I can hear their voices—Joe's low, authoritative, and soothing; the other guy's angry and steadily rising—but I can't make out their words. Then the handsome stranger makes a wild gesture with one hand, and I see the bloody track marks on his face.

Holy mother of God.

At that exact moment, the audio station in my head tunes in to his frequency and I can understand every word he says. "I'm telling you, asshole, she turned into a *lion*. We were making out, and she—she wasn't a *person* anymore, she was a *lion*, like a *mountain lion*. She *scratched* my *face*! She—crap, how can something like that happen? She, like, she—she wasn't human! She was this—she was like this *animal*—"

Oh my God oh my God oh my God.

I'm not the only one inching nearer to the confrontation. All around me, smokers and romantic couples are drifting over, trying to get close enough to hear, their faces reflecting fascination and amusement. Joe's voice sounds again, still untroubled, soothing.

"I'm sure that was quite a shock. You look like you've been injured, maybe we—"

"Fuck *yeah* I'm injured! She tried to claw my *eyes* out!"

"So maybe we should get those injuries looked at, Bobby. I'm just sayin'."

Bobby. So either Joe knew the guy's name before or he was able to extract it a few seconds into the encounter and is using it now as a way to keep the man calm. Either way, I'm impressed.

But the tactic isn't working on Bobby, whose voice gets angrier. "What you should be *doing* is looking for a crazy woman who turned into a lion right here in the middle of the city!"

That's sort of what I'm doing. I've gotten to the edge of the alley by now and I'm squinting at the pile of shadows behind Arabesque, behind the nearby buildings, looking for the chatoyant glint of cat's eyes staring back at me. I don't really expect Celeste to have stuck around this long, but I'm not sure where she could have gotten to safely in the minute or so that's passed. I'm as worried about that as I am about what the *hell* she's just done.

She changed shapes? In the arms of a stranger? Okay, sure, I'm not surprised he got fresh and he might even have gotten rough and maybe she panicked, but she *changed shapes*? It's axiomatic that shapeshifters don't tell ordinary people who and what they are unless they have absolutely zero choice or they have absolutely perfect confidence. So much is at stake—not just their own lives, their own secrets, but the lives and secrets of the entire community of shifters who have existed for thousands of years beside their human brethren, unknown and unsuspected. She has jeopardized everyone.

She really must have been afraid of him.

In my scrutiny of the alley's likely hiding places, I must have missed a couple exchanges, because now I hear Joe's voice raised a little louder in response to something Bobby just said. "I said, we'll look into it. But I can smell the booze on your breath and—"

Bobby shoves Joe hard in the chest. "I am *not* drunk, motherfucker! That woman, she—" He is clearly tired of repeating himself, so he makes his point by throwing another punch.

Joe moves fast, catching Bobby's arm and twisting it behind Bobby's back, so the guy howls in pain again. But there's a lot of fight left in him, drunk and mad as he is, and he lurches around, trying to shake Joe off, trying to kick him. I hear someone in the crowd yell, "Call the cops!" and there's a general movement of people, some running back inside, some pattering closer, ready to help or interfere.

I sink deeper in the shadows, waiting for it all to get sorted out. It's only a few minutes before Bobby is more or less subdued and a small crowd, mostly male, accompanies Joe as he marches his captive to the front of the building and back inside. Seconds later, a police car arrives, complete with sirens and flashing lights, and I see a couple of uniformed men get out of the car and head for the door of Arabesque.

I slip into the alley and start looking around. By now my eyes have more or less adjusted to the dark, which is only faintly broken by a string of old white Christmas lights hung above Arabesque's back door. I'm not watching for Celeste anymore; now I'm searching for her clothes. When shape-shifters transition from human to animal form, their accessories don't transition with them. If they make the transformation before they have time to disrobe, they leave behind little piles of jeans and skirts and underwear. If they change into something much bigger than their human selves, they leave behind *ripped* piles of clothing.

I'm guessing Bobby was so unnerved by the appearance of the

bobcat he didn't even notice that Celeste's clothes were littering the ground—a little supporting evidence that his story might be true. It doesn't take me long to find the items she's discarded. I pocket the gold necklace and the navel ring, because I know these are among her favorites, but I stuff the tight jeans and the strappy top and the feathered headpiece into the nearest Dumpster. I can't exactly carry them back into the bar with me but I prefer that they aren't found by anyone making a casual survey of the alley.

I look around some more but don't see anything else I should take care of.

The next trick will be finding Celeste. In her alternate state, she can make her way back to her apartment easily—well, in the sense that the journey won't be too taxing *physically*. But a bobcat on the loose in the streets of Quinville might find the trek dangerous. There are a lot of streets to cross and plenty of places where the ground cover is thin. Bobby isn't the only loud, stubborn drunk she might encounter on the way.

She could turn human again at will, of course. Celeste is blessed in that regard. But I'm not sure how much safer a beautiful naked woman would be, trying to cross Quinville at night.

Time to gather my highly questionable reinforcements.

I step briskly out of the alley, around the building, and back into the bar, which, after the dimness outside, suddenly seems too bright. It's also a scene of chaos. The band has stopped playing, though the musicians are clustered together on the stage, looking uncertain. Groups of customers have gathered around tables and in corners, huddled together as if for warmth. Most people are drinking something. Many of them, primarily the women, keep glancing over their shoulders as if they're afraid something is stalking up from behind. Joe and the two cops are making dark, burly shapes around the table where Bobby, his brother, and his sister-in-law are seated. Bobby's still mad; I can see his mouth working fast and his arms gesticulating wildly. In the bar's smoky light I can also see the four slim lines of blood across his cheek.

No doubt someone has said something like, "She sure cut you up good, dawg, but those are just the fingernail scratches from an ordinary girl." Because who could possibly believe anything else? But to me, they look like claw marks, thin and nasty.

I make my way to the table where Ryan, Rain, and the other blondes are standing, as uncertain and unnerved as everyone else. "There you are," Rain says in exaggerated relief as she sees me. "*What is going on?* Do you have any idea?"

The only person in this whole room who can provide me any assistance is Ryan, so for the first time in months, I actually think I could find shelter by burrowing into his embrace. I don't do it, of course, but I do meet his eyes and we trade a look. He knows exactly what has happened and, like me, will do everything in his power to help Celeste escape this night unscathed.

I make my voice puzzled and a little alarmed. "No! I went out for a walk and when I got back the cops were here and people were acting all crazy. What happened? Where's Celeste?"

Rain's eyes are huge. "She started dancing with that cute guy, that Bobby?" She doesn't quite point, but her vague gesture indicates the table where the cops and the troublemaker are still arguing. "And when the music stopped, they went outside, you know? To talk? And suddenly he starts screaming and saying she turned into a lion and scratched his *face* up? I mean, what's that about?"

"And now the cops are here and they want people to stick around if they have any information, but *I* don't know anything," says one of the other blondes. "I just want to go home." Belatedly she adds, "I'm worried about Celeste, though. I mean, of course."

"Of course," I echo. "So what do you think happened?"

Ryan speaks up. "He probably tried to cop a feel and Celeste didn't like it and she scratched his face up." He shakes his head admiringly. "She's done it before. The girl knows how to take care of herself."

Ah. That's the tack we're going to take. I say, "Oh man. I remember that one time. Where were we—down on Washington Avenue in St. Louis, right?"

"That's right," Ryan confirms.

"And this guy had been bugging her all night. And finally she agreed to dance with him, and then she kneed him right in the balls. On the dance floor. I mean, *hard*. He fell down and was writhing around like a baby."

"They called the cops then, too," Ryan says in a reminiscing tone.

"Bobby's face looks pretty bad," one of the blondes says in a nervous voice.

"Well, I guess he was pretty violent with *her*," I respond. "Celeste doesn't take much shit."

"So are you going to stay and talk to the police?" Rain asks me. "I mean, I want to do the right thing, but I didn't *see* anything. I don't *know* anything. I don't even know if she's ever met Bobby before in her life."

"Sure, we'll stay," Ryan says. "You guys go home. We'll take care of this."

Rain turns to her fellow beauty queens. "Or, you know, we could head on over to Black Market. I think they're still open for another couple of hours."

"Oh, hey, yeah," one of them answers. "My car's right over there, too."

"Great!" Rain answers. She gathers up her purse, then says to me, "Tell Celeste we're worried about her and she should let us know as soon as she's home." Then she flashes a white smile at Ryan. "Call me," she tells him.

She follows the other girls out the door. The place has largely emptied out in the past five minutes, and now it's maybe one-quarter full. I see the musicians on stage packing up their instruments. Nothing like a little mayhem to kill the mood.

I smirk over at Ryan. "Call me," I simper.

He grins. "Women love me."

"She's so not your type."

"I don't have a type. I like everyone."

It's not worth trying to find an answer to that, and anyway, Joe and one of the cops are headed our way. Someone must have pointed us out as the people who were hanging out with Celeste before the evening deteriorated.

I recognize the cop, and I want to start swearing. He's actually the sheriff of Quinville, a transplanted Southerner with a soft voice and sharp mind. Every time I've had a conversation with him I've felt guilty and nervous, like a schoolgirl trying to hide a misdeed from the principal. He and Janet were friends, sort of—she would come into town specifically to make house calls on his three German shepherds. She always said it was a good idea to do favors for powerful people, but I've found it impossible to take over that responsibility. I keep expecting him to ask to see my vet's license or my school diploma; I keep expecting him to expose me as a fraud.

Though that is not my primary concern right now.

"Good evening, Miss Karadel," he greets me in a pecan-pie drawl that from anyone else I would find seductive. He's good-looking in a beefy sort of way—maybe six feet tall, solidly built, with deep blue eyes looking out from a tanned and strongly molded face. His closely cropped black hair is starting to gray at the temples, and he looks like he's about forty, but Janet always said he was younger than he seemed. *It's the kind of job that ages you,* she had observed.

"Hey, there, Sheriff," I reply.

He pulls over one of the empty stools and half sits on it—like Joe, I think, attempting to seem less intimidating. Joe ranges behind him, but I keep my focus on the man right in front of me. "Kind of got a weird thing going on tonight," he observes, squinching his face up to indicate it's all just a little outside his normal purview.

"I'm not even sure exactly what's happened," I say.

But he's looking over at Ryan. "Don't think I know you, son. I'm Malcolm Wilkerson."

"Ryan Barnes. Sir."

Wilkerson spreads his hands. "So here's the situation. That young man over there—Bobby Foucault—he apparently met a young lady here tonight. Woman named Celeste Saint-Simon. People here say she's a friend of yours?"

"That's right," I reply. "I came with her tonight. Ryan joined us later."

"Ahuh. Well, Bobby took Celeste out to the back alley to get friendly, only he got too friendly and she didn't like it. She scratched his face and ran off."

"Sounds like Celeste," Ryan says.

"Here's the weird part. He says she turned into some kind of wild cat before she scratched him. She was a woman—and then she was a mountain lion. Or something." He looks between us with his blue eyes at their widest. His voice is dripping with Southern honey when he says, "You ever hear of such a thing before?"

Ryan opens and shuts his mouth, then looks at me. His expression says, *How can I tell the sheriff he's talking like a lunatic?* "No, sir," he says cautiously.

"This Celeste Saint-Simon never—never went through any kind of permutations like that when you could see her?"

Ryan looks at me again, so this time I answer. "No. Does he really think—do *you* really think—I mean—*what*? She changed into an animal? That's what he's saying?"

"Ahuh," the sheriff drawls again. "I have to admit, those scratches on his face look a little—different—than what I've seen in domestic disputes in the past. She clawed him in the chest, too. Got him real good. And those wounds don't look like your average fingernail marks, either."

For a moment I cast around for explanations that might sound logical. Maybe *Celeste has been filing her nails to super sharp points. She thinks it's fashionable.* Or maybe *She's been carrying a can of mace and this knuckle bar that looks like cat's claws. She says you can never be too careful when you meet people at a bar.* But I don't have the energy to maintain the lies. Let Celeste figure out what to tell the cops if they decide to follow up.

"I don't know what to tell you, sir," is all I come up with.

He nods and devises his own plausible alternative. "Maybe she had car keys or something in her hand, and she used those as a weapon. Because—mountain lion? Unless I can get a witness or some corroborating testimony, it's just not credible. I think I'm going to have to write him off as a drunk."

Ryan and I both nod, but prudently remain silent.

"So *now* the question is, where is this Celeste Saint-Simon?" the sheriff asks. "She hasn't come back inside, and the manager tells me there's no one out in the alley. I'm a little worried about the young woman's safety."

Oh, crap. I hadn't expected that. "Maybe she just went home," I say.

He nods. "Could be, and we want to send a squad car out there to check on her. But if she's not there we might need to start looking a little harder." He jerks his head back to indicate where the other officer is still standing guard over Bobby Foucault. "Don't want to let him go home until we're sure no one's been seriously hurt."

Worse and worse. Now we not only have to find Celeste, we have to get her back to her apartment in human shape, clearly safe and unharmed. "That makes sense," Ryan says, sounding deeply appreciative though I'm sure he's just as alarmed as I am. "Thank you."

"You happen to know her address offhand?" Sheriff Wilkerson asks.

It seems pointless to stall, so I reel it off. He doesn't write it down, so either he has an excellent memory or he already knew it and was just testing me to see if I'd tell him the truth. Why would he do that? I have no idea. But that's how Wilkerson always makes me feel.

"All right. We'll go look for her." He reaches into a breast pocket of his khaki uniform, pulls out a couple of business cards, and hands one to each of us. "Meanwhile, if you happen to find her before we do, tell her to give us a call or come down to the station, in case she wants to give us a statement."

"Yes, sir. We'll do that," Ryan says.

We all stand up, we all shake hands, and I settle my purse on my shoulder. Is this it? Can we go? Ryan nudges me with his foot and nods down at the floor, where I see Celeste's shiny silver handbag nestled against the base of the table. I think quickly but see no reason I can't admit it's Celeste's and take it with me, telling anyone who asks that I'll return it as soon as I see her. The sheriff turns away to say something to Joe, and I bend over to retrieve the purse. When I straighten up, I find Wilkerson has turned back to me with a smile.

"I forgot to ask you," he says. "You heard from Miss Janet lately? I sure do miss her."

I smile brightly in return. As part of maintaining the fiction that Janet is still alive, I frequently field such questions from her former clients. I'm constantly inventing news about her travels, phone calls, and occasional visits. "I got an e-mail from her this morning. She's doing great."

"She going to be back in town anytime soon?"

"Maybe. I didn't ask."

"Well, you tell her to come on by my place and say hi next time she's here. My dogs miss her even more than I do."

"I'll tell her you said that! How are they doing—I know she'll ask me."

"Babe's getting kind of old and gimpy. I don't think she'll be with me much longer. But the other two are just as healthy as can be. Barking their heads off last night at a squirrel got caught in the garage. Almost had the neighbors calling the cops on *me*."

Ryan and I both offer polite laughs. "She'll be glad to hear that," I tell him.

He nods at each of us, a silent good-bye, and this time he really does walk away. I glance quickly over at Joe, who gives me a small smile and a slight shrug. I read it as *Whaddya gonna do?* I smile and shrug in return. *Nice to meet you. Strange how the evening ended up. Whaddya gonna do?*

"All right, then, I think we can go," Ryan says in an undervoice. I nod and adjust my grip on the two purses, mine and Celeste's. Ryan puts his arm around my waist and guides me to the door. I try not to lean on him for support or shelter, but it's been that kind of night. I need a little of both.

The air seems sharply cooler outside, as if autumn has swirled through while we were inside lying to the police. Or as if the weather is turning ominous just as a reflection of our lives. Synchronicity.

"So now what?" I murmur to Ryan. "Do we look for Celeste? *Where* do we look for her?"

"I've been thinking. What would I do if I were her? I'd go hang out at my car and wait for my friends to drive it home for me."

That sounds reasonable, so I pull myself free of Ryan's grip and lead him several streets over to where Celeste and I found a parking spot. We're a few avenues from the main drag, so there isn't much activity and the street isn't particularly well-lit. Unfortunately, her car is under one of the few lampposts, so anyone watching from nearby storefronts or apartment buildings would definitely notice if a bobcat was lurking nearby. However, there are plenty of promising bushes and city trash cans and bus-stop benches along the street, throwing a modicum of shade. I dig through her purse to find her keys, and the electronic locks make a little chirp as they release.

"You drive really slowly," Ryan orders. "I'll watch for her along the sidewalk. When you get to a dark stretch, come to a stop for a few minutes and I'll get out."

We put this admirable plan in action, and I roll down the street at exactly two miles per hour. At the first intersection, there's a nice little wooden stockade to hold a collection of Dumpsters and recycling bins, and Ryan hops out to look around. I bend down to peer out through the passenger's side window.

And there's Celeste stepping out past the stockade's wide door, sleek and naked and human in the patchy light. Her skin is only a shade lighter than the wood of the fencing and her hair is as dark as night. She could have hidden here till morning and never caught anyone's attention.

"Celeste!" I exclaim as she slides into the backseat and hunkers down. "Are you all right?"

"I'm fine. God, that Bobby is such a prick. What took you so long? Get in the backseat with me. And turn up the heat," she says rapidly, all the commands and questions running together.

Ryan's already circled the car and opened my door, so I quickly yield my place and jump in back with Celeste. She's not embarrassed about being nude, because nothing embarrasses Celeste, but even in the inadequate light, I can tell she looks chilly and pissed off. I scoot close enough to wrap my arms around her and rub her back for warmth. Ryan puts the car in drive and begins cruising out of the neighborhood.

"I don't suppose you keep spare clothes in the trunk," I say.

"No, but I think I'd better start! I'm not that cold—I just changed shapes when I saw you guys pull up—but what a fucking stupid way to spend my evening."

"Well, and it's going to get even stupider because the police are sending a squad car to your place, and if you show up without any clothes on, they're going to ask a *lot* of questions."

"You guys called the *cops*?"

"*We* didn't," Ryan says from the front seat. "But there was a certain amount of commotion after you disappeared, and the police were most definitely summoned. And they were very interested in Bobby Foucault's story about the woman who changed into a mountain lion when he tried to kiss her. Either he doesn't recognize a bobcat when he sees one, or he didn't think a bobcat would sound all that scary," he adds.

I can hear the grin in Celeste's voice, and it makes me want to slap her. "Yeah. I figured changing shapes right then might not be such a good idea."

"Then why did you do it?" I demand. I'm still rubbing her skin to help warm her, but my voice isn't very friendly. "I mean—you shifted in front of a stranger? Are you *crazy*?"

"I know, I know. But I was so mad I wasn't thinking straight."

"Why? What'd he do?" Ryan asks.

"He assaulted me! He had one hand up my shirt and his other

hand unzipping my jeans and he was, like, slamming me into the wall. I mean, seriously, I thought he was going to rape me there in the alley."

I pull back to look at her as hard as I can in the dimness, because Celeste is prone to exaggeration. But she looks completely serious. And maybe a little bit frightened. "Why didn't you scream?" I ask slowly. "You knew there was a bouncer at the door. You knew there were a lot of people around."

"I panicked, okay? I mean, he had his cock *out*, you know, and he was hard. He was ready. I panicked, and I defended myself, and, well, I shifted. And I clawed him up pretty good," she adds on a note of satisfaction.

I glance toward the rearview mirror, where I can see Ryan's eyes, trained on Celeste. His face looks grim. "You need to tell that to the cops," he says.

"I'm not talking to the cops. Anyway, nothing happened. I got away from him and everything's fine."

"Well, you *are* talking to the cops, because they're coming to your place and they want to be sure you're all right," I say. "And you should tell them what kind of monster Bobby is, so that in a few weeks when he assaults *another* girl, and maybe does even worse, they'll believe her story."

She glances down at her nude body. "Well, I can't exactly talk to them dressed like this," she says. "And if they're already waiting for me when we drive up—"

I'm stumped. The local Walmart closes at ten and I don't know where else we might buy clothes at this hour. I can hurry into her apartment to grab jeans and a T-shirt, but if a cop has already staked the place out—and if he recognizes me from the bar—

She makes a *gimme* motion with her right hand. "Take off your clothes and let me put them on."

"What? No! How is it any better if *I'm* the one who's naked?"

"Because *you* don't have to get out of the car and walk up the sidewalk! As soon as the cop follows me inside you can jump in your car and drive away."

"Naked. All the way down Highway 159."

"I'll give you my shirt," Ryan says from the front seat.

"Give it to Celeste!"

"It doesn't look like something I'd wear to a bar," Celeste says impatiently. "But it will be decent for just driving home. You'll still have on your panties. You'll be just fine."

I argue feebly for a few more moments, but it was obvious from the minute she proposed her plan that Celeste would get her way. She always does. Ryan pulls over in some deserted parking lot, and we all start stripping down and swapping clothes. Ryan's short-sleeved polo shirt is still warm from his body and fragrant with masculine scents—soap, aftershave, sweat. I try not to inhale too deeply. Celeste has a pile of cloth grocery bags stuffed under the seat, so I spread a couple of them over my thighs to hide my bare legs.

"I hate this," I grumble, but of course no one listens to me. A few minutes later, we're on our way, and soon enough we're pulling into Celeste's apartment complex.

Where, indeed, there's a cop parked in front of her building, waiting with the determined patience of a man who could watch icebergs form. "Showtime," Celeste murmurs as Ryan brings her car alongside the police car. She rolls the window down.

"Officer—were you looking for me? I'm Celeste Saint-Simon."

He's out of the car in about three seconds flat, and it's clear he wants to take a statement and maybe look her over. I can't figure out the logistics of the next few minutes, but Ryan's way ahead of me. He practically pushes Celeste out of her car so she can confer with the police, then drives over to my Jeep at an angle that ensures Celeste's car hides my body when I step out.

"Wait for me," he says, then parks, returns the keys to Celeste, and jogs back to the Jeep and climbs in.

To my delight, I remember I have a pair of jeans in the backseat, and I don't waste any time grabbing them and slipping them on. When I'm dressed I feel a hundred percent better about the evening. This whole time, I'm watching Celeste in my rearview mirror. She's talking with her usual animation, smiling with her usual charm. She doesn't look worried or upset or frightened about any of the things that might have been set in motion this night.

"Should we wait till he's gone, then go in and make sure she's all right?" I ask.

"I don't think so. When I handed her the keys she said, 'Talk to you guys tomorrow. Drive safe.' So I think she's ready for us to go home."

I'm trying with limited success to suppress a yawn. "And I am so ready to *go* home," I say. "What a night." I switch on the ignition and back out. "So where are you parked?"

"Over by the Square. About a block from where you guys were. But you don't have to take me back to my car."

"Sure I do. It'll only take a few minutes."

"I meant—maybe we could go somewhere else. There's a Denny's that's still open. We could get breakfast. Pancakes, yum."

"No shirt, no service," I remind him, because I can't remember the last time I was in a restaurant that admitted half-naked customers, even if they were as finely sculpted as Ryan. "Besides, if I eat pancakes at one in the morning, I will fall asleep at the wheel."

"Then don't go home. Stay at my place. Go home in the morning."

By this time I've pulled out onto the street and am traveling back toward the Square. I glance over just as a streetlight flashes its illumination through the windshield, and I can see Ryan smiling at me.

I try to clamp down on the sudden bounding of my heart. "I don't think that's such a great idea," I say.

His smile widens. "Hey, you can have the bed to yourself. I'll sleep in the living room."

"Yeah. Still not a great idea. Anyway, I can't. I have all the animals to take care of."

I see the annoyance flit across his face. "You'll be back in the morning."

"Yeah, but I don't like to be gone more than twelve hours. Stuff happens. If Daniel was there, he'd shift back to human shape and feed everybody if I didn't show up on time, but he's not. There's no one on the premises right now I trust to take over if I'm gone."

Ryan lifts a hand and strokes my cheek with his knuckles. "That's Karadel for you," he says softly. "Always taking care of everyone else. Not letting anyone else take care of her."

I jerk my head away. "I don't need to be taken care of."

"Doesn't everybody? Some of the time?"

I force a laugh. "This from the man who's not famed for his caretaking skills."

"I don't want to be responsible for the whole world, that's true," he acknowledges. "I don't want to build a private *zoo* on my property and take in every distressed animal or shape-shifter in the bistate area and nurse it back to health. But one or two people? Yeah, I think I could watch over them."

I hold my peace. We've had this conversation before, only it was much more heated. *You're so selfish. You don't give a damn about anybody or anything but yourself* had been my contribution. He had volleyed back with *You're just afraid to* live! *You hide here at this clinic and pretend it matters because you can't face what waits out in the real world!* I doubt

Ryan has forgotten the specifics of that exchange any more than I have.

I turn off the main drag and into the honeycomb of streets that make up the Square. Still pretty lively, even at this hour. "So where *exactly* are you parked?" I say.

"Left here, then right on Maple. About halfway down. So, still 'no' on the pancakes? Have some coffee, you'll stay awake for the drive."

I've spotted his car, a black convertible. He drives it with the top down even in January. Ryan's never so happy as when he's got the wind in his face. That means he's in motion. That means he isn't trapped somewhere. Even better if he's not trapped *with* someone. I bring the Jeep smoothly alongside his car.

"Still no," I say. "But thanks for the offer."

He doesn't open the door right away, just watches me in the yellow light coming from a beer sign in the window of a nearby bar. "Can I come out one day next week and visit?" he asks.

I try not to show how much this flusters me. Like Celeste, like Alonzo, he used to pretty much have the run of my place. I assume he still has a key, as they do, and if he doesn't, he knows where I keep a spare. But he hasn't been out to the property for two months now, not since our last disastrous fight. We've talked on the phone, e-mailed, seen each other a few times when Celeste was around, but we've kept a physical distance along with the emotional one.

"Sure, yeah, anytime," I say.

He's smiling again. "I need to get my shirt back," he says.

"Oh! Yeah, but— Hey, I have an old sweatshirt in the backseat. If you wait a minute I'll just—"

"It's fine," he interrupts. "Keep it. Anyway, that's not all I need."

I take a deep breath. Surely he's not going to launch into an *I need you in my life* speech. That's not Ryan's style. "Yeah? Then—?"

"Last spring. You made me some kind of drug. I think I want more."

I turn my head to appraise him. I like the change of topic. It toggles me back into a professional mode, puts me at ease. "I thought it made you too sick to your stomach. You stopped taking it."

"Yeah, I did, over the summer, but I started using it again in the past few weeks. I still feel like I'm gonna puke, but that feeling wears off a little faster each time. And the drug works. I don't mind throwing up a couple of times if it gives me a little more control."

Ryan's particular shape-shifting pattern is one I've never found in anyone else. Every five days, he switches to one of three animal shapes—cat, fox, or falcon—and he holds that shape for twenty-four to forty-eight hours. Once he returns to his human form, it'll be another five days before he'll shift again. Though his body takes the three animal shapes in a set cycle, and he can't influence that, he has a little say in the timing, because he can transition out of his human body anytime he chooses. So if, for instance, there is some event occurring on a Saturday for which he absolutely must be human, he can shift on a Tuesday, return to his own form on Thursday, and be certain of being a man over the weekend.

My drugs successfully provided him with more time between transformations. Up to two weeks, if he injected himself every day.

"Well, great. I'd be happy to mix up more formula for you. Might take me a couple of days, though."

"Okay. So I should come see you—Tuesday? Wednesday? How does that sound?"

"Sounds good."

He smiles, and again touches my cheek with the back of his hand. His fingers are so warm they scorch my skin. "Sounds good to me, too," he says. For a moment he just watches me, and I think he might lean over and kiss me. Then he shakes his head, drops his hand, and climbs out of the car.

"See ya," he says. "Drive carefully." And he shuts the door and vaults into the convertible. By the time I've made a U-turn, he's already pulled out of the parking space and shot down to the end of the street.

The entire drive home, down 159, down W, past sleeping houses, empty cornfields, and moon-washed trees, I can feel the touch of Ryan's hand upon my face.

CHAPTER FIVE

The next few days pass in a blur of activity. Aurelia brings Alonzo out to spend the weekend and stays to chat for about an hour. She's so different from Bonnie that I sometimes wonder how they ended up together. Whereas Bonnie usually looks like she's dressed for hiking through the Rocky Mountain National Park—a little rumpled and über granola—Aurelia's image is cutthroat Wall Street or high-stakes politics. She's always wearing expensive tailored suits, full hose, designer pumps, and carefully understated jewelry; of the five closets in their house, three are hers, and some of her wardrobe leaks into Bonnie's as well. Her fine hair—a delicate flame-red that's entirely natural—is usually pulled into a sleek bun or clipped back with a matte gold barrette. I envy her skin, a translucent milk-white that I have never seen marred with a blemish. Her eyes are a guarded gray.

Everything about her screams heartless bitch, which I've told her a million times, but she just smiles. "Some of the people I face in court are soulless bastards, and I have to make them think I can play their game." She *can* play it; she was profiled recently as the Illinois lawyer with the best win-loss ratio in the state. She looked great in the photos, too.

Most people who know her only from the courtroom would be astonished at her softer side, which is on full display today. She's wearing comfortable jeans and an untucked denim shirt, and her red hair is in a long braid that hangs over her left shoulder. I watched from the window when she drove up in her BMW and she and Alonzo climbed out. Before she let him run off to the kennel, she caught his arm, drew his head down, inspected some mark on his forehead, and kissed him on the cheek. When she pulled back, she was smiling up at him as if he had brought her the secret of eternal life. He ducked his head, offered the tiniest of smiles in response, then ambled off with Scottie to feed the dogs.

"How's he doing?" I ask her as we sip tea at the big oak table in the big airy kitchen.

"I'm not sure. He's studying, so the home schooling is turning out to be okay from an academic standpoint, but I can't tell if he misses his routine at school. Sometimes he plays pickup basketball games down at the high school, so we thought about putting him in a league somewhere, but we haven't done it."

"Bonnie said he has friends who come over."

"He does. Not good friends. No one I think he's really close to."

I make a derisive sound. "Do men *ever* allow themselves to get close to anybody?"

Her smile is instant and wicked. "Well, I'm not an expert on men, but most of the ones I know are emotionally—What's the politically correct term?—delayed."

"So maybe Alonzo's just being a guy."

"Maybe. But I think we need to find something he really loves—something he can pour his energy into—and then he'll start finding soul mates."

"When is he happiest?"

Aurelia shakes her head. "Still figuring that out." She glances around the kitchen. "He likes being here, although when I asked him if he'd want to live here full time—"

"What? Oh, I don't know that I'm ready for that."

"Don't worry. He said no. He said it wouldn't be special anymore."

"Well, he's only, what, fourteen? How many of us knew what we were going to love when we were that age?"

"I did," Aurelia says. "I knew I wanted to be a lawyer. I watched lawyer TV shows and read lawyer books and had mock trials with the dolls and the stuffed animals."

"Dolls and stuffed animals," I repeat. "Wow. So girlie."

She laughs. "Well, the dolls usually ended up going to jail while the stuffed animals were set free, so, I don't know, maybe there was some racial or diversity bias there. You know. Always working on behalf of the 'other,' the one that doesn't quite fit in."

"That's my Aurelia," I say admiringly.

She looks at her watch, mutters, "Shit," then shrugs and refills her teacup. "What about you? What did you want to be when you were fourteen?"

Oh, that's too easy. "Normal."

She tilts her head to survey me. "Not a shape-shifter?"

"Hell, yeah, not a shape-shifter. I was turning into dogs and goats and deer and ostriches and an elephant once—an honest-to-God *elephant*. I hated my life and I hated myself. There's nothing you could have asked me to do, *nothing*, that I would have refused if it had meant becoming an ordinary girl with an ordinary body."

Her gray eyes glitter. Aurelia loves exploring people's personal limits. "Would you have killed someone?"

"At the time I told myself I would," I answer honestly. "I even went through the list of people I would and wouldn't kill. There were a couple of neighbor kids I would have been totally fine with murdering in cold blood. But my dad? My aunt? The cute guy three houses down? No. I knew I couldn't hurt them." I sigh. "And I'm sure I couldn't *really* have done it, even if the opportunity arose. At least, that's what my adult self likes to believe."

"So when did you come to terms with it? When did you say, 'This is who I am, I love myself, I will make the most of my life'?"

It's a long time before I reply. I swirl the dregs of tea in my cup, I look away, I look back. But Aurelia has infinite patience; she'll wait through the apocalypse if that's what it takes before you answer. "I haven't," I say at last.

"Really? But you seem so—I guess the word is content. You have friends you care about, a job you love, a house that I personally would kill for, and I say that knowing all the drawbacks to homicide—"

She makes me laugh, but in my head I'm replaying that old argument with Ryan. *You hide here at this clinic and pretend it matters because you can't face what waits out in the real world!* "I'm here because I'm protected here," I say softly. "It's a bonus that I have the skills and knowledge to help other people who are like me. Even if I didn't, I'd still be here. There's no place else that's safe."

"Do you fantasize about running away?"

"All the time." I would never admit that to Ryan, of course, but it's a relief to speak the words aloud to Aurelia. She's so familiar with the world's evil that nothing shocks her. "And if I ever perfected the serum that would let me wholly control my shifting? I'd be gone. I'd lock up this place and go."

She nods. "It's interesting that you think so."

I'm a little affronted. "What? You don't believe me?"

"I think maybe your circumstances helped mold you into a certain kind of person, but I don't believe that person could be pried out of you now if you took a chisel and split your body in half. Okay, maybe you could walk away from this clinic—but you'd set one up somewhere else. Or open a stray rescue foundation. Or start working with hunger charities. I don't believe you know how to live a life without meaning."

"That's not true. I can be shallow. I know I can."

She smiles. "Well, then. I hope you find the right medical formula so you get a chance."

Once she's gone, I work alongside Alonzo in the barn until the first client of the day shows up, leading a dachshund with a bad limp. Three more people from town arrive before the day is over, but their animals are simply animals and their problems are routine.

Right around nightfall, when I've released Alonzo from work and let him start playing his video games, a couple of shape-shifters come to the porch. One's a black wolf, and he looks so much like Cooper that for a moment my breath catches in my throat. He even has a little silver around his muzzle, like Cooper did in those last couple of years, but this one is still strong and healthy. He has a good five years left, I'm guessing, maybe more.

His companion is a mixed-breed dog, maybe part shepherd, part chow, with rough curly dark hair and root-beer-colored eyes. She's got a gash in her left foreleg that's deep, ugly, and not very old, but it's already starting to show signs of infection. Not fatal, though, not yet; she's arrived in time.

I'm pretty sure I've never seen either one of them before, and neither one chooses to or is able to take human form and talk to me, but I'm positive they're shape-shifters who know about me through the informal grapevine of our strange community. For one thing, true wolves don't generally show up at my door and look around with quite this degree of focused curiosity, showing no alarm when a woman steps outside and begins speaking to them. For another, feral dogs don't usually extend their injured limbs in a silent request for attention, then wait patiently when I say, "Let me get some supplies— I'll be right back."

I clean and bind the wound, giving my patient care instructions that include "Come back and see me in a few days and I'll change the dressing for you." I also give them a tour of the compound, showing them where they can sleep if they want to spend the night. When they settle into one of the unoccupied lean-tos, lovingly outfitted with blankets and other amenities, I say, "Give me a minute and I'll bring food and water. You can stay as long as you want. And if you're here in the morning, I'll check your leg again."

Alonzo puts the video game on pause so he can help me bring out bowls of supplies. He seems fascinated by the wolf, but he doesn't get too close. He pets the dog, though, and she licks his hand. *Just another instance of women being more open and approachable than men,* I think with a grin. But, honestly, even I find the black wolf a little intimidating. He's a man at least some of the time, yes, but that doesn't mean he's civilized. In this state, at any rate, he looks as wild as they come.

When I wake up Sunday morning, I'm instantly aware of the weight of another living creature on the end of my bed. Too small to be Scottie, too big to be one of the cats. I sit up and peer through the half-light permitted by the curtains. A not-quite-full-grown raccoon stares back at me, his dark eyes unblinking. Between his front paws rests an apple that he probably stole from the bowl in the kitchen.

"Alonzo," I say. "I'm guessing this is a surprise."

I yawn and reach for the cell phone I keep on my bedside table. It's barely 8 A.M., but Bonnie answers on the first ring. She's probably been up before dawn, re-siding the house or serving breakfast at the homeless shelter.

"Hey. Alonzo shifted overnight. He's a raccoon. Isn't this a little early for him?"

Bonnie's voice is concerned but not anxious. "It is. We thought he had another three or four days."

"Well, you know. Teen hormones. They can interfere with everything."

"I was going to pick him up this afternoon, but should I come get him right now?"

"He's probably better off out here, don't you think? He can stay until he shifts back."

"If it's not too much of an imposition."

"Not at all. Hell, I won't even have to feed him, since it looks like he can forage pretty well on his own."

"It's usually two or three days before he's human again. Call us when he's ready and one of us will come get him."

"All right. And don't *worry*. We'll be fine."

Alonzo, in fact, seems quite happy. He scurries out the front door when I open it for him and immediately heads over to the trash containers. I take a shower, eat a quick breakfast, and make my rounds among the animals, Scottie at my heels.

The shape-shifters are gone, which I take as a good sign. If they were worried about the leg wound, surely they would have stuck around longer. Daniel, on the other hand, is back, again in Doberman shape and again not looking very congenial. I refill his water bowl and leave him in peace. The puppies bark hysterically after I let them out into the fenced run and Alonzo sidles up on the other side.

"Oh, you're just trying to rile them up," I say in exasperation. "I should drop you over the fence and see how amusing you think it is then." But of course I don't. The turtle seems immune to all the commotion.

Once all the animals are taken care of, I spend a couple of hours in the lab, mixing up more serum for Ryan. And another few doses for myself. I take another injection of the Baxter-and-Isabel mix, though I'm thinking I might want to try a different formula later in the month, maybe mix a little of Lanita's blood into the formula and see if that helps me control the shapes I take. Or maybe I'll design a number of different concoctions and start alternating doses—one week the serum that limits how often I change, one week the formula that turns me into a cat. Might be safer, and might be just as effective.

Sounds like a brand of birth control, I think, and snort with amusement. *Better living through chemistry.*

I'm all for it. Better living through whatever method it takes.

Monday and Tuesday pass without incident; it's Wednesday when life gets interesting again.

For starters, Alonzo is human in the morning, which doesn't seem to make him happy. Well, maybe he's just suffering from the disorientation of transformation, which is harder on some than others. But he's silent during breakfast and spends most of the morning skulking in his room. I wonder if he actually *prefers* being animal to being human, and I think maybe he does. Life is drastically simpler in that alternate shape, as long as you aren't afraid for your life. When

I check up on him right before lunch, I can't resist giving him a hug, which he tolerates but does not reciprocate.

"I'm going to make us a couple of sandwiches, okay? So finish up whatever you're doing in here and then come out to the kitchen."

We eat in silence—well, Alonzo's listening to his iPod, so I suppose he has music in his head—and we're just finishing up when I hear the sound of tires on the gravel. A second later, the puppies start barking. I tap Alonzo's arm to get his attention, because he doesn't like being surprised by the sudden arrival of outsiders.

"We've got company," I say.

He strips out his earbuds and gets to his feet so he can look out the kitchen window. "It's Ryan," he says without inflection.

I used to be surprised that Alonzo didn't seem to feel for Ryan the level of hero worship that he displays for, say, Celeste. Ryan saved his life, after all, rescued him from unimaginably awful circumstances—and Ryan's one of those people who seems to naturally gather friends and disciples. He's charismatic, vibrant, exciting to be around. I couldn't figure out why Alonzo wasn't crazy about him. It wasn't the racial divide, because Alonzo has white friends as well as black ones, and race doesn't seem to keep him from forming at least tenuous attachments to Bonnie, Aurelia, and me.

Then I realized: It's because Ryan never pays any attention to Alonzo. I mean, he usually offers a friendly *Hey, Zo, how are you?* But he doesn't really listen to the answer. It's not a surprise, of course; Ryan's never been particularly interested in children and he's not great at maintaining relationships even with emotionally healthy people who don't require special handling. But it's one of the many things I find infuriating about Ryan. With the tiniest bit of effort, he could have made Alonzo adore him; he could have been the male role model the kid so desperately needs. But Ryan did his good deed and then just shrugged it off. He didn't let Alonzo change his life, and so Alonzo won't let Ryan matter in his.

"That's right, he said he'd be coming out today," I answer. "Maybe he can take you back to Quinville when he goes."

"I already talked to Bonnie. She's planning to come get me," he replies, and pushes out through the screen door. I hear Ryan greet him, hear Alonzo offer a monosyllabic reply. And then Ryan's in the kitchen, brightening it up with his blond hair, teasing smile, and electric presence.

"Your turn to babysit?" he asks lightly.

I strangle my urge to say, *You could be nicer to him, you know.* Ryan is who he is, and that's never going to change. "He comes out a lot to help me with the animals and I pay him a pittance for his time. It works for both of us." I stand up and start gathering the dishes. "We just finished lunch, but there's plenty of food, if you're hungry."

He shakes his head. "I ate on the way."

I dump all the dishes in the sink with a clatter, then turn back to face him. "So I mixed up a couple of vials for you. Did you bring a cooler? Because they should be kept refrigerated."

"I did. It's on the porch."

"Great. I can give you the first injection, unless you'd rather do it yourself."

"I'd be happy to have you play nurse, but can't we just sit and talk for a few minutes? You know, 'Hey, how was your day?' and 'Gee, I've missed you, it's been so long.'"

I'm forced to smile. "Well, I just saw you a few days ago, so I haven't had that much time to miss you, but I'd be happy to hear how your day has gone."

He grins and heads to the fridge, pulling the door open. "Can I have something to drink?"

"Of course."

There's a pause while he studies his choices, which include caffeinated and decaffeinated brands of cola, lemon-lime soda, juice, and flavored carbonated water. Ryan prefers to drink Coke out of a glass bottle, and I used to keep six-packs on hand just for him. Two months ago I pried the top off the last remaining bottle, poured the contents down the sink, and threw the bottle into the recycling bin so hard that it shattered.

He selects a can of Diet Coke and opens it without complaint. "So how was your day?" he asks.

"Very exciting. I released a couple of injured wild rabbits that had been with me for a week because they're fine now. I had someone drive in from town with her cat, whose paw was all swollen from a bee sting. I answered some e-mail. How was *your* day?"

"Wow, I don't think I can top that." He sips from the can. "Today's been kind of lackluster, but over the weekend I was in St. Louis and I spent a few hours at Lumière Place." I recognize the name as being that of a huge casino complex down on the St. Louis riverfront, though I've never been there. It totally fits Ryan's personality that he loves to gamble.

"Did you win?"

"I did. Five thousand dollars at blackjack."

"Wow! Good for you. You going to be sensible and save it or spontaneous and spend it?"

He grins. "What do *you* think?"

"Um. Let me see." I tap my chin. "Which option sounds more like Ryan? I gotta go with B."

His grin widens. "Five thousand dollars isn't enough to change my life, but it could sure help me make a pretty big splash if I spend it all in one place."

"That it could. So what are you going to do?"

He takes a few swallows of soda, watching me over the rim. "Thinking about driving down to New Orleans for a few days. Staying at a fancy hotel. Eating at the best restaurants. I bet I could go through five grand pretty fast."

"Good thing I got your serum ready. Take a shot every day, and who knows how long you could stay down there, partying all night long."

"Won't be any fun to go by myself, though," he says. "You want to come along?"

He says it so casually that at first I hardly register the words. "Come along—come to *New Orleans* with you?"

"Sure. Probably take us a couple days to drive down. We can bring camping gear, in case we need to—" He makes an undefined gesture. *In case we need to wait out a couple of days while one of us is in animal shape.* "Then spend a glorious few days in the most decadent city in America."

"I can't be gone that long," I say.

A look of irritation crosses his face, but his voice is coaxing. "Sure you can! Hire someone to stay with the pets for a week. You cannot be the only person on the planet who knows how to turn on a water hose and open a few cans of dog food."

I laugh but I'm far from sold. "Yeah but—some of my animals aren't really animals. They wouldn't be comfortable with a stranger around."

"Then hire Alonzo! Or Bonnie! Even Celeste, though you'd have to offer her something other than money."

"Really? She's always broke."

He's grinning. "Guess how much money *she* won in the Illinois lottery this week."

"Five thousand dollars," I say. He nods. "You're kidding. Wow, even by your standards, that's kind of spooky."

"So you'd have to bribe her with something else, but I'm sure you'd figure it out."

"Maybe but—Ryan—I don't know if it's such a good idea. For you and me to go away on a romantic trip together."

There. I've said it out loud, though my spare and awkward sentences don't come close to laying out the whole situation. *I'm still half in love with you, but I'm pretty sure you'll break my heart, and I just don't have the energy to try to believe in you again. It's almost more than I can manage to be your friend, but I care about you so much I can't bear to cut you from my life altogether. You are the problem I cannot solve, the knot I cannot untie. I don't think spending a week with you in New Orleans would make it any easier for me to find my way.*

He doesn't look angry, but he doesn't look convinced, either. "I know we said some pretty bitter things to each other last time," he says softly. "But can't we get past that? You matter to me, Kara. You're the one I keep coming back to. If I thought I was going to die tomorrow, you're the one I'd want to say good-bye to tonight. I just think—that kind of emotion is powerful enough that you shouldn't just walk away from it when it gets too hard."

Almost, he persuades me. Almost, I believe him. With Ryan, I always feel like I'm in some low-budget thriller where the heroine is on the run, surrounded by perils, and the handsome, exotic stranger shows up and promises to keep her safe. I can practically re-create the theater experience in my head, the dim lights, the bright screen, the smell of stale popcorn and spilled soda. Sometimes the audience members are shouting, *Don't you trust him, girl! Run the other way!* and sometimes they're calling, *Believe in him! Follow your heart!* But I don't know which kind of movie I'm in.

I take a deep breath. "I'm as far past it as I'm able to be right now," I say quietly. "I'm sorry. I'm doing the best I can. I want you in my life,

I just don't know if I can ever be more than friends with you again. And I'm sure not ready to go away for the week."

He stands a moment, stiff and unmoving, then he gives one sharp nod. "Fair enough. Not yet. Maybe not ever." Now he offers me a clipped smile. "But maybe."

"I'm sorry."

He sets down the empty can of Coke and stretches his arms as if his shoulders are tight. "Hey, if you were easy to win over, you might be a lot of fun, but you wouldn't be Kara."

I'm able to snort in amusement. "Who isn't fun at all."

His smile is wider this time. "I didn't mean that. Exactly."

"C'mon," I say. "Let me get you your drugs."

In a few minutes, I've administered a shot, slipped the rest of the vials into his cooler along with some baggies full of ice, and handed him another can of soda for the road.

"So you going to go to New Orleans anyway?" I ask as I walk him out the door and over to his car.

"I don't know. Maybe. I might think of some other spectacular way to blow my money."

"Well, drive carefully. If you do go. Or if you don't. Just—you know. Be careful in general."

He lays a hand on my shoulder and smiles down at me for a moment. "So should *my* parting exhortation to *you* be, 'Don't be so careful. Go wild'?"

I smile reluctantly. "I guess I'm just as likely to follow your advice as you are to follow mine."

He bends down and kisses me on the forehead, his lips lingering a moment longer than I expect. It is all I can do to keep from pulling my head back, rising on my toes, and pressing my mouth heavily against his.

Maybe all that stops me is the sound of another car pulling onto the gravel. A truck this time, and the sunlight hits the windshield in such a way that I can't tell who's behind the wheel.

Ryan and I fall apart. "Another client for Country Mouse Vet," he says. "I'll see you in a few days, I guess."

"Let me know if you have any problems with the serum. Or if you run out and need more. Or—you know. If you need anything."

He smiles, waves, and hops into the black convertible. He's in motion and out of the compound before the other vehicle has even come to a complete standstill. But then the truck's emergency brake squeals, the engine cuts, and the door opens. To my complete surprise, the man who steps out is the guy from Arabesque. The bouncer, the bowhunter, my onetime dance partner. Joe.

CHAPTER SIX

Joe stands for a moment with one foot on the running board, one hand on top of the door, looking like he's ready to turn around and go home if I so much as blink at him. "Hey," he says. "Is this a bad time to drop by?"

I want to give my head a vigorous shake to clear it. There is too great a contrast between the complex emotions I experience as I watch Ryan leave and the simple pleasure I feel as I identify Joe. I'm not sure how quickly I can make the switch, how far I've retreated behind my guarded walls, if my voice will seem strained and unfriendly. I swallow hard to clear my throat and offer a smile.

"Not at all," I say, sounding normal enough. "Did you bring Jezebel?"

His round face shows happy surprise. "You remembered her name."

My smile broadens. "Sometimes I remember animals' names better than their owners'."

"Yeah, I guess that makes sense." He steps away from the door and gives a soft whistle. "C'mon, girl."

A thin but well-cared-for black Lab climbs gingerly out of the extended cab of the truck and looks around, scenting the air. Her eyes are bright and her coat is shiny, but I can tell just by the way she holds herself that she's in a little pain. I drop to my knees to coax her over. When she trots forward to investigate me, she's favoring her right hind leg a little. I run my hands over it, feeling for scar tissue, but there's nothing obvious. I'm guessing her main complaint is old age.

I offer my hands, then scratch the top of her head, murmuring little doggie endearments. She drops to her haunches and watches me with a quizzical expression so pointed that I can almost read her mind. *You're not fooling me, you know. I know I'm old and I don't have much longer to live, so don't give me any of this "good doggie" crap.* I'm smiling as I come to my feet again.

"She's smart—I can tell by the look in her eyes," I say.

Joe laughs. "*So* smart. It's so easy to understand what she wants that I sometimes think she's got ESP or something. She just puts thoughts in my brain. 'Let's go for a walk!' or 'Feed me *now*' or 'You see that kid? He's in trouble!'"

"Really? Like 'The barn's on fire and Jimmy's inside'?"

He shuts the truck door, strolls forward, and leans down to rub the sleek black head. "Yeah, one summer I was spending the weekend with my brothers out at Carlyle Lake. All these kids going by on Jet Skis and a bunch of other people water skiing. Every time someone would wipe out and be splashing around in the water, Jez would jump in and swim over like she was gonna rescue them. We had to head her off and haul her back to shore. Except once she got away from us and she *did* make it out to some poor boy deep in the water. She saved the kid's life, because he'd lost his life jacket and he didn't swim very well and he was terrified. And Jez just towed him back in. It was pretty awesome."

"I love stories like that," I say. "Animals saving the day."

He's taking a moment to gaze around the compound, at all the buildings and fenced enclosures. From where we're standing, we can see the aviary, the dog run, and a few cages where I keep the wildest animals separate from the rest.

"Wow, look at all this," he says in an admiring voice. "You're like the witch in *Thomasina* or something."

"What's *Thomasina*? Wait, did you just call me a witch?"

"She's a good witch. It's a movie about a cat. You've never seen it?"

"I guess not."

"Old Disney movie. Really good. Do you have a bear?"

"Why would I have a bear?"

"There's one in the movie."

"I thought it was about a cat?"

"Well, there's a bear in it, too."

I can't help myself. I start laughing. "You're funny," I say. Jezebel has angled her head and is looking up at him, one ear pulled back to express polite disbelief. "Your dog thinks so, too."

He bends down and tugs on her ear as if to pull it back in place. "She just can't believe I sound like such a goofball when I'm talking to a pretty lady. She thinks maybe I should have practiced some better lines when I was driving out here."

"Oh, that's what she's telling you with her ESP, is it?"

He straightens up and grins at me. "Something like that."

"Well, you're doing just fine." I nod toward the house. "Come on. Let's take her to my office so I can look her over."

We circle around the porch toward the separate side entrance that leads directly to my office and exam room. Joe has to lift Jezebel to the metal table, but once there she submits with a dignified resignation to my poking and prodding.

"I don't think she's torn anything," I say finally. "I think she's just suffering from old age and the beginnings of arthritis. I can give you some anti-inflammatories, some glucosamine and chondroitin. You also want to make sure she eats right and gets at least a little exercise every day. Nothing too vigorous, but the more she moves, the more she'll be able to keep moving." I shrug. "Same thing is true for humans."

He takes her face between his hands and leans down to touch his nose to hers. "You hear that? No complaining when I say it's time to go for a walk." He laughs when she twitches her eyebrows at him. "Okay, maybe *I'm* the one who's too lazy to go for a walk. But that changes right now."

I make a spur-of-the-moment offer. "Not sure this is a good idea, but I have a couple of puppies who are ready to go off to good homes. If you think she'd tolerate another dog in the house, that's one surefire way to keep her active. Because these puppies are nothing *but* active."

He looks uncertain. "I don't know. I'm gone a lot. Not sure I have time to train another dog. Are they Labs? I've always been partial to big dogs."

"Beagles. Well, part beagle. Part God knows what."

He shrugs. "I can take a look, maybe. They're here?"

"Yeah, they're in the fenced area you saw as we came in."

"Sure. I'll meet them, anyway."

He lifts Jezebel from the table, then follows me to the tiny sitting room where I keep a desk, a filing cabinet, pharmaceutical samples, dog treats, and cleaning supplies for wiping down the exam room. He drops into the chair across from me while I rummage in the cabinet for some drug samples, and even though I'm not looking at him, I can tell the exact moment his eyes fall on the painting behind my desk.

"Oh, wow," he says. "That's you."

I glance up at him, over at the long horizontal painting, and back at him. I'd guess only about one percent of the people who come into my office realize that I'm the subject in the image. Even people who know me well sometimes don't recognize me in this pose. I'm on the floor, asleep, a colorful quilt covering my body, my dark hair fanning out behind me. There's one kitten curled up next to my stomach, another one balanced precariously on the mountain range of my hip and rib cage, and a third one batting at one of my loose curls. Sunlight is streaming in from an unseen window, turning the hardwood floor to amber, the colors of the quilt to jewels.

"Yeah," I say. "Painted a long time ago. I think I was eighteen."

"Why are you lying on the floor?"

"I was playing with the kittens and I fell asleep."

True as far as it goes. I had, in fact, *been* one of the kittens earlier in the day, and we had been romping around with the boundless energy of youth until we all collapsed in a heap in the middle of the floor. As happens to me so often, I transformed in my sleep. Janet had covered me with the blanket, because, of course, I was naked. Cooper had snapped a photo, and later recreated the scene in oils. I appear in about a dozen of his other paintings, but this one is my favorite.

"Who's the painter?"

"Cooper Blair. He lived here with Janet Kassebaum—you know, the vet who used to own this place. He was an artist."

"That's right. You told me about him. That's a great picture."

"Yeah, I love it. No matter how broke I am, I'm never going to sell that piece."

Joe has come to his feet and leaned over the desk to get a better look, but now he pulls back and studies me. "Would it sell for a lot of money? *Are* you broke?"

I offer a lopsided grin. "Not really broke. But this place doesn't bring in a whole lot of cash, and things are always breaking down and needing repair, and there's taxes every year and a new car every so often and—" I shrug. "So I think about money a lot."

He gestures at the painting. "I don't think you *should* sell it, but how much would it be worth?"

"Mmm, the last Cooper Blair original went for fifty thousand dollars, and that was smaller, so—maybe seventy-five thousand? Enough to buy me a few years, don't you think?"

"Man, I changed my mind! Sell it now!"

I laugh. "Well, I have almost fifty other paintings I could put on the market first, so I'm not destitute yet."

He looks puzzled. "I don't understand. Is he dead? Are you the executor of his estate? Why wouldn't Janet be handling all this?"

Because Janet is dead, too. I curse myself for being careless, but I think I sound unruffled as I respond. "Yeah, he died a few years ago. That's the real reason Janet retired—she just wanted to get away from this place and all the memories. I think I mentioned that my dad repped Cooper when they were both alive, and I know all his gallery contacts, so Janet just turned the artwork over to me. Anytime I sell something, I put the money into a fund she set up to support the property—but it's really all her money." Or it would be, if she were alive.

"What'd he die of?" Joe wants to know. "How old was he?"

Again, two very complicated questions, if I were to answer with the truth. *He was in his late thirties, but he died of old age, because shape-shifters beat up and batter their bodies so much that none of them live past fifty.* "Cancer," I say. "Right before he turned forty."

"That's sad."

"Yeah," I say. "But he left his mark on the world. He left something behind. People will remember him. That's something most of us can't say, even if we live to be a hundred."

"I'd like to see some of his other paintings."

"Sure. We'll take the whole tour. You can meet the puppies and the bunnies and the turtle." Joe laughs, and I go on. "And then we'll look at the paintings."

"Any chance of getting something to drink first? I forgot to bring water with me on the drive."

"Of course! Here, this door takes us into the house. There's soda and tea and everything else in the kitchen."

I can tell he's doing a quick study of the house as we trek down the hall, through the living room, and into the kitchen, Jezebel at our heels. Maybe he's more curious than thirsty and he just wanted a better look at the place I call home. But it doesn't bother me to show it to him. He's a comfortable sort of guy and I kind of like having him here.

The message light is blinking on the answering machine in the kitchen, so I wave at the fridge and say, "Help yourself," then hit play. The message is characteristically brief. *It's Celeste. What are you doing this weekend? Call me.*

I turn back to face Joe and find him sipping a Snapple, watching me. His face is alight with interest. "Celeste? Your friend from Arabesque the other night?"

"That's her," I say.

"So everything turned out all right? You found her and she was okay?"

"Well, she was a little shook up. That guy—Bobby?"

He nods. "Bobby Foucault. Kind of a troublemaker."

"She says he practically raped her. So she scratched him and then ran off."

"Did you tell her what he said? About her turning into a mountain lion?"

I laugh. "Yeah. She said—and I quote—'The guy's a fucking moron.'" I can't remember if she actually said that, but she certainly called him a lot of other names.

He takes another sip, his expression meditative. "That'd be something, though, wouldn't it? If people could turn into animals?"

I'm not sure how to answer that, so to buy time, I motion him away from the refrigerator and pull out my own drink at random. Turns out to be a Diet Dr Pepper, which I don't even like. I open it anyway and take a couple of swallows. "Well, it would be pretty cool, I guess. I mean, it's *impossible*, of course, but it would be an extraordinary thing to be able to do. See the world from a wholly different perspective."

"I mean, say, if you could turn into a bird. What would *that* be like?"

It's amazing and exhilarating and terrifying all at once. The world is so enormous, the winds are so capricious, and you're so small. So small. And yet you know precisely how to settle onto a vagrant breeze, exactly how to position your wings to make an elegant landing. Nothing is out of reach; no place seems too far. "It would be great," I say.

"Yeah, especially if you had to get somewhere really quick. You know, a friend calls you up and he's in trouble, but he lives thirty miles away. You could just say your magic words and turn into a hawk or an eagle, and off you go. Faster than driving, I'll bet."

I'm not so sure about that. Hawks don't reach their top speed unless they're diving on prey; otherwise, they cruise along at around forty miles an hour, and I've seen drivers double that speed along the interstate. But it seems more prudent to agree. "And you arrive and everyone says, 'How did you get here so fast?'"

"'And where's your *car*?'" Joe adds.

I laugh. "So you don't tell any of your friends that you're a shape-shifter?" I ask.

"*I* wouldn't," he says. "They'd think I was crazy."

"Unless they were all shape-shifters, too. Unless everyone was."

He wrinkles his nose in dissent. "Nah. It wouldn't be special if everyone was."

"Pretty big secret to keep," I say.

He nods, but it's clear he's started thinking along different lines. His face is creased with an old memory. "I know people can't really turn into animals, but there sure have been moments in my life when that was the only explanation that would have made sense."

I take another sip of the diet soda. God, I hate fake sweeteners. "Like when?"

"Back in Joliet, when I was on the force. Couple times, we'd be chasing a perp down a street or into a building—someplace where we knew for a fact there was no way out—and we'd turn the corner or bust into the building and—" He makes a *poof!* gesture with his empty hand. "The guy would be gone. Nowhere to be found."

"He probably climbed a fence or ran through a door you didn't know about."

"Sure, yeah, what else? But if he could turn into an animal—it would sort of make sense. There was this one time. Three of us, we had a guy cornered in an alley. I mean, there was *no* way out of that alley, there were ten-story buildings on three sides. It was like being in a horizontal well. The guy dives into a Dumpster and starts burrowing into the trash. We could see all these cans and soda bottles and old newspapers flying up as he dug down. We were kind of laughing because, you know, pretty gross, but where did he think he was going?

"So he digs in and he doesn't come out, and we're all like, 'Shit, man, we are going to have to dig in after him.' So we did. We emptied out that whole entire Dumpster. And that man was not in there. There was a *squirrel* about halfway down, and it about scared the crap out of us when it came jumping out, but there was no *person*. We dug all the way to the bottom. And he was gone."

He sips from his Snapple and focuses on me again. "But if the perp had been able to turn himself into an animal whenever he felt like it—well, maybe he *was* the squirrel. Maybe we'd caught him after all, we just didn't know it."

I'm absolutely positive that that's what happened, but I'm certainly not going to say so. "Well—the likelihood is that he got out some other way. Maybe there was a loose panel at the back of the Dumpster and he crawled out that way while you guys were digging in from the top. Or something."

"Yeah, I mean, we had to assume that's what happened. But it was still pretty damn weird."

"I can imagine."

There's a short silence and I'm trying to think of a natural segue to any other topic, when Jezebel comes to my rescue. She's been lying quietly on the kitchen floor, but a noise at the door catches her attention. She levers herself awkwardly to her feet with a little whuff of warning.

"Easy, girl. It's just my dog. Scottie," I tell her. "He wants us to come out and play."

Joe sets his empty bottle on the counter. "Yeah, and we want to take that tour now anyway. Let's go."

We all step outside, and Scottie and Jezebel sniff at each other and decide to make nice. I pat Scottie heartily on the shoulder and say, "What do you think? Shall we introduce our guests to the puppies? Maybe they'll want to take one home. Life would be a lot calmer then, don't you think?"

Scottie offers a short bark of approbation and we head off in the direction of the kennel. But Joe's already been distracted by something else. "Who's that?" he asks in a quiet voice.

He's spotted Alonzo shooting baskets at the forlorn hoop by the patio. There is no possible way that Alonzo—who is preternaturally aware of the exact whereabouts of anyone in his vicinity—overlooked Joe's arrival. Unlike Scottie, Alonzo hasn't come forward to investigate because he doesn't actually *want* to meet Joe or Jezebel. He doesn't even look in our direction as he sinks another basket.

"Alonzo. He's the foster son of some friends of mine who live in town. He comes out sometimes and helps me with the animals."

"Shouldn't he be in school about now?"

"Once a cop, always a cop," I say lightly.

He grins faintly, but his eyes are still on Alonzo. "Hey, I know a truant when I see one."

"He's having some troubles at school," I say quietly. "So they're teaching him at home. So far it's working out."

"He doing any extracurricular stuff? Playing soccer or whatever? 'Cause otherwise it's hard to make friends."

"He plays basketball sometimes, I think."

Joe nods, watches Alonzo for another moment, and then puts his attention back on me. "So. The puppies," he says.

Scottie and Jezebel follow us through the gate into the dog run, and we're instantly surrounded by a frisking, leaping, yapping vortex of canine excitement. Scottie lopes off to the side, away from the frenzy, but Jezebel stands her ground. Her lip curled, she gives a very slight growl, warning the puppies to keep their distance. They're less interested in her than in the humans, anyway.

Joe is laughing out loud. He drops to his knees, patting the top of his thigh, and all three puppies instantly pounce. The littlest one takes Joe's wrist in a mock bite, the middle one leaps up and tries to lick his face. The big one, the one with all the personality, jumps on

Joe's lap and jumps away, back and forth, back and forth, as if trying to convince this new playmate to chase him around the enclosure.

"Oh, he likes you," I say.

Joe grabs the puppy's face and ruffles his ears. "You got a ball? You got a stick? You know how to fetch?" The dog barks and pulls away, rushing around even more ecstatically. Joe laughs again.

"Oh, man, he's a charmer. Make you crazy, though, all that energy."

I find a ball and toss it halfway across the grass. All three of the dogs run madly after it, but of course it's the biggest one who reaches it first, snatches it up, and carries it back. He doesn't even look at me; he drops it in front of Joe, then waits expectantly, practically dancing with impatience. Joe obligingly hurls the ball even farther away, and the dogs go scrambling off.

"Hope you've got a good throwing arm," I say. "They can keep this up all day."

Joe doesn't seem to mind, and for the next ten minutes they engage in an energetic game of fetch. By this time, Jezebel has lost her aversion to the youngsters. She comes and settles beside Joe, seeming to watch with interest as the puppies chase down the ball, a chewed-up old rag doll, and various sticks that I scrounge up. She doesn't even seem to mind much when the obnoxious puppy pauses in his frantic running to investigate her some more, sniffing at her face and backside, then barking in her face. She merely pulls her ears back with a pained expression, then drops her muzzle to her paws.

"I think she likes him," I say in a hopeful voice.

"That seems a little strong. I think maybe she's tolerating him," Joe answers.

"Take him home. See how they get along over the long haul."

He hesitates and I realize, to my surprise, that he's actually considering it. "I would, but—I'm gone so much. I don't have time to train him and make sure he's housebroken."

I glance skyward and turn a hand palm up as if testing for rain. "Pretty nice weather this time of year," I say. It's mid-September and the days have been warm more often than not, though obviously that pattern will eventually change. "You could leave him outside most of the day, at least for a couple of months."

The exercise has tired the puppies, and now they've all come to rest, panting, sprawled out on the grass between Joe and me. The big one has rested his nose on Joe's knee and is gazing up at him with soulful adoration. As if he can't help himself, Joe is smoothing the soft fur on top of the dog's head.

"What do you call this one?"

I shake my head. "I haven't given any of them names. Once I name them, I love them, and I find it harder to give them away."

He turns his head to give me a curious look, half smile, half specu-lation. I can almost see his brain working through the analogy. *Is that how it always goes with you? You try not to let anyone in because once you do, you know you can't kick them out?* But if that's really what he's think-ing, he doesn't say so aloud. "Well, I think we should call him some-thing. Something that fits him."

"Godzilla," I suggest.

He wrinkles his nose. "Not the sort of name that would make me want to adopt him."

"You're right," I say. "Sweetie Pie. Lambchop. Mellowhead."

Now he's laughing. "'Mellowhead'? That's the dumbest thing I ever heard."

"There is *no* pleasing you."

"Well, but a name is important."

"Then you come up with one!"

"I'm still thinking."

"You can name the other two while you're at it. And then you can take them home with you, too."

He shakes his head. "I really couldn't handle three puppies, but my buddy might want one. Actually, he might want both. His kids have been bugging him for a dog, and he said the other day he'd get two so they could keep each other company."

For a moment—and it's so ridiculous—I have an actual physical pang at the thought of losing all three puppies at once. They're so exhausting but they're so adorable. I know I'll miss them.

Then I harden my heart. "Great! Fabulous! Do you have a camera? Take photos. Bring your friends out here this weekend to meet the puppies. I would love for all of them to go off and live happy lives—somewhere else."

"Yeah—hang on," he says, and shifts his weight so he can pull a smartphone from the back pocket of his jeans. He snaps a few shots of each of the dogs, and then, before I realize what he's doing, lifts the camera and clicks a photo of me.

"Hey," I say.

He's grinning as he studies the digital image. "That's a cute one. You've got a little mud on your face and dog hair all over your shirt."

"Great. Be sure to show that to your friend when you're trying to convince him he wants a couple of dogs."

Joe leans over and scrunches up the big one's ears again. "So what do you think? What should your name be, little guy?"

"Snoopy," I say. "Isn't he the world's most famous beagle?"

"Something more original than that," Joe says. "And it should begin with a J. Like Joe and Jezebel."

My mouth falls open and I can feel my face light with amusement. "You've got to be kidding. *That's* why you named her Jezebel?"

He glances over at me, trying to look quelling, but he's laughing. "*No.* That was the name she had when I got her. But I don't want the puppy to feel left out if everyone else in the house has a name that starts with J."

"Jujube," I say, the word just popping out of my mouth. The next ones that present themselves are equally inappropriate, but they come spilling out anyway, as unintentional as toads and snakes. "Juilliard. Jabberwocky."

Now he's really amused. "You're terrible at this. If you ever have kids, you better ask for input from your friends before you write anything down on a birth certificate."

"Jared," I say defiantly. "Justin. Jasper."

"Better," he concedes. "But not really dog names."

"Jinx."

"Oh, I like that," he says, and puts his nose close to the puppy's. "Hey, Jinx. Have you been chewing up the furniture? Have you been chasing the squirrels?" The dog wriggles free and barks in his face. "Is that your name? Jinx? Jinxie?" The puppy barks again.

"Maybe that's a girl's name," I say, beset by sudden doubt.

"Too late," Joe replies, heaving a ball so far across the enclosure that it almost goes over the back fence. "I think it's his name now."

I watch as the puppies tear after the ball and then fight over it before Jinx wrests it away from his sister and comes loping back. "So does that mean you want him? You'll take him?"

"Yeah, I think it does. Not today, though. I've got to get some supplies and puppy-proof the house and see if the neighbor kid will come by on days I'm going to get home late."

"Well, this is great news! Now if you can only convince your friend to take the other two, my life will be blissfully peaceful. Should we come up with names for them, too?"

"I thought we already had names," he answers, straight-faced. "Jabberwocky and Jujube."

I swat him with the mangled rag doll. "Don't say that. Joke names have a weird way of sticking."

"Oh, they were *jokes*! I thought you were *serious*!"

I laugh and climb to my feet. "Come on. I'll show you the rest of the property while Jinx spends a little more quality time with his siblings."

Jezebel and Scottie follow us out of the enclosure and through the barn, where I point out the other transitory animals that are here to be healed and released, or raised long enough to find homes elsewhere. We've just stepped outside into the sunshine when Daniel moseys over from wherever he's been all day. I hold the door open for him so he can find his accustomed spot in one of the unused stalls. He barely even looks at any of us as he slips past, though I observe that Jezebel focuses on him with a sudden, sharp attention. She makes no effort to get close enough to scent his body. In fact, she backs away from him, slowly and unobtrusively. Joe doesn't seem to notice.

"Is that one a pet or a stray?" he asks.

"Stray. He kind of comes and goes. I put out food for him, let him sleep here, but I don't know that he really considers this place his *home*."

Joe nods and says nothing as we cross a wide strip of lawn toward the art studio that's on the back edge of the property. The silence unnerves me a little. I wonder if he's regretting agreeing to adopt Jinx or if he's thinking about some upcoming trip he's going to take for his trucker friend or if he's just tired of making conversation with me and trying to figure out a polite way to say good-bye. But we're stuck with the art tour now. The studio is the one building I always keep locked, and we pause for a moment in front of the weathered wood door as I fish my keys out of my pocket and sort through them for the right one.

Abruptly, Joe voices the thought that must have been on his mind. "So is that your boyfriend?"

I'm so astonished that I drop the keys. *Does he mean Daniel? Oh my God, he realized Daniel was actually a man, not a dog?* I feel a sudden bloom of terror, and it's all I can do to keep from exclaiming, *How did you know?* "Is *who* my boyfriend?" I manage to ask in a cautious voice.

"That guy who was here when I pulled up." Even I can tell that he's making some effort to keep his tone casual. "You were with him at the club, too, last week."

Relief rushes through me like storm water through a drain. "Oh. Ryan." I bend to pick up the keys. "No. But it's complicated."

"He used to be your boyfriend," he guesses.

I shrug, unlock the door, and step inside, gesturing for Joe to follow into the still and lightless space. The temperature in here is perfectly controlled; the lights are always off unless I'm showing the art to someone. From my father I learned a thing or two about the best conditions for preserving artwork. When Cooper was using this space to paint, he let light pour in from windows on all sides, but I keep the heavy curtains drawn against the sun. Cooper wasn't Picasso, maybe, but I consider his artworks true treasures. Not least because they're really all I have left of either Cooper or Janet.

"Ryan and I have known each other a long time," I say. "And we've never gotten the relationship quite right. Shield your eyes. I'm about to turn on the lights."

Joe doesn't cover his eyes, of course, so when the whole space flares with illumination, he stands there squinting, trying to take in everything at once. There's a lot to see. There are five or six paintings on each of the four walls, plus covered crates that hold maybe two dozen more canvases, as well as a metal cabinet with close to a hundred original prints. Whenever I start worrying about money, I calm myself by slowly going over the math. *Forty-five paintings times fifty thousand is more than two million dollars . . . If I live another thirty years, that's more than sixty thousand dollars a year.* Who couldn't live on that?

And the chances are slim that I will live another thirty years.

Joe is studying each bank of images, then making a quarter turn to gaze at the next wall of paintings. I see his eyes flick between a few of the major pieces as he identifies a recurring model. Eventually he points to the largest canvas, the one that hangs in the center of the back wall, the pride of place. It features a small, dark-haired woman sitting on the porch of the main house. It's autumn, so the background is filled with flaming trees and bushes in every gradation of orange; the hues are almost as violent as a van Gogh. But Janet sits in a calm oasis of shadow, protected, or so it seems, by the bulk of the two-story house and the overhang of the roof. She appears to be the still, calm center of a frenzied kaleidoscope, a point of serenity in a world of frightening wildness. It's hardly even a metaphor; I'm convinced that's exactly how Cooper viewed Janet.

"That must be the painter's girlfriend," Joe says. "She's everywhere."

I nod. "Janet used to say, 'I can't imagine why people would want to buy pictures of *me*,' but of course what they were buying was the emotion that came through whenever Cooper would paint her. My father tried to explain the value of what he called the recurrent muse. You know, Andrew Wyeth's Helga pictures, Dante Rossetti's canvases with Jane Morris. I'm not sure she ever really got it. But she never minded posing for him." I shrugged. "She buried her life in Cooper. To the point where it wasn't really healthy, maybe."

He turns his head to glance over his shoulder at me. "So how's she handled his death?"

She died right alongside him. "By running away. So I guess you'd say she hasn't handled it at all."

"Still? Five years later?"

"Still," I confirm. "Probably forever."

He puts his hands in his back pockets and rotates to study another painting. Janet again, outside again, this time kneeling in one of the flower beds that she was able to maintain and that I have let go to weed and bramble. The hollyhocks and clematis make vivid reds and purples against her black hair. "I like the *idea* of a love that's all-consuming," he says. "But it seems like it'd be awfully hard to maintain day-to-day. I mean, sometimes you have to be shopping for groceries or fixing the flat tire or balancing the checkbook."

"Or arguing about money or arguing about values or accusing each other of being selfish," I add.

Now he grins at me briefly before returning his attention to the canvas. "It's *your* turn to do the laundry. No, we went to your mother's *last* week. Why do *I* always have to do the dishes?" he says.

"I see we're both romantics."

He waggles his head from side to side. "Or we hide behind old hurts to keep from stumbling over new ones," he replies.

That surprises me, and I respond with a faint laugh. "Art and philosophy," I say lightly. "Not quite what I expected from you."

Another quarter-turn and he's facing me. His hands are still in his pockets, his pose is utterly relaxed, and yet I feel my pulse thrum up a level as if I were gathering my strength to flee from danger. "What did you expect of me?" he asks casually.

It takes an act of will not to step back from him. Belatedly, I recognize the sensation of champagne in my veins. Not fear, but excitement. "Good ol' boy, salt-of-the-earth dependability," I answer honestly. "Kind but not particularly articulate."

Now he laughs. "Well, that doesn't sound so bad," he says. "Can I be all that but *better*?"

"Maybe," I say, smiling. "I mean, it's too early to tell."

"I'd be happy to give you a chance to find out more," he offers. "Take you to dinner next time you're in town."

I assume a demure expression. "It sounds good, but I don't come to town that often. I mean, it might be *weeks*."

"Uh-huh," he says, amused. "Well, maybe you could make a special trip. To see me. If we make actual plans."

"Maybe I could do that," I allow. "What did you have in mind?"

"There's a restaurant right off the Square. Pub food and good beer. Not too noisy, so you can hear yourself talk. Not too fancy, so you don't have to get all dressed up." He nods in my direction. "Don't even have to pick the dog hair off of your sweater."

I glance down and make a feeble effort to brush some of the fur and mud from my clothes, before giving it up as hopeless. "I might make a special effort, though," I say. "You know, since I'm driving into town and all."

"So how about this Saturday night? I could meet you there at, say, six o'clock?"

"Sounds good," I answer. "Should I bring Jinx with me?"

He laughs. "Uh—not quite yet. I need to get the house ready first."

"You're not going to renege on me, are you? Pretend you want the puppy just so I'll like you a little better?"

"Does that seem like the kind of behavior you'd expect from a salt-of-the-earth, dependable guy?"

"Not really."

"Then, no. Not going to change my mind. I just need a little time. Anyway, if I have to pick up Jinx myself, I have an excuse to come back here again. It all works out."

I feel like the grin on my face makes me look silly, so I head for the door as I try to summon a different expression. "So what's the name of this place where I'm meeting you? I don't think you actually said."

"Paddy-Mac's. I can draw you a map."

I wait at the door till he's stepped outside, then I turn off the lights and lock up the studio. "Not necessary. I've driven by it a dozen times, I've just never been inside."

"I hope you like it."

"I'm sure it'll be great."

Silence falls between us as we head back toward the center of the property, trailed by Scottie and Jezebel. It feels like the conversation is winding down, and I can't tell if he wants to leave or hopes I'll ask him in for another Snapple and maybe an early dinner. You'd think there would be an easy way to transition to a new conversational topic, but my mind goes utterly blank. I find myself proactively despairing over the Saturday night date, which will clearly be a disaster if neither of us comes up with anything to talk about. I can only pray that a place called Paddy-Mac's features Celtic music, maybe bagpipes, something loud and wailing and difficult to speak over. No, he said it was a quiet place. We're doomed.

I sneak a glance at him, thinking I might see embarrassment or regret on his face, but he's not paying attention to me. His eyes are fixed on Alonzo, who's practicing three-point shots from the dirt apron around the patio, and missing every other one.

"Okay if I talk to him?" Joe asks, and I wonder how he knows that it might not be all right.

"You can try," I say. "He doesn't like strangers."

"Introduce me, then."

Alonzo sees us approaching and waits before taking his next shot, dribbling the ball with a fast steady rhythm that is no doubt intended to communicate impatience. There is absolutely no expression on his face.

"Hey, Alonzo," I say. "This is Joe, he works in town. He brought his dog out for me to look over."

Alonzo nods without speaking. The ball continues to make its hollow racket against the pavement, against his hand.

"You named after Alonzo Mourning?" Joe asks.

Surprise flickers across the boy's face and he actually answers. "Yeah."

I'm astonished. The only Alonzo I'd ever come across before was in the *Little House on the Prairie* books, but it had always seemed unlikely that my Alonzo had been named after that one. "Who's that?" I ask.

Joe doesn't answer, so Alonzo does, as briefly as possible. "Played for the Heat."

"The who?"

"The Miami Heat," Alonzo says, enunciating each syllable with exaggerated care.

"Is that a sports team?" I demand.

Joe is grinning. "Yes, ma'am. Basketball. He played at Georgetown before he went pro, won all kinds of awards."

He glances at Alonzo, and I'm suddenly terrified that he'll ask the next natural question. *Was your dad a fan?* My brain freezes as I try to think of a way to head him off.

But he surprises me again. "You ever see him play?" he asks instead.

Alonzo shakes his head. He's actually stopped dribbling the ball for the moment. "I don't watch the pros much."

"You watch college hoops?"

"Some," Alonzo admits. This is a lie; he *loves* college basketball. He and Celeste will stay glued to the TV set during all of March Madness. Sometimes I sit and watch with them, just to be sociable, but I don't have the patience to endure the whole tournament. "Final Four, anyway."

"I know we're all supposed to like Duke, but, Jesus, can somebody else be ranked number one? Just for a little variety?" Joe exclaims.

Alonzo actually cracks a smile. "Who do you follow?" he asks.

"Should be U of I, because they're so close, but it's usually the Jay-hawks."

"Kansas is good," Alonzo agrees. "I like Mizzou."

"Sometimes yes, sometimes no. They can be pretty uneven."

"Depends on the coach," Alonzo says. "I like the new one."

Joe jerks his head toward the ball in Alonzo's hands. "So do you play?"

Alonzo shrugs. "A little."

"Up for some one-on-one?"

Alonzo eyes him, so obviously cataloging Joe's strengths and weaknesses that I can't help grinning. I don't know enough about the game to weigh the relative advantages of size and age. Joe's an inch or two taller and obviously stronger, which would seem to give him the edge, but Alonzo's slimmer and probably faster. "Sure," he says, and flings the ball straight at Joe's midsection.

Joe catches it and immediately feints to one side, dribbling with his left hand. Alonzo moves with him, close as a tango partner, his eyes never leaving Joe's face. Joe pauses, pivots, and changes course, bouncing the ball to his right hand and charging toward the basket. But in a blur of motion that's too fast for me to follow, Alonzo suddenly takes possession of the ball. He whirls, jumps, and sinks a perfect shot.

I think Alonzo's trying not to smile as he retrieves the ball and passes it back to Joe. "So that's how it's going to be, is it?" Joe says, dribbling left-handed again. Alonzo creeps closer, watching for an opportunity, and this time I see his hand snake in as Joe continues to bounce the ball. But Joe whips it behind his back and suddenly he's got it in his right hand. He points his shoulder toward the basket and edges closer, while Alonzo gives ground inch by contested inch. When he's near enough, Joe simply pauses and tosses the ball over Alonzo's head. It hits the backboard and drops through the hoop.

"Two-two," Alonzo says.

Joe scoops up the ball and lobs it to Alonzo, who's already in place at the top of the key. "Play to twenty?"

"Sure," Alonzo says. He rises to his tiptoes and throws a graceful perfect curve that makes no sound as it clears the rim.

"Son of a bitch," Joe says.

And Alonzo laughs.

I'm still in shock at that unexpected sound when I hear much more familiar noises behind me—tires crunching through the gravel, a car door slamming. I tear my eyes away from the action to see Bonnie striding away from her station wagon and over in our direction. Her eyes are fixed on Joe with such intensity that I'm surprised he hasn't lost all ability to concentrate on the game. I move to intercept her and we end up standing about ten feet away from the court.

"Who's that?" she asks in a low voice.

"Joe McGinty," I say, grateful that I learned his last name as I was filling out Jezebel's paperwork. "I met him last week, and today he brought his dog out for me to look over."

"Yes, but who *is* he?" she demands.

What she means is, *Can I trust him with Alonzo?* And, honestly, I don't know. I like his smile. I like his mix of openness and humor and insight. I like his tenderness with his old Lab and his playfulness with the young puppies, because I'm predisposed to think well of anyone who loves animals. I like that he flirts with me and makes me feel fizzy as a dropped can of soda. But none of that would offer any reassurance to Bonnie.

"He's a bouncer at a club in the Square. Used to be a cop in Joliet," I say. "He's lived here about a year, holds down a couple of jobs. But I don't have any other details."

She nods briskly. She's never taken her eyes off him, and now she strides forward again, clearly intent on disrupting the game. Alonzo has just called out "eight-four" and received the ball back from Joe, but as soon as Bonnie stalks up, he stops all motion and merely waits.

"Good afternoon," she greets Joe in a neutral tone of voice. "I'm Bonnie Logan, Alonzo's foster mother. And you are?"

He offers her his hand, which seems to disarm her a little. "Joe McGinty," he replies. "Nice to meet you. My buddy and I coach in a basketball league at the Y, and I was just asking Alonzo if he might want to try out. We have our first practice for the season this Friday night."

She makes no pretense at subtlety. Well, I'm not sure subtlety is a skill Bonnie has ever mastered. "Certainly, if he's interested, but not until I know more about *you*," she says. "Why are you coaching young boys? How do I know there's not something *wrong* about you?"

Alonzo bounces the ball exactly once. *"Bonnie,"* he says in a choked voice.

I'm sort of amused that even Alonzo can be embarrassed by a parent, or someone who's acting in that capacity, but Bonnie doesn't glance his way. "All kinds of sick and twisted men take jobs as priests and coaches and youth advisors just so they can get close to children. I will *not* have a pervert around my kid."

Now Alonzo looks down at the ground, shaking his head, but I think I can see the ghost of a smile on his face. I think it's the phrase *my kid*. It pleases him. Someone claiming him, someone fighting for him. It's something he might never get used to.

Not looking remotely offended, Joe nods and assumes a serious expression. "No, you're right, you can't be too careful," he says. "We meet at the Y, and there are always two adults with each team at all times, and no adult is allowed to be alone with one of the players. If you want to have a private conversation with one of the kids, you have to do it where everyone can see you, even if they can't overhear."

"Who's the other coach?" she asks.

"Mark Carson. He owns Carson's Trucking, has two boys who are going to play on the team."

Bonnie relaxes a little. "I know Mark. His oldest daughter was in some of my classes when I was teaching middle school."

"I think he'd vouch for me," Joe adds.

Her gaze sharpens again. "Why do you *want* to be coaching young boys?" she asks. "Do you have kids of your own?"

Joe scratches the back of his head. I don't think he's at a loss, exactly, he just hasn't had to articulate his reasons before. "Mark asked me last year if I wanted to be his assistant. I hadn't lived in Quinville that long, I was kind of bored, I know a little bit about basketball, and I thought it might be fun," he says. "And I didn't have anything else lined up for Friday nights and I wanted to do something but sit home and feel sorry for myself. All of that still holds true *this* year. And no, no kids. Not yet."

"Well—it sounds all right," Bonnie says grudgingly. "If Alonzo's interested."

Everyone looks Alonzo's way. He handles the pressure by keeping his eyes down and dribbling the basketball a couple times. "Sure," he says offhandedly. "Might be fun to try."

"You know Mark's youngest boy, what's his name?" Bonnie says.

"Dillon," Joe supplies.

Alonzo nods. "He's cool."

"And you practice at the Y on Friday nights?"

"Yes, ma'am. Seven P.M. Practice is scheduled to last two hours. There's an ice cream place next door, and last year we'd all go over afterward to get a cone. But you can pick him up right at nine, if you'd rather."

"We'll see how it goes," Bonnie says. "Thank you for including us." She holds out an arm as if collecting Alonzo. "Go get your things. Aurelia's making dinner and you've got lessons tonight. Time to get going."

Alonzo nods, makes a bounce pass to Joe and says, "See ya," as he heads toward the house. A few minutes later, they've bundled themselves into Bonnie's car, waved good-bye, and set out for Quinville.

Not until then do I trust myself to speak. "I suppose I should apologize for her rudeness," I begin.

"She wasn't rude," Joe interrupts. "More parents and guardians ought to be that—that *fierce* when they're sending their children off to be with strangers. Might save a lot of heartache down the road."

I glance up at him and find his expression perfectly sincere. "I think Bonnie would be that protective of any child who fell under her care, but Alonzo's a special case," I say. "I don't want to go into the details, but he was badly abused. And if Bonnie has anything to say about it, *nothing* bad will ever happen to that boy again."

"I liked her," he said.

I smile. "She's one of my favorite people in the world."

He smiles back, but the expression is speculative. "So is she that protective of *you*?" he asks. "Can I expect another inquisition if she thinks we're dating?"

I'm surprised into a laugh. "No, it's Aurelia you'd have to watch out for then. Her partner."

I see him register the fact that Bonnie's gay, but he merely nods. Just another piece to fit into the human puzzle, another stray bit of information to help explain the world. "Well, it's good to know you have somebody watching out for you. Everybody should."

"Do you?" I ask.

He whistles and pats his thigh, and the black Lab trots over and lifts her head to be petted. "I have Jezebel," he says.

"I meant, someone who could visit you in the hospital if you ended up in traction."

He laughs. "Sure, the whole family would caravan down from Joliet if they thought I needed something. Otherwise they leave me to my own devices."

I'm dying to ask if any of them would interrogate a new girlfriend, should he happen to acquire one, but I don't know if he's looking for a girlfriend or if I'd want to be that girl if he was. So I leave the words unsaid.

Instead I glance at the sky as if I am trying to judge the passage of time by the angle of the sun. "It's getting late," I say. "Should I invite you in for something to eat or—"

"Nah, I need to get back," he says. "I'm doing a short run for Mark up to Chicago tomorrow, and I need to get organized."

I'm half relieved and half disappointed. It's been such a chaotic afternoon that I need a little solitude to review it and decide what I think about my several visitors. But I'm not nearly tired of spending time with Joe.

"Well, travel safely," I say. "And I'll see you Saturday."

He grins down at me. "Can't wait."

CHAPTER SEVEN

I e-mail Celeste to tell her I have a date for Saturday night because that's a rule we established long ago: Never go out with a strange man without telling your best friend who might have slit your throat when you turn up dead. I can't keep up with Celeste's dizzying assortment of boyfriends, but I do always save the e-mails she sends with the relevant information, only deleting them once she's dropped that particular guy from her life.

Practically the moment I hit send, my phone rings. It's Celeste, of course, wanting to discuss my wardrobe options, but I steadfastly refuse to let her bully me into wearing something from her closet. I also won't tell her where we're meeting for dinner because I don't want her "accidentally" running into us while we're at Paddy-Mac's, something she's entirely capable of.

"Honestly, you'd think I'd never gone out with a guy before in my life," I complain as she starts giving me advice about topics to avoid and precautions to take.

"Well, gee, let's see. How many people have you dated in the past five years? Two? *Including* Ryan?"

"Three. You're forgetting Luke."

"Who—oh, the shape-shifter dude who looked like your dad."

"He did *not* look like my dad!"

"Well, he was at least ten years older than you."

I shake my head. "Hanging up now. I'll call you sometime Sunday."

"Not too early. I'm going out with Rain and some of the other girls Saturday night."

"Celeste. I would *never* call you early on a Sunday morning."

I hear the laugh in her voice. "Have fun."

Saturday morning I feed and water all the animals, clear out my e-mail, completely discard the outfit I had decided to wear and put together an entirely new ensemble, which I also discard after lunch. This is ridiculous; my guess is that Joe won't even *notice* what I have on, so any carefully calibrated nuance of presentation will be wasted on him. But the high-necked white turtleneck seems too virginal, the tight black cashmere sweater too come-hither, the red blouse with the denim vest too hoedown, the twin-set too librarian. And I'm *not* wearing a dress and pumps to a pub. In the end, I go back to the black sweater, but cover it up with a casual jacket, and complete the look with black jeans and a pair of boots. I do change belts three times, and necklaces twice, but in the end I'm reasonably satisfied with my appearance.

Before I leave, I track down Daniel, lying in his usual morose state in the barn. I crouch down by him and lift his muzzle so his eyes meet mine and I can be certain he hears me.

"I'm going into town," I tell him. "My *plan* is to come back tonight, but if I die on the road, you have to shift into human shape and feed everybody. You got that?"

He beats his tail once against the floor, wearily, then yawns in my face. I take that as a yes. "See you later," I tell him, and then I'm on my way.

I've allowed way more time than I need to get to town, so the sun is still shining mightily as I speed down the empty expanse of W and turn onto the more crowded lanes of 159. I'm happy—I'm actually dancing in my seat a little when the oldies station plays a Go-Go's song. I laugh out loud when "Footloose" comes on. It seems like a sign.

I kill time at Walmart when it turns out I'm forty-five minutes early, but even so I'm parked and walking into Paddy-Mac's about ten minutes before the hour. I like the place the minute I step inside. It's mostly dark paneling and low lighting augmented with a few neon brewery signs, but it has a warm, welcoming vibe to it, a little rumpled, a little mischievous. It makes you feel like it should be easy to have a good time here.

I hadn't even looked for Joe's truck on the nearby streets, so I'm surprised to find him already at a booth, nursing a beer and perusing a magazine. I slip into the seat across from him before he realizes I'm even in the restaurant. "What is that, *Guns & Ammo*?" I say in a teasing tone.

He looks up, a smile breaking across his face. I can hardly describe how good it makes me feel to know that someone is so delighted to see me. "No, *Soldier of Fortune*," he retorts.

"I'm not sure I know what that is."

He laughs. "All about mercenary soldiers and militia for hire."

I feel my eyes widen. "*Really?* That's what you're reading?"

He holds it up so I can see the cover. *Consumer Reports*. "Just joking. Though I *have* leafed through the occasional copy of *Guns & Ammo.*"

A young waitress has materialized at our table. She's got dyed red hair pulled back in a ponytail, a fleur-de-lys tattoo on each wrist, and three silver hoops in each earlobe. She's wearing a hand-lettered name tag that says RACHEL; it's decorated with ink drawings of cats. I like it that Paddy-Mac's doesn't make its employees conform to a conservative dress code. "Can I get you something to drink?" she asks.

"Definitely," I say in a faint voice. "Something with alcohol. Beer or—I don't know."

"This is our first week to offer a new hard cider, and it's been pretty popular so far," Rachel answers.

"Oh, that sounds good. I'll have that."

She drops off a food menu and heads back to the kitchen. Joe and I regard each other across the table.

"So how've you been?" he asks. "In the—let's see, seventy-two hours since I've seen you last?"

"Good. Nothing too exciting has happened in the past three days, though, so we'll have to talk about the way more distant past if you're hoping I'll say anything entertaining."

"Nothing exciting has happened to *you,* maybe," he says. "But *my* life has been full of drama."

I laugh and settle back against the padded bench. "Do tell! How was your trip to Chicago?"

"Not bad until I got on the Dan Ryan Expressway to find traffic at a dead standstill. Some big accident just off the highway. Three hours, just sitting there, nobody moving an inch. Drivers started getting out of their cars and talking to the people around them. Sharing food, sharing water bottles. I think I saw one couple meet, fall in love, and decide to get married while we were all just waiting."

"Sounds horrible."

"It was that," he agrees. "On the other hand, none of us were dead, and it turned out that six people died in the crash. So it was hard to be too upset after we heard that."

"Well, now I'm depressed."

"Sorry," he says. "That was meant to be more of an I'm-grateful story than a life-sucks story."

The waitress brings my cider, which is amazingly good. When she recommends the beef stew and biscuits for dinner, I instantly agree. Clearly this girl knows what she's talking about.

When she leaves, I pick up the conversation exactly where we left it. "I try to do the grateful thing instead of the bitter thing," I say. "When I have a bad day—when I'm worried about money—when things just go wrong, I try to count up all the ways I'm lucky. It helps me shake off the mood."

"Living in America in the twenty-first century," he says instantly. "Running water, penicillin, and the Internet."

"I usually count up more specific blessings," I say. "Good friends, a wonderful house, and work I love."

"Good health," he adds. I nod, but inwardly disagree. I'm *not* thankful for my body, and that's the truth; I feel like I live with a severe disability that has shaped every single aspect of my life. Not that I'm planning to admit that to Joe at the moment.

He sips at his beer. "So what sorts of things put you in a bad mood?" he asks. "What makes a 'bad day' for you?"

"Stupid things, usually," I say. "Long lines, heavy traffic, ungrateful clients, automated voice menus when I'm trying to reach a live person, tax bills that I'm not expecting. Flat tires. Broken air conditioners. Dropped cell phone calls." I take another swallow of the cider. I *love* this drink. "Like I said. Dumb stuff."

He leans back and considers me for a moment. "Yeah, none of those seem all that terrible," he says. "I have to think there's other things that bother you and you just don't want to talk about them."

I pause with the cider bottle halfway to my mouth and regard him in silence. How would he react if I listed for him all the issues that really depress me, all the details that scare me and worry me and tear at my heart? *Turning into a wild animal in my father's backyard. Living in fear that someone will discover that I am living a lie. Seeing everyone I love die too young because shape-shifters have short and violent lives.*

"Well, I guess we all have things that bother us that we don't like to talk about," I say quietly. "I mean, what makes a bad day for *you*?"

"When I was on the force, it was seeing the awful things people could do to each other," he answers readily enough. "Murders. Abuses. Stuff I sure don't want to talk about *now* when we're supposed to be having a nice conversation. These days— Well, if I read about some of those same things in the news, it'll get to me, but not as much. These days, what bothers me tends to be more personal. You know, what am I doing with my life, have I totally screwed it up, will I ever figure it out? That kind of stuff."

"You don't *seem* to have totally screwed up your life, but I don't know what you left behind in Joliet," I say cautiously.

"Busted marriage," he says. "And a job I was good at, but couldn't take anymore."

"I knew about the job," I say. "I guessed about the marriage. What happened?"

He shrugs and looks away. "She wanted a bigger house and I didn't. She wanted to move to Chicago and I didn't. She wanted to go out five nights a week and I didn't. She was a lot *livelier* than me all the time, if you know what I mean. She used to say that she brightened me up and I steadied her down. But after a while I think she started feeling that I was *pulling* her down. Holding her back. I was a lump and she was a butterfly."

I am listening sympathetically until the very last line, and then I have to strangle a laugh. "I'm guessing that's something she actually said to you."

He nods. "Yeah, there was a lot of stuff along those lines, but that's the phrase that sticks in my head."

"Well, so far you don't seem like a lump to *me*," I say. "But I don't know you that well."

"And you don't seem like a butterfly," he replies. "Good as far as it goes."

I've actually been a butterfly once, as it happens, and it was as carefree an existence as I can ever remember. But overall, I don't consider my transformations as some manifestation of my basic temperament. I'm just not that random and experimental. "What *do* I seem like?" I ask.

He studies me a moment, either trying to figure it out or trying to put it into words. "The high school valedictorian who turns out to be a racecar driver in her free time," he answers. "You know, someone who works hard and is super responsible, but then turns out to have this really unexpected secret life."

It's all I can do not to choke on my cider. He's got the specifics wrong, but he's dead on target in the general sense. "Wow, that makes me sound more interesting than I ever thought I was," I reply.

"Oh, I think you're pretty interesting," he says. "I figure the more I learn, the more interesting you'll get."

That might be true, if I had any intention of letting him learn exactly what my secret life entails. "But we were talking about you," I say, turning the subject. "And whether or not you've screwed up your life. What would you want to do if you were starting over?"

"Still working out that part," he says. "In the meantime, I do odd jobs and hang out with friends and let the days go by."

"And you coach basketball, too," I remind him. "Speaking of that, did Alonzo come to practice last night?"

"He did."

"How'd it go?"

"Not bad. He was pretty quiet—waited for me or Mark to tell him what to do, didn't trash talk with any of the other kids, kind of kept to himself. But he played pretty well and he seemed to enjoy himself and he said he'd be back next week, so I figured it was a win."

"Did he go out for ice cream with everyone else?"

Joe shakes his head. "Nah. Bonnie came in with him and sat in the bleachers and watched us the whole time. I swear, she didn't blink once. Then she took him straight home afterward."

I muffle a laugh. "Did any of the other parents stay during practice?"

"Sure. A half dozen, maybe. Though most of them were on their phones or their laptops instead of watching the kids play."

"Well, maybe next week she'll let him stay for ice cream."

"Not sure he wants to," Joe answers. "He doesn't seem like the kind of guy who just hangs out. Some kids, you know, they have no interest in talking to adults—they just want to be with their peers. Other kids seem kind of awkward with boys and girls their own age. They want to be with the grown-ups having grown-up conversations. But Alonzo didn't really seem comfortable with kids or adults. He didn't seem to hate being there, but he didn't—he didn't seem like he was going to fit in anytime soon."

I sigh. "Yeah. I'm not sure where Alonzo is ever going to feel like he belongs."

I don't have to elaborate, because this is the moment the waitress chooses to bring over our meals, so we lose the next few minutes to rearranging plates and pushing glasses out of the way and taking our first bites of the food. The beef stew is delicious, and Joe's hamburger and fries smell just as good.

"I love this place," I say. "I'm never eating anywhere else."

"Fine by me."

I take another bite. "Though I'm not sure I can convince Celeste to come here very often," I add.

"Celeste—" he says, like he's trying to remember who she is.

"My best friend." I glance at him. "The one who had the little incident with Bobby Foucault at Arabesque."

"Oh, right. The one who turns into a mountain lion."

Again, I almost choke. I'm tempted to correct him—*bobcat, not mountain lion*—but, of course, I don't. Instead I swallow hastily and answer, "Exactly! She prefers establishments that are a little more upscale."

"As any wild animal would."

Now I'm laughing. "Do you think so? Wouldn't they be more comfortable at more casual venues? Picnics, hot dogs from food trucks, that sort of thing?"

He's grinning. "I never gave it any thought. I suppose so. We'll have to ask her."

I try to imagine that conversation and decide I can never introduce the two of them. There's no telling what kind of answer Celeste would give to that question. "Well, I'm not sure this is her kind of place. But *I'm* coming back here sometime."

"Next week, maybe?" he says easily. "We can meet for dinner again."

A glissando of pleasure tingles up my spine. "That would be fun," I say.

"We might even make it a habit."

Before I can respond to that, one of the other patrons stops by our table on his way out of the pub. The friends he's with pause at the door, talking among themselves as they wait for him.

I'm not thrilled to recognize Sheriff Wilkerson, looking every inch the benign Andy-of-Mayberry-style representative of the law. The skin crinkles around his blue eyes as he offers me a warm smile. "Well, hello there, Miss Karadel," he says in that soft Southern drawl. "Good to see you back in town for the evening."

"Good to see you, too, Sheriff," I say, my voice as friendly as I can manage.

He jerks his thumb in Joe's direction. "What are you doing hanging around with questionable characters like this fellow? Don't you know he's nothing but trouble?"

He says it in such an exaggerated way that I'm pretty sure he's joking, and the amusement on Joe's face makes me think I'm right. I assume an anxious expression.

"Oh no, I scarcely know him," I answer. "Tell me, quick! What's so terrible about him?"

"I had him watch my dogs for me one week when I was out of town, and when I got back, they wouldn't give me the time of day. Just sat at the door all night, whimpering and pining away, hoping Joe would come back. He alienated their affection, that's what he did."

"That *is* pretty bad," I reply.

"And then, when I tried to convince him to sign on as a deputy, he turned me down! What kind of man doesn't want to protect and serve? 'Specially a big man with an excellent understanding of firearms." He shakes his head. "I have to figure he's up to no good. I just don't know what it is yet."

I cut my eyes over at Joe. Sheriff Wilkerson tried to hire him, and Joe turned him down? It reinforces my belief that Joe's one of the good guys—albeit a somewhat lost and uncertain good guy.

"He does sound suspicious," I say. "I'll see what I can find out."

"Would you do that for me? And then report anything you've learned."

"I will."

"Good girl." He actually pats me on the shoulder as he turns to go. But I'm not surprised that, one step from the table, he turns back. "Have you heard from Miss Janet lately?" he asks.

"Not this week."

"Well, next time you do, you be sure and tell her I said hi."

"I'll do that."

This time he does depart, and a *whoosh* of street air comes wafting through the door as he and his friends exit.

"You refused a job as deputy?" I say the minute the door is closed again.

Joe shrugs. "I'd just quit the police force a couple months before that. I didn't think I was ready for the same kind of job, just in a different place." He glances around the pub. "Though Quinville isn't much like Joliet."

"Probably more about rescuing stray kittens and less about solving homicides."

"Still gotta be ready to deal with the homicides," he says quietly. "And I'm not sure I am."

"Well, I can't say I blame you for that," I say on a long sigh.

"And we're back to dreary topics," Joe replies. "Come on. Let's think of happier stuff to talk about."

"Dessert might be a happier topic," I suggest.

"Yes. Dessert. We need that."

We wave the waitress over and she reels off the selections. We go from thinking we'll split one to agreeing we each want our own to wondering if we might get *three* and share them all.

"You're going to be bad for me, I can tell," Joe says as soon as the waitress departs. "You heard Wilkerson call me a 'big man,' right?"

He glances down at his stomach. "I keep eating three desserts every night, I'll be a *huge* man."

When I throw my head back and laugh, the pain is so sudden and so intense that for a second I think I've cracked my skull against the back of the bench. It's so overwhelming that I'm disoriented for a moment—I can't figure out what's happening or why.

Then the nausea slams like a fist into my stomach and I think I might throw up right at the table. "Oh my God," I say, and I can hear the stark terror in my voice.

Joe's instantly concerned. "Karadel? What's wrong?"

I put both palms up to my face so I can support my head, which is shrieking with agony, but then I don't have a hand free to cover my mouth in case I start vomiting. "Joe. I'm going to be sick. Really sick. I have to leave right now."

He's digging into his pocket with one hand and wildly waving at our waitress with the other. "Do you think you got food poisoning? Were you allergic to something?"

I think I'm about to change shapes. Sooner than I expected and much faster than I usually do, and holy God, my head might explode before I transform. "No—it's a migraine—I get them all the time, but they're usually not this sudden." My voice comes out almost as a gasp.

The waitress has jogged up to the table, and Joe throws a few twenties at her. "Cancel the dessert. My friend's sick, and we've got to leave."

"I'll be right back with your change."

"Keep it," Joe says, pushing himself out of the booth. "I have to get her home."

Solicitous as an undertaker, he bends over me and eases me out of my seat. "I'm not sure I can make it home," I say shakily. "I might just drive to Bonnie's."

"You're not driving anywhere," he says flatly. "I'll take you wherever you want. There's an urgent care center just down the street—or the hospital, if you'd rather—"

God, no. The last thing I need is to be in a public facility. My head is pounding so hard I can't think straight, and my one clear thought is that I have to get out of sight as quickly as possible. "I just want to get to Bonnie's," I say.

He's ushering me out the door, where the fresh air makes me momentarily feel better. But as soon as I take a deep, hopeful breath, the nausea roils more violently in my stomach. "God," I say.

He has one arm around my waist, the other holding on to my elbow, and he's urging me toward his truck, parked across the street. I resist as best I can. "I really think I can drive myself," I say, though I am not positive this is true.

"Well, you're not going to," he answers. I don't have the strength to pull away from him and head to my own car, so I just give in. He practically lifts me onto the seat and actually fastens the seat belt around me. I lean my aching head against the headrest and pray I can hold on for another ten or fifteen minutes.

"Where to?" he says as he climbs in next to me.

"Take 159 to Mannheim. Right on Mannheim, left on Poplar," I whisper. "They live just off Poplar."

"Are you *sure* you don't want to go to the hospital?" he asks as he pulls away.

"I'm begging you. No hospital."

I close my eyes, hoping the motion of the car doesn't upset my stomach even more, and try to gauge from distance and the turns he makes when we've arrived at Poplar. I guess right—he's just swinging through the intersection when I look at my surroundings again.

"Three blocks down. Little street called Blossom. Turn left. They're the third house on the left. Blue shutters," I croak out, then I close my eyes again.

Only as I feel him turn into the driveway does it occur to me to wonder if anybody's home. I have a key to their place, but Joe seems worried enough about me that I'm not sure he'd be willing to leave me alone. An attitude I would find sweet if it wasn't, in this situation, highly inconvenient.

But I open my eyes again as he cuts the ignition, and I can see lights on in various windows in the two-story brick house. It's almost full dark, so the rose garden and the porch swing and the small fountain are practically invisible, but even so the house manages to project an air of hospitality.

He's out of the truck before I've taken a breath to thank him, so I wait for him to come around to my door and help me climb out. Impossible as I would have thought it, my head hurts even more, and I briefly entertain the idea that I have an aneurysm, something even more deadly than my usual malady. Even with Joe's help, it's hard to stand upright, hard to navigate the three concrete steps that lead to the wide porch. The button for the doorbell is tricky to find, as it's usually hidden behind a curtain of ivy, and Joe doesn't bother hunting. He just pounds furiously at the door with his left hand while supporting me with his right arm. I can't hold my head up, so I'm resting it against his shoulder.

Alonzo opens the door, takes one look at me, and calls "Bonnie!" even as he pushes the door wider so I can come in. Joe helps me over the threshold and then stands there while I sway against him, not sure where he should escort me next. We've stepped just inside the living room, an elegant place of antique furniture and muted pale-winter hues. If I could speak and gesture, I'd point Joe's attention to the Cooper Blair original on the wall. But at the moment, all I can think is how bright the room is, how pulsing with color. I stand mute, ready to crumple to the floor. I think all that's holding me up is Joe's arm around my waist.

Bonnie bustles into the room, drying her hands on a kitchen towel. "For heaven's sake, Alonzo, what—oh."

The minute I hear her voice, I know I'll be all right.

"We were out to dinner," Joe says. "And suddenly—she says she got a migraine—she says she doesn't want to go to the doctor. But I don't know, she's acting so funny—"

"No, no, this is fairly common for Karadel," Bonnie says briskly. "Alonzo, take her to the guest room. Right now. Bring her some water and—well, you know what to do."

It might be my fevered imagination that Joe releases me with some reluctance into Alonzo's hands. But Alonzo's arm around my waist is as steady as Joe's, and he leads me with infinite care out of the room and down the shadowed hallway. I catch echoes of the conversation between Joe and Bonnie. I think he's explaining again that I just suddenly got sick, and she's assuring him that I'll be all right, that this has happened to me before, that she will take care of me. I hear something about my car and I think Bonnie is promising him she'll fetch it from in front of Paddy-Mac's.

I don't know. Their words are muffled by our distance from the front door and the escalating throb of blood in my head. Without warning, I drop to the floor, right there in the hallway, curling in on myself, clutching my head, biting my lips to hold back the moans. It feels like a saw blade is ripping down my spine—it feels like a tourniquet has been knotted around my lungs. My fingers splay and contract; my hips pop apart and recombine. I lift my head to howl—

And then everything is fine.

Pain gone. Body light. Bones aligned and muscles perfectly balanced. I blink once and look around.

I'm low to the ground and flooded with sensory input, sounds and scents particularly sharp. I extend my right front leg and am not surprised to see it covered in fluffy orange fur. Apparently, my new hybrid serum is still allowing me to turn into a cat, like Isabel—but the addition of Baxter's blood has had some unexpected and unpleasant side effects. I might need to rethink my formulas.

But I can't force my mind to stay on that subject. I'm distracted by a noise in the other room—the sound of the door shutting—and by the rich smells drifting down the hallway. Fish and bread and cheese, among other inviting scents. Bonnie must have been in the middle of making dinner.

Moments later, she appears in the hallway, palming a light switch to illuminate the dark space. "That was cutting it close," she observes, bending over to pick up my clothes, my purse, and my shoes. "I take it you didn't expect to change quite so rapidly."

I burble a response, which is unintelligible, and she sighs. "I'll put your things in the guest room," she says. "And I'll make up a bed for you in there. Though, of course, you can sleep anywhere you like."

Alonzo squats down beside me. "Are you hungry?" he asks.

"Your coach said they just had dinner," Bonnie tells him.

He glances up at her. "Yeah, but sometimes it takes so much energy to change that you're starving right away."

I mew politely, my way of conveying that, *Yes, please, I'd like a little something to eat. Some of that fish would be especially nice.* Bonnie sighs again.

"I think you're right," she says. "So perhaps you could get out a food plate and a water bowl."

He stays on the floor a moment longer. "What about the animals?" he asks me.

Mwwrrr, I reply.

He thinks about it a moment, then holds his hand out, palm up.

"If Daniel's there and the animals will be all right, touch my hand," he says.

I bat at his fingers with my right paw, careful to keep the claws sheathed. He pats my head before coming to his feet again. "Everything's fine," he says to Bonnie, and then saunters toward the kitchen.

Because in this shape I'm unable to summon the level of anxiety that I know the scary world requires, I find myself agreeing with him. Everything *is* fine. I follow him down the hall.

CHAPTER EIGHT

Sunday passes in a hedonistically leisurely fashion. In the morning, Aurelia finds me still half asleep on the bed in the guest room and pauses to scratch under my chin.

"Look at you, your fur is almost the same color as my hair," she says. "Did you do that on purpose?" Then she laughs because she knows that I have done no part of this transformation on purpose.

"I'm sure you'd like to go back to your own place as soon as possible, but I don't think it will be today," she goes on. "Bonnie's at church this morning, I've got a Women in Law luncheon this afternoon, and we usually try to make sure Alonzo does homework on Sunday evenings. Is it okay if we take you back tomorrow? We did go fetch your Jeep this morning, though, so it's in our driveway as I speak."

I offer a chirping little meow meant to express agreement, and she grins. "Guess it doesn't matter if you approve or not," she observes. "Not much you can do about it anyway. See you later."

After I've refreshed myself with another nap, I go exploring, eventually locating Alonzo in his room on the second floor. He's sitting at his desk, reading a book, though his expression indicates it's something he's doing because he has to and not because he wants to. I tense my muscles, gauge the distance, then make a perfect leap from the floor to the desk. Moving with great delicacy, I pick my way through the books, pens, action figures, and electronic devices scattered across its surface until I come across a stack of papers that might be completed school assignments. The perfect spot. I sniff at them briefly, then settle on top of the pile, wrap my tail around my feet, and look around me.

Alonzo's room has a lot more personality than it used to. When he first moved in, every single item in it had been picked out by Bonnie or Aurelia, from the furniture to the bed coverings to the books on the shelves. It was about a year before he added anything he chose for himself—an *Avengers* poster, hung so that the only way to see it was from inside the room with the door closed. Since then, he's slowly amassed a more personal collection, but the additions are sparse. A stack of comic books. A handful of DVDs, most of them with science fiction themes. Another poster, this one featuring some sports star I don't recognize. *Lord of the Rings* memorabilia.

None of it looks like something he loves so much he couldn't leave it behind if he had to vanish in the middle of the night.

"Don't mess up my homework," Alonzo admonishes me, but otherwise doesn't seem to mind my intrusion. He even reaches over to pat me on the head and allows me to nuzzle his wrist before he goes back to his reading.

Maybe an hour goes by before I hear Bonnie's footsteps in the hallway moments before she sticks her head in the door. "Have you seen— oh, there she is. I wanted to make sure she was all right."

"She's fine," Alonzo says, not a trace of doubt in his voice. He understands that on a level that Bonnie, despite her long association with shape-shifters, simply cannot. It's the transitions that are so hard, at least for some of us; the existence itself, assuming you're in a safe place, is almost carefree.

"How's the book going? How many chapters have you read today?"

"Two," Alonzo says.

"Do you like it?"

"It's all right, I guess. It's kind of boring."

"Maybe it would be more exciting if you read it out loud," Bonnie suggests. "Karadel might enjoy the story."

"Okay," he says without much enthusiasm. "How much should I read to her?"

"How about ten pages? Then you can come down and we can discuss it while I make dinner. Aurelia ought to be home in a couple of hours."

He nods and waits for her to leave before picking up the book again. Any other kid might pretend to do what he's told, figuring his foster mother wouldn't know if he'd actually read out loud to a cat or not, but of course Alonzo does it. He wouldn't dare upset the precarious balance of his life by rebelling; as far as he knows, this small haven of kindness where he has so miraculously come to rest could be barred to him if he makes the smallest mistake. He wouldn't risk it.

Alonzo's voice is soft.

Sydney Carton looked at his punch and looked at his complacent friend; drank his punch and looked at his complacent friend.

"You made mention of the young lady as a golden-haired doll. The young lady is Miss Manette . . ."

The first name clues me in that today's assignment is *A Tale of Two Cities*. A story of brutality and hope, sacrifice and redemption. A glimpse at the cruelties people are capable of inflicting on each other, a reminder that the world still produces heroes, flawed and ordinary as they might be. Alonzo reads with little inflection, stumbling over some of the more complicated words, but with a dogged focus that makes it clear nothing will prevent him from finishing this particular task. For the first time since I've known him, I experience a profound sense of conviction that Alonzo will be all right. He doesn't know much about joy, he doesn't entirely believe in goodness, but he knows how to persevere. He knows how to hang on and keep going and power through. He learned long ago how to simply endure.

The half hour before dinner is so exquisite that I wish with all my little feline heart that I were human. Aurelia's home from her event, still dressed in a suit and heels, telling stories about her fellow lawyers in her usual dry and acerbic fashion. Bonnie's laughing out loud at some of her descriptions, and even Alonzo is grinning. The three of them are finishing up dinner preparations with the ease of long familiarity, moving between the kitchen and the dining room to set the table, carry in serving dishes, open and decant the wine. The whole event reeks of *family*, of companionship and affection and belonging, and it's something I've missed almost as long as I've been alive.

"It's a merlot, do you want a small glass?" Aurelia asks Alonzo. "You liked it the last time we had it."

I know he's too young to drink alcohol, but there's something about the ritual that seems to please him, Bonnie had told me not long ago. *I don't know if it's because it's something that we share with him, and that makes it special, or if it's because he knows wine is for adults, and he likes to think that's how we see him. We just give him a couple of ounces. I don't think it's hurting him. I think it can't be hurting him* if it helps convince Alonzo that he matters to them.

"Sure, I'll take some," he says, and Aurelia pours an inch of wine into the gold-rimmed goblet. It's a casual family dinner on a random Sunday night, but trust Aurelia to have gotten out the good dishes. She requires elegance like other people require air.

Bonnie stands at the table, hands on her hips, looking everything over. "Have I forgotten anything? Bread! In the oven. Alonzo, could you take it out and put it in a basket? Then I think we're ready to eat."

Almost on the words, the doorbell rings. "Oh, Lord," Bonnie says on a sigh, but Aurelia's expression is almost angry. For someone who so willingly does battle on the public stage, she is ferocious about guarding her private time.

"I'll get rid of whoever it is," Aurelia says, striding into the living room. Since I'm a cat, curiosity is my besetting sin, so I mince along after her. She opens the door and gazes out into the gathering darkness. "Yes?" she says in a forbidding tone.

"Hi. I'm Joe McGinty," says the visitor. I'm so surprised at the familiar voice that I freeze midstep, then drop into a protective crouch. My tail twitches as I stare at the door, though I'm at the wrong angle to get a good look at the man on the other side.

"Yes?" Aurelia repeats, her voice even more frigid.

"I'm Karadel's friend. I was with her last night when she got sick."

Aurelia's transformation is so sudden and so complete that you'd think she was a shape-shifter changing from ice princess to earth mother. "Joe!" she exclaims, now radiating warmth. "Yes, I've heard about how kind you were."

"I just wanted to know—is she feeling better? She hasn't answered her phone all day."

By this time, Bonnie has joined Aurelia at the door. "She's better," Bonnie tells him. "But it might be a couple of days before she's fully recovered."

"I saw her car outside," Joe says. "Is she here? Could I come in and say hello?"

"Oh, I don't think that's a good idea," Bonnie says, clearly caught off guard.

It's Aurelia, always more adept at lying, who expands on the answer. "She's sleeping," she says. "She was awake all night—throwing up—really miserable. I think it was dawn before she fell asleep. She got up for a few hours, ate something, but she's back in bed now."

"That sucks," he says.

"I know, the poor thing," Aurelia replies. "She gets these migraines—oh, every few weeks, I suppose. She has drugs, you know, but nothing seems to stave them off completely."

"Will you tell her I came by?" he asks. "And maybe have her call me when she's feeling better?"

"We certainly will," Bonnie says.

Then Aurelia, who truly has an evil streak, says, "Oh, why don't you come in and have dinner with us? We've just put the food on the table."

There's a short silence while Bonnie probably tries to telegraph her disapproval and Joe probably tries to figure out if she's sincere. "I don't want to impose," he says at last.

Aurelia opens the door wider. "Nonsense. We'd love to have you." She turns her head to call over her shoulder. "Alonzo! Set another plate. We have company for dinner."

I spend most of the next hour crouched in a corner of the dining room behind a huge potted peace lily, watching Joe.

I'm tense, ready to spring, though I'm not sure if I want to pounce on prey or flee from peril. Human emotions don't always filter clearly through the animal instincts, so all I know is that I'm on high alert, and it's difficult to say exactly why.

Nothing about the meal itself would seem to offer any danger. Alonzo doesn't say much, though he answers direct questions, but the rest of them are all capable of carrying on a civil conversation, even with a total stranger. At first the talk is general as Joe politely inquires into Aurelia's line of work and they go over the ordinary niceties about weather and gas prices and road construction headaches. But I'm not surprised when Aurelia commandeers the conversation and begins asking Joe more personal questions: *Where are you from? Why are you here? What happened in Joliet?* Within ten minutes she's learned all the basics about his former job, his broken marriage, his family relationships.

"How do you know Karadel?" she asks next.

I think he surprises her. "Oh, that's right. She warned me about you," he says.

She sips from her wine and arches those thin red brows. "How foresighted of her," she drawls. "What exactly did she say about me?"

"That you'd be the one to interrogate me. If you thought we were dating."

"And are you dating?"

"I hope so," he answers, which makes her laugh.

"But how did you meet?" Bonnie asks.

"I was working at a new club in the Square. Checked her ID, learned she was a vet, asked if I could bring my dog out. We seemed to hit it off."

"A new club," Aurelia repeats. "Arabesque?"

"That's right."

"Didn't they have some—altercation there a couple of weeks ago?"

He nods. "The night I met Karadel, in fact. One of her friends was involved."

"Celeste," Bonnie says. I see the look she gives Aurelia then, and it's not hard to interpret. *Better drop this right now.* Clearly she remembers all the details we told her about that night.

But Aurelia isn't done probing yet, poking at this fascinating new specimen, seeing how it reacts to unfamiliar stimuli. "Yes, Celeste! She said this yahoo took her out back and tried to feel her up and then she created a scene? The police were called? It sounded very dramatic, even by Celeste's standards."

"Bobby Foucault. Not exactly a yahoo. More like someone who's straddled the line between deadbeat and criminal for most of his life. It's just a matter of time before he ends up in jail. I think he tried to do more than feel her up."

"I wonder how she got away from him."

Joe snorts. "*He* says she turned into a mountain lion. *She* says he's a crazy drunk. But she did scratch the hell out of him."

Alonzo might not have known that part of the story, because he shoots a quick glance at Joe then trains his eyes on his plate. Bonnie's face assumes a masklike expression, but Aurelia wears the proper look of astonishment.

"He says she—what? Turned into an animal?"

Joe nods and sips his wine. "Said we had a shape-shifter right here in Quinville, Illinois."

"How on earth did you respond to that?"

"Well, Sheriff Wilkerson was the one who questioned him. His deputy and I just stood there trying not to laugh. I thought it would be cool, though."

"What would be cool?"

"To be able to do that. Become something or someone else. Especially in a situation like that, you know, when you needed to defend yourself."

Aurelia's voice is quizzical. "But, of course, you know that's not possible."

He grins. "I know. Doesn't make it any less cool."

Unexpectedly, Alonzo joins the conversation. "What animal would you be?" he asks. "If you could choose?"

Joe thinks long enough to show he's giving the question serious consideration. "A dog, probably. One of the bigger breeds—shepherd or Lab. Collie. How about you? What would you be?"

I don't think anyone has ever asked Alonzo this question, either, because he takes a moment to ruminate. "Wolf, probably. So no one would want to mess with me."

"Yeah, but if you're a wolf and you're living in the city, it's kind of dangerous, don't you think?" Joe argues. "Better to be a dog. Nobody will shoot at you when you change shapes."

"I wouldn't live in the city if I was a wolf," Alonzo said. "I'd live in the country. Out by Karadel."

The briefest look of alarm crosses Bonnie's face. This conversation is getting too close to the truth and she wants to end it now. "We've got ice cream for dessert," she says. "Does everybody want a bowl?"

Everybody does. Bonnie and Aurelia come to their feet, and I think they're both going to scoop and serve, but Aurelia surprises me by stopping next to the peace lily, bending over, and picking me up. I'm too stunned to contort in her arms, trying to get free, though I let loose a piteous little wail. She returns to her seat and settles me on her lap, stroking my fur. Which is practically standing on edge because I'm so agitated.

"Do you like cats, Joe?" she asks.

He makes an equivocal sound. "They're okay. I'm more of a dog guy."

"Too bad. This one's a stray and we've been trying to find a home for her."

At that, Alonzo is unable to repress a sound that I recognize as choked laughter.

Joe smiles sympathetically. "Yeah, if you feed them a few times, you find it hard to get rid of them," he says. "And then pretty soon you get attached to them and you can't bring yourself to give them away."

"Exactly. Are you *sure* you don't want this one?"

I want to kill her. If I were a proper size, Celeste's bobcat, I swear I'd do it. She lifts her hand to stroke me again and I turn my head fast enough to nip her wrist. When she mutters, "Ouch," and raises her hand to her mouth, I take the opportunity to hiss and jump from her lap. The minute my feet touch the floor, I practically teleport into the kitchen, where I take refuge under the small desk built into one corner.

I can still hear Joe's voice, and he sounds amused. "No, ma'am. I'm going to be bringing home a puppy in a few days, so the timing seems wrong. Besides, she doesn't seem very friendly."

"She might not like *me*," Aurelia says. "But I bet she'd be nicer to you. I really think you ought to find out."

It's barely dawn Monday morning when Bonnie and Aurelia take me back to my place. I ride with Bonnie in my Jeep, while Aurelia follows in her BMW. Aurelia has a court date at nine, which is why we leave so early, but once I get over my disgruntlement at being woken up, I don't mind. I want to go home. I want to be in my own place, surrounded by my own idiosyncrasies. I am tired of depending on the kindness of friends.

Though I am unutterably grateful for those friends.

Bonnie sets the emergency brake on the Jeep, unlocks the house to pile all my belongings on the kitchen table, then heads back to the BMW. In minutes, they're on their way back to Quinville, the luxury car almost soundless as it pulls away. I roam the property just to make sure everything is in order—not that I could do anything about it if it wasn't—but I don't see anything amiss. Jinx and his littermates bark at me furiously as I pass by, which rouses Daniel, who pokes his head out of one of the trailers to see what all the commotion's about. When he spots me, he just nods and goes back inside. He's about as communicative in human state as he is when he's a dog.

Scottie's happy to see me, though—he comes trotting up just as I'm nosing open the barn door, and he gives me a happy sniff of welcome. I bat playfully at his ear and he barks, but his tail is wagging. He follows me on the rest of my rounds and then we head for the porch, where we curl up side by side and take a nap. It's not even noon yet, but already I feel like I've had a full day.

By nightfall, I'm human.

It's wholly unexpected. I can't remember the last time my animal stage was as brief as forty-eight hours. I had been ignoring the twinges in my skull and the spates of blurry vision that usually presage my transformation back to my human form—a process that is always much less violent than the shift to animal. So I am sitting outside, in full view of anyone who might happen to drive up seeking veterinary advice, when my body goes through a single, painful convulsion and I am suddenly a naked twentysomething woman shivering in the twilight chill.

"Son of a bitch," I say to Scottie as I jump up, almost lose my balance, and dive through the door. The change has been so rapid that I'm clumsy in my own body, and I bump into two door frames and one kitchen counter before I realize I'd better slow down. I'm so happy to be human again that I don't want to start looking for darker meanings, but I can't help but wonder if I've entered a new phase in my shape-shifting. More frequent and more difficult transformations into animal shape, offset by shorter periods in that alternate state.

I'm not sure I want to make that trade-off.

And if that *is* my new pattern, is it a naturally occurring one, or has it been catalyzed by my experiments with the blood of other shifters? But if I stop the injections altogether, will I go back to my wildly unpredictable schedule of transformations into a bizarrely diverse set of creatures—some far more challenging than marmalade house cats?

Damned if I do, damned if I don't, I think as I skid into the bathroom and dial the shower water up to the hottest temperature I can stand. The operative word is *damned.* No poet ever dreamed up this particular circle of hell.

I step into the shower and try to wash away the despair.

The blinking light on my answering machine shows that I have ten calls to answer, but I don't play any of the messages back just yet. Instead, while my hair is drying and I'm sipping a cup of tea, I make the call that seems most important.

Joe answers on the first ring. "Are you all right? I've been so worried."

It's not much effort to sound a little wan and stretched out. "You must have Caller ID."

"Everybody has Caller ID. Are you all right?"

"Yeah," I say. "But it'll be another day before I feel a hundred percent. It's like I have a migraine hangover."

"Aurelia said you get them all the time. That's terrible."

"Well, I wouldn't say all the time. Every two or three weeks, maybe."

"That sounds pretty often to me! What does the doctor say?"

Oh, what *would* a doctor say about a condition like mine? "Doesn't seem to be curable, so the best we can do is try to control it with drugs."

"But you *do* take drugs? You aren't just—just—trying to live with it and be brave?"

"Oh boy, do I take drugs," I answer, though I know my invented concoctions aren't the kinds of medicines he's referring to. "I am so far from being brave about this. There are days I want to just throw my head back and howl"—which, in fact, I *have* done, in certain incarnations—"and rail at the injustice of the world. Why me? Why should *I* have this stupid condition? But I do have it, and I handle it the best I can, and there's no point in feeling sorry for myself."

"Okay," he says. "I'll just feel sorry for you instead."

I smile. "But I mostly called to apologize," I say.

"For getting *sick*? Don't be dumb."

"It's just—that's not the way I wanted it to go. Our first date."

"Yeah, well, you know, I have a theory about that," he says. His voice changes in timbre a little; I get the notion that he's shifted positions, maybe stretched out on the couch to get comfortable for a long conversation. "Everyone's always on their best behavior on a first date. They want to make a good impression. But maybe that's the wrong way to go about it. Maybe we should show our worst sides on those first dates, so there are no nasty surprises in the future."

"Unfortunately, I think there are worse things about me than a predisposition to migraines," I reply. "So you still have a lot to learn."

"Ready and willing," he says.

I laugh. "But it doesn't seem fair," I say. "I didn't get to see *you* in crisis mode Saturday night."

"Are you kidding? I was flat-out terrified. Thought you were going to have a stroke or something. Trying to decide if I should take you to the hospital even if you didn't want to go. I *hate* being dumb and helpless."

"Well, you seemed calm and collected, and I wanted to thank you for being so nice about everything."

He laughs. "Wow, what kind of asshole would have done anything else? 'Okay, you're sick, buh-bye. And, by the way, you *ruined* my dinner.'"

"Well, and then you came by Bonnie and Aurelia's house the next day to ask how I was doing. *That* was nice."

"Oh, yeah. Did they tell you they invited me in for dinner? You were right about Aurelia. Just zeroed right in on me and wouldn't let up."

"I thought you handled her really well, though," I say without thinking. "Never lost your cool."

"How would *you* know? You were sleeping in the other room. At least that's what they told me."

Crap. "Bonnie repeated the entire conversation to me," I say weakly.

"Yeah, right. You were probably sitting there in the hallway, listening to the whole thing. You probably *told* Aurelia to give me the third degree."

I manage a laugh. We seem to have eased right by my careless remark. "Didn't have to. She took up that duty all on her own."

"She asked if we were dating."

"And you said, 'I hope so.'"

"So let's plan another date."

I smile into the phone. "Let's do it."

Celeste wants to hear every single detail of the calamitous dinner and the follow-up phone call, so Thursday I meet her in town for lunch. She's chosen the most relentlessly feminine establishment in Quinville, a tea room filled with antique furniture, lush stained-glass panels, and snatches of love-is-grand poetry stenciled on the lavender walls. The only men I see in the whole place are a couple of patrons I would bet are gay and the busboy I know is the son of the owner.

Celeste is wearing a long, flowing sundress printed with tiny pink flowers and a pair of embroidered flats that make her feet look no bigger than a child's.

"It would be easier to be your best friend if I were blind," I say as I drop into the chair across the table from her.

She looks first surprised at such a greeting and then deeply amused. She shakes her hair back, and the wispy dark curls seem to float around her face. "Jealousy only makes you less attractive," she answers.

"Bitch," I say obligingly.

She laughs heartily. "Besides, you've got this very sexy vibe going on and you know it. Bonnie told me you looked pretty hot Friday night, despite being on the verge of puking your guts out."

"Bonnie doesn't talk like that."

"Well, okay, she described what you had on and *I* said it sounded hot, but can we get to the important stuff? Tell me about Joe. What was he like? What did you talk about? Do you like him?"

There are few more pleasant ways to pass the time than talking about someone who's been on your mind almost incessantly since you met him. No detail is too insignificant for Celeste, so she wants me to recount whole conversations, complete with my interpretation of his accompanying expressions and descriptions of my own care-fully hidden reactions. Given the fact that our evening out was cut short, I think my recitation to Celeste actually takes longer than the dinner itself. At any rate, talking about it takes us all the way through lunch at the tea room and a follow-up cup of frozen yogurt that we buy from a nearby shop.

We carry the fro-yo as we promenade through the little city park that is sandwiched between the fire station and the VFW hall. It's a little chilly out, but sunny, and the park is packed. Within ten minutes, we meet six people Celeste knows and two who are clients of mine.

"If I ever develop amnesia, this is where I'm coming," Celeste observes after an old man selling soft pretzels calls her by name. "*Someone* here will be bound to recognize me within five minutes."

"Well, *I* recognize you," says a voice behind us, and we both turn, smiles already on our faces.

They're instantly replaced by scowls when we identify the man who's accosted us. It's Bobby Foucault, the long, lean, walking pack of trouble Celeste tangled with at Arabesque. He's still handsome, but in a sinister sort of way, or maybe it's the bitter sneer that makes me think I see darkness in his features.

"What do *you* want?" Celeste says in a hard voice.

"How about an apology?" he answers. He gestures at his face, and we can see the thin red scars of multiple scratch marks across his cheek. Much faded, but maybe never to go away.

"The way I remember it, you attacked me," Celeste says. "So you're the one who should be apologizing."

He's shaking his head in angry admiration. "I never did see such a prick-teaser in all my life."

She puts her hands up in a gesture that might simply signal she's done with the conversation—or might be designed to remind him that she's capable of clawing his eyes out. "Look. We don't like each other, so let's just avoid each other from here on out. I'm walking away."

She turns aside, but before she can take a step, he plants himself in her path, crowding her off the sidewalk. "Maybe I don't feel like avoiding you, *Celeste*," using her name like it's an insult. "Maybe I think you owe me a little something for treating me so bad."

She stares him down. "If you think I'm too ladylike to start screaming bloody murder in a public place, boy, have you got me wrong," she answers. "Get away from me. *Now.*"

He backs up just a step. "Maybe you won't be in a public place next time I see you, Celeste."

"And maybe you'll be in jail the next time I see *you*," she shoots back.

This time, when she tries to brush past him, he makes no move to stop her, and the two of us hurry down the path fast enough for him to figure out he's rattled us. "You have to tell Sheriff Wilkerson," I say.

"I already filed one report about him. They already know he's a creep."

"Yeah, but he just threatened you! And he knows your *name*! What if he comes to your apartment?"

"I didn't tell him my last name. I'm not that stupid."

I glance somewhat fearfully over my shoulder and see Bobby Foucault in conversation with the pretzel man. Maybe he's just buying the mustard special. Or maybe he's getting exactly the information he needs. *Oh, that pretty lady? That's Celeste Saint-Simon.*

"I don't like it," I mutter.

Celeste shakes her hair back and consciously shakes off the mood. "You worry too much," she says, and gives me a big smile. "I'll be fine."

CHAPTER NINE

The second date with Joe starts out exactly like the first one. We meet at Paddy-Mac's at six on a Saturday night, I order cider while he opts for beer, and we talk as easily as if we have known each other since we laid our mats side by side during naptime in kindergarten.

I don't change shapes, though. Nothing at all goes wrong. We stay through dessert, we linger through coffee (in his case) and decaf tea (in mine). We decide the cool evening isn't too cool to make the thought of a walk enjoyable, and we stroll at a dawdling pace past every single establishment in the Square. We pause for five minutes to talk to the guys who are checking IDs at Arabesque; we think about stopping at one of the quieter bars to get another nightcap. But we're hooked instead by the music boiling out of Black Market, a Train tune that has both of us executing little dance steps right on the sidewalk.

"You wanna?" Joe asks with a grin and I giggle and nod.

Inside, it's a chaotic swirl of too many bodies and not enough lights, and, of course, there isn't a table free in the whole place. But I find a rack to hang my coat on and I sling my purse strap across my body so my handbag won't get in my way, and we head directly to the dance floor. It seems the set has just begun, so we romp through eight or ten songs, barely needing to take a break between numbers. The band mixes it up, old songs segueing into new ones, but we're happy either way; we just want a danceable beat. I'm not quite sweaty but I'm certainly a little heated by the time the lead singer pauses at the mike and says, "Now we're going to slow things down just a little bit."

"Damn," I say, just as Joe says, "Wish they wouldn't do that."

But the song they pick is "You Send Me," one of my favorites, and I can't help an involuntary *oh* as the crooning starts.

"Well, this one isn't too bad," Joe decides, holding out his arms. "Should we try it?"

I adjust my purse so it's behind my hip, and I step into his embrace.

It's like the longest and best hug I've ever had in my life. We move with the music, slowly, barely taking a step in one direction and then another; we're swaying more than dancing. His arms are around my back and my head lies on his chest, and it's not too much to say I feel cradled against him, a sensation I had never expected to find so delicious. I can smell the detergent he's used on his laundry, the deodorant and aftershave he's used on his skin, and the faint scent of perspiration caused by exertion, all of them unexpectedly enticing, comforting, familiar. That's it exactly—he seems familiar to me. And yet I still barely know him.

I want to groan out loud when the music stops, and this time he's the one who says, "Damn." The lead singer shouts into the microphone, "Thank you all very much! We're going to take a quick break now, but stick around and we'll be back in fifteen minutes!"

Joe lets go of me—with some reluctance, or so it seems—and I look up at him. "Want to stay or want to leave?" I ask.

"Hardly seems like we could top that," he answers.

"I agree. Time to go."

Once we step outside, I realize it's both much colder and much later than I'd thought. In fact, it's edging up toward 1 A.M.; it'll be close to two before I make it home.

"I feel like I'd be pushing it if I tried to convince you to go for a drink somewhere," Joe says. "But I really don't want you to leave."

"Pretty much exactly what I was thinking," I say.

"We could get coffee," he offers. "Make sure you're awake for the drive."

I shake my head. "I'll be fine. But I do need to be on my way."

We turn in the direction of Paddy-Mac's, where we left our vehicles, but we walk really slowly. "I can't help feeling this is bad planning," Joe says. "You having to make such a long drive after we've had such a great night. Could you—I mean, if you wouldn't feel weird about it—would you feel comfortable staying at my place?" He glances down at me. "I'd sleep on the couch."

"It requires a little more planning than that because of all the animals," I explain. "If I'm going to stay in town, I need to make sure someone can come in and feed them."

He nods and then asks, "What happened last week? When you were sick?"

I don't miss a beat. "Bonnie called a guy named Daniel, who lives down my way. He's the one who usually covers for me in emergencies."

Joe stops me with a hand on my arm. "I think it's an emergency," he says, and bends down to kiss me.

It's better than the dance that seemed like a hug. Better than hard cider or ice cream or my first human meal after shifting back from animal shape. Better than oxygen.

"Yeah, wow, maybe," I murmur when he finally pulls away. "I can see where an emergency might be right around the corner."

"So you want to stay?" he asks, his voice husky.

But I'm not ready, not yet, not so soon. Pleasure and desire are singing an operatic duet in my head, but I need to think this through. I'm a shape-shifter, for God's sake. How can I even consider falling in love with a human man? Or letting him fall in love with me?

"Not this time," I say, my voice still almost a whisper.

He lifts a hand to stroke my hair, the side of my cheek. "I could come out to your place," he offers. "Follow you there, or just take one car. You'd have to come back to town tomorrow morning if we did that, though."

I swallow a laugh. "Not this time," I say again. "But maybe we can figure something out next time."

He kisses me again, just a swift little reminder kiss, a placeholder, maybe. "All right. But you have to call me when you get home so I know you're safe. That's a long, dark drive."

I take his arm as we recommence walking even more slowly back to our cars. "You don't need to worry. I've made that drive more times than I can count."

"I can worry if I want to. So call me. Promise."

"Promise."

Another block, and we're at my car. Another kiss and then I pull away, a little shaky, and make myself climb into the Jeep. "Talk to you later," I say.

"See you soon. *Really* soon," he answers, and I laugh and drive away.

Though all my thoughts remain behind in Quinville.

* * *

Naturally, Ryan is not happy about recent developments—the ones in my life, the ones in Celeste's. I hadn't thought he would be in a position to approve or disapprove of anything I've been doing, but apparently Celeste has been filling him in on a regular basis.

I find this out Tuesday afternoon when I'm in Quinville getting supplies and Celeste meets me for coffee at the only Starbucks in town. You'd have thought a Nordstrom had moved in the way Celeste celebrated its arrival a few years ago. Whenever I'm in town and she's not at home and she doesn't answer her cell phone, I come here. She's usually sitting in one of the big soft chairs, venti double espresso latte in one hand, iPod in the other, blissfully drowning in music and caffeine.

On this particular day, it's where she suggests we meet, though she doesn't mention that Ryan will be joining us. Still, I'm over Ryan, right? I'm thinking about hooking up with a new guy. I shouldn't feel this sudden breathlessness followed by an adrenaline rush. I shouldn't be thrilled or panicked or—who knows?—maybe both.

"Hey," I say coolly as I join them. They're sitting at a cozy round table made for two, but they've borrowed a chair from a nearby table to make a place for me.

Ryan's on his feet almost as soon as I'm seated, and I can't tell if I'm relieved or disappointed that he's leaving so soon. But I am not so lucky.

"I need a refill," he says, briefly laying a hand on my shoulder. "What can I get you?"

"Um—how about tea and a cookie? Decaf."

"I'll have a cookie, too," Celeste says.

There's a certain amount of settling and desultory so-how's-it-going talk as we wait for our orders and rearrange ourselves around the table. But soon enough Ryan's blowing on his coffee and I'm watching my tea steep and all the preliminaries are abruptly over.

"So you've got a boyfriend," Ryan says to me.

"I—what?" I shoot an accusing glance at Celeste, who just smiles. "I've had a couple of dates with someone, yes."

"Tell me about him."

"Oh, I'm sure Celeste has supplied all the relevant details."

"I want to hear all about him from you."

I make a big production of removing the tea bag, squeezing out the last drops, and placing it on a napkin, where it instantly stains straight through to the table. "Well, you're not going to," I say sweetly. "And aren't you glad? That means I won't talk to *him* about *you*."

He grins, but there's a calculating look in his eyes. Like he's trying to figure out what persuasion will work on me. "Well, I think I know the most important thing about him already," he says. "He's not one of us."

"One of our small circle of petty, judgmental, and gossiping friends?" I can't help asking.

"Hey, I'm not petty," Celeste says. She's grinning, too. She thinks this is funny.

Ryan leans closer, easy to do considering our cramped quarters. "Not like us," he says in a voice of quiet authority. "And you *know* what I mean."

I sip my tea even though it's too hot. "Maybe that's what I like about him."

Ryan shakes his head. "People like us should stick with our own kind. It's too dangerous otherwise."

"Is that right?" I marvel. "Wouldn't know it by your behavior. You're forever picking up cute little chickies, brainless and beautiful, and I'm pretty sure you're not finding out how much they're *like you* before you start getting friendly."

"That's different," he says. "I'm not getting serious with them."

"That's worse," I say, in the exact same tone of voice. "It makes you an asshole."

"Children, children," Celeste chides us. "Do I have to separate you?"

"Maybe," I say. I'd thought I was keeping my cool, but I am definitely ruffled. Who is Ryan to tell me what to do and who to date? "Or maybe you should just stop talking about me behind my back."

Celeste shrugs, unconcerned. "I talk about everyone. It's what makes me such a delightful conversationalist."

Ryan isn't ready to let it drop. "All I'm saying," he insists, "is that people like us are different. We have to be more careful. We have to know our boundaries. We have to know where we can put our trust. And it's not with outsiders. The only ones we can *really* trust are each other."

"That's a bunch of bullshit," I say. "What about Bonnie and Aurelia? What about Janet? We've had plenty of *outsiders* as friends and they've never betrayed us."

A girl at a nearby table gives me a curious look, and I wonder how much of our conversation she's actually overheard. I wonder if she's trying to figure out what qualities differentiate "outsiders" from "people like us." Does she think we're gunrunners or drug smugglers or prison escapees? I take a moment to imagine her reporting us to Sheriff Wilkerson and trying to explain what, exactly, made us seem so suspicious. I can almost hear him saying: *Ahuh. And do you think they would consider* you *an outsider? And did you ever believe yourself to be in danger?*

"We didn't meet Janet and Bonnie and Aurelia when our judgment was clouded by lust," Ryan answers.

"Oh for God's sake," I snap. I turn to Celeste. "Change the subject, or I'm leaving right now. And maybe I'll go straight to the home of my outsider boyfriend so I can pant my lust all over him."

Joe happens to be in Joliet at the moment, attending a nephew's birthday party, but I haven't mentioned this to Celeste and am not about to say so right now.

She smirks at Ryan. "I told you it wouldn't be a good idea to give her a talking-to."

He shrugs. "Had to say it. Friends speak up when they're worried about their friends, even if they know the conversation will make everyone angry."

"That's it," I say, and make a show of gathering up my purse and jacket.

"No, no, no," Celeste says, placing a hand on my arm. "Stay. We'll talk about other things." She nods at Ryan. "How are the injections working?"

He makes a visible effort to lighten his expression. "Good. I had a week of nausea, but then everything settled down and I haven't had any side effects."

I'm still too annoyed to shift mental gears, but Celeste keeps the conversation going. "And you haven't had any of your usual—symptoms—since you started the shots?" *You haven't changed shapes as long as you've been using the serum?*

"No. It's been remarkably efficacious." He risks a look at me. "I was thinking I needed to ask Karadel to mix up another batch for me. Next time she's speaking to me."

"I'll speak to you when you have something interesting to say."

"Well, I'm running low," he says in a placating voice. "So if you have time to make some more for me, I'll be grateful."

I'm still too irritated to be polite. "So here's what I want to know," I say. "Do you talk to Celeste the way you talk to me? Do you deliver a lecture to *her* every few weeks, which is about how often she starts dating some new guy who doesn't meet your criteria?"

"I thought we were done with this topic," Celeste says.

"Celeste's more careful," Ryan answers.

"Celeste is the least careful person on the *planet*!"

He laughs. "Well, she has more control, if you know what I mean. She doesn't suddenly find herself in—difficulties—like I hear you did."

"Really? And who is it who *deliberately* found herself in 'difficulties' just a couple of weeks ago?"

"Celeste can take care of herself," Ryan says firmly.

I eye him over the rim of my cup. "And I can't?"

Now he gives me a warm smile, full of tender fondness and intimate memories. "Sometimes you can be a little vulnerable," he says. "Sometimes you need looking after."

I will not let that smile melt my heart. "Really?" I say again. "And who got accosted in the park just the other day by a guy who looked ready to slit her throat right there in broad daylight?"

"That guy is a creep," Celeste mutters.

Ryan is instantly frowning. "Yeah, I'm not happy about him," he admits.

I glance at Celeste. "Did you report him to the sheriff, like I told you to?"

She shook her head. "I'd just as soon not get the law involved in my life if I don't have to," she says. "I'd just as soon not have Sheriff Wilkerson paying attention to me, if you know what I mean."

I do know what she means; I don't want Malcolm Wilkerson watching *me* any more closely than he already does, either. Still. "If this guy is going to be stalking you, you need some protection."

"Or someone needs to teach this guy a lesson," Ryan says. "Let him know he shouldn't try to take advantage of pretty girls."

"I thought Celeste already made that point," I say in a dry voice.

Celeste is digging something out of her purse. "I Googled him the other day," she says, pulling out a crumpled sheet of paper. "Couldn't find an address for him, but his brother owns that junkyard off 159."

Ryan laughs. "I did the same thing!"

"Two great minds," she says.

He leans in. "Are you thinking what I'm thinking?"

She leans forward, too, so close their foreheads almost touch. "Time to drive by the Foucault homestead?"

He nods, and, at the same moment, they both sit back, satisfied smiles on their faces. "Let's do it," he says. "Right now."

I think it's a terrible idea to cruise by the Foucault junkyard, "just to see what it's like," and I know I shouldn't even climb in the car with them. My one somewhat muddled thought is that they're less likely to get in trouble if I'm with them. It's odd that I'd think this, of course, because my presence has never before prevented either of them from pursuing unrestrainedly reckless behavior.

Bobby Foucault's brother—whose name appears to be Terry—owns property on the other side of town from where W intersects with 159, so I haven't been in his neighborhood that often. Still, everyone in Quinville knows where the junkyard is. It's a little west and north of the Strip, the cluster of pawn shops, liquor stores, and adult entertainment emporiums that huddle together on the north edge of town. I suppose the thinking is that someone might steer his 1987 Chevy off the main road to Terry's place, sort through the abandoned washers and broken-down muscle cars to find the perfect hubcap, then pause at the nearby establishments to pick up a sixpack and a dirty movie before heading home.

Of course, I'm probably being too harsh. Celeste says she's browsed through the adult entertainment store, even bought a few things there, "Though the places down in St. Louis are nicer." She's also pawned a few things—mostly jewelry and small electronics presented to her by lovestruck boyfriends who didn't get a chance to stick around too long—so she knows this corner of Quinville better than I do.

Ryan's driving his convertible too fast for the road, so his tires squeal when he makes a hard left onto the unmarked road that leads to the junkyard. I'm in the backseat, huddled up against the chilly wind of passage, so I didn't even know the turn was coming. I yelp in surprise, but they both ignore me.

"I think it's about a mile up the road," Celeste says.

"Have you actually been here before?" Ryan asks.

"Once. When I was seeing that guy who restored old Mustangs. It was a couple years ago, and I don't think Bobby was around then. Only Terry."

The area leading up to the property is lightly wooded, and between the stands of trees are swaths of failed crop experiments that have long since yielded to saplings and creeping ivy. Here and there, some distance off the road, I spot broken-down buildings—barns, outbuildings, single-family houses—that appear to have been abandoned. The whole scene looks like the perfect setting for a horror movie.

The junkyard itself, which eventually comes up on the passenger side of the car, isn't much more inviting. I'd guess it covers eight or ten acres, all of which are enclosed by a chain-link fence topped by a couple of strands of barbed wire. The wire sags down in a number of places and appears to be cut clean through in another, leading me to suspect that there have been a few break-ins recently, though I can't imagine what anyone would want to steal. Cluttering up the lawn from end to end is a truly eclectic tumble of machinery and vehicles. I spot tractors, threshers, and items I can't begin to identify in among cars, trucks, motorcycles, and Jet Skis. There are also a couple of mobile homes, and at first I think they're part of the junk. Then I notice that one of them has curtains in the window and a light shining through the cloth, and I realize that someone actually lives there.

Terry and his wife, probably. Maybe Bobby, too, unless the second mobile home—which is far more dilapidated but still seemingly whole—is actually functional.

Ryan slows to a crawl and we all gawk over the side of the car.

"Hey, look, that's a 1992 Camaro," Ryan says. "First car I ever owned."

"Me, *too!*" Celeste exclaims. "Mine was red, except the front bumper was blue."

"Mine was black. And orange, if you count all the rust."

"If I still had it, I could come here and get replacement parts."

They point out a few other objects that catch their interest. They seem to have completely forgotten what brought us out here in the first place. For my part, I can't stop staring at the mobile home, the one with the lights on; I twist around to keep it in view as Ryan inches past. I keep thinking about the woman who was sitting with the Foucault brothers at Arabesque that night, the one wearing the low-cut black shirt and the closed expression. Did she marry into the junkyard or is that where she and Terry ended up after other unsuccessful ventures? Did she think it was a temporary stopping point or did she unpack her bags expecting it to be her permanent home? Did she come from a worse environment, so that this ramshackle space seems like a haven of comfort and safety? Would she drive past my haphazard property on the other edge of town and feel sorry for anyone who ended up living as *I* do?

Ryan comes to a complete stop before we've quite passed the property. "I must say, this is even more picturesque than I remembered," Celeste says.

"All it's missing is a starved-looking dog lunging at us from a chain that's just a foot too short to let it jump the fence," Ryan says.

"You've got it wrong," Celeste answers. "It's off the leash and it's trained to kill anyone who comes through the gate after dark."

"I've seen prisons more welcoming than this," Ryan adds.

"I don't—" Celeste begins, but breaks off when the door to the mobile home opens and someone steps out. Not the weary, unhappy wife I've had so strongly in my mind, but the proprietor himself.

I sort of remember him from the night at Arabesque, but he comes back sharply into focus now. Like Bobby, he's tall and dark-haired, but more heavyset and not as good-looking. He can't be more than thirty-five, but there are deep lines etched around his eyes, gouged between his nose and his lips. I'm guessing they're the souvenirs of cigarettes and booze and a propensity to glare, as he's doing right now. He comes a few steps closer to the street.

"Hey!" he shouts. "You want something?"

Just as I'm thinking that's not the kind of friendly voice that would make *me* want to hop out of the car and go exploring through his offerings, a second figure sidles out of the trailer's metal door.

"Crap, that's Bobby," Celeste exclaims. "Let's get out of here."

Ryan hits the gas so hard that the convertible jerks into motion and we spurt on down the road. Not quite fast enough. I'm looking over my shoulder, and I see Bobby startle and then race toward the gate, shouting something and waving a fist. It takes no great intuitive leap to guess he's recognized Celeste.

"I *told* you this was a bad idea," I say as we jounce along the rapidly deteriorating road. Ryan is a fearless driver, but after half a mile, even he is forced to slow down to avoid potholes and buckled pavement.

"Do you think this leads anywhere?" Ryan demands. "Or should I just turn around and go back?"

Celeste has her iPhone out. "I was just getting into my map app," she says, flicking through images on the screen and frowning at the options she's given. "Well, hell. It looks like the road just *ends*. Unless this map is out of date."

Ryan's braking so hard I feel the seat belts cut hard swaths across my chest and stomach. Over his shoulder, I can see that the road indeed peters out ahead of us, the asphalt feeding into a stretch of dirt, then an empty field. When he's slowed to a reasonable speed, he wheels the car in a wide 180-degree turn, though his tires drop off the edge of the road for one terrifying moment. "Looks like we go back," he says.

"I hope they aren't in a truck coming after us right now," I grumble. "Since obviously *they* know this road leads nowhere."

"I think this car can outrun anything those hooligans might own," Ryan says in a supercilious way.

"Off-road?" I demand. "'Cause I don't know what they're driving, but I bet they'd have an advantage if they chased you cross-country."

He doesn't answer, so I know he's pissed, but I don't really think they're coming after us. I mean, I think they'd have caught up with us by now. Still, I'm not particularly looking forward to driving past their place again on the way to the highway.

Ryan stays at a relatively cautious rate of speed as long as we're on the crappy parts of the road, but he accelerates when the pavement smooths out, which doesn't happen until we're almost in view of the junkyard. Then he floors it, and my guess is we're going close to seventy as we zoom by the property.

Not so fast that I can't see the two men pressed up against the fence watching for us. Not so fast that I can't see Terry raise his rifle and take careful aim. Not so fast that we outrun the bullet. It grazes Ryan's right hand where it rests on the steering wheel before plunging into the dashboard and shorting out some circuitry with a sizzle of smoke and a sharp electric odor.

Ryan yells in pain and swerves dangerously close to the side of the road, but rights the car at the last minute. Celeste is screaming and I'm cowering in the backseat, my arms folded protectively over my head. I'm terrified, I'm furious, I'm worried about Ryan, and yet the thought topmost in my mind is: *This is a funny way for shape-shifters to die.*

Not from the physical demands of our impossible lives. Not from the frightened village mob throwing rocks and firebombs. Not from exposure, dehydration, rabies, tetanus, encounters with feral beasts, or unfortunate brushes with animal control.

But from behaving like idiots. From being human.

CHAPTER TEN

As far as I can tell over the next few days, there's no fallout from our brush with the Foucaults. Probably because none of the people involved mention it to anyone else. Obviously Bobby and Terry have no incentive to complain about us to Sheriff Wilkerson, and I'm kind of on board with Celeste's reasons for not talking to the law. Ryan absolutely refuses to go to an urgent care center, so once we're back at Celeste's, I bandage his hand as best I can with the supplies Celeste has in her medicine cabinet. The wound looks superficial, but *all* sorts of possibilities for infection present themselves. Ryan promises he'll seek professional help if there's swelling, heat, or pain, and he also promises to come out to my place early next week so I can change the dressing.

"And I can pick up more of the serum," he adds. "If you'll have time to mix some up by then."

"I'll make it a priority."

I don't know how he'll explain the bullet buried in the dash when he takes the car in for repair. I figure that's not my problem.

I also figure it's not my story. So when Joe calls me on Thursday and asks, "How was your week?" I say, "Oh, pretty quiet." I probably should feel bad about the lie, but as I've been lying since I met him, it hardly registers.

"I'm hoping there's going to be time to see you this week," he says. "I'm coaching Friday night, and Saturday I agreed to take a shift at Arabesque. I figure I have to work there *sometimes* or they'll quit asking."

"Makes sense."

"But I wondered if you were free Sunday? My buddy Mark wants to come and look over the other puppies, if that's okay, but I don't think he'd stay long." There's a beat. "*I* could hang out for a while, though, if you wanted me to," he adds.

I hesitate for a moment because I'm starting to get nervous. By Saturday, it will be two weeks since I last shifted, and lately that's been my limit. But the setting seems ideal. Even if I start getting warning signs that I'm about to transform, I'll already be at my place and Joe's already seen me come down with "migraines." It shouldn't be too hard to convince him to go.

"That sounds great," I say. "See you then."

On Sunday, Joe arrives at about three in the afternoon, his truck closely followed by a gold van. Inside the second vehicle I can spot an adult who looks to be in his forties and enough kids that I keep losing track. Eventually, they've all piled out and I do a quick head count—three girls and two boys ranging in ages from about seventeen to ten. The dad's got salt-and-pepper hair, a thick mustache, and a weathered face that I instantly like. The kids all have that lean look of teen athletes and the restlessness of people who have been cooped up in a small space for far too long. I can tell that all of them are yearning toward the enclosure where the dogs have started up an excited chorus, but they've been raised too well to scamper off without permission.

Joe makes introductions. "Karadel, this is Mark Carson. He owns the trucking company I work for, and he coaches basketball with me."

Mark's handshake is warm and firm; his smile is irresistible. "Nice to meet you, ma'am."

"Oh, please call me Karadel! And these are all your kids?"

He laughs. "Well, they're all mine, but it's not all of them. There's two more already old enough to have left the house." He identifies them quickly and I nod and smile, though I have no hope of matching names to faces.

"I hear you might want to adopt a couple of puppies," I say.

"We might," Mark says.

"Dad. You *promised*!" the youngest girl wails.

"Well, you gotta see if you like them first. See if you bond with them. Dogs, you know, they have personalities, just like people do."

"And these particular dogs have tons of personality," I tell them. "Come on. Let me introduce you."

That's enough to send the kids racing over to the enclosure, and in seconds they're sticking their fingers through the fence, petting the eager little muzzles that are poking out through the chain-link.

"Remember the big one is mine!" Joe calls after them.

I smile at Mark. "You're going to have a hard time telling them no after this."

He grins. "Already bought a couple dog beds and a bag of puppy chow."

Eventually, we're all inside the enclosure, and there are so many dogs and kids running around that I actually feel dizzy from the motion. Joe's made a point of separating Jinx out from the others, giving him undivided attention, and Jinx loves it. He watches Joe's every move, chases after every ball Joe throws and brings it straight back, then dances at Joe's feet, waiting for the next opportunity to show off his adorableness. Mark's down on his knees, letting the smallest dog gnaw on his knuckles and tugging on the silky ears. I feel like I've had one of those signs printed over my driveway—*Puppies! Free to good home!*—and people from the good home have fortuitously arrived.

"Can we have them, Dad? Can we have them?" the youngest girl is asking.

Mark looks over at me. "I'm guessing they've had all their shots?"

I nod. "I've started the distemper and parvo. You'll need to come back for rabies shots. And if you bring them back in a few weeks, I'll spay and neuter them for free."

He looks down at his daughter. "Then we can have them."

I try not to be depressed as the girl and one of her brothers gather up the puppies and carry them out to the van, arguing over who gets to sit in which seat and who gets to hold the animals on the way home. But as Mark backs out and waves one last time, I feel my heart shrink down and my throat close up and tears sting at the back of my eyes. I wave back, but it's the puppies I'm saying good-bye to, not the Carson clan.

It doesn't help that, when I turn back toward the dog run, Joe is standing at the fence, Jinx in his arms, and the puppy is whining and pawing at the chain-link as if he desperately needs to chase after something precious that has been whisked away.

"Well, I don't know who looks sadder," Joe remarks. "You or Jinx."

I put a hand to my heart and manage a laugh. "I'm going to start *crying*. How stupid is that?"

"Well, if you didn't love them at least a little bit, you'd be a terrible person to be raising animals, so I think it's sweet," Joe says. "But I'm kind of worried about this little guy. Can we let him out of the corral here?"

"Yeah—I don't think he'll wander too far from you this afternoon," I say. Just in case, I whistle for Scottie, who's usually a stabilizing influence on the younger dogs. He's sleeping in the sunshine pooling at the side of the barn, but he climbs to his feet and trots over as I open the gate to the enclosure and Joe sets Jinx down on the ground outside. They sniff at each other, and then trail behind us as Joe and I stroll over to the house and settle onto the bench on the porch.

"He's going to be pretty needy for the next few days," I warn. "He'll be lonely. I hope Jezebel is patient with him."

"Yeah, he might make her crazy," Joe says. "But I've been thinking. I have a couple of short runs down to southern Illinois next week. Maybe I could take him with me."

I'm not positive. "You might have to make a lot of stops. Let him run off some energy and do his business."

Joe shrugs. "Mark's paying me by the trip, not the time, so I can stop as often as I like. And there's a fair number of rest areas along the way. I think I'll try it at least once and see how it goes."

The afternoon sun is dropping closer to the horizon and bathing the whole property in gold. The air is unseasonably warm today, but you can feel the chill lurking in the shadows—autumn waiting to pounce the minute you turn your back.

"Want something to drink?" I say. "Water, soda, beer? Something to eat?"

"A beer would be nice," he decides. "Maybe some chips. But it's too nice to go inside."

"Be right back."

A few minutes later, I've brought out a tray bearing snacks for all of us. I toss rawhide bones to the dogs and hand Joe a beer, keeping a single-serving margarita bottle for myself.

"This is the life," Joe says, knocking his bottle against mine and taking a long satisfied drag. "You must love it out here."

"I do. But sometimes I'm overwhelmed."

"Really? By what?"

I make a broad gesture to include the whole property. "Sometimes there's more than I can handle. I mean, not just making sure all the animals are fed and cared for, but maintaining the property, too. Keeping the barn painted. Keeping the sump pump working. Changing the furnace filter. Just—everyday stuff, but there's a lot of it."

"You need a handyman."

"Yeah, I've thought that more than once! Alonzo comes out and works here a couple of weekends a month. Daniel—I told you about him, he lives down the road—sometimes he'll swing by and do some work. And I manage. Some days better than others."

He lifts his shoulders in a slight shrug. "I'm pretty handy. Tell me a couple of the projects you really want done, and I can come out some weekend and help you with them."

"Well, that would be awfully nice of you," I say. "But I don't think I know you well enough to take advantage of you."

That makes him grin. "Maybe that's the best way to get to know people," he suggests. "By seeing how they react when you *try* to take advantage of them."

I laugh. "Oh, so now you're thinking of ways to take advantage of me so you can find out what I'm *really* like?"

"No, I think I'll try to find other ways of getting to the real you. The Karadel at the core."

It's ever so slightly alarming to think that he might find out who I really am. "Well, I hope you like her when you find her," is all I say.

He shifts a little on the bench and seems to be shifting the topic as well. "I think I'll like her but I'm not sure she'll like me in a minute," he says ruefully.

I draw back a bit so I can bestow a mock frown on him. "And what terrible deed have you done that's going to turn me against you?"

"I'm going to be gone next weekend."

"I hardly think I'm entitled to demand that you see me every weekend—"

"Because I'm going bowhunting with a couple of friends," he adds.

"*Oh.*"

"Just going to bring down my one deer and get it dressed and then freeze it and eat it, every bit of it," he goes on in a rush. "It's no worse than eating a cow, it really isn't. Or a chicken. And I know it disgusts you and maybe I shouldn't do it if I want you to like me, but I—"

I fling out a hand. "You're absolved. This is part of who you are. As long as you commit to eating the game you hunt, I won't hold the hunting against you. Though you'd better not ever, *ever* ask me to go with you," I can't help adding.

"Yeah, that didn't even occur to me."

"So you'll be gone all weekend?"

He shakes his head. "Coaching Friday night again. We'll go out Saturday morning, probably come back Saturday evening if I get my deer. My buddies might stay out through Sunday, so I figured I'd take my own truck so I can drive back when I want." He glances over at me. "So maybe I could drop by on Sunday, if you were free."

"Maybe," I agree. I'm still wondering when my next transformation will hit—surely within the next week—and I hesitate to make too many plans. "Celeste mentioned some barbecue in the park thing she might want to drag me to, so call before you come out. Or I'll text you if I won't be around."

"Sounds good," he says. "Though you want to be careful at those barbecues."

"Really? Why?"

"Probably a lot of single guys looking to hook up with pretty girls. You just never know what kind of line they're going to hand you."

I grin. "Okay. I won't flirt with anyone. If someone tries to hit on me, I'll just give them a cold stare, like this"—I demonstrate—"and they'll leave me alone."

"Unless you meet someone who seems really great," he allows. "Unless you meet the perfect guy."

"Hmm," I say. "I'd have to think that over. I'm not sure exactly what I would consider perfect in a guy."

"Well, what sorts of attributes are you looking for? What kind of man do you want to be with?"

The answer is on my lips before I have time to think it over. "Someone who makes me feel safe."

He's silent so long that I think it might have been a stupid answer. I risk a sideways look at his face and observe, "You've gotten all quiet. Did that sound weird?"

"I can't decide between two things to say in response."

"Yeah? Like what?"

He spreads his hands as if to draw attention to himself. "*I'm* a big strong guy. I know how to handle myself in a fight and I'm pretty good with a couple different kinds of weapons. *I* could probably keep you safe."

My face burns because, of course, I realized all that as soon as I made the remark. "And the other one?"

He angles his head to look down at me. His expression is worried. "What are you afraid of?"

Now I feel my shoulders hunch with tension, but I don't look away. "I'm not *afraid* of anything," I say quietly. "But there are times I just want to—lay the burdens on somebody else's shoulders for a while."

I gesture toward the rest of the property, the barns, the corrals, the trailers, the acres that I have already indicated are sometimes too much for me. "Sometimes I feel like I'm responsible for too many other lives. What if *I* stumble? Who takes care of *me*? I know that sounds selfish."

"'Selfish' isn't really a word that comes to mind when I think about you."

I take a deep breath. Might as well say all of it, since I'm embarrassing myself with so much honesty. "And then there's Ryan," I add.

"What about him?"

"When we were dating. He was—he is—there's always a lot of excitement around him. He made me feel—fluttery. But I never felt safe. I always felt that at any moment everything could blow up in some spectacular fashion." I pause, then add in a rush, "Though to be fair, it never did. So I might not have had a reason to feel that way."

Joe's expression is neutral, but I think I can read behind the mask. He's only encountered Ryan in tangents—that night at Arabesque, that afternoon when he arrived as Ryan was leaving—but somehow I think Joe's conceived a dislike of him. "If that's the way you feel, that's the way you feel," he says. "Doesn't sound like he's the right guy for you."

"No," I say on a sigh. "I came to that conclusion myself." I make an effort to lighten my voice. "So what about you?"

He shakes his head. "I don't think Ryan's the right guy for me, either."

I'm tricked into a laugh. "No, I mean—your perfect woman. What would she be like?"

"She'd be happy I was in her life."

I wait, but he doesn't add anything. "That's it? That's a pretty low bar."

He grins. "You know, I don't think my ex-wife ever *was* that happy about me. I think at the beginning she thought she could make me over into someone more like she pictured. When it turned out I was too hard to change—"

"Too much of a lump."

He nods. "I just made her miserable. I remember coming home one day, a little earlier than she expected. She had some music on and she was dancing across the living room, laughing and shaking her butt. She saw me and all the joy went out of her face. I said, 'Hey, I like to dance! Let's put on some more albums!' but she just shook her head and turned off the stereo. I think that's when I knew we'd gone too far down that road to ever get back."

The story has sad little hands that twine around my heart and give it a hard twist. I slip my fingers around his wrist. "Hey, *I* like to dance," I whisper, standing up and tugging him to his feet. "Let's put on some albums."

J oe stays pretty late, but he doesn't spend the night. We dance for a while, fast music, then slow. We sit on the couch and make out for even longer. At one point, he's sitting there with his head thrown back against the couch cushions; I'm kneeling with my legs on either side of his, leaning in to kiss him, my hands on his cheeks.

I pull back just enough to whisper, "I'm not going to sleep with you."

"Ever?" he whispers back, barely opening his eyes.

I giggle. "Tonight. Just so you know. Takes the pressure off, don't you think?"

"I wouldn't have phrased it quite that way," he answers, which makes me giggle again.

"Sometime," I add. "I think. But tonight is too soon." I kiss him again. "This is good, though."

His arms rise to wrap around me and draw me into a bone-cracking hug. "This is *wonderful*."

It's not that far from midnight before he finally groans, heaves himself to his feet, and says he has to go. Jinx has fallen asleep next to Scottie on the living room rug, but he's quick to rouse and offer to play. We both laugh, but I feel like crying again as I see both of them to the truck. Ridiculous to feel bereft and abandoned since I was *trying* to get rid of Jinx and I defined my boundaries for Joe. But I do. Once they're both settled in the front seat, I lean in through the window to give Joe another kiss good-bye.

"See you next week," he says. "Remember what I said about those barbecues."

That makes me laugh, so I'm smiling as his headlights cut a thin swath of brightness through the absolute dark that crouches all around my property, just outside the reach of my house lights. But I'm depressed as I hurry back inside, and I can't shake off the mood as I brush my teeth and change into pj's and climb into bed. Scottie has followed me into my room, and I invite him to sleep at the foot of the bed, something I rarely do. But he makes me feel less alone. Less like the world is a big, empty echoing place and the sound of my voice cannot reach any other living creature.

Monday isn't much fun. Three clients arrive before noon, and although I need the business and I like their animals, I'm tired as hell and it takes a supreme effort to give them the attention they deserve.

I do spend a little more time with the last client of the morning, a long-haired Maine coon cat in calico colors. She's brought in by an older woman named Patti who's always collecting strays. "She hangs around the back porch a couple of weeks at a time, but she won't come in the house," Patti tells me. "She seems so tame, and she's so gentle I even let Hayley hold her, but she is definitely an outdoor cat."

What she definitely is is a shape-shifter. You wouldn't know it by the incarnation, which is perfect to the last detail, but I read the truth in the flecked amber eyes fixed unwaveringly on my face. In this form, she seems to be about eight or nine years old; in her human shape, my guess is she's in her late thirties or early forties. Starting to slow down a little as age or the wear and tear of transformation catch up with her. Probably has been used to foraging for herself but is starting to find the wild life a little too difficult, so she's looking around for a more permanent situation.

I wonder where she lives when she's human. If she's in cat shape for weeks at a time, maybe she's not human very often or very long.

"Definitely an outdoor cat," I agree. "I wouldn't try to make her an indoor cat after all this time. She'd probably be miserable—start peeing on the beds and the carpets. Maybe even stop eating."

"Oh, I wouldn't want that!"

"People think it's a kindness to try to domesticate animals that have lived in the wild, but sometimes it isn't," I add. "It works for *some* of them, don't get me wrong, but at her age—" I shake my head. "I wouldn't risk it."

"What should I do, then?"

"I'll check her out, give her all her shots, make sure she's healthy. And I'd suggest you bring her back every year for a check-up. But other than that, I'd say just do what you're doing. Feed her. Give her water. When it gets cold out, make up a bed for her outside, or put a cat door in the garage if you'd rather. She'll be fine."

Patti's hands are stroking the gorgeous multicolored fur, and a low purr rises from the examining table. "Should I put a collar on her? With her rabies tags? So people know she's not a stray?"

The purr abruptly stops. Most cat collars today have safety features that make them ridiculously easy to unsnap, but Patti seems like the type to have a few old-school buckle collars lying around. I take a moment to imagine the terror of transforming to human stage with a small leather tourniquet strapped around your throat. Would you choke to death before your hands were fully formed enough for you to rip away the collar? "Honestly, I wouldn't bother," I say. "She'd probably spend every waking minute trying to get it off, and she'd probably succeed. Just seems like a waste of money."

"That's kind of what I was thinking," Patti says. "But I didn't want to seem cheap."

I can hardly restrain my laughter when the cat starts purring again.

Finally, Patti and her unconventional pet depart, and I have time to devour a quick lunch. Ryan arrives about twenty minutes later, looking unexpectedly sexy in a tight black T-shirt and snug black jeans. His fair hair is tousled, as if he went to bed as late as I did and hasn't had time to shower today, and he hasn't bothered shaving, either. Combine this unkempt look with the bandage still wrapped around his right hand and he projects an aura of attractive menace.

"You look like you've had a rough few days," I greet him sympathetically. "Did something happen? I mean, other than getting shot at?"

He slouches at my kitchen table and guzzles a cola as if it's the first sustenance he's had for days. "Trouble sleeping," he says. "I stay up too late doing work stuff, then I can't get up in the mornings, so I drink too much caffeine so I can function, then I don't want to go to bed at night."

I sit across from him at the table. "Can you take a couple of days off? Kind of get back into a normal cycle again?"

He gives me a faint grin. "I don't *want* to take a couple of days off.

I wish I could just give up sleeping altogether. It annoys me that I can't."

"That's my Ryan," I say. It occurs to me that he's lying about the caffeine and that he might be using some more powerful stimulant to stay awake and focused. If he is, he clearly doesn't want to admit to it, so I don't ask.

"I'll be fine," he adds.

"How are you doing with the serum?"

"Great. Works like a charm. But it's all gone now."

"Maybe that's part of the problem," I say. "Maybe your body needs to shift or it gets all out of whack. When's the last time you changed?"

He has to think about it. "Two weeks ago? It's been fucking great."

The shape-shifter in me heartily endorses the sentiment, but the medical professional spots the flaw in the regimen. "Well, if you'll pardon me for saying so, you don't *look* great. Which you normally do. And if the only variable is the fact that you haven't shifted, my advice would be to stop the injections for a few days, let your animal self come out, and see how you feel when you're human again."

He gives me the bad-boy smile that has always been irresistible. To me, and to every other woman he ever met, I remind myself. "You think I usually look great?" he asks.

"Wow, way to skip over the most important part of my speech."

He shrugs impatiently. "Maybe you're right. I had the same thought. But there's so much else to *do* and I don't want to lose the two days and I—" He presses his lips together to force back the rest of the words. But it's easy to fill in the blanks. *And I don't want to be a fucking shape-shifter to begin with.*

I stop myself before I make an offer I know I'd regret. *You can stay out here while you shift if you want to.* He used to do that pretty often—head to my place as soon as his body started tingling with the warning of transformation, spend a couple days with me in his animal incarnation, and then a couple of days in his human form. He did that even before we were lovers, though his stays in human shape were much briefer back then.

I don't know where he's been going in the past few months when he feels the urge to shift, because there aren't that many places in the city where it's safe to suddenly be a fox or a hawk. Or that many places where it's safe to leave the fancy convertible that you've driven to this theoretical haven.

So maybe I should invite him to stay. Let him make the transition that his body craves, unencumbered by worries about his safety. Let him roam the property until he's back in human shape, then politely make it clear that I don't want him to extend his visit.

But I keep silent. It's not just that I think it's a terrible idea to slip back into habits of easy intimacy with Ryan—though I do. It's also that I don't know when Joe might call again, or even stop by, and I don't particularly want Ryan to witness our interactions. I don't want Ryan to see me girlish and happy, or flustered and tempted; I don't want him to get a chance to size up Joe's style of courtship, then drop little barbs about the way he speaks or dances or kisses. I don't want Ryan to watch me falling in love with another man.

I press my hands to the edge of the table, and then push myself to my feet. "Well, you have to do what makes sense to you," I say. "I'm the last one to tell someone *else* not to try to alter his fate, since I'm injecting myself with new concoctions all the time. But I think there are repercussions, and you want to be careful that you understand what they are."

He comes to his feet more gracefully than I do, and his smile is sardonic. "Everything has repercussions," he says. "The thing to do is to find the balance."

"Between pain and pleasure?" I ask, leading the way down the hall to my office. I want to change the dressing on his hand before I give him the newest batch of serum.

"Between Eden and Armageddon," he answers.

My eyes are wide as I look at him over my shoulder. "That seems a little extreme."

He laughs. "I've always been a man of extremes."

I flip on the light in my office and motion him inside. I don't answer out loud, but I'm thinking, *You're right. You always have.*

Monday afternoon, I change.

Like last time, there's only a brief and excruciating buffer between my animal and human states. I use it to take care of the most pressing tasks—making sure all the cages are secure and the animals have plenty of supplies; texting Bonnie and Celeste to let them know what's going on; unlocking the front door and taking up a position on the porch so I'm not trapped inside when the transformation occurs.

The last thing I do is text Joe.

Hope your trip is going well. Feel a migraine coming on, so don't worry
if you don't hear from me for a few days. Pat Jinx on the head for me.

Then I slip the phone inside and hunker down, waiting out the increasingly violent waves of nausea and sledgehammer attacks against my skull. Just when I really think I can't bear it any longer—when I'm thinking I'd rather die outright than suffer this agony—the release comes. The pain evaporates, my body snaps into place. I am whole, I am perfect, and I am beyond emotions like worry and fear. I simply am.

Scottie trots over to inspect me, and I scramble up to offer a friendly bark. That's when I realize I'm not the marmalade cat this time, but some breed of dog. My paws are thin and sinewy, covered with clipped black hair, and I'm not as big as Scottie. Beagle, maybe, or some kind of terrier.

Not one of the animals I've included in my most recent concoction. I know I should be concerned about that—my body is outmaneuvering its chemical overrides—but I just can't be bothered at the moment. The air smells fine, there is much to explore, and this body was made for running. I race across the central space of the compound—Scottie in more leisurely pursuit—and head for the open land beyond my property.

What's the point in fretting, after all? I can't answer e-mails, I can't update client reports, I can't wash dishes or paint the barn or tend the garden. I can chase squirrels and bark at passing cars and live in the moment. I can be happy.

Bonnie comes out the next day to check everything over for me and to leave Alonzo behind. "Although I don't know how much help he'll be," she tells me before she departs. "His schedule's been erratic lately, but I wouldn't be surprised if he shifts sometime in the next couple of days. So you might all just be living in one big wild game preserve before too long." She pats me on the head and tells Alonzo, "I'll be back on Sunday," then heads on home.

He spends a couple of hours working in the barn and corrals, though I follow at his heels, trying to convince him to come play with me instead. He pauses a moment at the enclosure where the puppies used to live, eyeing the empty space with what looks like regret before turning away without comment. There are baby bunnies in the hutch, though, and he spends extra time with them, his big hands unexpectedly gentle as he holds their small, quivering bodies on his lap and strokes the long silky ears.

He divides the evening between doing homework, playing a video game, and watching a movie, this last activity being the only one I find marginally entertaining. He doesn't speak a word until my cell phone rings at nine and he sees Celeste's name, so he picks up. Their conversation is brief—apparently she offers to come out and help but he tells her he's doing fine. His voice sounds cheerful enough, so I don't think he's sulking that he's here. He just hasn't felt compelled to share any of his thoughts with me.

Which, actually, is typical of Alonzo.

Wednesday is pretty much exactly the same, down to the phone call, except Alonzo watches two movies instead of doing any homework.

I wake up early Thursday morning to find myself lying on top of my bed, shivering with cold. I'm human, which delights me, but freezing, so I crawl under the blankets and fall back asleep. It's probably ten in the morning before I wake up again, embued with that restlessness that usually stalks me whenever I've shifted back to my natural state. I'm hungry, I'm craving a shower, and I'm desperate to know what's transpired in the real world while I've been in my own private alternate dimension.

Shower. Then food. Then phone calls and e-mails until I reconnect.

I'm standing in the kitchen—barefoot and with my wet hair dripping down the back of my sweatshirt—when Celeste calls. My mouth is full when I answer the phone and mumble, "I'm too hungry to talk."

She laughs. "All right, I'll talk. Alonzo texted me at midnight, said he thought he was shifting, he was going outside. I let him know I'd come out today but now I see I don't *have* to, since you are back among us again."

I swallow. "I haven't had a chance to go looking for him yet. I just got up. But he isn't immediately visible, so I guess he did change. I'll see if I can find him."

"Bonnie says he's been bigger animals lately. Like, the other day he was a mastiff. Took up a lot of room in the house."

"Maybe that's why she wanted him out here this week."

"Maybe. I think she's starting to worry about it. Like—is it time to think about moving somewhere a little more private? Or closer to woodland?"

I take a long swig of milk while I think that over. "They've been in that house for fifteen years. I'd hate for them to have to sell it."

"I think they'd hate it, too, but I don't think they'd hesitate," Celeste answers.

"We shape-shifters certainly don't make it easy on the people who love us," I say.

"See, you're just not paying attention," she says. "Nobody makes it easy on anyone. We're not difficult just because we're shape-shifters. We're difficult because we're people."

I laugh. "Maybe. I don't think I know enough regular people to judge."

"You know *one*," she says in a meaningful voice. "How's the romance going with the bouncer-slash-truck driver?"

"Fine, I think. I really like him."

"I think I need to check him out."

"You met him already."

"Once! For five minutes! Before I knew you were going to get all gooey over him."

"I don't want you to meet him. You'll say something embarrassing."

"I won't. And I won't bring embarrassing pictures, either. Like, say, the one of you in the striped dress—"

"Celeste!"

Our talk goes like this for the next fifteen minutes. I continue to eat the whole time I'm on the phone, so I'm pretty much finished with my meal by the time we hang up. I head outside to do my chores and to look for Alonzo. But I don't come across him the whole time I'm working. Not a squirrel or a raccoon or a small creature then. Something bigger and wilder and more predisposed to roam.

I'll leave some clothes on the edge of the property, a blanket on the front porch bench, so he'll have something to cover himself with when it's time to come home. Celeste and even Ryan and I are pretty cavalier about turning up naked around each other, and Cooper was never particularly shy, either, but Alonzo doesn't like anyone to see him undressed. I figure that would hold true for any fourteen-year-old boy, not just one who's covered with battle scars. Though my experience with teen boys is pretty limited.

I spend the afternoon mixing up new serums for Ryan and for myself, and answering electronic and voice mail. Janet's mother has sent me a short note, talking about the great weather in California and a new recipe she's tried, and my intention is to send back a reply that's just as breezy and superficial.

But I find myself telling her about Joe. I type out:

He's not like other guys I've dated. He's low-key and not very focused on a career and not the sort of guy you look at and think, "Oh, he's so cute." But when I'm with him, I feel so good. I don't know how else to explain it. I feel like my hand fits inside his hand.

I hesitate a moment before I send it; the sentiment is so girlish and uncertain that I can't imagine Janet would ever have come up with the words, and surely Nina Kassebaum will realize that. But I feel like I want to confide my thoughts to *someone*, and it's hard to think who else to tell. Celeste is too bawdy, Bonnie too brisk, Aurelia too sharp, to trust with such timid and wondering emotions. Janet's mother is the closest thing I have to a mother of my own.

I hit send and then log off my e-mail account immediately. Time to think about other things.

Friday I entertain a long stream of clients—three dogs, four cats, and a pair of pet rats with respiratory problems—so I'm glad when the day comes to an end. Gladder still that I've finally emptied out the waiting room by the time Joe calls, so I have time to sink to a chair and talk for a few minutes.

"Just about to leave for the Y, wanted to say hi and see how you were doing," he says. "Headache still better?"

We've talked twice since I shifted back, and each time he's asked after the migraine. I'm thinking I might have to come up with other reasons to explain my sudden absences. "Headache still gone," I say.

"Still up for having me come out Sunday afternoon?"

"Absolutely. Unless you'd rather have me come into Quinville?"

"I hate you making that long drive back at night."

"You're going to have to get over that. I drive at night *all the time* when you're nowhere around."

"Oh, sure. Give me something else to worry about."

But the truth is, I'm just as happy to have him come out to my place. I've never been the kind of girl who particularly enjoyed fancy dinners and loud entertainment. A fire, a pizza, a video, a bottle of wine—good times.

"Anyway, I owe you a meal," I say. "Let me cook for you."

"It's a deal," he says.

I can't bear to wish him good luck when he goes hunting the next day, but I do give him a generic benediction: "Hope you have fun on Saturday."

As I hang up, I comfort myself by thinking he might have fun even if he doesn't bag his deer. He'll be out with his friends, tramping through the woods, communing with nature. Who wouldn't enjoy that, even if the experience isn't completed by murder?

Saturday I have two clients in the morning, but the afternoon is free, and I've resolved to clean up one of the trailers. Until about six months ago, a young couple lived there—both of them shape-shifters—along with their baby girl. She had been sickly and frail and obviously having trouble dealing with her shape-shifter genes. One day she would be all human except for her left arm, which would have claws and fur like a cat; another day there would be a human head on an animal's body. When she died in her sleep one night, I wasn't sure if she'd been suffocated by her own ungainly body or by one of her distraught parents who couldn't bear to subject her to such a bizarre and nightmarish life. We buried her on the edge of the property, where there are dozens of unmarked shape-shifter graves. The next day, the parents were gone.

I'd done a superficial cleanup of the trailer in the following week, but I'd always planned to really scrub it down, disinfect any lingering germs, and wipe away what I could of the concentrated sorrow. I'm a believer in sunshine and fresh air. They don't always dispel the ghosts, but they soothe those grieving spirits, robbing them of some of their bleak power.

The day is chilly but bright, and I almost enjoy my task. I'm humming to myself as I swab down the tiny bathroom surfaces, spray Windex on the glass and tiles. I'm elbow-deep in a bucket of soapy water when there's a commotion outside. A car horn blaring repeatedly, becoming louder and more frantic as the vehicle grows closer—tires rattling on the rocks, a car door slamming—a hoarse voice shouting my name.

I rip off my rubber gloves and burst out of the trailer to find Joe's truck parked haphazardly on the gravel, both doors wide open. Joe is racing toward me, carrying a limp and bloody body in his arms.

It's Alonzo, and there's an arrow through his chest.

CHAPTER ELEVEN

My stainless-steel operating table isn't big enough for Alonzo's body, so Joe holds him in place while I run to find a card table as an extender. I don't have time to hear Joe's explanation first, though he looks as if he's witnessed the apocalypse and he's murmuring, "He just—he just—" so I'm betting I can guess what happened. On a bone-deep level, I'm utterly terrified, but on what I consider my conscious level, I'm gripped by professional calm. My hands are steady, my brain is functioning at a furious rate, and I know exactly what to do.

"Here—keep his chest and hips on the metal table, move his legs to the card table—that's right," I say as I return to the operating room and start setting things up. It's a small space at the best of times, and exceedingly cramped now, but Joe has also forced himself into a professional mode—officer in crisis—and he works with efficiency. "You might have to restrain him while I examine him."

Alonzo's awake, his wide, dark eyes watching me, but he doesn't speak. I've already ascertained that the arrow is in an optimal place—high up on the shoulder, not through the chest as I first feared. I don't think it's even cut through an artery, since he's already stopped bleeding.

Thank God he's stopped bleeding. I don't dare give him a transfusion.

"You doing okay, buddy?" I ask him. "I'm gonna give you a shot to help with the pain, then I'm gonna get this thing out of you. Still going to hurt like hell."

He just gives me the briefest of nods and continues to watch me.

Most of my medicines are designed for animals, of course, but I've been using them on shape-shifters for five years now and never had a problem. So I get to work with the supplies I have at hand. A little lidocaine to numb the area, a twilight cocktail to induce drowsiness, some antibiotic cream where the arrow pierces the skin.

"Cut off the tip then pull it back out," Joe suggests.

I nod. "Yep. As soon as I'm sure the drugs have taken effect. And when I can figure out what to cut it with." The arrow isn't wood, as I would have expected, but metal. A modern improvement to the traditional hunting method, I suppose.

"I've got clippers in the truck," Joe says. "If it's safe for me to leave for a few minutes."

I nod. "Go."

Alonzo is semi-unconscious by the time Joe reappears, and I move quickly to remove the arrow, flush the wound with disinfectant, then suture it up. While I work, I can't help but notice all the other scars cutting across his dark, supple skin. Burn marks. Knife wounds. Knobby lumps that might be souvenirs of untreated broken bones. One long, thin scar starts over his left rib cage and makes a jagged track toward his pelvis, disappearing under the blanket I've thrown over the lower half of his body.

Being shot by an arrow probably isn't the worst thing that's happened to this kid.

Now that he's sewed up, infection is my biggest worry, so I pump him with antibiotics. I *think* he'll be okay. I *think* Joe got him here in time. But oh my God, to have come so close to losing him . . .

"Can you carry him upstairs?" I ask Joe quietly. "I keep a room for him here. Just put him there."

He nods without speaking and gathers Alonzo in a careful lift. I grab my cell phone so I can dial Bonnie's number as I follow Joe through the house. She doesn't answer and neither does Aurelia, so I leave identical messages. "Call me as soon as you can. Everything's going to be okay, but . . . call me."

Upstairs, we settle Alonzo in his bed, and I check to make sure the jostling of relocation hasn't caused the wound to start bleeding again, but everything seems fine. I lay my hand on his forehead even though it's too soon to check for fever. I just want a reason to touch him again. His skin is warm and smooth. His eyes don't open, but his breathing is steady.

"Okay," I whisper to Joe, and he follows me out of the room. We go downstairs and I head straight to the kitchen, straight to the refrigerator, and pull out two beers. I drink about half of mine in one long, greedy pull before I sigh, lean against the counter, and give Joe a level look. "Tell me what happened."

He hasn't touched his beer, though he holds the bottle in his hand as carefully as if it's a nuclear warhead. His face is pale and his eyes are haunted. This is a man who has just witnessed the end of the world as he knew it.

"I don't *know* what happened," he says in a low voice. He's staring down at the bottle in his hand. "I can tell you what I saw, but I—I think it's true, but I—"

"Tell me," I say more gently.

"My buddies and I had split up. None of us had hit anything in the morning, so we took a break for a few hours in the afternoon, then they went off together and I went a different way. I'd found a good spot, and I'd been in place for a while, just waiting, when I saw the deer come through. Four of them—buck, doe, a couple younger ones. I had sighted on the buck when one of the other ones kind of leapt forward. Right in the way of my arrow. My first thought was, *Damn, ruined my shot.* I knew I'd only wounded him, knew I'd have to track after him to kill him clean. And then—and then—"

He lifts his eyes and stares at me. "He started flailing. Thrashing around. And he fell to the ground and he—he was a deer but then he—he was a *person*. He was a *child*. I saw a deer change into a human being, and it was Alonzo."

"Yeah," I say. "He does that."

He holds the stare for another long minute. "So it's true," he says at last.

"It's true."

"There are really people who can turn into animals."

"Hundreds," I say. "Maybe thousands."

"Your friend—the one at the bar—who turned into a mountain lion. She really did that."

"A bobcat actually, but yeah. She really did."

"So is that what—does it happen when they're in danger? Suddenly they find themselves transforming?"

I shake my head. "It's different for every one of them. Celeste can actually choose when to shift between states, though I wouldn't have said she picked a good time that night with Bobby Foucault. Alonzo's on a sort of unpredictable schedule, which is often what happens with teenagers. He'll be human for a few weeks, then animal for a few days. Different kinds of animals. I haven't seen him be a deer before."

"Why did he become human when I—when I shot him?"

"I can only guess. Most shape-shifters I know die in their human state. If they're dealt a mortal blow while they're in animal shape, their bodies transform during their last moments of life. I think Alonzo's body didn't know how desperate the wound was, so it automatically began the transformation."

"I didn't mean to hurt him," Joe whispers.

"I know. He knows."

"When I saw it—when I saw him—when I knew what I had done—"

"Terrifying. Horrifying. I know."

"All I could think of was I had to get him here. To you."

"I'm glad you were so close. I'm glad I wasn't in Quinville."

He focuses on me again. "At first I wasn't sure if you knew. About him."

I take another swallow of my beer, but my throat is tight. I know what's coming next. I nod.

"But then I remembered your friend. Celeste. And I was pretty sure you knew about her."

"That's right."

"So I figured you knew about Alonzo. And then I thought—"

I wait.

"Your migraines," he goes on in a thread of a voice. "What if that's not what they really are?"

I want to lie. I want to reassure him that I'm normal, a little sickly, maybe, but perfectly human. I'm not a strange, fantastical creature whose hybrid body appears on ancient temple walls as the manifestation of evil. But the secret's already out in the fresh air and bright sunshine. Like a ghost, it can't survive long without the dark.

"I don't really have migraines," I say quietly. "I'm a shape-shifter, too."

For a moment, he doesn't move or speak. Then he lifts the beer bottle to his mouth and swallows down most of the contents without pausing for breath. The whole time he doesn't take his eyes off my face.

Then he sets the beer on the table, pulls out a chair, and drops down, gesturing for me to take a seat as well. I warily comply, though I'm tense as hell. Waiting for what he'll say next.

It's simple. "Damn. Tell me about it."

There's not that much to my story, after all. "I was born to a couple of shape-shifters who lived up in Chicago. My own transformations were so erratic that I couldn't be in public much. My mom died when I was young, but my dad moved heaven and earth to find someplace where I could live in safety." I glance around the kitchen, but I'm really indicating the whole property. "He met Janet, who was studying to be a vet. She was human, but she was in love with Cooper, who was a shape-shifter, and he needed a safe place, too. So my dad and some friends bought this place and set Janet up in her practice, and I came to live here."

"How'd you get the schooling you needed to be a vet?"

I smile. "I didn't. I learned everything from Janet. I'm not licensed. I'm not legal. I live in terror that Sheriff Wilkerson will find out and shut me down." I rub a hand across my forehead. "Well, it's just one of the many things I live in terror of."

He's gone to the fridge to get another beer for each of us, and he unscrews the cap before handing mine to me. "What else?"

I exhale a breath that's almost a laugh. "That someday I'll be out in public and I'll need to change and I won't be able to get to a safe spot. That some crazy fear-mongering bastard will find out I'm a shape-shifter—or that my friends are—and start hunting us the way you were hunting deer. That something will happen to Alonzo or Celeste or"—I manage to stop myself before outing Ryan—"or any of the others." I glance at him. "That you'll find out. And you'll hate me."

He shakes his head. "That won't happen. I won't hate you. But I'm still trying to get my mind around it."

"A process that might take you a while," I say.

He settles back in his chair and takes a meditative sip of his second beer. "So Bonnie and Aurelia. Are *they* shape-shifters?"

"No."

"But they know about you—Alonzo—all of you?"

"Yeah. There are always some—some—normal people who know about us. Usually they're family members or lovers or people who just somehow find out. Well, most shifters I know try very hard to keep the secret, because they're all afraid. They know that once the world starts asking questions, life could get very dicey."

"Seems pretty dicey anyway. I mean—" He gestures toward the door, in the direction of the woodland some miles away where the hunting accident occurred. "If you're running around as an animal half the time, people could kill you. Like I almost killed Alonzo. I mean, *anything* could happen."

"Believe me, I've thought about every possible terrible scenario," I say ruefully. "Each one scarier than the last." I produce the barest laugh. "I suppose the only good thing is that I won't have that long to be afraid."

"What's that supposed to mean?"

I'm already sorry I said it, so I try to speak lightly. "Oh, you know. It's a hard life, and lots of shape-shifters don't live that long."

Now his attention, which has been pretty diffuse as he tries to chase down all his chaotic thoughts, suddenly concentrates on me. "What's *that* mean? You don't live long?"

I just say it straight out. "Every shape-shifter I've known has died before turning fifty. Some a lot sooner. Cooper wasn't even forty. A girl Janet was treating a few years ago—I think she was twenty-two. They didn't come down with diseases—we don't seem to get cancer or diabetes or pneumonia. Our bodies give out on us. We die of old age when we're young."

His eyes still fixed on mine, he frowns. "That's terrible. I hate to hear that."

I manage a light shrug. "Lot of ordinary people die young, too. Children. Babies. Young mothers with everything to live for. Newlyweds. None of us is guaranteed a long life. I try to remember that. I try to make peace with that—with all of it."

He leans back in his chair. Still watching me. "That sounds like you don't much like being what you are."

"I hate it!" I burst out. "I hate being *different* and *strange*. I hate the fact that my body is completely out of my control, that these transformations will take me over whenever they want to, and I can't guess when and I can't stop them. I hate living in fear. I hate lying to everyone I know. I want to be normal and ordinary."

"Nobody's normal," he answers, "and you'd never be ordinary."

My smile is bitter. "I'd like to give it a try."

Something occurs to him; he sets the beer down and leans forward. "So you resent all the time you spend in animal shape," he says.

"I do."

"But maybe you're thinking about it the wrong way. What if you were born to be an animal? What if that was your natural state? And all the time you're human—*that's* the special time? *That's* the gift?"

I stare at him, because this has literally never occurred to me. "I would—I don't—that doesn't make sense."

He leans back again. He's almost smiling. "It makes as much sense as the rest of it does."

But I'm not ready for paradigm shifts. I rub my head and feel, suddenly, exhausted. Not for the first time, my day has gone far from the way I planned.

My gesture concerns him. "Are you getting a headache? Are you about to shift shapes?"

I look up. "What? No—*no*. I'm fine."

"How does it work? When you change?" he asks. "What does it feel like?"

I stare at him. "It feels—there's a lot of pain. I actually *do* get headaches, horrible ones. I'm sick to my stomach. I feel like all my bones are stretching or squeezing down. It's like—have you ever seen pictures of those contortionists who can fold their bodies down so they fit into a tiny box? That's what it feels like is happening to me." I spread my hands. "Then suddenly I'm something else and I feel fine."

"What something else? What animal?"

"A lot of different ones. I've been almost everything over the years. Dogs, cats, deer, raccoons, monkeys, birds—everything." I sip my beer. "Lately I've been trying to control it a little. I've been taking injections. Making a serum from the DNA of other shape-shifters, trying to replicate their patterns. Trying to see if I can mimic their timing or mimic their shapes."

"Wow. I'm impressed. Is it working?"

"I thought so. The past few times I changed, I was the same animal—an orange tabby. But this week I was a dog, so I don't know."

It takes me a moment to realize why he suddenly looks so startled. "An orange cat?"

"Yeah."

"The one at Bonnie and Aurelia's house?"

I'm surprised into a laugh. "Uh. Yeah. That one."

"Aurelia was trying to convince me to take you home!"

"Nah. She was trying to piss me off. Which she managed to do. Aurelia—she likes to see what people will do or say under stress. It intrigues her. Don't be mad at her."

But he's wearing a look of unholy amusement. "It's pretty funny, though, when you think about it. Kind of like, if you could turn invisible, you could be in the room with other people and hear what they were saying about you."

"Trust me. It's not as much fun as that."

"Well, I don't think the whole thing is as awful as you seem to."

"That's because it's not happening to *you*."

But he's right. Once he made it past his initial shock, Joe has been remarkably at ease with my astonishing tale. Maybe because I didn't have to first battle his disbelief—he'd already found out in the most dramatic fashion possible that shape-shifters really do exist. Now he just has to figure out how they fit into his worldview.

I tilt my head to one side to consider him. "You're taking this so well," I say. "Why aren't you more freaked out?"

He rubs a thumb along the corner of his mouth, mulling it over. "I've been thinking about it, I guess," he says. "Ever since the night your friend Celeste made such a scene. You and I talked about what it would be like. It's not like, boom, one day I shoot an arrow into a deer and it suddenly becomes a person and it's never occurred to me such a thing could happen so I think I'm hallucinating. It's like"—he squinches up his face—"when you do a crossword puzzle and one of the answers is a word you've never heard before, so you look it up. And then the next day, you hear it on the radio, so you already know what it means."

I'm laughing. "It's *way* weirder than that."

He grins. "Well, it is," he admits. "But it's along those lines."

I shake my head and pick at the beer label with my thumb and don't look at him. "So—now that you know—you still want to hang out with me?"

"Hell, yeah!" he exclaims. "This makes you the coolest girlfriend *ever*."

I grin briefly. "It doesn't make you think—I don't know—I'm kind of creepy?"

"No," he says positively. "It makes me worry about you more—and I was a little worried, anyway, thinking about you living out here all on your own, so far away from town. Now I know *why* you're out here, but that doesn't make me feel any better. Anything could happen to you when you're in another shape. I don't like that at all."

"I have a network," I tell him. "I usually have time to call or text someone right before I shift, and a lot of times Alonzo or Celeste will come out when I'm in another shape. And there are a couple of other people I can call on when I need someone to take care of the animals."

"It's not the animals I'm worried about," he retorts. "It's you."

I toss my head in a sassy-independent-woman way, but to tell the truth, it gives me a warm glow to think he's fretting about me. When's the last time *that* happened? "I've made it this long," I say. "I'll be fine."

He lifts his shoulders in a slight shrug. "Maybe—next time you're about to change you could call me? And *I* could come and help out?"

I stare at him. "I don't know."

"Why not?"

"It might be too strange."

"For you or for me?"

"Both of us."

He puts his elbows on the table and leans forward. "So what's it like for you in animal shape? Are you still you? Do you feel the same? Remember everything?"

"Yes and no. I remember who I am and where I am and who people are and all of that, but it feels distant. Not always very important. I'm always thinking about more immediate things—what I'll eat, where I'll be safe. My senses are different. I pay attention to different things. I'm easily distracted."

I gesture, trying to explain. "But I can still think through a problem the way an animal wouldn't. For instance, if I'd been a deer out in the woods this afternoon, and I'd realized there were hunters nearby, I'd have found someplace to wait out the day. I'd have kept away from the usual trails or water spots. Actually, I'd probably have come back *here* where I knew I'd be safe, and no real deer would do that. So I'm a crossbreed, basically."

"Huh," he says. "So why would it bother you to have me around?"

"Because you'd be looking at me, wondering what I was thinking! Because either you'd pet me on the head like I really was a cat or a dog, or you'd try to talk to me like I was a person. Because I usually transform back to human state when I'm sleeping, and I wake up naked."

"Now, that I wouldn't mind seeing," he says with a grin.

"Because I don't know you well enough," I add. "It's too personal. Shifting."

He eyes me for a while, weighing his response. "Someday you might know me well enough, though, don't you think? You might not mind getting—personal."

"It's more intimate than sex," I tell him bluntly.

But he's already gotten my drift and isn't about to be rocked off balance now. "Baby steps," he says affably. "We'll have sex first."

I laugh and I blush and I jump to my feet, all at the same time, just because I'm too wired to sit there. "I'm going to check on Alonzo," I tell him. "Stay here."

Upstairs, I find Alonzo still in the grip of sedatives; his body is lax, his face inexpressive. Once again, just to have an excuse to touch him, I check his skin for fever, but nothing registers but his usual warm temperature. I make sure the blanket is pulled up to his chin before I leave the room and head back downstairs.

The minute I rejoin Joe in the kitchen, my cell phone rings. "It's Bonnie," I say.

"She's going to flay my skin off."

"I wouldn't be surprised," I reply as I accept the call. "Hey, Bonnie."

"Good afternoon, Karadel," she says in her formal way. "We were at the movies with our phones turned off. What's wrong?"

"Listen, Alonzo's going to be fine, but there's been an accident."

There's a two-second delay before she responds, and then her voice sounds slightly more distant. I'm pretty sure she's put me on speakerphone so Aurelia can hear. They're probably still in the car, heading back from the theater. Great. Bonnie will skin Joe, and Aurelia will grind down his bones.

"What kind of accident?" Bonnie says, sounding calm.

"He was hit by a hunter's arrow."

"Fuck. Is he all right?" Aurelia's voice.

"It went through his shoulder, didn't hit anything vital. He's here, I've got him sedated, and I'm not sure there's much you can do for him right now."

"We're coming out there," Bonnie says.

"You're welcome, of course, but—"

"How did you find him?" Aurelia interrupts me. "Was he able to get back to your house under his own power?"

I lift my eyes to Joe's and give him an apologetic smile. He can't hear their side of the conversation, but I'm sure he can fill in the blanks. "He was a deer when he was hit. He shifted. The hunter brought him back to me."

There is absolute silence on the other end.

Joe motions for me to give him the phone, but I switch it to speaker before I hand it over. It's like the worst conference call you can imagine. Joe says, "It was me. I shot him. I'm so, so, so sorry."

"Who is this?" Bonnie demands.

Aurelia, of course, is the one who remembers. Aurelia remembers every face, every voice, she's ever encountered. "It's that Joe fellow. The one who's dating Kara."

"You shot our boy?" There is no leniency in Bonnie's voice at all.

"I was aiming at a different animal. He jumped in the way. Almost like he did it on purpose."

"That excuses nothing," Bonnie says sternly, but Aurelia has a different take.

"He probably did do it intentionally," she says. "Alonzo hates to think of animals getting hurt. Of anybody getting hurt."

"We'll be out there in a half hour," Bonnie says.

"Forty-five minutes," I correct her, but she's already hung up. I look over at Joe. "Better run while you can."

He shakes his head. "I'll stay. Gotta man up."

It's what I expected him to say, but the reply pleases me anyway. This is someone who doesn't run from the consequences of his actions. "Then can I feed you something? Fortify you against the ordeal to come?"

"That would be great," he says. "And I'd love another beer but I think I'd better not."

"Yeah, the only thing Bonnie would hate more than someone who hurt Alonzo is someone who hurt Alonzo and then got drunk."

Turns out the anxieties of the past hour have burned through all my reserves, so I'm starving, too. I'm not up to cooking, so I defrost some chicken casserole and open a bag of chips. We talk quietly as we eat. Mostly Joe asks more questions about my life, my transformations, my injections, my limitations. He seems more intrigued and less astonished with every passing minute, so I find myself relaxing, growing more eager, *wanting* to tell him the minutest details. I can't help wondering if this is what it was like for Bonnie's old girlfriend Derinda when she first told an outsider her own story. Terrifying and exhilarating and, in the oddest way, comforting. *I don't know how I know this, but I believe this person will never betray me.*

Bonnie never betrayed Derinda, of course. I guess it's too soon to know about Joe.

"You can't tell anybody, you know," I say as we gather up the dishes and put them in the dishwasher. "*Anybody.* Mark. Your brothers. Your next girlfriend. Whoever you marry. Even if we have a huge fight and you decide you never want to see me again, you can't get back at me by talking about this."

"First, really hoping we never have that kind of fight," he says, closing the dishwasher door and snapping it in place. "Second, I tend not to be a big blabbermouth anyway. Third, nobody would believe me. So I'd look like an idiot if I talked about you."

"Ah, male pride," I say. "The one thing I can rely on even if everything else fails."

I've been watching the clock, so I'm not surprised by the sounds of tires rolling across gravel and car doors slamming shut. Bonnie bursts through the kitchen door first, her bony face set in grim lines. I'd lay money that she was the one driving.

"Where is he?"

"Upstairs in his room."

She gives Joe one look of burning reproach before hurrying toward the stairwell. Aurelia enters just as Bonnie exits, her pace more leisurely and her pose a little less strained.

"Bonnie's convinced he's at death's door, but I'm thinking you didn't lie to us," she says. "And he really will be okay."

"I'm worried about infection, and there could be some damage to his shoulder muscles, but aside from that, I swear to you I think he'll be fine."

Joe came to his feet the minute they drove up, and now he squares his shoulders. "I can't apologize enough," he begins.

"Probably not," she says. "But I don't see how we can blame a hunter for shooting a deer. And believe me, I would blame someone if I could."

Joe risks a quick look at me, unprepared for the reasonable tone. I give him a faint smile. "Aurelia's done some hunting in her time."

"Rifle," she says. "Never had the patience for a bow. It's been years, though."

"This will be my last hunt," Joe says.

Aurelia nods. "Yeah. Meeting shape-shifters is what turned me off of it, too."

She heads out the door toward the stairs, and Joe watches her with a hopeful expression. "Maybe she'll keep Bonnie from killing me," he says.

"She's the only one who could."

Joe remains behind in the kitchen while I join the others in Alonzo's room. Bonnie's perched on the edge of his mattress, one palm pressed against his cheek, her eyes unwavering as she watches his face. Aurelia's standing at the foot of the bed, her hands in her back pockets, her expression soft as she gazes at the two of them. It's impossible to ever guess what Aurelia's thinking, but I make a stab at it. *These are two of the people I love most in the world. It will not be because of my negligence that either one of them ever comes to harm.*

Bonnie turns her head when I step into the darkened room. "How long will he sleep?"

"At least a couple hours. Longer if I give him another shot."

"Can you bring a chair or a cot in here so I can sleep in his room?"

"No," I say firmly. "He's not in mortal danger. I'll make up a room for you down the hall and you can get up as often as you like to check on him. But I think he'd rather sleep by himself."

"He would," Aurelia agrees. "Don't smother him."

Bonnie's lips tighten, but she gives a sharp nod. I'm glad Aurelia said it; I don't think Bonnie would have heeded anyone else.

"Are you staying, too?" I ask Aurelia.

She shakes her head. "I don't want to smother him, either. I think one of us hanging over his bed will be plenty."

Since I'm pretty sure they came in the same car, I'm instantly thinking about logistics. I say, "I can bring them to Quinville tomorrow or the day after, unless you want to come back for them."

She turns to give me a wicked smile. I think her red hair throws a rosy light on her face, because I can see her expression perfectly. "No, I'll leave the car for Bonnie. I'm going to ride back to town with Joe."

Alonzo and Bonnie stay with me through Monday afternoon. Alonzo is, as you might imagine, the perfect patient. He never complains about pain. He accepts every treatment in stoic silence. He refrains from thrashing in the bed, mussing up the sheets; naturally he doesn't vomit on the bedspread, or anywhere else. He even manages to avoid coming down with an infection, though that might be my drugs, not his willpower.

Bonnie, of course, cannot contain herself enough to sit quietly at his bedside for all the hours of the day, though surely that is what she envisioned herself doing. Instead, she checks on him a couple of times an hour, feeds him, helps him to the bathroom, and even reads to him for an hour at night. But mostly she strides around the property, fixing things. The loose towel rack in the guest bathroom. The burned-out bulb in the living room chandelier. The rickety kitchen chair. All repaired or replaced.

Then she cleans out my pantry, throwing out expired spices and organizing cans alphabetically. She cooks massive meals from the ingredients I have on hand, and freezes most of them in single-serving containers. She scrubs every room in my house. She changes the furnace filters. She dusts the miniblinds. The whole place is filled with the inviting scents of fresh bread and pine-scented cleaners.

"Can I hire you?" I ask. "You could be the live-in caretaker. I'd give you one of the trailers."

She barely smiles. "*You* could have the trailer. Aurelia and I would take the house."

"Deal."

Joe calls multiple times a day to check on Alonzo's progress. He still hasn't told me what he and Aurelia talked about on the drive back to Quinville. When I asked Aurelia, she just laughed like a cartoon villain. I figure I'll never know.

"What can I do to make it up to Alonzo?" Joe asks me Sunday night. "Buy him a video game? An iTunes card? A car?"

"A video game, maybe. But I don't know that you have to buy him anything. He knows you didn't do it on purpose."

"I still feel horrible."

"I think even Bonnie is starting to forgive you," I say. "Everything will be all right."

"It doesn't feel like I've suffered enough for it to be all right."

"There are always plenty of other chances to suffer," I tell him. "Don't be sad when one of those opportunities passes you by."

Monday afternoon he sounds unexpectedly cheerful. "Hey, does Alonzo know how to ride a bike?"

I happen to know that he does, because I happened to be there when he learned. Celeste brought him out to my place about two months after he came into our lives, back when he didn't speak and wouldn't meet your eyes and always appeared to be waiting for the next blow to land. She'd bought him a shiny red ten-speed and spent a solid week teaching him how to ride it. He didn't seem to have the requisite sense of balance at first, and I wondered if he'd gotten one too many concussions or maybe he'd suffered inner ear damage after a particularly savage beating. But then one day all the components just clicked for him—weight distribution, muscle coordination, and forward momentum—and he went racing down the road. When he came back, pedaling as furiously as his legs would take him, his face wore the closest thing to a smile any of us had seen so far.

"He does," I say to Joe. "Why?"

"I think I may have found him a job. If he wants it."

"Riding a bike?"

"You know the little pharmacy on the corner of Baker and Horseshoe? Q-Ville Drugs and Gifts?"

"Yeah. The owners have a couple of collies and an ancient Siamese cat."

I can hear his grin. "Well, I didn't know *that*, but they're looking for a part-time person who can deliver orders around town."

"Huh. That sounds like something Alonzo could do. Except—well—he can't always be sure he's going to be available. You know."

"Right. And Rich said—Rich Hogarth, he's one of the owners—"

"Right. I know them," I say patiently.

"Rich said they didn't need someone every day, anyway. He said maybe Alonzo could call every Monday, or whatever, and talk about the days he'd like to work that week. I don't know if he can tell how far in advance he's going to change, but maybe they could work something out."

"Maybe. I'll talk to Bonnie about it. And Alonzo, of course. He'll be pleased you thought of him."

He blows his breath out in a way that's half laugh, half sigh. "Still trying to make it up to him. So I think about him a *lot*."

"They're planning to go home tonight. So maybe you could swing by sometime this week and apologize in person."

"Do you think Bonnie would let me in the front door?"

"Maybe. Maybe she'd make you wait on the porch and just let Alonzo peer out through the screen."

But Bonnie, when I talk to her a few minutes later, merely nods. "I think it would be good for him to come by and express his remorse to Alonzo directly," she says. "A man should own up to his misdeeds, and it will be good for Alonzo to have that role model."

She's intrigued by the notion of the part-time job with Q-Ville Drugs, but, of course, she sees all the obstacles as plainly as I do. "We would have to let the Hogarths know that he is sometimes—and quite suddenly—unavailable," she says. "Perhaps we could come up with an arrangement, however. On the days Alonzo is scheduled to work—but can't—I could complete the deliveries for him. That shouldn't happen more than once or twice a month, if we pay attention to when his next cycle is about to start."

I agree. "There seems to be no reason not to *try* it," I say. "And if it doesn't work out—well, he's no worse off than before. I suppose the Hogarths are inconvenienced if they have to look for another delivery boy, but—"

"But we can't worry about their problems as well as our own," Bonnie concludes. "So let's give it a try."

I've prepared quite the cornucopia of drugs for Bonnie to take back with her and administer as needed, but Alonzo is doing remarkably well by Monday evening. He even sits at the dinner table and eats with us, though he's quieter than usual and doesn't have a huge appetite. He lets me hug him, though, before he gets in the car.

"You call me the minute the pain gets worse, or the wound looks funny, or you spike a fever, or *anything*," I tell him, sticking my head through the passenger-side window to give my final instructions. "Don't try to tough it out. I am *here* for you."

That elicits a faint smile. "I know. Thanks."

I pat his cheek, then step back. "You are absolutely and completely welcome."

They drive off into the gathering dark and I head slowly back to the house. Scottie follows me as I move from room to room, straightening up and locking up and generally making sure everything is in order. But despite his faithful presence, despite the fact that I am so relieved at Alonzo's quick recovery, despite the fact that I am glad to have my house back to myself, I realize that I'm feeling at loose ends. A little lonely. Depressed, even.

I recognize the emotion, of course. It's loss. Bonnie and Aurelia and Alonzo are the closest thing I have to family these days, and despite the terrors of the situation, it was rather lovely to have them around for the extended weekend. I've become something of a hermit since Janet and Cooper died, and I was never the kind of person who liked big crowds and noisy gatherings. But I don't think my natural personality is a solitary one. Under other circumstances, I believe, I would be the kind of woman who hosted Saturday dinners for all the cousins or plotted the annual family reunion. I might have had only a few close relationships, but I would have treasured every connection; I would have poured my heart into each one.

Well. Fewer relationships now, but still that willing heart. I collect a beer from the fridge, pick up the cell phone from the kitchen counter, and go settle on the couch to call Joe.

CHAPTER TWELVE

Celeste wants to meet Joe.

"You've met him," I tell her, as I've told her before. It's Monday, more than a week after Alonzo's accident, and she's disgruntled that I haven't had time for her in all these days. So she's driven out to my property to demand lunch and conversation.

"For five seconds! When we were walking in the door at Arabesque! That doesn't count."

"I'm not ready for you to meet him."

"Why? You think I'll tell him things about you?"

I wave my hands. "Because you're so—you're such a force of nature. People find you overwhelming."

"People find me charming."

"You're deluded."

She grins. "If you won't introduce me, I'll just find a way to meet him on my own. He coaches Alonzo at the Y, right? I'll go hang out with Bonnie some night so I can introduce myself."

"Why would you bother?" I demand. "I never force myself on any-one *you're* dating."

She makes a dismissive gesture. "None of them mattered. Joe seems to matter to you. So I need to know him. Decide if he's good enough for you."

I point at her. "See? Right there. That's why I don't want you to meet him. If you don't like him, you'll be horrible."

"If me being horrible to someone is enough to scare him off, then he wasn't the right guy for you to begin with."

We're still arguing when I hear the sound of a car pulling onto the gravel. I'm not expecting any clients, so it might be an emergency—a dog that swallowed something toxic, a cat going into renal failure. Even my most devoted clients tend to take their animals to vets in town when the situation is dire enough, but maybe one of them risked the mad dash out here because he just didn't trust anyone else.

I head to the kitchen door and wait to see who steps out of the car. It's got Missouri plates, which is my first clue that this isn't one of my regular visitors. I don't recognize the driver, either, when he emerges a moment later. He's a slim, dark-haired guy of medium build and handsome features, and he doesn't have a pet with him. But he strides straight up to the porch as if he's been here before. Something about him is teasingly familiar, and nothing about him screams *danger*, so I open the door and motion him in before he's even had a chance to knock.

"Can I help you?" I ask.

He glances quickly around the kitchen as if to check it against his memory, nods casually at Celeste, then addresses me. "You might not remember me, I used to know Janet Kassebaum," he says. His voice is so attractive I think he should be a singer, or maybe a radio announcer. "My name is Brody Westerbrook."

"Brody!" I exclaim. "Of course! I'm Karadel."

He smiles. "I thought you must be, but you were just a skinny kid last time I saw you."

"Come on in. You want a drink? Something to eat?"

"A soda would be great," he answers, moving toward the table.

"That's Celeste, by the way," I add. "A friend of mine. Shape-shifter."

That elicits a laugh from Celeste, who has been lounging in her chair looking the visitor over with frank interest. "Well! I suppose we don't have any secrets from *Brody*," she says.

I bring over sodas and chips and cookies for everybody, then sit down next to Celeste, so we're both facing him. "Brody used to be a TV reporter," I tell her. "He and a cameraman filmed a shape-shifter transforming from animal to human—on live television."

"Holy shit," she says. "So how come we weren't all part of some media circus?"

Brody waves this off. "No one believed it. Thought it was some big hoax. But the whole experience got me curious, so I started looking for evidence that such creatures existed." He glances around the kitchen again. "One thing led to another, and I met Janet and a few of her friends. And a few other shape-shifters."

One of them had been a laughing blond girl whose body was deteriorating under the stress of constant transformation. Brody was dating the girl's sister and he's the one who introduced them to Janet. Janet tried to treat her, but she died when she was in her early twenties.

My age.

"So how was Africa?" I ask. "Isn't that where you went for a couple of years?"

"It was amazing. Spectacular. Eye-opening. Everywhere you'd go, there'd be these animals—cheetahs sitting on rocks, like they were just *posing* for you—"

"They probably were," Celeste says with a laugh. "Probably half of them were shape-shifters just trying to act the way you'd expect."

"I bet some of them were," he agrees.

"I saw a review of your book," I tell him, and then explain to Celeste, "He and his wife worked at a charity school in Tanzania. Brody wrote a book about what they're doing to help kids born with disabilities—the review was really positive."

"Yeah, not quite a bestseller, but I did get some attention and we set up a fund for the school with some of my royalties. Which made me feel really good about the whole thing."

"Wow, an author. I'm impressed," says Celeste. She leans forward a little, fixing her dark eyes on Brody's face. I recognize this as her seductive pose; I've seen her employ it often enough on men she thinks are cute, and Brody certainly fits the description. "Are you going to write another book?"

He glances at me. "Actually, that's what I'm here to talk about. I wanted to get Karadel's opinion."

I raise my eyebrows. "Really? I'm not much of a literary critic. Actually, I don't read a lot. I'd rather watch movies."

"*I* read all the time," Celeste says. It's true, as it happens, but she'd say it even if it wasn't. She's flirting.

"When I first met Janet, I wanted to write a book about shape-shifters," he tells us. "Nonfiction. Describe their lives, their challenges, explore how they live among us in secret and have *always* lived among humans, even though we didn't know it."

Now Celeste frowns and pulls back. "That's a terrible idea."

He nods. "I finally realized that. Even if I used pseudonyms for the shape-shifters I interviewed, even if I didn't give details about where they lived, the book could have put all of them in danger. If people believed it, of course, which they probably wouldn't have."

Celeste leans forward once more, liking him again. "So what's your new idea?"

"Write a *novel* about shape-shifters. Use what I know, but make it clear the story is fiction. My sisters tell me there's this whole paranormal craze in the market right now—my book would fit right in."

"That's brilliant," Celeste says.

Hard to believe, but Brody ignores her. "So what do you think?" he asks me. "Would it be okay?"

I'm still a little puzzled. "Sure. I mean—I don't know why you even think you'd have to get my opinion."

"I want to tell Janet's story."

"Ahhhh . . ."

For a moment there's silence between us, as I contemplate Brody and he waits for my answer. Well, it's a compelling tale, that's for certain, and no one who read it would possibly believe it was true. But that doesn't mean it's safe to tell. And then there's something else to consider. As she lived her life, Janet was a very private person; she was only close to a few people, including Cooper, my father, and a couple of college friends. I don't know how she'd feel about hundreds—thousands—of people helping themselves to the details of her unconventional life. If Brody even knows those details.

"Are you sure *you* know the story?" I ask him quietly.

He nods. "She sent us her journal. Right before we left for Africa. The only thing I don't know is how it ends. If the experiment worked."

I nod slowly. "It did."

"How long did she have?"

"Longer than she expected. Fifteen months."

"But she—she did die, after all?"

"About a week after Cooper. I think she could have survived longer, but she chose not to."

Brody takes a deep breath. "Then that's the perfect ending, don't you think?"

I know Janet thought so. I truly believe that, for that last year and a half, she was as happy as she'd ever been. She was never the jump-up-and-down-with-delight kind of woman; her early life had imbued her with a wary reserve that made it hard for her to be wholeheartedly joyous. But she had been deeply content. She had been exactly where she wanted to be.

"If she sent you her journal," I say, "I think she probably wanted you to tell her story. So I think you should go ahead and write the book."

"Thank you."

"*I* think you should write it, too," Celeste says. "I make my living doing freelance editing, so I could look it over for you once you've got a rough draft done."

For the first time since he's been here, really, Brody gives Celeste his full attention. I'm surprised it hasn't happened sooner; guys are usually caught by Celeste's exotic face and soulful expression within the first thirty seconds of meeting her. But Brody was a reporter for years. My guess is that his bullshit detector is calibrated pretty high.

Now he's grinning. He holds up his left hand to show off a wedding band. "Married," he says. "But thanks."

Celeste's face dimples into a naughty smile. "How married?"

"*Very* married."

"I could still help you with the editing. If you wanted."

I give her a light punch on the arm. "Behave yourself."

She shoves me back. "I never behave myself."

"Which is why I think I'll ask one of my friends to be my beta reader," Brody says. He's still grinning.

"Wise man," I say. "But feel free to call *me* anytime you have a question. Or come visit the property if you want to get some detail right."

"I'll do that," he says. "I thought I might get some photographs today."

"Sure," I say, coming to my feet. Both of them follow suit. "But you have to promise you won't be specific enough about this place that anyone would recognize it. Or could find it."

"Promise." He hesitates a moment before turning to the door. "It was good to see you, Karadel. You look like you're doing well."

"I am," I say, smiling back. "Thanks for noticing."

It's another three days before Celeste actually meets Joe, and it's perilously close to a disaster. Though it's not her fault. It's mine.

It's Thursday night and I've come to town because I won't have a chance to see Joe again for a couple of days. He keeps apologizing that his Fridays and Saturdays are taken up by other commitments—coaching the basketball team and working at Arabesque—but it doesn't bother me at all. Living as I do, I don't care much about weekends. I'm more focused on a different kind of calendar: my internal clock that decides when it's a good time to shift. I'm closing in on two weeks again, and I might not have much longer before the change occurs. So I want to see Joe while I still can.

We've gone back to the little pub that he has started to call "our place." Tonight Paddy-Mac's is about half full and we get the goth waitress who seems to have no other life, since she's there every time we are. We sip our drinks until the food arrives, talking with the ease of old friends and the excitement of almost-lovers. We laugh so much the air around us seems charged with hilarity, a not quite perceptible glittery shine.

I don't know about Joe, but I haven't been paying attention to anyone else who might be in the restaurant, so I don't realize Celeste is there until she slides into the booth next to me.

"Hey," she greets us cheerfully. "Fancy meeting you here."

"Hey," Joe replies, surprised but cautiously amiable.

I'm the one who's frowning. "Go away," I tell her.

"Well, that's rude," she says, turning toward Joe. "Don't you think so?"

"It is."

"Seriously. Go away."

She picks a French fry off my plate. "I just want a few minutes. Want to get to know Joe a little." She smiles at him. She is, as she says, charming. "It *is* Joe, right?"

"Yep. You must be Celeste."

She laughs. "Kara must have described me. What did she say?"

"That you were worse than Aurelia. I find that hard to imagine."

She turns sideways to give me an indignant look. "I am not! No one is!"

"When you want to be, you're worse than anybody," I inform her.

"You're also a bobcat," he adds.

Celeste rolls her eyes at me. "Jeez, are you spilling secrets to *everybody* these days?"

"I was at the bar when it happened," he reminds her. "I just didn't believe it then."

"So you can blame yourself if he already thinks you have a hot temper and you lack judgment," I say.

"I hope you also mentioned that I'm loyal and funny and I've saved your ass more times than I can count."

"I don't think I got that far."

Joe leans back in the booth like a man preparing to be entertained. "So how do you two know each other?"

Celeste eats another French fry. The goth waitress comes over to see if Celeste wants any food of her own. "I'll have some of that cider."

"And her own order of fries," I add.

She folds her hands on the table and returns her attention to Joe. "We met out at Janet's place. Karadel had sort of taken up residence there one summer because she was—" She waves her hands. "Changing like a maniac. Never knew what she'd become or when it would happen. So she had to hide away so no one could see her."

"How'd you know Janet?"

Celeste wrinkles her nose, like she's trying to remember. "Through my mom. I don't know how *they* first met. But there was this whole network of—of people," she says, glancing around to see how close anyone else is sitting. She doesn't want to say *shape-shifters* out in public. "They all knew about Janet. If one of us got sick or hurt or whatever, we'd go to her for treatment."

"So your mom was the one who—" Joe lets his voice delicately trail off.

Celeste nods. "She was like me. Had complete control. Could choose when to change from one to the next."

"The easiest possible life," I grumble.

She grins. "I *am* the golden girl."

He studies her a moment, and I get the feeling he's doing the math. *Celeste looks to be about Karadel's age, so her parents would probably be in their fifties.* And he sure hasn't forgotten what I've said about the life span of shape-shifters. "Is she still in Quinville?" he asks. Nicely phrased, I think.

Celeste shakes her head. "Nah, she's been gone for years. I don't even know if she's still alive."

That widens his eyes; not the answer he expected. I fill in a little. "Celeste's mom wasn't really the maternal type. Not too interested in raising her kids. Always trying to find somewhere to stash them so she could go off and do what she wanted."

"Kids?" Joe repeats.

Celeste nods. "Yeah, apparently I have a half sister somewhere up near Chicago. And, who knows, maybe a couple other brothers and sisters scattered across the Midwest. I've never met any of them."

"That would make me curious," he says. "I'd be tempted to track them down."

"Would you?" she says. The waitress arrives just then with her order, and she thanks the girl with a smile. As soon as she leaves Celeste says, "I've never seriously considered it. I figure they're all probably as unstable as I am, and hardly worth the trouble of getting to know."

"You're not unstable," I say. "You're just annoying."

"So the two of you hung out at Janet's and started arguing with each other," Joe says, "and that led you to realize you were meant to be best friends?"

Celeste laughs. "We're so different," she admits. "But we got along from the beginning. Kara seems so meek and quiet, but there's a lot of fury under that calm exterior."

"Fury," Joe repeats, looking at me. "I would have said longing."

"Ooooooh, that's good," Celeste says. "But she's way more discontented than she seems."

"Let's go back to talking about you," I say.

"No, we're supposed to be talking about *him*," she exclaims. "I got distracted!"

"What do you want to know?" he asks. "No secrets."

I rattle off the basics. "Divorced, no kids. Lots of brothers. Good family relationships. Ex-cop. *Now* will you go away?"

She ignores me. "So what do you like about Karadel? What attracted you to her?"

"Initially?" he says. "I thought she was cute."

"Smokin' hot bod, right? She does *not* take advantage of it."

He's grinning. "That's part of what made her cute."

"So then? After that?"

"I liked the way she talked to me. Like she thought I was interesting. I thought *she* was interesting. She seemed very authentic."

"Yeah, she was lying to you the whole time, you know that, right? Because unless she was telling you all about her *other life*, she was just making up stories."

"Well, everybody holds back at the beginning, don't you think?" he says. "You show part of yourself, and if someone likes it, you show a little bit more."

I can tell she likes that answer, but what she says is, "What have *you* been holding back?"

He narrows his eyes and seems to consider. Then he smiles. "Stuff I'd probably tell Karadel before I'd tell *you*."

She makes a little disgruntled noise, but she doesn't seem displeased. "Well, I hope it's nothing too terrible."

"I think I'm basically a decent guy," he says. "Whether or not you like me."

She laughs. "You want to know something amazing? *Aurelia* told me she liked you, even though she didn't want to. And Aurelia likes maybe two percent of the population."

"That *is* amazing," he agrees. "I feel like ordering champagne or something to celebrate."

"No, let's go over to Black Market instead," Celeste says.

"*You* can go," I say. "*We'll* stay right here."

"It'll be fun," she says. "There's a DJ. People might dance."

"I like to dance," Joe says.

"Nobody dances on Thursday night."

Celeste jumps to her feet and tugs on my arm. "It's not like it's a *rule*," she says. "People dance all the time. Come on."

Joe's already throwing money on the table. "I got yours," he says as Celeste reaches for her wallet.

"I'll buy the first round at Black Market," she says. "Let's go."

In fact, there's a rehearsal dinner or family reunion or something at the bar, because people *are* dancing at Black Market, but most of them bear a vague resemblance to each other and they're taking up one whole section of the seating area. I've never particularly liked this place, because it's got low ceilings and sticky floors and a sort of depressing ambiance, but at least there's no cover charge and you don't have to worry about looking good enough for the rest of the clientele. Celeste tows us to an empty table against one wall and says, "A pitcher okay?" When we nod, she heads up to the bar.

Joe smiles at me. "I like her. She's fun."

I nod gloomily. "Everybody loves Celeste."

"Hey, I didn't say *that*."

"Well, don't like her better than you like me or I'll probably never get over it."

He reaches across the table to take my hand and give it a squeeze. He doesn't bother to release it. "*You're* the one with the smokin' hot bod," he reminds me.

That makes me laugh. "And the authentic personality."

"That's right. It's no contest."

Celeste is back at our table a minute later, followed by a waiter with the requisite pitcher and glasses. None of us have taken more than a few sips before a Maroon 5 song comes over the speakers, and Celeste gives Joe an I-dare-you look.

"Dance with me?" she invites him.

He glances at me, but I wave them toward the floor. "Go on. Have fun. I'll people-watch."

"Come on," Celeste says, pulling him out of his chair. "Don't waste the music."

I sit at the table by myself and try not to feel like a wallflower. Just to have something to do, I observe the cluster of tables holding all the family members and try to guess the reason for the gathering. Are they celebrating the old woman's eightieth birthday? The young couple's engagement? The middle-aged couple's silver anniversary? It's easy to pick out the spouses, the ones who look bored or irritable or long-suffering. One of them, a good-looking power-suit type who's probably in his mid-fifties, catches my eye and gives me a wink.

Not wanting him to come over and start making conversation, I shift in my chair to look away, and find myself staring straight at Ryan.

"Hello, sweetheart," he says, and bends over to kiss me on the cheek.

Instantly, my skin is aflame with reaction to his presence and worry that Joe will have seen the gesture. I laugh, hoping the sound seems casual instead of rattled.

"Ryan! What are you doing here—or, no, let me guess. You and Celeste cooked this up between you."

He grins and settles into the chair next to me. Joe's place. "Nothing so specific. She said she knew you had a date tonight and she was going to try to track you down. I said I'd be here or at Arabesque. Looks like we both picked Black Market."

"Because you're twins."

"Something like that." The waitress materializes at his shoulder and asks if he'd like a glass, which she conveniently already has on her tray. He glances at me and I shrug, so he accepts the offer and pours himself a beer.

"Won't your date think you're rude to go off and talk to another woman?" I ask.

"Not on a date. Here with clients," he says. "And they left five minutes ago. It's just me."

"How's your hand?"

He holds it up for me to inspect in the low light. He's dispensed with the bandages, so the wound is plain to see—mostly healed, but still an angry red surrounded by slightly puckered skin. "I think I'll live. Now, whether Terry Foucault will live, that's another story."

"Haven't you learned your lesson about going out and stalking people on their own property?" I demand. "Isn't there some kind of my-home-is-my-castle law that allows people to shoot intruders? We were intruding."

He sips his beer, watching me over the rim of the glass. There's something about the look on his face that gives me a momentary chill, and I try to identify the expression. Menace? Calculation? Conviction? I have the wayward thought that, if I was running down a dark alley, I'd rather meet up with a Foucault brother than with Ryan. I shake it away.

"We were driving down a public road, which we had a right to do," Ryan finally says. "If we'd climbed the fence, then maybe they'd have a right to shoot us. If that gun's even legal."

"Well, hey. Unregistered firearms. Tell the sheriff."

"I don't talk to the law."

"Phone in an anonymous tip."

"We can take care of ourselves and our problems," he says. There's an ever so slight emphasis on we.

"Shape-shifter vigilante," I scoff, too annoyed to be cautious. But no one can hear me over the music. We can barely hear each other.

He smiles faintly. "If necessary."

Just then one song ends and another begins—a Jessie J piece, I think, though I don't recognize it. Danceable, though, which means there's no chance Celeste will release Joe for the duration. I try to muffle a sigh.

Ryan sets down his beer and slips to his feet. "Come on," he says, holding out his hand. "Just a dance."

My glance strays toward the family reunion table, where the restless stockbroker type is still watching me. I get the sense that if I don't accept Ryan's invitation, this guy will come over and offer to buy me a drink. Maybe my shirt is too tight.

"Fine," I say ungraciously and scramble to my feet. "But just one song."

It is, of course, impossible for me to adhere to the one-song rule. Ryan's a great dancer, lithe and sexy, and he always focuses his attention wholly on his partner. A bit like a lion stalking its prey across an African veldt, maybe; I always get the feeling it's too late to get away. I shake my head to flick away the thought and shake my hips to the upbeat music.

There are maybe five other couples on the dance floor, as well as a group of twentysomething girls from the family group, forming their own private dance hall and raucously egging each other on. Still, it's not hard to get a look at everyone else who's out there swaying to the music. Joe and Celeste look like they're having a great time, strutting and pointing and snapping their fingers as the beat dictates. She's tossing her hair and giving him sultry looks over her shoulder, but she's playacting; that's the way she always dances, even when it's with me. Joe sees me watching them and gives me a big smile. If he doesn't like that I'm partnered with Ryan, he doesn't show it.

I see someone from the family group cross the floor to request a song from the DJ—even looks like there's a five-dollar tip involved—so I'm not surprised when the next chord progression elicits exclamations from the whole party and most of them surge to their feet. It takes a moment for me to recognize "Stand by Me," which maybe was the theme song at someone's wedding. At any rate, they're all planning to dance to it.

I turn back toward the table, but Ryan catches my wrist. "C'mon. You love this song."

I used to. It was playing on the radio the first time Ryan and I made love, and I can't ever hear it without remembering that. When we first broke up, I stopped listening to both oldies stations and country music for fear it would come on the radio in one of its cover versions.

"Ryan—" I say.

"C'mon," he repeats, tugging me closer.

I could break free, but I don't want to have a wrestling match here in Black Market and I don't want Joe to see me struggling in Ryan's hold. It seems easier to acquiesce, to let him pull me against his chest, put his arms around me, and rest his cheek against my hair. Unexpectedly, I am engulfed in such deep and complex emotions that I think I'd lose my balance if I wasn't already leaning against him. I'm sad—so sad—I miss him so much, I miss *this*, the shape of his body against mine, the sense of excitement, desire, and belonging I feel whenever his arms are wrapped around me. The song speaks of faith and trust, the singer offering himself up as a bulwark against despair, and for a moment I can't remember that Ryan cannot be counted on for any of those things. For a moment I remember only how much I loved him and that I can't have him anymore, and the sense of loss is devastating.

By the time the song ends, I feel like I've shrunk into a fragile collection of sticklike bones and dried-leaf skin; squeeze me too tight and I'll crumple into dust. As the last notes sound, all the couples on the dance floor stand motionless, still embraced. It's as if we've all been frozen by the cessation of music. I suppose it's only three seconds before the next song starts, but it feels like an eternity before Bruno Mars comes wailing out from the speakers. The people around us shake themselves back to life.

Ryan lifts his head, pulling back a little, though he doesn't release me. Wordless, I glance up at him, not even attempting to arrange my expression into something less exposed. Maybe he can't read my face in the dark, but I can tell he's smiling.

"That was nice," he whispers, and drops a kiss on my mouth.

My whole body trembles as someone takes hold of Ryan and gives him a hard shake. "Hey! No making out on the dance floor!" It's Celeste, of course, and she pries Ryan's fingers off my arm. "My turn. I want to dance, and Joe says he's done for the night." Now that I'm liberated from Ryan's embrace, she pushes me back in the direction of the table. "But I bet he'd dance with *you* if you wanted."

I stumble for a step or two, then have to twist out of the way of three young girls who are gyrating together more wildly than the music would suggest. By the time I'm back at the table, I feel a little less dizzy, but my brain is still in something of a whirl.

Joe's lounging at his ease, sipping from a water glass instead of his beer. From his expression, I can't tell if he didn't witness Ryan's kiss or he just didn't think it was any big deal. "Not exactly the way I expected the evening to wind up," he says over the music.

"That's what happens when Celeste is in the mix." My voice sounds normal enough to me.

He holds his arm out to show me the watch on his wrist. Past eleven. "I've got a drive to make tomorrow, and I have to get back tomorrow night before basketball," he says. "Probably time to leave."

I am so ready for this night to be over. "Just what I was thinking. Let's go."

"What about Celeste?"

"Ryan'll take her home or back to her car. She'll be fine."

But I wave to her anyway as we head toward the door and she waves back, clearly unconcerned. A few minutes later, Joe's truck has pulled up next to my Jeep where we left it outside Paddy-Mac's.

"Here's the bad part," he says. "Me dropping you off at your car and worrying about your long drive home."

"I'll be fine. I'll text you when I get in."

"You do that. Or, you know, you can always sleep at my place. On any piece of furniture you choose."

"I know. Don't worry."

He hesitates a moment, and I think he's trying to figure out how to express something unpleasant. I tense up. But all he says is, "You know I'm busy the next couple of days."

"Yeah. And—I don't know about me. Maybe Sunday or Monday or Tuesday—the change will happen. I can't tell."

"So it might be a few days before I see you again."

"Yeah."

"So that'll give you a little time, I guess."

"Time for what?"

"To think about Ryan."

There's dead silence.

"I don't want to think about Ryan," I manage at last.

He gives me a small smile. Lighting in the truck, under the streetlights, is just about as poor as it was in Black Market, but I can see the unhappiness on his face. "Well, I think you do sometimes whether you want to or not. And he's sure thinking about you."

"Ryan's not the right guy for me. I'm positive of that."

"Sometimes we want stuff even if it's wrong for us."

"Joe—" I put my hand on his arm. He doesn't pull away, but he doesn't draw me closer, either. "I confess, when Ryan's around, I still get muddled a little. But—"

"You're not over him."

"Maybe not, but I *want* to be over him. I want to move on with my life. I want him in my past, not my present. I want—I want *you* in my life."

He's been gazing out the front windshield, but now he looks at me again. "And I can't tell you how much I want you in mine," he says. "But I don't want to fall in love with someone who isn't ready to fall right back. I've done that. And that's about the worst place anyone can be."

It's the first time the word *love* has come up for air during our conversations, but it's been swimming around just under the surface for a couple of weeks now. I feel a small, hopeful smile come to my face, and I squeeze his arm tighter. "Well, I don't want you to be in that dark terrible place," I say softly. "I want to fall when you do."

Unexpectedly, he leans forward and gives me a brief, hard kiss. It's a ghostbuster of a kiss; it chases away the lingering wraith of Ryan's memory. "Don't wait too long," he says. "I've already started falling."

CHAPTER THIRTEEN

I don't change for another seven days.

It's weird. I feel like I'm in a state of suspension, as if I'm waiting to hear the results of a medical test or a bar exam—as if I can't move forward with my life until I get some resolution on a current problem. Don't get me wrong, I'm happy to keep my human incarnation, and even hopeful that my modified injections have bought me more time in my natural state, but I'm unsettled, too. The only thing I want more than a normal existence is a little consistency in my abnormal one.

Joe calls every day, even comes out Monday and Tuesday evening, because I don't want to be caught in town when the change comes over me. He seems to be in a good mood, but there's a little distance between us. We cook meals, we watch movies, we talk easily, we make out a little—but there's a suspension in the relationship, too. Waiting for something.

Bonnie brings Alonzo out on Wednesday and I pronounce him fit to resume light exercise, though I don't think he should be playing basketball yet. "He could dribble and shoot with his right hand, but what if someone knocks him to the floor? It could tear his wound right open."

Alonzo, who makes it a point not to want anything enough to beg for it, is clearly disappointed, so I relent a little. "Well," I say. "You can go to practice and do the passes and the shootarounds, you just can't play in any of the games where you might get hurt. And I'll tell your coach the same thing."

"That's cool," he says, seeming satisfied.

Except for the fact that he's been recently shot with an arrow, Alonzo's in a good place right now. He enjoys the basketball team; he's started taking a math class at the middle school, and he's unexpectedly good at it; and he got the job with Q-Ville Drugs. Before I cleared him to start riding his bike again, Bonnie took him around in her car to make deliveries, just so he could get a feel for the route.

"That Rich Hogarth—the guy who owns the drugstore?—I think *he* thinks Alonzo has Asperger's," Bonnie says. "He said something the other day, like, 'I have a son who's on the spectrum, too. It gives me hope to see Alonzo doing so well.'"

"Huh. I wouldn't say that's Alonzo's primary disability, but maybe it's not a bad thing if people think it," I reply. "It makes them more willing to make accommodations."

"Well, he doesn't need any accommodations in math. He's blowing everybody away. It makes me so proud."

But the most interesting thing that happens this week is that I acquire new tenants.

It's Friday evening, and I've just spent a couple of hours cleaning the barns and rearranging cages. Two different sets of people dropped off puppies earlier in the week, so now I have seven tumbling around the enclosure—three that look like setter/Lab mixes, and four that might be half poodle and half God knows what. The poodles were brought by a longtime client who said her neighbor had threatened to drown them; the other three were left at the house in the middle of the night. Scottie woke me up with a warning growl, so I got to the door just in time to see a shadowy shape dash from the porch to a waiting car, leaving the box of squirming dogs behind. I wished I'd woken up in time to get the license plate, because the puppies looked like they were barely three weeks old, and the night was unexpectedly cold. If Scottie hadn't sounded the alarm, they could have frozen to death by morning.

They're young enough that I start to get anxious about what will happen when I change shape and no one else is around. I bottle-fed them that first morning, then coaxed them to eat real food by night-fall. Still, they won't survive long without constant care. At the moment, Daniel isn't on the premises, so I can't even beg him to stick around until they've grown up enough for me to stop worrying.

But then this particular problem—of all the ones in my life at the moment—chooses to solve itself.

I'm just getting ready to leave the barn and head for the house when I hear car tires scrape across the gravel. Now that we're almost through October, night falls so early. It's almost full dark when I step outside and try to figure out who's arrived.

The car is a big old clunker, white with a lot of rust. It's not too hard to imagine that it's just managed its very last burst of effort and will never be able to move again. A woman is climbing out of the driver's side door, and I note the head of someone else, maybe younger, in the passenger's seat. If there are any others in back, I can't see them.

I stroll close enough to talk, stay back far enough to not seem threatening. It's hard to tell in the dark, but the woman looks edgy to me, nervous, like she's not sure she wants to be here. "Hi, I'm Karadel, can I help you?" I ask.

"I'm looking for someone named Janet," she answers. There's a slight quaver in her voice. Could be fear, but I'm betting exhaustion. Like the car, she seems to have been pushed to the limit

"Janet's been gone awhile. She sold the place to me. But I know all about her particular—clients," I say delicately. A down-on-her-luck after-hours visitor is likelier than not to require specialized services, but just in case this woman isn't a shape-shifter, I don't want to be the one to say the word out loud.

She comes a little closer, moving into the circle of my perimeter lights. She's a short, plump, tired-looking woman who might be in her mid-forties; she clearly hasn't spent much time on her hair or clothing. Or maybe she's just been driving for days.

"My dog's sick," she says abruptly. "Can you look at her?"

"Of course," I answer. "Is she well enough to walk inside, or can you carry her? Or do I need to get a cart?"

"I'll carry her," she says.

A few moments later, we form a procession from the car, across the yard, and through the side door into the office. Scottie's right behind me, followed by the nervous woman, who's holding in her arms a Dalmatian that's maybe halfway to adulthood. Bringing up the rear is a teenage girl. I didn't get a good look at her except to notice her fine dark hair, her pale white skin, and her sulky expression. Neither of the newcomers speaks until we make it to my office.

The woman lays the dog on the examining table and leaves her hand resting on the animal's thin shoulder. Just from the way she's breathing, I'm betting that the Dalmatian has a respiratory problem; she lies on the table with the listlessness of a creature too miserable to care what happens to it next. But her dark eyes are intelligent and alert, and they meet mine with a preternatural self-awareness.

The woman might not be a shape-shifter, but her dog is.

I check the patient's vitals, listen to her lungs, and manage to induce a cough. My diagnosis is tracheal bronchitis, and she's a pretty sick little girl, but some oxacillin and prednisone ought to help her mend quickly enough. I give her an injection, which she endures with utter stoicism, then I offer her mother a choice.

"I can write you a prescription for pills you'd need to administer daily. She looks like she'd be pretty good about taking them," I say. "But if you're planning to be in the area for the next few days, I can give her shots till she's well."

"But she's okay? She's not—" She doesn't complete the sentence, but it hangs in the air: *She's not dying?* "We've been on the road for a week, and she just kept getting worse—"

"She should be fine," I say gently. "Better if you stay put for a while."

The woman sags against the table and buries her face in her hands. "I would. I would. But we—I don't know where we can go, and I—it's just been so *hard*, it's so much *harder* than I thought it would be—"

I can't help glancing at the dark-haired girl, who's pressed up against the wall as if she's hoping she'll turn into some kind of vaporous matter that can leak right through the plaster and wood and into the night air outside. Her eyes are fixed on her mother. For a moment, her stony expression holds, then she presses her lips together, pushes away from the wall, and comes over to give her mother a hug. "Everything will be all right once Desi is better," she says. I can't tell if she believes it. I *can* tell that she's said some version of this sentence maybe a thousand times in her life. *Everything will be all right. Just wait and see.*

"Let me give you some tea and maybe a little dinner and we can talk about your options," I say quietly.

The girl gives me a sharp look. She's not used to random displays of generosity, and she's already wondering what the catch is. But the woman takes a deep breath that's just this side of a sob and nods. I hand the daughter one of the rag blankets I keep in a basket and say,

"Let's all go to my kitchen. Take this and make a bed for Desi. She probably needs water and a little food, too, and then a place to sleep. Come on. You all look like you're starving."

In a few minutes we're settled in the kitchen. The Dalmatian is curled up in the corner, the blanket beneath her and Scottie lying close enough to provide warmth and comfort. The three of us are seated at the table, where I've set out bowls of microwaved soup, fresh rolls, and mugs of tea. It's the most unalarming scene you can imagine, so I figure it's safe to say the scary things.

"So the dog's name is Desi," I begin.

"Desdemona, actually," the woman answers.

"Very pretty," I approve. "What about the two of you?"

"Helena," the woman says, gesturing at herself. "And this is Juliet."

"And are all of you shape-shifters, or just the dog?"

Helena drops her spoon with a clatter. *"What?"*

Juliet stiffens and stares, but doesn't speak.

I continue to calmly eat my soup. "Shape-shifters. People who transform into animals and back. Desdemona is one, but I don't know about you two."

Now Helena is staring as hard as Juliet is. "How do you—why do you—"

"That's who Janet treated when she owned this practice. That's what half of my patients are. I recognize them in animal shape." I smile slightly. "Not always in human shape." They still don't seem ready to trust me, so I add, "I'm one, too."

"Ohhhhhhhh—" Helena lets her breath out in a long sigh. "Oh God. So that's how you know."

Juliet doesn't stop watching me, but the quality of her gaze goes from hostile to considering. "Mom isn't," she says. "But I am. Desi and I are twins."

"Do you turn into a Dalmatian, too?"

She nods. "But hardly ever. Three days a month. And Desi is human three days."

"The same days?"

"Sometimes. Usually we have one day where we overlap and we're both human."

"Those must be special days," I say.

She nods again, but doesn't elaborate. I think there must be a whole dense, intense, wonderful and sad story behind her determined silence.

"We'd been living in Massachusetts," Helena says. "And it was going okay, but I started getting depressed. So I thought we'd go to New Mexico and stay with my sister for a while. But then Desi started getting sick, and I didn't know what to do, and I remembered that I'd brought the girls by to see Janet, oh, eight or ten years ago. They were just little then. I didn't even know if she'd still be here."

"No, she's been gone about five years. But she trained me, so I can look over both the girls before you go."

Helena gives a heavy sigh. "I don't know if that damn car can make it all the way to New Mexico, to tell you the truth. And my sister—well—I mean, she has to take us in, right?"

Juliet flicks an unreadable look at her mother, then returns her attention to her soup.

"You can stay here awhile, if you like," I say. "I have an empty trailer and that's what it's for—to give shape-shifters a place to live when they're sick or in trouble."

Now Juliet's face gets that sharp look again, while Helena's just looks eager. "I could pay you," she says. "Not very much, but maybe I could get a job."

Juliet's voice is challenging. "Why would you be so nice to us? We're strangers."

"Juliet!"

"People were nice to me when I needed help."

"We could steal things," she warns me.

I glance around. "Not much here to take that's worth any money."

"We could *murder* you."

"*Juliet!* The things you say!"

"I suppose you could," I agree. "But I'm going to live a short, odd life anyway, so at least I'll live it trying to do good things instead of holding back when people need me." I sip my tea. "And the truth is, I could use your help. I have a bunch of animals that I care for on the property, and when *I* change, I worry about them. I have friends who can cover for me—but only if I have enough warning to call them. And lately, sometimes I don't get much warning. If there was somebody else living here who could feed and water the puppies and the rabbits and the birds, well, that would ease my mind."

"We could do that," Helena says eagerly. "Juliet loves animals."

I look at Juliet. By her expression, she doesn't love animals. And she doesn't trust strangers and she's worried about her sister and she's tired of being stronger than her mother but she doesn't think she has a choice. My guess is that she's about fourteen, but she's already been forced to function as an adult for far too long.

"We could try it for a couple of weeks, see how it goes," I say softly. "If you guys don't like being here, or I don't like having you, you can move on. But if you decide to stay, Helena can look for a job in town and Juliet can enroll in school, and Desi can just hang out here on the property. I don't need rent money, but I *do* need your promise that one of you will feed the animals anytime I'm not able to."

"Of course! Absolutely," Helena says.

"What do you change into?" Juliet asks.

"It could be almost anything. Lately I've been an orange tabby more often than not—but last time I was a dog. No idea what it will be next time."

"How often do you change?"

I shake my head. "That varies, too. Hard to predict."

"That kind of sucks," Juliet says.

I laugh. "It *totally* sucks. Which is why I need friends."

"Everybody does," Helena answers. But Juliet's face hardens and she looks away.

So I might become the first friend she's ever had.

It takes about an hour to get them settled into the trailer and then, even though it's pretty late by now, I walk Juliet through the barns and enclosures, pointing out all the animals and outlining their care. When she starts to look a little overwhelmed, I say, "Just remember two things. Give all of them water, even if you aren't sure what to feed them. And Bonnie's number is programmed into my cell phone, which I'll leave lying on my kitchen table. Call her if you need any help."

"How will I know you've changed? I mean, if you could be any animal—how will I know it's you?"

I've never had to think about this question before, and it makes me laugh. "I don't know! I guess I'll follow you around until you realize I'm there, and you can actually *ask* me. 'Karadel, is that you?' And then I'll bark or meow or something and you'll know."

"All right."

"I'll see you in the morning. Come for breakfast and we can go over everything I told you tonight."

"All right. And—thanks. You know. For all of it."

I want to pat her on the arm and tell her everything will be just fine, but she already knows it won't. So I just say, "Hey, we all take our turns helping each other out. Your turn's coming."

"Can't wait," she mutters, and turns toward the trailer. I head for the house, but call out cheerfully over my shoulder, "Talk to you in the morning!"

Of course, I don't talk to her the next day, because I shift overnight.

The pain of impending transformation wakes me around one in the morning. My hands shaking, I text Celeste, Bonnie, and Joe, informing them of my new tenants and letting them know that I won't be available for a while. Then I scribble a note for Juliet and leave it on the kitchen table along with the cell phone. That's all the prep I can manage before I run outside into the cold night, doubled over with agony. I drop to my knees and clutch my head in my hands, fighting back nausea and despair. When the transmogrification finally occurs, I'm so relieved to be out of pain that I merely lie there a moment, panting, before I extend my right forearm and try to determine what I've become. Thick brushy fur, sinewy leg, clawed and padded foot. Oh, this can't be good.

I push myself to all four feet and trot around to the side of the house, where I propped up a small mirror last week for just this purpose. The perimeter lights barely extend this far, but the moon is shining brightly, and anyway, my eyes are marvelously adapted for the dark.

I'm a wolf. Not Cooper's solid black, but a grayer creature with a white face and black-tipped fur. No wonder Scottie didn't accompany me outside; no wonder the puppies, locked inside the barn for the night, have started a frightened chorus of howling. I imagine the bunnies are cowering in their cages as well, and any small nocturnal creature that happens to be awake right now is slinking off to the safest place it knows.

A wolf. Swell.

It's different being a wild animal. Especially a predator—a fox, a coyote, an eagle. When I'm a dog or a cat, something with thousands of years of domestication built into my evolution, I have a greater affinity for humans. I like to be around them, take food from their hands, sleep curled up on the ends of their beds. I'm more social, maybe, more trusting.

When I'm wild, more feral instincts take over. I'm at a higher state of alert, jumpier, more inclined to melt into the woodlands and live by my wits. I have a harder time connecting to the Kara at the core.

I'm more inclined to run away and never come back, leaving all my unsolved human problems behind me.

In fact, I have a strong desire to do that right now—jog off the property and disappear into the patchy treeline just to get away from the smell of civilization. I'm not exactly hungry, but I'm already thinking about food, and the odor from the rabbit hutch reminds me of how many delectable treats might be found just off the edge of the property. I'm still human enough that I have no intention of trying to break through the cage and snack on the creatures that have been so long under my care—but wild enough that I can imagine just how delicious they would taste if I did.

Every instinct in my body, civilized and feral, shrieks at me to leave.

But I ought to stay, to let Juliet know what I've become.

The dilemma leaves me agitated and on edge, and I'm not really thinking clearly. With a snarl at my own reflection, I turn away from the mirror and lope across the back of the property, away from the animal enclosures and their rich scents. I will stay away until daybreak, finding somewhere to sleep away the rest of the night, and return in the morning.

And if I forget, or can't bend my body to my will, then so be it. Juliet can muddle by as best she can, or call Bonnie for help, or break down in tears and beg her mother to leave as soon as they can load the car. I can't worry about it.

I see a flash of movement in the distance, a small shape darting from a cluttered field toward the shelter of an oak. I bound across the field, thinking of nothing but the hunt.

As with my most recent transformations, my time in animal state is short, but turning human again presents a few logistical problems. That is, less than thirty-six hours later I wake up in broad daylight, more than a mile from my house, buck naked on a chilly October morning. Well, hell.

It's too cold to simply sit there, shivering and waiting till nightfall, so I just have to make my way homeward and hope my new tenants aren't too freaked out when I show up nude and dirty and covered with scratches. I'm only a *little* worried about running into a concerned citizen—a hunter or a hiker or some misguided birdwatcher—who would either run shrieking in the opposite direction or believe me to be an assault victim and come to my aid by calling the cops. I'm some distance from any major roads and I know all the back ways to my property. So it's not total strangers I'm concerned with. I just don't want to embarrass Helena and her girls.

I make it without incident to the border of my property and pause a moment in the shade of a flaming maple to assess the situation. There's no one immediately visible in the open area, which is good—but Joe's truck is parked next to Helena's white car.

Which is bad.

He has come here to help out while I'm gone or to await my return, either way determined to show me that he wants to support my alternative lifestyle. Though I am not ready for him to be quite this supportive. I don't mind so much that he will see me naked, since we've been heading in the direction of clothing-optional for a couple of weeks now, but I'm not ready for him to see me so raw from my animal state, still marked by traces of wildness. There is a scent, an aura, a patina that clings to me for a few hours after I change back. I feel like I am waking up from a bender and I am not yet completely myself.

Or I am entirely myself and have not yet had time to reset the filters that help me make it through normal human interactions.

Either way, I don't want to see him. But I'm cold and my feet hurt and I'm on the edge of miserable, so I have no choice. I push myself away from the tree and dash the final fifty yards as fast as I can manage.

Someone has left a blanket on the porch, and I snatch this up moments before all the doors on the property seem to open at once—the one to the barn, the one to the trailer, the one to the house. Juliet, Helena, and Joe.

I stick one hand out of the blanket that I have hastily wrapped around my body, and I wave a little frantically at the women. "I'm back—I'll talk to you as soon as I've showered," I call, then I turn toward the kitchen door.

"Hey!" Joe says, sounding delighted to see me. Jinx is frisking at his feet, and he greets me with a few friendly barks. I can see Jezebel and Scottie sitting more sedately inside.

I pause long enough to scratch Jinx on the head, but I don't make eye contact with Joe when I straighten up and push past him into the house. "I am *not* talking to you until I've cleaned up," I say. "Do *not* follow me out of the kitchen."

"You want something to eat?" he shouts after me.

"Yes! I'm starving! Carbs. Bready things."

Twenty minutes later I've showered away my latest adventure, brushed my teeth, pulled on jeans and a sweater, and tied my wet hair back in a ponytail. I'm still ruffled, but human. It's an improvement.

I head to the kitchen, where I can smell toast and oatmeal. Joe doesn't listen when I ask him to keep his distance, but apparently he pays attention when I talk about food.

"God, I'm so hungry," I mutter, plucking a piece of bread from the toaster and cramming half of it into my mouth without waiting for butter or jelly. He's pulling a pot off the stove and spooning a big mess of oatmeal into a bowl, but he turns to give me a smile. As soon as I've swallowed the bread, he leans over to kiss me, not even bothering to set the pan down first. I'm still annoyed that he's here, but I have to admit the kiss is nice.

"I've missed you," he says.

"We have to talk," I say, "but first I have to eat."

He's already set a place for me at the table, and my plate is filled with all the things I crave most when I first shift back—bread, cheese, eggs, fruit, the quickest foods to deliver carbs and protein in a few hearty bites. I gobble down the oatmeal first, since it's steaming hot and he's sprinkled it with brown sugar and raisins.

Harder and harder to hold on to my irritation when he's doing such a good job of easing me through the transition.

It's not a proper mealtime, so he's not eating anything, but he sips a soda and watches me. I think he's trying to gauge my mood. Or maybe he's just cataloging the unfamiliar expressions and mannerisms I exhibit when I'm so fresh from changing.

"My mouth is full," I say around a big wad of toast. "*You* talk." Jinx is sitting as close to me as he can, his face hopeful, so I toss him a small chunk of cheese. I know, I know, but Joe doesn't stop me; it's pretty clear Jinx is used to getting scraps from the table.

"I had a chance to visit with your new tenants when I got here last night," Joe tells me. "Interesting family. Juliet was wonderful with the animals, by the way, especially the puppies. Didn't talk much, though."

"Yeah, I think it'll be great to have them here for a while. Give me more freedom." I swig down half a glass of orange juice, then remember something. "Weren't you supposed to be working at Arabesque last night?"

It's probably my imagination that he hesitates a second before replying. "Marcus wanted the hours, so I gave him my shift."

This doesn't seem to require an answer, so I just nod and take another bite.

Joe continues to fill me in on the events of the past couple of days. "Let's see, Alonzo put in a full day at his new job on Saturday—delivered about fifteen prescriptions. So far he seems to be really pleased with how it's going, Bonnie said."

I laugh. "So now you're checking in with Bonnie every week? That's funny."

"Well, we had stuff to talk about," he says.

I finish the bowl of oatmeal and the last of an apple, then look around, trying to decide if I want another piece of toast. Or more cheese. A glance at the clock shows me that it's about ten-thirty. I can probably hold out until lunch and then get back on a normal schedule.

"That was good," I say, relaxing enough to lean back in my chair. I put my hand down and Jinx edges forward to lick my fingers. "How did you know *exactly* what I'd want to eat?"

"I told you. I talked to Bonnie."

"Listen. It was sweet of you to want to be here waiting for me, but—I have to tell you, I'm not sure I'm ready for this. I need some time to get back to myself, you know what I mean? It feels a little—a little pushy for you to be here without an invitation." It sounds awfully mean, but I try to harden my heart. I have to set boundaries and I have to make him respect them. As I would respect his.

He nods soberly. "I know. I'm sorry. But something's happened and I wanted to be able to tell you in person and I didn't know when you'd change back."

The oatmeal turns to iron in my stomach, and every muscle in my body cords with fear. I sit up straight and stop paying attention to the dogs. "What happened? To who?" I demand. If he was just talking about them so casually, it can't be Bonnie, it can't be Alonzo . . . "Celeste?"

"She'll be okay," he says quickly. "But yeah. She was assaulted last night and she—"

"Assaulted?" I interrupt. "*What?* What happened?"

He starts speaking in precise words and sentences; I suppose this is how policemen communicate. "She was getting out of her car in the parking lot by her apartment. It was about seven in the evening—dark. Two men jumped her. One held her from behind, the other started hitting her in the head with PVC pipe. She thinks he was trying to render her unconscious so she couldn't change shapes."

"Oh my God," I whisper. My hand is at my throat. I think I'm going to throw up. But he's quoting her observations; he's already said *she'll be okay*. So surely this doesn't have the very worst ending.

"Naturally, she was struggling and screaming," Joe continues. "The man holding her started dragging her toward another vehicle—a van, she believes—while his accomplice continued to strike her head with the piping. He also swung at her ribs and her knees a few times, but mostly her head. She believes she was very close to going unconscious—"

"*Jesus!*" I exclaim. My body is prickling with adrenaline; I'm practically jumping out of my chair. "Why didn't she change? She can do it whenever she wants!"

"She says she wasn't thinking clearly. She also says she could smell something her abductor was holding—she thinks it might have been chloroform—and she thinks that might have been causing her some confusion."

"So how did she—what did they—"

"Luckily, your friend Ryan arrived on the scene," Joe says, and there is no inflection at all when he says Ryan's name. "Apparently he and Celeste had dinner plans. He was able to wrestle the pipe away from the one man and turn it against both of them. They released Celeste and ran for their vehicle. Ryan chose to stay with Celeste rather than chase after them."

My hands are in the air, my fingers spread as wide as they will go, and my mouth is hanging open. The word *dumbstruck* circles through my brain. "Then she's—but she's—how badly is she hurt?"

"Ryan took her to Bonnie and Aurelia's house," Joe continues. "She was conscious enough to say she did not want to be taken to the ER. Bonnie thinks she has a concussion and a couple of broken ribs, but, of course, she's not a doctor. Celeste made it through the night without getting worse, which everyone seems to think is a good sign, but—" He shakes his head. "I know that concussions are tricky. Even a couple of days later—" He shakes his head again.

Even a couple of days later, the internal bleeding can continue and your brain can swell and you can die. He doesn't need to say it.

"She needs a CT scan," I say as calmly as I can. "And someone needs to call the sheriff."

"Even this morning, she was refusing medical treatment," he tells me. "And she doesn't want the cops involved."

"They *should* be involved!"

"They should," he agrees in a quiet voice. "But I can understand why she wants to keep off the radar. Why all of you want to keep off the radar. And if she goes to any medical facility looking like this—"

"Was it the Foucaults?" I demand.

"Neither Ryan nor Celeste could see their faces—the attackers were wearing ski masks—but that's what we all assume. Ryan told me he saw a van on their property the other day, when the three of you apparently did a drive-by."

That time it's easy to read his opinion in the tone of his voice. "Yeah, it was stupid. They shot at us."

"So I hear."

I push myself up from my chair. "Let's go. I need to see her. Since I'm the closest thing to a doctor we've got."

He comes to his feet as well. "That's what we all figured. Pack an overnight bag. Now that you have caretakers living here, you can stay in town a couple of days."

"Almost makes you believe there's a divine plan," I say.

I take a step toward the door, then turn back, dive around the table, and throw my arms around Joe. The world feels bigger and meaner and scarier than it ever did, and I was telling the truth the other day when I told him I want someone to make me feel safe.

His arms come around me and he hugs me so tightly that all the wolf is squeezed right out of my body. I do feel safe; I feel at home; I feel like I've found the place where I belong.

CHAPTER FOURTEEN

Juliet is not thrilled to learn that she'll be feeding the animals for another couple of days, but her dark eyes get big when I tell her the reason I'm abandoning her again so soon.

"Sure, yeah, I'll take care of everything," she says. I believe her. I believe, like me, she's been responsible for so much for so long that it wouldn't occur to her to shirk even the most unpleasant duty.

Joe and I have a brief disagreement when it comes time to climb in our cars and go.

"Ride with me," he says. "You're going to stay in Quinville a couple of days anyway."

"But then you'll have to bring me back."

"Well, I'm going to bring you back anyway. Or follow you out here."

"What? Don't be ridiculous."

He just looks at me over the roof of the truck. "These two crazy backwoods yahoos are out to get revenge on Celeste any way they can, and they already know you're a friend of hers. They were willing to attack *her* right in the middle of town on a public parking lot. What's to stop them from coming out here, where there's not a soul around for miles, and beating up on *you*? I'm not leaving you alone for a while."

"Well, unless someone is willing to talk to the cops, I bet they'll be hanging around for longer than a *while*," I reply with some heat. "You think you can just follow me back and forth forever?"

His grin is lopsided. "Maybe. We'll talk about it. But for the next few days I'm making sure you're never alone. So drive your own car if you want, but I'll be right behind you."

I heave a dramatic sigh, but, truth be told, I kind of like the protective attitude. I like the notion that someone thinks I'm precious. But. "What about Helena and the girls?"

"They're not you," Joe says. "Bobby and his brother don't have an argument with them."

Does that keep them safe? Maybe yes, maybe no. I don't have time to think it through; I have to get to Celeste as quickly as I can. It doesn't feel worth the energy to keep arguing with Joe, so I climb into his truck without another word.

He covers the distance even more quickly than I usually do, and I tend to ignore speed limits, so we're at Bonnie and Aurelia's in record time. I note Ryan's convertible parked in front of the house, Alonzo's bike on the porch, Bonnie's station wagon and Aurelia's BMW both in the driveway. Everyone's still here, then.

"Karadel. Thank God!" is Bonnie's greeting when she answers the door, which—I can tell by the clicks and rattles—has been triple locked. Seems like a wise move when there's an injured shape-shifter inside and crazy assholes roaming the streets.

"How is she?"

"No worse. Maybe better. Hello, Joseph."

"Hey. Listen, I have my dogs with me. Should I leave them in the truck, or can I put them in your backyard?"

"Oh, by all means, in the yard. There are water bowls out there already."

I don't stay to watch Bonnie help him settle the animals, I just head to the spare bedroom. It also functions as the overflow space for the roughly ten million books that are in the house, so it kind of looks like a library with a bed in the middle of it. Noon sunlight is pouring in through the lacy curtains, which gilds the room in optimism, but I still feel punched in the gut when I get a good look at Celeste's face.

The café au lait skin is covered with welts and bruises; there's a lump the size of a golf ball on her forehead. She's sitting up in bed, but the covers are pulled to her waist and she's wearing a bright pink bathrobe, so I can't see much below her collarbone. Her throat, though, is a mass of marks and bruises. Even her hands, curled around a mug of tea, are purple and red with defensive wounds.

But damn if she isn't smiling. Throw her into the scalding pit of hell, and Celeste would laugh in your face.

"Look who's back from Alternate World," she says. Her voice is a little hoarse. I can't tell if it's emotion rasping her voice, or pressure from trauma to her throat. "Good to see you."

The small room is overfilled with people. Aurelia's sitting in a chair right beside the bed; Ryan and Alonzo are leaning against bookshelves on opposite walls. That doesn't keep me from marching right in and dropping onto the mattress next to Celeste.

My hand goes instantly to her forehead, since, of course, I'm worried about fever, but when I speak, my voice is as light as hers. "I never saw a girl who got into trouble as often as you do," I say. "Could you maybe, just for one week, try to lead a calm and sane existence?"

"It would be too boring," she replies. She leans back against the pillows that are propped up against the headboard. I think I can see dried blood matted into the flyaway curls. "Though this hasn't exactly been fun."

"You don't seem to have a fever," I say. "Does anybody have a flashlight?"

"I checked her pupils last night," Bonnie says from the doorway, where she and Joe have just arrived. But Alonzo stirs and hands me a flashlight that's been conveniently stored on the bookshelf on his side of the room.

"I want to check again. Ryan, could you close the curtains? Bonnie, the light?"

We darken the room as much as we can, and I shine the beam in Celeste's eyes. She doesn't have any difficulty following the light, and her pupils react as they should, so that's encouraging.

"Does your head hurt?" I ask.

"Fuck, *yes*, it hurts, what do you think? But it's not unbearable. It's no worse than my average falling-estrogen headache every month."

That actually makes me grin. "Are you nauseated? Have you thrown up?"

"No. In fact, I'm getting hungry but Bonnie will only let me have gruel."

"I don't even know how to make gruel," Bonnie says. "I gave her chicken broth."

"Are you drowsy? Having a hard time staying awake?"

"Again, Bonnie wouldn't let me *sleep* last night, so yeah, I'm tired."

"I let you sleep after midnight," Bonnie says a little defensively. "But you know lethargy is a sign of concussion, and I wanted to be sure."

"And then you kept waking me up!"

"*I* woke you up," Aurelia says. She glances over at me. "She never had any problem coming to consciousness."

"These are all good signs," I tell the room.

"Hallelujah," Ryan mutters.

"But I want to check on the rest of her injuries. So all of you get out."

Alonzo doesn't need to be told twice. He's the first one out the door, and Joe follows, talking to him in a low voice. Ryan more slowly straightens up and stares down at Celeste.

"She wouldn't let me take her to a doctor," he says. "I didn't know what I should do."

Aurelia comes to her feet and puts her hand on his arm. Her glorious red hair is tied up in a messy knot, and I see signs of exhaustion on her porcelain skin. My deduction is that she and Bonnie split the watch last night, and Aurelia's only had a couple hours of sleep out of the last twenty-four.

"You brought her here. That was the right thing to do," Aurelia says. "Come on. Give Kara some privacy."

Bonnie looks like she might want to stay, but Aurelia tugs both Bonnie and Ryan out of the room and shuts the door behind them.

"Get naked," I tell Celeste.

She sets down her mug of tea. "Oooh, and here I thought you weren't interested in me. After all these years—"

"Get naked, comma, *bitch*," I say, and she laughs.

The rest of her body doesn't look quite as awful as her face, but the injuries are bad enough. Lots of bruising on the arms and chest, one big ugly spot over her left hip, a long scrape down her right leg. I poke around a little on her ribs, and she curses in pain as I touch one particularly tender spot.

"I'm guessing it hurts to take a deep breath?" I ask.

"Oh, it does."

"Are you short of breath? Have you been coughing up blood?"

In answer, she takes a couple of long inhalations and shakes her head.

"Any blood when you pee?"

"Not that I've noticed. Can't believe Bonnie didn't make me piss in a bedpan so she could check it herself."

There's a tube of Neosporin on the nearby table and I'm guessing someone already spread some on the worst injuries, but I smooth on a little more. Then I gesture at her to pull the robe back on.

"Well, if you have a concussion, it's probably a mild one, and there is literally *nothing* I can do about it. If you start to get worse—if the headaches are crippling, if you're dizzy, if you fall unconscious, if you start throwing up—you really really *really* need to go to a hospital. Because I can't do brain surgery, and that's what you'd need."

"Great. Glad we called you out here. You've been so helpful," she says as she slips her arms back in the sleeves of the robe and pulls the covers up over her legs again.

"You also appear to have a broken rib," I go on. "Can't do anything about *that*, either. The real danger is that you won't breathe deeply enough to clear the crap out of your lungs, so you could get pneumonia. So even though it hurts, try to take deep breaths as often as you can. Also, get up and move around a couple of times a day."

"Can you tell Bonnie that? Because she wants to chain me to the bed."

"Hey. Bonnie's kept all of us alive plenty of times before this. Show a little appreciation."

"I will, I swear, but can you at least make her let me take a *shower*?"

I hesitate. "I don't want you to get dizzy and fall over."

"I'll sit on the floor of the tub! You can get in the shower *with* me! I just want to get *clean*! I want to get this blood off—I want to wash away the feel of their hands—I want to—I want to—"

Her voice gets more ragged and then chokes off. She drops her face in her hands and starts sobbing—Celeste, whom I have never seen cry. I loose an exclamation of dismay and wrap my arms around her, pulling her against my shoulder and patting her back.

"It's going to be okay. You're going to be okay," I tell her.

She fights the tears as valiantly as she can. "God*damn* it, I already look like shit, and now I'm crying on top of it," she says, straightening up and wiping her hand across her eyes. "This day couldn't get any worse."

I hand her a Kleenex from the bedside table. "That's right, it can't, so it's going to get better," I agree. "Think how good a shower will feel! And then *lunch*! Think how happy *that* will make you!"

"All right. I'm getting out of bed. Let's see how shaky I am."

But she stands without assistance and looks pretty steady on her feet. I'm already feeling hopeful about her chances of total recovery, when she stops at the door and gives me a naughty smile.

"So I'm liking your new boyfriend more and more," she says. "Sleep with him yet?"

"That's it," I say, opening the door and almost shoving her into the hall. "You're obviously going to be fine."

Lunch is a pretty festive affair. There's something about remembering how closely we are all stalked by death that makes people want to party. Bonnie's still restricting Celeste's intake, but the rest of us feast on baked chicken and homemade bread and all sorts of side dishes. Aurelia has a glass of wine and, after a moment's debate, so do I.

"Hey, I'll have some of that," Celeste says. She doesn't seem surprised when Bonnie and I cry "No!" in unison.

"So what happens next?" Joe asks as Bonnie dishes up ice cream for dessert. "If you're not going to tell the cops about the Foucaults, how do we keep Celeste safe?"

"She can stay with me for a few weeks," Ryan says.

"I'd hate to cramp your style," she jokes. He doesn't smile in return; he's about as serious as I've ever seen him.

"You can't go back to your apartment," Ryan tells her. "So you're going to have to move. There are a couple of vacancies in my building, so I could keep an eye on you."

Celeste usually shrugs off any notion that she might need anyone's care, but this incident has really spooked her. I see her actually pause to give the idea consideration. "Maybe. I'll think about it. But can't I go back just to get some *clothes*?"

"No," we all say at once. I add, "I'll go pick some stuff up for you this afternoon. Just make a list."

"Take somebody with you," Joe says quietly.

Aurelia throws him a sharp look. "You think Kara's in danger from these hoodlums as well?"

Joe nods. "The night they met Celeste, Karadel was in her company, so they know her. Karadel was also along for the joyride past the Foucault property the other day."

"The what?" Aurelia says.

"Oh, it was just a little fun!" Celeste exclaims. "We wanted to see what Terry Foucault's junkyard of doom looked like, so we drove by."

"And they saw you," Aurelia says. Her voice is dripping with *are-you-really-this-idiotic* disbelief.

Ryan and Celeste and I briefly exchange glances. No one mentions the gunshot. "They saw us," Ryan says.

Aurelia gives him a look of withering scorn. "*You* were along as well?"

"I was driving."

Joe looks at Ryan for what might be the first time today. "Which leads me to the next thing. *You* might be in danger, too. Because you were also with Celeste the night she met Bobby Foucault."

Ryan meets his eyes and says quietly, "I can take care of myself." There's something in his tone of voice, in his expression, that gives me a chill; even though he's not exhibiting any overt signs of aggression, something about him is exuding menace. With a shock, I realize that he's not stunned and horrified about what happened to Celeste, as the rest of us are. He's furious.

Joe doesn't glance away. It occurs to me that he's got a better read on Ryan than I do—that he probably picked up on that fury the minute he walked in the door. Old cop instincts coming to the fore, helping him identify the likeliest source of trouble. "I'm sure you can," he answers, his voice just as quiet. "But don't do anything stupid."

"It's obviously too late for that excellent advice," Aurelia says dryly.

Joe looks at her, and some of the tension goes out of the room. "I still wish you'd tell the cops," he says. "Or let me do it. Sheriff Wilkerson knows me. He'd believe me if I said the Foucaults had beaten up a girl last night."

"But wouldn't you need to produce this girl?" Bonnie says.

"Not necessarily," Aurelia answers. "There's a lot of reasons a victim won't step forward. She's afraid for her life—she's got outstanding warrants of her own—she's a junkie. While upstanding citizens occasionally get attacked by random strangers, the truth is that a lot of violence is perpetrated by people who know each other and who are sometimes living desperate lives." She glances at Celeste. "Unless there's proof that a crime occurred, the sheriff can't arrest the Foucaults, but he can certainly watch them a little more closely. Keep them under surveillance."

"Probably already doing that," Joe agrees. "They've both got 'lawbreaker' written all over their faces."

"So for the short term, Celeste stays here," Aurelia says. "And Kara?"

"If you have room for me, I'd like to stay a couple days and look after Celeste," I say. "After that . . ."

"You're welcome at my place," Ryan says warmly. I can't tell if he makes the offer to embarrass me or annoy Joe.

Who answers, "Or mine," in a similar tone of voice.

Alonzo, who's mostly been concentrating on his ice cream, glances up at that. His eyes go from Ryan to Joe and back to Ryan, until he sees me watching him. Then he focuses on his ice cream again.

"*I,*" I say in a hearty tone, "am going to stay here a few days and then go back and feed my animals and resume my normal life."

Bonnie shows me a worried face. "Maybe we should talk about that."

"Well, then, we'll talk about it later. Let's just get through the immediate crisis."

"I'd feel better if someone in this house had a gun," Joe says.

The rest of us look at Aurelia.

"Oh," he says.

"I don't think we have anything to worry about while we're all together *here*," she says. "So let's just make sure everyone is abnormally careful and observant whenever we're out and about."

We all murmur agreement, and then people start stirring and stretching. It's time for the meal to be over. Alonzo's the first one to his feet.

"I have deliveries to make this afternoon," he says. "If it's okay for me to go."

"Of course it's okay!" Celeste exclaims. "I want you to start earning a paycheck! Then you can pay to rent the movies next time we have an *X-Men* marathon."

He grins at her. "You have to buy the popcorn, then."

"I will. Later, my man."

He nods at the rest of us and ambles out the front door. Moments later, from the dining-room window, I catch a glimpse of him streaking down the street on his bike, headed toward the drugstore.

"I think I'd better be going, too," Joe says, levering himself up. "Bonnie, thanks for the meal. Celeste—you be good." She sticks her tongue out at him, and he laughs, then he glances at me. "Walk me out?"

We swing through the backyard to collect Jinx, who bounds out of the gate ahead of us, and Jezebel, who moves with her usual regal calm. The sun is still beating down like a midsummer day, but it's probably no more than forty degrees out, and I'm instantly cold. I wrap my arms around my body for warmth and follow Joe to the truck.

He opens the door and motions the dogs inside, then turns back to me. "She going to be all right?" he asks in a low voice.

"I think so."

"Close call. If Ryan hadn't been there—"

"I don't even want to think about it," I interrupt.

He peers down at me; he looks concerned and uneasy. "But you'll stay here, won't you, until I come get you? You won't do anything stupid?"

"You haven't been paying attention," I reply. "I never do anything stupid. I'm too responsible."

He grins faintly and says, "I've got a trip tomorrow. Out to Topeka. Be back Wednesday evening. Will you stay here till then?"

"I might go out to my house in the day—*with* Bonnie and Alonzo and plenty of protection—but I won't spend the night," I promise.

He looks like that's not quite good enough for him, but finally nods reluctantly. "And then maybe we can go out to your place and stay a few days."

"Poor Juliet will be ready to kill me by then, I'm sure," I say. "If she hasn't run off already."

"Nah, she's like you. Too responsible."

I put one hand on his shoulder and rise to my tiptoes to give him a kiss. "Drive carefully. Call me from the road."

"Every hour too often?"

"I don't know," I say. "Try it and see."

The next couple of days are little but healing and boredom, sprinkled with random irritability. Celeste has never been a good patient, because she's constitutionally incapable of sitting quietly, and Aurelia has never bothered hiding her moods or softening her opinions. It's easier during the day, when Aurelia leaves for work, but there are still too many people in the house.

"You have to work today?" I ask Alonzo around noon on Tuesday.

"Already did some deliveries this morning," he tells me.

"Then can you come out to my place for a few hours and protect me while I get some work done?"

"Aurelia keeps the gun locked up."

He says it absolutely straight-faced, and for a minute I think he's serious. But my expression must be all he hoped for, because then he cracks up. "Sure," he says. "I'll bring my baseball bat."

We take Celeste's car, which Ryan and I fetched from her parking lot Monday afternoon. Alonzo has his iPod with him, but consents to listen to the radio as long as I let him change channels every time a song comes on that he doesn't like. Driving down 159 on a sunny day, communicating only by singing along to the radio, is a pretty good way to hang out with Alonzo. We're both feeling fairly mellow by the time we arrive at my place.

Everything appears to be in good shape. Some dogs barking, some dogs sleeping in the sun, rabbits sleek and healthy, tenants not murdered by backwoods assassins. The best possible scenario.

Scottie accompanies me as I make the rounds, cleaning up cages, double-checking water levels, and spending extra time with the youngest puppies. So does Helena. She'd been pretty quiet the other night, but now she's talkative and full of questions. I wonder if this is her natural personality, which only comes out once she's rested and free of fear, or if she's in the manic phase of a mild bipolar condition. I only listen with half an ear. I'm a little surprised to see Juliet and Alonzo sitting together on the porch holding a quiet conversation, Desi sleeping at their feet. Juliet doesn't seem any quicker to warm up to strangers than he is. But maybe when you're always surrounded by adults, your only defense is to retreat into silence. You can put away that armor when you get a chance to talk to someone your own age. Or maybe each one thinks the other one is cute.

I listen to my voice mail, arrange to make a couple of house calls in Quinville "since it turns out I've got some business in town," and clear out my e-mail. A lot of junk mail has piled up in the past four days, because I haven't checked my account since before I changed shapes.

The most interesting piece of new mail is a message from Janet's mom, who hasn't communicated since I confessed that I thought I was falling for Joe. She writes:

Sweetie—I'm so glad to hear you've met a nice man. I know I'm not the best role model for how to pick a life partner, but I think you're being very wise. It's not the dashing, exciting, handsome man who will stay with you and love you to the end. It's the sincere and thoughtful man, the one who maybe isn't so good-looking but who has the bigger heart.

My eyes widen at the next paragraph; it was something I'd known about, but nothing she'd ever mentioned before.

I was always so crazy for your father, and he was such a bad person. Bad to me, bad to everyone. But I forgave him over and over, because of how he made me *feel*. I was dizzy when he walked into the room; I just couldn't wait for him to put his arms around me. But he could be so awful sometimes. He drove you away. He broke my heart. Well, he almost killed me more than once. My life was so much better once I left him. You know I've been seeing Bradley for a couple of years now. Not nearly as attractive as your father, but I've been so happy with him. I hope you can be just as happy with your new guy.

I hope I can, too, I think. *I'm almost ready to try.*

Joe's back Wednesday by five, and *everyone* agrees that it's time for me to move from Bonnie and Aurelia's place to his.

"Don't even stay for dinner," Celeste tells me, practically pushing me out the door. "Seriously. Just leave."

We haven't even backed out of the driveway when Joe says in a solemn voice, "Of course, if you're staying at my place, we have a pretty big decision to make."

"Oh?" I say. I'm both nervous and excited, but I try to make my voice nonchalant. "What's that?"

"Eat out or pick up enough food to make dinner at home."

I had been expecting him to make a crack about sleeping separately or together, so this makes me laugh, which makes me relax a little. "Make dinner at home," I say. "I'm dying of curiosity to see how you live."

We purchase a few groceries and head to his house, a rented bun-
galow on a run-down street where there are no sidewalks and the
front lawns just end in a tired interface of dirt and asphalt. Most of
the houses are built of white siding, and little distinguishes one from
the other except small touches like green shutters or an orange roof.
None of them have garages, and few of them have flower gardens or
decorative shrubbery to brighten their dull exteriors. I figure Joe
would have been just as happy in an apartment or a townhouse except
he needed a yard for Jezebel, and now Jinx.

He lets the dogs out of the truck and into the backyard. It's bigger
than I would have thought, enclosed by a chain-link fence, and Jinx
immediately goes chasing after squirrels. Jezebel trots over to investigate something hiding under a rusty black metal table that's set out
on the cracked patio. There are no chairs to accompany the table, but
I do spot a small barbeque grill.

"Cozy," I comment.

"Yeah, it's about the same quality inside."

He's right. The neutral interior has been listlessly furnished with
beige carpet, off-white drapes, and eggshell-colored paint. In the small
kitchen, the flooring is green and the wallpaper features faded images
of tomatoes, parsley, and corn. Joe hasn't made much attempt to decorate. The brown couch is clearly secondhand, and the scarred coffee
table probably fifth-hand; there's not a single piece of artwork on the
walls. On the other hand, the widescreen TV is almost as big as my
barn.

"I can see what matters to *you*," I say.

He grins. "*And* it's high-def."

There are two bedrooms down the dark and narrow hall, though
one is functioning as a storage unit, since it's so crammed with boxes
and luggage and unused furniture that you can hardly make your
way through it. But he actually seems to have put a little effort into

the room he sleeps in. The blue-and-white striped bedspread looks new, there are six big pillows piled against the headboard, and the curtains match the linens. On the dresser there's finally some evidence of his human connections—framed photos of what I take to be family members, plus a couple of sports trophies and a stack of magazines. There's another small TV in here, easily visible from the bed.

"Welcome to my palace of seduction," he says in a deep voice dripping with meaning.

"Yeah, unless there are condoms in the bedside table, nothing about this room really screams *seduction* to me."

"Oh, there are all *sorts* of fun things in the bedside table," he answers, which makes me laugh again.

"Will it hurt your feelings if I say this is the most depressing house I've ever been in?" I ask.

"Nah," he answers, urging me back down the hall toward the kitchen. "I think it is, too."

"So why don't you do something to fix it up? Or at least give it a little personality?"

He shrugs. "Because I don't have any attachment to it. Because I don't *live* here. I'm just staying here. I'm not going to put any effort into it because it doesn't matter to me."

"I think, even if I was staying someplace temporarily, I'd have to beautify it a little," I reply. "If I didn't do anything except put up a poster of bright red flowers. *Something.*"

"All right," he says amiably. "You can decorate. Buy anything you like. Anything that makes the place feel comfortable to you."

"Oooh, Lady Gaga posters and calendars of puppies and kittens?"

"You bet. *Mi casa es su casa.*"

"This will be an interesting challenge."

The kitchen is reasonably well stocked with pots and pans and dishes and glasses, so my deduction is that his ex-wife wanted to start all over when it came to cookware and china. We both sip beers while he makes sloppy joes and I toss a salad.

I'm getting ready to set out plates and silverware when I realize, "You don't have a table. Where do you *eat*?"

He gestures out the kitchen door. "In front of the TV. Just carry everything to the coffee table."

He lets the dogs in, so pretty soon we're all curled up in the living room, relaxed and happy. There's a baseball game on—neither the Cubs nor the Cards have made the playoffs, so I don't really care about the outcome, but I like the background noise of strikes and balls and crowd reaction. Jinx has his head on my knee and watches me with soulful desperation until I give him the last bite of my sandwich.

"I wouldn't think a vet would spoil animals as much as you do," Joe says. He doesn't have much room to talk; he's set his own plate on the floor so Jezebel can lick it clean.

"I remember what it's like to be in dog form, and I *loooooove* human food," I tell him. "It's the shape-shifter in me, and not the medical professional, who does the spoiling."

"Probably better for a shape-shifter to eat people food than a real dog."

"Probably," I agree.

He collects the dishes and takes them to the kitchen, returning a couple of minutes later with a pair of longnecks. He sets these on the table as he settles next to me on the couch.

"Want another beer?" he asks.

"No," I say, and scoot around to kiss him.

He doesn't need a second invitation; he scoops me into his lap and returns the kiss with enthusiasm. For a moment, the heady combination of heat and touch and excitement and desire leave me dizzy. But underlying the wild thoughts, the passionate ones, is a whole other layer of emotion. I feel at ease, I feel protected, I feel like I could strip down to my naked soul and Joe would just gather me closer, hold me tighter, make a safe and solid place for me to come to rest beside his heart.

"Do we have to watch the rest of the ballgame?" I whisper.

"Well, I was really hoping to see if the Yankees could manage to win it," he murmurs against my mouth. "But I suppose I can catch it all on DVR."

I giggle. "There's a TV in the palace of seduction."

"Damn. It doesn't work. We'll just have to settle for a different kind of scoring."

I'm still laughing when he sweeps me up in his arms and comes to his feet.

"My big strong hero," I coo, wrapping my arms around his neck.

He drops a kiss on my mouth. "My sweet little darling," he says, and he suddenly sounds serious.

"You asked me before," I say. "I think I'm falling."

His arms tighten as he negotiates around the coffee table and carries me down the hallway to the bedroom. "Oh good," he says, "because it's no fun to fall all by yourself."

Joe loves like he dances. With all his heart and with a great deal of laughter. He doesn't worry about seeming silly or being out of practice or getting it exactly right the first time. All he needs is a partner who looks like she's having fun. Who looks like she can't think of any place else she'd rather be.

Who loves him right back.

*   *   *

When my cell phone rings, I can't for a moment orient myself. I know I'm with Joe—that part is vividly obvious, with his big warm body next to mine and my own body pleasantly sore from the exertions of the past few hours. But the room is dark and I don't know where my purse is and I don't know what time it is and I haven't had enough sleep and who the hell would be calling me, now, when I don't want to think about anything except Joe?

He stirs as I fight to extricate myself from his embrace and the sheets, which seem to be balled up around my shoulders. "What is— is that your phone?"

"Yeah—hang on—I have to find it—"

"I think you left it over by the dresser—" He stretches out to turn on a bedside lamp, and I catch a glimpse of the clock. A bit after five in the morning. This can't be good. The ringing has stopped by the time I stumble across the room, grab my purse, and return to bed to snuggle beside Joe.

"Shit," I say when the phone shows me that I have one missed call from Aurelia. Now I'm wide awake. Something must have happened to Celeste. My stomach is one big knot of terror when I hit redial, and Aurelia picks up within two seconds. "What's wrong? Is it Celeste?"

"No," she says, and her voice is as clear and hard as a statue of ice. "Bobby Foucault turned up dead, and the cops have arrested Ryan for murder."

CHAPTER FIFTEEN

The case against Ryan is about as solid as it could be, Aurelia tells us a half hour later. We're all gathered in the kitchen at her house—Bonnie, Celeste, Alonzo, Joe, me—looking as shocked and confused as tornado survivors. Celeste, of course, looks like a survivor who was tumbled around pretty badly by the high wind, though the red welts and purple bruises are starting to modulate to shades of pink and green. Only Aurelia looks wide awake and at the top of her game. She's dressed in a black pinstripe pantsuit and her red hair is perfectly styled; she's wearing full makeup, down to the lipstick and eyeliner. She could walk into a courtroom right this minute and not be out of place.

When Ryan got his traditional one phone call from the police station, he picked Aurelia. Anybody's best choice.

"It appears that yesterday afternoon around three, Ryan went to the property owned by Terry Foucault and entered the premises," Aurelia says in a precise voice. "Neither Terry nor his wife were at home, but Bobby answered the door. Ryan shot him three times with a small-caliber pistol and immediately left the scene. Terry's wife found the body when she got home a couple of hours later, and she called Sheriff Wilkerson."

"How do they know it was Ryan?" Bonnie demands.

"Because it seems Terry has had a few robberies in the past couple of years, so he's installed security cameras in strategic places."

"You'd think Ryan would be smart enough to look for those," Celeste mutters.

Aurelia gives her an unreadable look. "Apparently he was. Two of them had been disabled. However, there was a third one concealed in some piece of would-be junk sitting just outside the door. Sort of like a nanny cam that people install in their houses to check up on the babysitters."

"And there's no doubt that it's Ryan?" Bonnie asks.

"I haven't been permitted to see the video yet, but I'm guessing it's pretty convincing footage."

"Where'd he get the gun?" Joe wants to know.

Now she gives all her attention to him; again, her expression is impossible to decipher. "I believe it's mine. At any rate, mine is missing."

Joe's eyebrows shoot up. "He knew where you kept it?"

She nods. "And yes, it's always locked up. But the lock was forced."

"Did they find the weapon at the scene?"

"No. And they didn't find it in his car or his apartment, either. But that's probably not going to matter much."

"You've reported yours missing?"

"I had to. Might not be mine, but—" She shrugs. *Probably is.*

Now Joe looks at Celeste. "I suppose Ryan was here yesterday."

She looks stricken. "Yeah. All morning. Everyone was gone but me, and I spent half the time sleeping. He could have stolen anything in the house."

"Means and motive," Joe says.

"*Motive!*" Bonnie exclaims. "For cold-blooded *murder*? I don't think so!"

Now Celeste and I exchange glances. "It wasn't cold," I say. "Ryan was angry with them for what they did to Celeste. So incredibly angry."

"So were we all!" Bonnie replies. "But we did not take that anger and go out in the world and commit unforgivable acts!"

"You don't understand," Celeste says. "With Ryan it's all about—all about the dividing line between human and shape-shifter. The sting of being different. Of having to lie and connive and pretend that he's just like everyone else when he's not. It makes him angry. And it makes him proud. And it makes him look for ways to right the balance."

"It's more than that," I say quietly. "He thinks he doesn't have to operate by society's rules because he's not a part of that society. He's special. He's different."

"Standard sociopathic markers," Joe comments.

"He's not!" Celeste cries. "Yes, he knows that he's different, and yes, he doesn't always play by the rules, but he's not—*evil*. He's not *uncaring*. He cares too *much*, and he feels rage when he feels helpless. Like he felt helpless when I was attacked."

She's sitting next to me at the table, and I can see her hands clenched around the brightly patterned cloth napkin that Bonnie set out when she made tea for all of us. Tea. As if we were having just any regular early morning confab among friends. I place my hand on Celeste's forearm.

"Sweetie, that's how *you* feel," I say. "You're angry and helpless because you're different, but you *do* care. You *do* feel deeply. You get frustrated because you know the world can't be changed—but he thinks the rest of the world doesn't matter."

Her eyes are full of agony; she didn't look this wretched the day she was beaten up. No matter what the circumstances, she would be upset to learn Ryan had done something so impossibly awful. But she knows she's the reason he's done it, and she can't bear it. "But we're the same. Ryan and me. We always have been."

Now I put my arm around her shoulders and hug her to me. "No, you're not. You think alike, sometimes, but you don't feel alike. You never have."

There's a moment of silence while we all try to marshal our thoughts. Then Joe starts questioning Aurelia again. It occurs to me that they're the only two who really understand what happened, in the sense that they're the only two who have actually had conversations about and with murderers before. This has made them allies, I think. Unless it's made them adversaries.

"So Terry's wife calls the sheriff, shows him the tape," he says. "When did they arrest Ryan?"

"Last night around midnight. Apparently they went by his place a couple of times but he wasn't home until then. They had a search warrant, too, and they've impounded his car. Though I imagine he got rid of other evidence when he got rid of the gun."

"Other evidence?"

"Bobby came at him after he'd been shot. There's probably Bobby's blood somewhere on Ryan's clothing." She pauses for a beat. "That clothing was not found in his car or apartment, but there might be traces of blood in the car."

"Sweet Jesus," Bonnie says.

"I have to say, this strikes me as being pretty stupid on Ryan's part," Joe says. "I'd take him more as the guy who'd wait for you in an alley and strangle you with his bare hands under cover of darkness when no one was around. Not the kind of guy who walks up to your house in broad daylight and shoots you when *anyone* could have seen him."

"Nobody would have known anything without the nanny cam," Aurelia points out. "That junkyard is in the middle of nowhere—unless someone happened to be driving by, no one would have witnessed a thing. And there would have been no other reason to suspect Ryan. Since neither the Foucaults nor our friends reported the shooting at the drive-by, there was no history of disagreements between them."

I glance at Celeste and she nods. Sometime this morning she'd fessed up about what really happened when the three of us drove by the Foucault property. I can only imagine what Aurelia had said when she learned about the gunplay.

"Ryan was with Celeste the night Bobby got fresh with her," Joe says.

"But he didn't even have a conversation with Bobby that night, from all I hear. Never threw a punch. No, this would have looked much more like a robbery gone wrong, or a dispute between buddies who had a falling out. They'd have been looking for known associates who held a grudge."

Bonnie opens her hands like someone who can't even imagine how to hold on to anything anymore. "So what happens now? If Ryan killed him and there's proof Ryan killed him—how can you even attempt to defend him?"

"I don't have much maneuvering room," Aurelia admits. "I'm trying to decide whether it's a good idea or a bad idea to introduce Celeste to the case."

Celeste looks apprehensive. "What do you mean?"

"If he was avenging your attack, that gives him motive. On the one hand, that's bad. On the other hand, sometimes jury members are more lenient when they believe a man was protecting his loved ones. A passionate revenge killing plays better than cold premeditated murder."

"But no one saw Celeste get beaten up," Bonnie says.

"Right. So we might have to take her to that urgent care clinic after all. Get some documentation after the fact. It might weigh in our favor when it comes to sentencing."

Joe gives Aurelia a long, considering look. "So you're going to defend him."

"It's the American legal system, Mr. McGinty. Even the foulest criminals you can name deserve the best defense the law will allow."

"And if there wasn't this—this overwhelming evidence against him—would you try to get him off? Knowing he was guilty of murder, would you try to ensure that he went free?"

Alonzo, who has not said a word this whole time—who has, in fact, spent most of the hour staring down at the tablecloth—now lifts his head and divides a glance between Joe and Aurelia. He still doesn't say anything.

Aurelia meets Joe's narrowed speculation with a hard gaze of her own. "Fortunately, I don't have to try to solve that dilemma. Because unless Sheriff Wilkerson and his men are staggeringly incompetent, I believe there is no way anyone could be convinced Ryan didn't commit this crime. So my job now is to try to soften his sentence as much as I can."

"I would," Celeste tells Joe defiantly. "I'd try to set him free if I could. He did a terrible thing—but Bobby *tried* to do a terrible thing. Bobby's worse than Ryan."

Joe looks at her but he doesn't answer, doesn't press her. But I feel a little chill wiggle down my spine. Before the day is too much older, Joe's going to ask me the same question, and I have no idea how I'll answer.

Knowing Ryan deliberately killed a man, would I try to protect him from the consequences of his actions? Even if that man deserved killing?

Did Bobby Foucault deserve killing?

Even if he deserved killing, was it Ryan's right to carry out his punishment?

I don't know. I'm too horrified to think it through.

"We can all debate the ethical dilemmas another day, I suppose," Bonnie says at last. She sounds weary, Bonnie who has enough physical energy to personally power the state of Illinois. "But what happens next? Will Ryan get out on bond? Will he stay here in Quinville or be sent to prison somewhere to await his trial?"

"I'll ask for bail, but we won't get it. My guess is they'll keep him here at the holding cell for a couple of days, then send him to the Madison County jail to await trial. Which could take months."

Alonzo looks up again and this time he decides to speak. "What happens when he changes?"

For a moment, there is absolute dead silence around the table.

"Fuck," Celeste says at last.

You wouldn't think we could have forgotten this central, this calamitous aspect of the situation. I have the fleeting thought that Ryan can't be the first shape-shifter who's ever been arrested, but he's the first one I happen to know. He's in jail, and within a few days he's going to transform into an animal shape, and if we thought we had a crisis on our hands before, it's nothing to what will happen to him—to all of us—once that occurs.

"He can't change," Aurelia says flatly.

"Good luck with that," Alonzo mutters.

Celeste is looking at me. "He said—didn't you make him a potion of some sort? To slow it down? To help him control his shifting?"

I nod. "I did. He said it was working. I can—I'll go home today—

right now—and mix up another whole batch for him." I appeal to Aurelia. "Can I just take it to him at the police station? Will they let me give it to him?"

"You can try, but I doubt it. Some jails have awfully strict rules. Like, you can't mail someone a book from your house—it has to come from Amazon.com or some recognized commercial outlet. And with drugs—well—it seems unlikely a private citizen could just waltz in and hand over a vial of something she claims is medically necessary. There could be anything in that bottle."

"I'll try," I say. "The sheriff knows me. Maybe he'll let me—" I don't complete the sentence. *Maybe he won't.* What then?

"When can we go see him?" Celeste asks.

"I wouldn't go before eight or nine. The police station is open all night, of course, so theoretically the holding cells are, too, but they don't like civilians cluttering up the place outside of normal working hours."

Celeste clutches my arm. "You and me. We'll go this morning and see what we can find out."

I nod and look over at Joe. "And then will you take me back to my place so I can mix up some serum?"

Like Aurelia, he's wearing an opaque expression, and I'm not entirely certain what he's thinking. *Let the bastard rot in jail,* maybe? *Hell, no, I won't do a damn thing to make it easier for you to save your lying, murdering ex-boyfriend.* But even if he thinks Ryan should be tried, convicted, and executed without delay, surely he realizes that the story gets exponentially more terrible if Ryan shifts shape while he's in a small-town prison and everyone starts wondering what he really is.

And what his friends are.

"Sure," he says. "I've got to run some errands and pick up some stuff from Mark, but I'll be back by three, will that be okay?"

"That sounds great," I say. "See you then."

He pushes himself to his feet and the rest of us stand up, too, though no one else seems to have the first idea of where to go next. "See you later," Joe says, kisses me, and leaves.

The rest of us just stare at each other for a moment.

"Bad day," Aurelia finally says.

I nod. "Gonna get worse."

I look almost as rough as Celeste does when we leave the house a few hours later. I left most of my clothes at Joe's, and the ones I threw on when the phone call came in aren't entirely clean, so I end up borrowing pieces from Celeste and Aurelia and hoping for the best.

Aurelia walks out with us into the cold morning sunshine. "Are you coming with us?" I ask.

"Not right now. I've got an appointment with another client and I'm already late."

Celeste insists on driving—"I'm not an invalid!"—though I have to Google the address of the police station because neither of us has been there before. Turns out it's not that far from the Square, which makes sense, since the cops are probably constantly coming in to the area to pick up drunks or break up fights. It's a squat brick building with shabby concrete sidewalks leading up from the parking lots on either side. There are a few bushes, a few patches of decorative grass, but they're all dead. Three poles are planted out front—one holding the American flag, one the Illinois state flag, and one a pennant that I don't recognize. Maybe Quinville's own civic crest and motto, which I have never to my knowledge laid eyes on before.

Inside it's all linoleum flooring, fluorescent lighting, pressboard furniture, and anxious people. It's probably fifteen minutes before the gatekeeper—a desk sergeant? a dispatcher? an ordinary cop who pulled this duty for the day?—has time to ask us our business and find someone to take us to Ryan. We surrender our coats and purses and walk through a metal detector before we're escorted down a brightly lit hallway fronted by a series of closed doors. Within a few steps we find ourselves on what looks like the set of a bad TV movie.

The Quinville police station boasts three holding cells, each about the size of a small bathroom. They're all constructed of cinder blocks on five sides, including the floor and ceiling; the sixth side is a barred door set with a heavy lock. Each cell holds nothing but a bunk, which also appears to be made of cinder blocks, and a metal toilet bolted to the corner. All the walls are inexplicably painted a bright yellow. Since obviously no one chose the color to make the place seem more cheerful, I assume it's to camouflage traces of urine and maybe vomit, both of which scent the air.

In the far left cell, a teenage boy is sleeping on the cinderblock bed, his back to us. The middle one is empty. Ryan is in the far right cubicle.

"Thank God," he says when he sees us, and his hands grip the bars, just like the prisoner in every jailhouse movie you've ever seen.

"You're only supposed to stay a half hour," our escort tells us, but with such detachment in his voice that I have a feeling he doesn't care if we're here all day, singing camp songs and picnicking on the floor, as long as no one complains. "Make sure you sign out when you leave."

Celeste practically flings herself against the bars, thrusting her hands through so she can give Ryan an awkward hug. "Oh, Ryan, what did you *do*?" she wails into his shoulder.

"Hush," he says sharply, glancing up at the discreet little camera set at the join of the wall and ceiling. "Aurelia says you have to assume everything is being recorded."

A little late to think of that, I want to point out, but this doesn't seem to be the time for recriminations. Or maybe it is, I don't know. I'm still so much in shock that I can't figure out how I should feel about the situation. Or how I *do* feel, if that's different from how I *should* feel.

Celeste pulls back a little and gives him the fakest smile ever. "Aurelia's the best," she says in an encouraging voice. "If anyone knows what to do, she will."

He surveys her for a moment. "You look a little better," he says. "But you're gonna have a scar. Right there." He lifts a hand and traces a wound that runs from her left temple down to her ear.

"I know," she answers. "I'm just going to have to grow my hair out so no one sees it."

He looks over the top of her head and gives me a solemn nod. "Hey, Kara. Thanks for coming."

I step close enough to take his hand, which closes on mine with an almost convulsive grip. I can tell he's working hard to hold it together, but he's worried. This is a bad spot and it could get worse fast, and he can't control what happens next.

But he's not a total wreck. He's not despairing. Which means he thinks he has options. Which means he might have some kind of crazy plan.

"We thought you'd like to see a couple of friendly faces," I say. "Is there anything we can do for you?"

"Yeah," he says, his voice heavy with meaning. "I need my prescription. And I need it really fast."

I nod. "We were just talking about that. I'll go to my house this afternoon and bring you all that I've got."

Celeste glances toward the other cell, where the young man may or may not be sleeping. "When's the last time you took any?" she asks delicately. "I mean—how much longer could you hold out if you had to?" *When did you change last?* is what she means. Or, more accurately, *How soon before you change again?*

"I think I have two days," he says. "Not much time."

"And then—what comes next?" Celeste wants to know. Again, she's speaking vaguely to confuse any eavesdroppers, but Ryan and I understand the question: *What animal will you become next?* His cycle is fixed, inflexible: cat, fox, hawk, cat, fox, hawk. My serums have bought him time, but I haven't tried to mess with his menagerie.

"Cat," he says, barely breathing the word.

"Could be better, could be worse," Celeste decides.

"I thought so, too."

"How long do you think you'll be here?" I inquire. "Aurelia seems to think you'll be transferred to the county prison soon."

"No one's told me anything."

Celeste seems to be thinking it over. "Big prison might be better," she offers. "If you aren't in a small cell when—something happens—and if there isn't a camera on you and if you don't draw attention to yourself—" *If you're not locked up and videotaped when you change into a cat, you might be able to escape the building without anyone realizing what's happened.* Would have been easier to do if he were a hawk, harder if he were a fox.

"I know. I thought of that," Ryan says. "That's why I need the drugs now. While I'm here."

"Is there anything else we can get you?" Celeste asks, and there's an urgent undertone in her voice. "Or anything we can do for you? At your apartment or wherever?"

It takes a while for me to realize what she's asking. *Is there any evidence we can dispose of for you? Just let us know.* Looks like Celeste has come down hard on the side of justifiable homicide. She's going to stand by her friend no matter what his crime.

Ryan gets her meaning, too, and he gives her a lopsided grin. "Thanks, but I don't think so. You've got to take care of yourself right now. Let Aurelia take care of me." He glances at me. "And Kara. She's the only one who can really help right now."

As it happens, we don't stay any longer than our allotted thirty minutes. There's just not much we can say, especially knowing that our conversation might be monitored, and the place is so depressing that the air has an actual weight to it, crushing my lungs, making it hard to breathe. I feel guilty for so many reasons when I reach through the bars to hug Ryan good-bye. Because I'm so relieved to be able to walk out when he can't. Because I don't hate him for killing Bobby.

Because I do hate him for killing Bobby.

Because I don't know how I'm supposed to deal with a friend who is also a murderer.

As luck would have it, Sheriff Wilkerson is just arriving at the police station when Celeste and I step out into the bright, blessed, clean, fresh, beautiful sunshine of freedom.

"Well, hello there, Miss Karadel," he says with his usual avuncular charm. "What brings you to the station on this pretty day?"

"Visiting a friend of mine who got picked up last night," I say.

"Now, who might that be?"

"Ryan Barnes."

His face doesn't lose its usual friendly expression, but I think I see his eyes sharpen with interest. "Ah, that's right. In connection with the murder of Bobby Foucault. That's a sad business."

"Listen," Celeste says. "Ryan's got a medical condition, and he needs to take a daily injection. Can we go to his place and pick up some drugs for him?"

She instantly has the sheriff's full attention, which, despite his aw-shucks demeanor, is searching and smart. "Well, we'd need to talk about that," he says pleasantly. "I don't think I know you, young lady."

She smiles with her usual patented brilliance, though I have the feeling it doesn't have the typical effect. "My name is Celeste Saint-Simon. I'm a friend of Ryan's, too."

"How do you do?" he says, and shakes her hand. "You're the girl who had the dustup with Bobby a few weeks back, aren't you, over at Arabesque?"

Fuck. Who'd have expected him to remember her name? But it's obvious his mind is quickly connecting all the dots. Celeste is the link between Bobby and Ryan. Aurelia hadn't been sure if we should offer up Celeste as motive for Ryan's actions, but right now it looks like we're not going to have a choice.

Celeste casts her eyes down in embarrassment and confusion, but I know she's furiously trying to think it through. "That's right," she says, very low. "That's the first night I met Bobby. He tried to—hurt me."

"Looks like someone else tried to hurt you recently, too," he observes in a gentle voice.

When Celeste lifts her eyes again, they're swimming with tears. The girl is the best actress I've ever seen. I can tell she's come to the same conclusion I have, so she's just going to fling herself into the inevitable. "Bobby and his brother," she says, barely above a whisper. "They thought I deserved to be beaten up for what happened that night at Arabesque."

"Now, when did this happen?"

"Saturday evening."

"Did you file a report with my officers?"

She shakes her head, her expression utterly woebegone. "I thought that would just make things worse."

"People like Bobby Foucault do not take kindly to police interference, that's a fact," the sheriff agrees. "But the police are the ones who should be dealing with men like him, so young ladies like yourself aren't repeatedly put in danger."

"I suppose. I didn't know what to do."

"Ahuh. Did your friend Ryan know that they assaulted you?"

Celeste gives a frightened start, as if it's just now occurred to her that it might not be a good idea to be confiding in cops, and looks at me with beseeching eyes. I put my arm around her shoulders.

"I'm not sure what Ryan knew," I say. "I'm not sure his lawyer wants us to be talking about stuff. I'm sorry. I don't mean to be—what's that word?—obstructive."

"Well, you talk to Miss Aurelia and get back to me," he says.

Celeste turns away to pull out a tissue and surreptitiously wipe her eyes. I take a deep breath and say, "So. Sheriff. About the medicine."

"Oh, that's right. The medicine." He gives me a rueful smile. "See, I can't just let people bring random drugs into the station and hand them out to prisoners. I don't know what all could be in those pill bottles."

"It's an injection."

"Well, that could be even worse," he says humorously.

"But he needs the medicine," I say, my voice gaining intensity. He hasn't asked me what Ryan's condition is, thank God, because I haven't figured out what answer I should give. All I can think of is diabetes, but I don't want some prison doctor to suddenly start injecting Ryan with insulin. "Isn't it a crime to withhold life-saving drugs?"

"I don't want to withhold anything. Have a doctor or pharmacy deliver the meds and we'll happily administer them. But failing that—"

I'm about to argue the point when Celeste clutches my arm. "We'll do that," she says. "Thank you so much. It was good to meet you, Sheriff."

"It was very interesting to meet you, Miss Celeste." He actually tips his hat to us and saunters on into the station.

Celeste tows me to the car without speaking, but her face is full of determination and shows no traces of her recent tears. Once the doors are safely shut and no one can overhear us, I burst out, "What are we going to *do*?"

"We're going to call in a prescription to Q-Ville Drugs," she says in a triumphant voice. "And Alonzo will deliver it—*after* you've switched the medicine in the bottle!"

"Great idea—except I'm not a physician! I can't get prescriptions for *people* filled at a pharmacy."

"*Someone* can. We'll figure that part out. Alonzo is our ace in the hole."

She drives back to Bonnie and Aurelia's at a furious pace. Alonzo's gone, but Bonnie's home, and the house is rich with the scents of baking bread and simmering soup. Bonnie cooks when she's troubled; it's like she's preparing for war, and she needs to lay in supplies for the troops.

The three of us sit around the kitchen table, put Celeste's cell phone on speaker, and call Aurelia. For a wonder, she's actually in her office and not, at the moment, consulting with a client, so we quickly recount our adventure at the police station. She agrees with our assessment that we had no choice but to explain to Sheriff Wilkerson that the Foucaults attacked Celeste. And she very much likes the idea of using Alonzo to deliver the necessary serum to Ryan.

"But I told Celeste. I can't write the scrip," I say.

"I can take care of that part," Aurelia answers. "I know someone who will do me a favor."

"Prescribing unnecessary drugs?" Bonnie demands. "That seems morally questionable."

"I'll make the case that they're necessary but, for various reasons, unobtainable through the ordinary channels," Aurelia replies. "Which has the advantage of being the truth. Don't worry."

Bonnie sighs and looks weary. When, a few minutes later, we cut the connection, she continues to sit and just stare at the phone.

Celeste watches her a moment and then says, "You hate this."

Bonnie looks up, some of the usual fire in her eyes. "I would think we *all* hate this."

"You think Ryan did this terrible thing and he deserves to be punished for it," Celeste challenges her.

"And you don't?"

Celeste flings her hands in the air. "I think he did a terrible thing for reasons I understand. He did a terrible thing, but he's still *Ryan*. And he's still my friend and I want to help him if I can. I do *not* want him to go to prison. I'd lie for him. I'd set him free if I could. I'd help him leave the state, or leave the country. If you hate me for that, I'm sorry. But I'd do the same thing for you if you murdered somebody."

I expect Bonnie to retort *I would never murder anybody!* But her fierce eyes grow fiercer and she stares Celeste down. "I believe that, in certain circumstances, any of us can be moved to violence," she says in a steely voice. "If someone threatened Alonzo's life, for instance, and I had the means at hand, I would kill that person if it was necessary to save my boy. But deliberately seeking a man out to take his life because you believe he does not deserve to live—that's something I can't countenance. Something I can't forgive."

"Don't you think—" Celeste begins, but Bonnie overrides her.

"If Ryan can decide Bobby Foucault deserves to die, why couldn't Bobby's brother decide you should die? If vengeance is always an acceptable motive for murder, *all* of us will be gunned down at some point. And if we give the individual the power to make those life-and-death decisions—if the single, armed vigilante can take it upon himself to rid the town of monsters—how can we make sure the individual correctly identifies the monsters? Some people would call *you* a monster. So does that give them a right to shoot you on sight?"

Celeste's face is stormy. "No—I don't believe in vigilante justice. I don't think we should all be armed and shooting at people because we don't like them. But this is *Ryan*. And so it's different. I can't explain."

"Situational ethics," I say in a muffled voice.

They both look at me. "Well, don't you agree with me?" Celeste demands.

"I don't know," I say. "I'm so shocked I have no idea what to think. And I don't expect to figure it out anytime soon."

Bonnie gives a heavy sigh and appears to deflate a little. "In the meantime, there are mouths to feed and people to care for and ordinary days to get through," she says. "Maybe we can solve this problem tomorrow. It will certainly be waiting for us then."

CHAPTER SIXTEEN

It's a relief to get out of the house when Joe arrives a little after three, Jinx and Jezebel peering out happily from the backseat of the extended cab. There's a little coolness between Bonnie and Celeste after the argument about Ryan, and I can tell Celeste is thinking it's time for her to return to her own apartment or at least find another place to recuperate. I wonder if I should bring her back to my property for a few days. Surely between the two of us—and Helena and her girls—and Daniel, if he's around—we could fend off the remaining psychotic Foucault brother.

I mention this idea to Joe once we're out of the main traffic of Quinville, not quite to highway W.

"Sure, if you want," he says. "But I'd like to stay, too, if I can." He glances over at me, and his smile is warm. "It would be nice to find out what it's like to wake up next to you and not go rushing off to some disaster."

"Things *have* been pretty exciting with my friends lately," I agree.

I keep my voice light to camouflage the sudden wild excitement of my heart.

"Of course, you're practically running a bed-and-breakfast these days. Not like we'd have much privacy."

"The doors lock. We'd have privacy."

"Then let's do it."

We travel a couple miles without exchanging any more words. Joe is a relaxed driver, his right hand loose on the wheel, his left elbow resting against the door frame. I lean back in my seat and try to convince myself the silence is companionable. But despite his casual pose, I think I feel tension emanating from him, or maybe it's disapproval.

Or maybe I'm the one feeling tense.

"You haven't said what you think about this whole Ryan situation," I say finally. My voice sounds overloud and almost accusatory. I feel like I have blundered into this conversation, but I don't know how else to begin it.

He gives me a brief glance before returning his attention to the road. "I think it sucks."

"Bonnie thinks we're wrong to even try to help him," I say, my words still bald and bumbling. "She thinks there shouldn't even be any thought of mercy for a murderer."

He nods. "Lot of people feel that way."

"But how do *you* feel?" I persist. "Will you be mad at me if I do something to help Ryan?"

He gives me another quick glance, switches hands on the wheel, and reaches over to squeeze my fingers, which are knotted together in my lap.

"I think whenever we see someone we love do something terrible, we're faced with an impossible dilemma," he says quietly. "You can't stop loving people on the spur of the moment. And if you understand why they've done terrible things, it's even harder to turn against them. So it's your job, in a sense, as Ryan's friend, to still believe in him."

There's obviously a *but* coming, and I wait for it in silence while he collects his thoughts.

"But just because a mother loves her son who's gone out and shot ten people, it doesn't mean that boy shouldn't go to prison," Joe continues. "It's her job to love him. It's society's job to punish him. I understand that you want to help Ryan, and I'm okay with that. But I think he belongs in jail."

I turn a little in the seat to get a better look at his face. I'm still holding on to his hand with both of mine. "But he's a shape-shifter. He can't *be* in jail."

"Why not?"

"Because—because—what happens when he changes shapes? The world goes crazy! The sheriff calls in the FBI, and Ryan gets sent to some secret laboratory in Washington, and suddenly there are doctors and government agents and I-don't-know-who-all swarming all over Quinville, looking for other shape-shifters. We live in *terror* of being discovered, don't you understand that? Discovered and—and—" Bonnie's word comes back to me. "Viewed as monsters. Hunted down and killed, or locked up and experimented on."

"Pretty scary. I absolutely agree," he says. "But just because they find Ryan doesn't mean they'll find you."

"I can't control my shifting! I don't even know when it'll happen! When those FBI agents start snooping around Ryan's life, don't you think they'll start investigating me? And I'll be in the middle of an interrogation and the change will come over me and—oh, you have no idea. This is what my nightmares are made of."

He squeezes my fingers again then releases me and puts both hands on the wheel. "Maybe it would go a different way," he suggests.

"Maybe the government would protect you. The doctors and scientists would ask permission to study you. They'd see you as—magical. Creatures with phenomenal possibilities. The military would want to hire you to deploy in delicate operations. You could all come out of the shadows and live in the light. Maybe *that's* what would happen instead."

"Maybe," I say, "but I think it's more likely that some deranged survivalist would creep out one night and put a bullet in my head because he thinks I'm an abomination."

"Well, that's about the worst thing in the world that could happen," he says in a soft voice. "Makes my heart almost stop to think about it."

"And that's why Ryan can't be in jail," I finish up.

He nods but doesn't answer. He's turning from 159 onto W, and there's a fresh pothole right at the intersection, which requires a little negotiating. I look out the window and realize with a shock that autumn is almost over. There are a few defiant elms and maples still madly clinging to their scraps of color, but most of the trees have been stripped bare. They stand like grim gray ghosts beneath the unforgiving sky, the wraiths of summer haunting the gloomy season.

Winter soon enough. Winter too soon. But then, I always think it's too soon for winter.

When Joe speaks, it's in that faraway voice people use when they're concentrating on a memory, trying to bring it more clearly into focus. "I never gave it much thought before, but if you were trying to commit the perfect murder, a shape-shifter would be the one to do it," he says. "There was one time—back when I was on the force—we never could figure out how this crime was committed. How the killer got away. But if the guy had been a shape-shifter—"

I bring my attention away from the trees, back to Joe. "What happened?"

"Couple different people called us one night from the same neighborhood. They'd heard shouting and crashing noises from this one house, like there was a fight going on. Well, my partner and I were only one street away—we got there in, like, two minutes. Kind of a shabby house in a shabby part of town. Bunch of people standing in the yards nearby when we pulled up, pointing at the house in question. We were just going to ask the name of the homeowners when we heard shots fired inside.

"My partner called for backup and I ran up to the house, shouting, 'Police!' No one came out, no one answered. We waited until a couple other units arrived, then we all went in at the same time, front and back, guns drawn. I was with the group going in through the front, and the minute we opened the door, a couple of animals came streaking out—a cat and a dog, I think, though they went by so fast I really couldn't tell you. Figured they were spooked by the gunshots and wanted out bad.

"We didn't find anything in the house till we got to a back bedroom that had been turned into an office. And there was the body, pooling with blood. So freshly dead you could almost think you could bring him back to life. Gun was on the floor right next to him, but it was clear he hadn't killed himself, 'cause he was shot in the back."

Joe's quiet a moment before he resumes his story. "We looked through every inch of that house, from the basement to the attic, and we never found the shooter. He was gone, but we couldn't figure out how he could have gotten out without being seen. The back door was chained shut—we had to break it open to get in. All of the windows were locked from the inside. The only way out would have been through the front door—where I was standing from the moment the shots were fired. The shooter was *not* in that house, but there was no way he could have gotten past us." He glances at me. "Unless he was a shape-shifter."

I nod. "The cat. Or the dog. He shoots the victim, he changes shape, he runs out the door when you open it. Why would you think to stop him?"

Joe nods. "The perfect crime."

"Did you ever figure out who he was? The shooter, I mean? If he left the gun behind—"

"We lifted his prints, but they weren't a match for any we had in the system. And they've never turned up again."

"So you never found out who killed that poor man."

Joe makes a sound something like a snort. "Well, if ever anyone deserved killing, it was him. We found the most god-awful setup in his basement. Horrifying. Some blankets and some water bowls and a terrible smell of piss and shit and rotted food. There was a chain wrapped around one of the weight-bearing poles in the middle of the basement, with a collar on the end of it. On the floor there were a couple of belts, and a whip—like the kind of whip you'd see in an *Indiana Jones* movie. There were matches and cigarettes and something that, I swear to God, looked like a cattle brand.

"You know, your first thought is, 'What's all *this* shit for? Is he keeping *animals* down here?' And then you start looking at the size of that collar, and you realize that the food on the floor is in McDonald's wrappers, and you see a pair of blue jeans that are way too small for the body upstairs, and you think, 'Was he keeping a *person* down here?' And pretty soon the forensics guys are there and they start taking evidence and looking at samples, and they say, Yeah. Yeah, there was a person down here. And you start talking to neighbors and they say, Yeah, used to be a kid who lived here, but they haven't seen him around for a while—a boy, maybe ten or twelve years old. Gosh, it's been a couple of years since they've laid eyes on him."

By this time, we've traveled all the way down W to the edge of my property. Joe makes a smooth turn onto the gravel, cuts the motor, and twists in his seat to give me a serious look. "And you think—you think—it can't be possible, but this *motherfucker* was keeping his son chained in the basement for *years*. And somehow that kid got free and he killed the son of a bitch and he got out of the house before anybody saw him, and you're glad. You hope he never gets caught. You only wish you could have gotten there sooner, so you could have shot the prick yourself."

I am staring up at Joe with so much horror on my face that he instantly dissolves into remorse. "Christ, I shouldn't have told you that story. It's a shocker, I know. Worst thing I ever saw when I was on the force—and I saw a lot of bad things."

I shake my head, but I can't answer. I can't speak. I almost can't breathe.

I suppose there could be two stories so awful, so similar, but I don't think so. I think that was Alonzo's house. I think that was Alonzo's father.

I think it was Ryan who shot him.

He's not just a murderer. He's a serial killer.

I tell Joe it might take me a couple of hours to mix up the drugs for Ryan, and he agrees to confer with Helena and the girls to see what needs to be done around the house. I head back to my lab, Scottie at my heels, and when I shut the door behind us, I throw the inset lock.

Then I stand in the middle of the room and stare sightlessly at the silver-toned refrigerator that holds my samples and experiments.

Ryan killed Alonzo's father. After somehow learning of Alonzo's existence, he gained admittance to the house, freed the boy and shot the father, probably right in front of Alonzo. That certainly explains why Alonzo has always been so wary of Ryan. Sure, Ryan rescued him, but he hadn't presented himself as any less brutal than his dad.

Maybe murder had not originally been on the agenda. Maybe Ryan had just planned to rescue Alonzo, hoping the two of them would simply vanish into the night, but the dad had come home unexpectedly. There had been an argument, Ryan had snatched up the man's gun—

That doesn't make sense, though. If they'd found Alonzo's dad in the basement, or the hallway, maybe you could make the case that he had arrived inopportunely and Ryan had been forced to kill him just so they could get away. But they found the body in a back room, which argues that Ryan went looking for him. And if I ask Joe, I'm betting I'll learn that the victim didn't own the gun used in the shooting.

I'm betting that Ryan came to the house armed and intending to kill Alonzo's father. Because he thought the man deserved to die.

For the crime of abusing a shape-shifter.

For which he also believed Bobby Foucault deserved to die.

I have no way of knowing if Ryan has encountered other humans that he also brought to justice for similar crimes. But it seems very, very possible to me.

I put a hand to my mouth, because I don't want to be making that sound—that slight whimpering that could build into a full-fledged sobbing if I don't hold it in. Scottie comes over and presses against my legs, offering a wordless comfort for distress that he can sense, though he can't understand it. I drop to the floor and wrap my arms around his neck, burying my tears in his rough fur.

God, if I could do it, right now, I'd shift to animal shape and never shift back.

I don't come out of the lab for the next three hours.

Most of that time I'm sitting on the floor, my back against the wall, my legs straight out in front of me. I stare out the window, but I don't register much beyond weak sunlight slowly fading over bare trees and dying grass. Scottie lies beside me, his head in my lap, my hand stroking his ears.

I'm trying to think it through.

I can mix up potions that will allow Ryan to stay human until he chooses to shift. If he's transferred to the prison in Madison County, there will surely be a day when he's out of his cell, perhaps in a prison yard with access to a delivery truck or with knowledge of some small break in the fence where a cat could squeeze through. He could be gone in five minutes. He'd never be able to return to Quinville, of course, but he's a clever man; he'd be able to make a life for himself somewhere else.

A life that very easily could include more murders.

If I don't give him the potion and he transforms while he's in a small cell under constant surveillance, my life—Alonzo's life—Celeste's and Daniel's and Juliet's and that of every shape-shifter I have ever treated—all careen into danger. Is it more urgent that I protect the secret of all the people under my care, or that I ensure a killer stays in jail?

If I don't give him the potion, he will know that I have set myself against him. He will know that I no longer trust him, and he will no longer trust me. If he somehow gets free without my assistance, will he exact some kind of vengeance?

Maybe that's what I should hope for. Maybe I should pray that he takes cat shape this very night when the camera is not turned his way. Surely he'll manage to slip through the iron bars and sidle out of the police station before anyone notices. Let him come for me, let him kill me. At least whatever happens next won't be my fault.

My hand freezes on top of Scottie's head. He lifts his muzzle to give me a questioning look.

Is it my responsibility to stop Ryan? To make sure he never harms anyone again?

I could do it, I think. Mix up a lethal potion and swap it for whatever drug the legitimate pharmacist supplies. Ryan would inject it without hesitation and die within hours. I could even pick something that would cause him very little physical suffering.

I see huge logistical problems with this plan, of course, the primary one being that the pharmacist himself would instantly be under suspicion if Ryan mysteriously died. And if he could prove his innocence, Alonzo would be the next one under investigation. But surely there is some other way to slip Ryan the fatal dose, even if I merely smuggle it in past the police guards at the station.

But if I execute Ryan for the crime of murder, how am I any better than he is?

Who *does* have the right to decide who lives and who dies?

Displacing Scottie, who scrambles up to a sitting position, I draw my knees up and rest my head on top of them. I don't know the answers to any of my questions. I have spent the past eight years of my life healing people, helping people; I have dealt in life, not death. I don't want to turn my gifts to other uses.

But I don't know what to do.

In the end I call the one person I can always count on for clarity. Aurelia's assistant tells me she's on the phone, but she'll call me back within the hour. I'm still sitting with my back to the wall, Scottie stretched out beside me. There's nothing to see out the window now, since it's past six and night has already fallen. But I don't move from my spot on the floor. It seems like the safest place to be when the world is rocking off its foundations.

Barely five minutes pass before Aurelia returns my call. "I'm on my way out the door," she says. "What's up?"

"I think Ryan killed Alonzo's dad two years ago. Which makes me wonder if he's killed other people, too."

There's the briefest of silences while she processes this information. She doesn't ask how I know. "What method did he use to commit the crime?"

"Handgun. Left on the scene. There were fingerprints, but they were never identified."

"Because he wasn't in the system—but he will be *now*," she says.

This hadn't even occurred to me, but of course I am not the only one who will make this connection if the connection exists. "I don't know what to do," I say. I can hear the hysteria rising in my voice. "It's even worse than I thought. I don't want to help him—but if he changes while he's in jail—Aurelia, what do we do?"

"We focus," she says quietly. "We determine what course of action serves the most people."

I press my fist to my forehead. "I think—I think more shapeshifters will come to more harm if Ryan is discovered. I think the greater evil is Ryan changing shapes in a public place."

"I think so, too," she says. "So you mix the potions."

"But if he goes free—and he does it again—"

"We will deal with that eventuality when it arises."

"I haven't told anybody else," I say.

"Good. For now, keep it that way. Where are you?"

"At my place. Joe's here."

"Maybe you should stay there tonight. Come back in the morning with the serum. Alonzo already picked up the order from the pharmacy and it's ready to be delivered."

"I can't think straight," I say.

"No," she says. "It's been that kind of day."

I emerge from the lab around seven, having spent the last hour finally carrying out my appointed task. I've mixed up three vials for Ryan, enough to get him through a couple of weeks, I think. Surely by that time he'll have been relocated to the prison in Edwardsville. He'll have found his chance and shed his human shape and slipped away.

Joe has made dinner, but before we sit down to eat, I take a few minutes to tour the animal cages, pausing longest at the enclosure holding the puppies. Even the smallest ones, the ones abandoned at my door one cold night, seem to be gaining weight and thriving. I have been so wrapped up in human affairs that I have had no energy to spare for these tiny creatures entrusted to my care. I scratch their heads and tug gently on their ears and promise I will be more attentive in the coming days. I only hope I can keep my promise.

Then I join the others inside the house. Joe has invited Helena and Juliet to eat with us, but the human contingent is matched by the canine one, since Scottie, Jinx, Jezebel, *and* Desdemona share the supper hour with us. As you'd expect, Desi is the most well-behaved of the lot, followed closely by Jezebel. The two of them don't bother begging for food, but curl up on the floor nearest the people they love the most—Juliet and Joe, respectively—and are rewarded for their patience with some of the best scraps from the table. Jinx and Scottie both focus on me, since I'm clearly the easiest mark.

It's hard to make conversation, because Helena and Juliet are virtual strangers and I obviously can't discuss the subject that obsesses me. But Helena is a talker, and Joe is exerting himself to ease the situation for me, so he starts drawing her out with gentle questions. She prattles away willingly, and even Juliet contributes a few observations. I think maybe she likes Joe, so she doesn't want to appear too sullen.

As the meal draws to a close, I say, "You two have been lifesavers this week when so much has been going on in town. Can I offer you anything? Pay you a salary? Do you a favor?"

"Oh, heavens, you've done us the biggest favor already by letting us use the trailer!" Helena exclaims. "We're still in your debt! But I do need to take a day or two and go to town and see if I can find a job. And, of course, I need to get Juliet registered for school."

"What kind of work can you do?" Joe asks.

"Secretarial and light bookkeeping," she says. "A little website maintenance. I have references."

"I'll ask my buddy Mark if he's heard of anything. He runs a local trucking company, and he knows *everybody* in town."

Juliet looks at me and asks a rare direct question. "Where does Alonzo go? Will I go there?"

She's only met him once, so at first I'm surprised that she'd want to follow him to school. But then I figure she wants an ally. If there's another shape-shifter on campus, life could get exponentially easier on the days that turn out to be dicey.

"He's homeschooled," I reply with a smile. "But maybe Bonnie would take you on as a student, too."

Her face turns wistful. "Maybe. But I like school. I like being with all the other kids."

Well, that makes sense, too, since her shifting cycle is apparently under much better control than mine ever was. She can pretend to be normal most of the time, and what's more normal than public school?

"I think you'll probably do just fine," I say, "even if Alonzo isn't there."

Helena and Juliet offer to help clean up after the meal, but I'm desperate to have my house to myself, so I refuse all offers of aid and they finally leave. Once Joe and I have loaded the dishwasher and tidied up the kitchen, we head to the living room and collapse on the couch. I sag against him and he puts his arm around me and for a moment—just a moment—the perilously teetering world settles onto a stable axis.

"Day from hell," I say.

"Week from hell, really."

"And hell yet to come."

He leans in to kiss my cheek. "So you've got your special injections all ready for Ryan?"

"I have."

"Tell me again what they do for him?"

"They inhibit his transformation. Ryan normally changes shapes every five days and stays in animal state for twenty-four to forty-eight hours. If he takes the serum, he can hold that off for another few weeks."

"Hey, maybe you should take some of that potion sometime."

I laugh softly. "Oh, I take all *kinds* of drugs, trying to control my shifting. I'm trying to find just the right formula that gets me both a predictable cycle and an acceptable alter ego. You know—trying to find a way to guarantee that I'll turn into a cat every three weeks. Then my life would still suck, but it would suck in a way that allowed me to make plans."

He takes my chin in his hand and tilts up my face to meet his gaze. "Your life does *not* suck," he says, and he sounds deadly serious. "You have friends who love you. Work that matters. A roof over your head, enough money to live on, and plenty to eat. So many people would envy you."

"Yeah," I say on a sigh. "I know you're right. It's just—"

"You're also as cute as can be," he says, giving me a quick kiss. "*And* you have a pretty hot boyfriend. I don't think your life sucks. I think your life is *great*."

Now my laugh is more genuine. "If my boyfriend is so hot, why are we just sitting here on the couch instead of making out in the bedroom?"

"Because he was trying to seem like somebody who could be emotionally supportive. Somebody who cared about *you*, who wasn't just interested in sex."

"But he *is* interested in sex?"

"Oh, yeah."

I put my arms around his neck and give him a deep kiss, as suggestive and full of promise as I can make it. "So am I," I whisper. "Let's get to it."

T his time it's almost eight in the morning when the phone rings. Joe and I are still asleep, curled up together in a warm and blissful tangle, when my cell starts pumping out the piano riffs of my ringtone.

"Seriously?" he groans.

"Swear to God, this only happens when I'm with you."

I grope for the phone, which I've left on my nightstand, and feel deep apprehension to see Aurelia's name on the screen. "What happened?" is my greeting.

"He's gone."

"Ryan? How?"

"Sheriff Wilkerson was pretty pissed off about it, because it sounds like it was all his fault. They'd decided to transfer Ryan to the Madison County jail today, so right around seven A.M., Wilkerson takes him from the cell and brings him outside. Ryan's in manacles, the sheriff says—feet and hands—so he thinks it's safe to leave him standing by one of the squad cars because it turns out he's brought the wrong set of keys. Wicked stupid, huh? When Wilkerson gets back outside less than two minutes later, Ryan's gone. Manacles are on the ground, still locked shut."

"Ryan saw his chance and he shifted," I say. That gets Joe's attention. He's lying back on the pillows with a forearm thrown over his eyes to block out the sunlight, but now he lowers his arm and gives me a questioning look. I nod.

"Looks like it," Aurelia says. "Sheriff doesn't know that, of course. He thinks Ryan's some kind of Houdini who managed to slip the cuffs somehow."

"Wonder what he thought when he saw the pile of clothes right there by the squad car."

"I don't know, and we have more important things to worry about," Aurelia says impatiently. "Such as the desperate manhunt that's currently under way. If there's not a cop at your place now, I'm sure one's going to show up within a few hours. Your place, our place, Celeste's place—they're going to be on us like white on rice."

"Surely Ryan knows that. Surely he won't come to any of us for help."

"Well, he hasn't exhibited much intelligence so far, so I wouldn't rule it out. But, yeah, the more likely course is that he's long gone. On the road to Chicago or Canada or God knows where. Someplace he can start over."

I take a deep breath and slowly let it out. "And we didn't have to choose," I say.

She sounds ever so slightly amused. "Our hands are clean."

"I feel horrible about all the rest of it, but kind of good about that part," I admit.

"I think Bonnie's relieved, too. Though, of course, she feels terrible that she feels relieved. She believes she should be strong enough to make tough moral decisions and stand by them."

I can't help grinning at that. "But why did they decide to move him so soon? I thought he'd be in the holding cell a while longer."

"Because you were right. They fed his fingerprints into the system and they got a match. To a crime scene up in Joliet."

Even though the information is hardly news, it still hits me like a punch in the stomach. It's a moment before I can draw in any air. "Then he better keep running," I finally say.

"That's what we all hope."

"So is there any reason I need to come to town today? Can I just stay here and live my own life for a few days?"

"I think that would be best. Celeste wants to go back to her own place and we've about decided she should. With the cops all over all of us, she'll probably be safer than she's been in years."

"That makes sense. All right. Good. Thanks for calling."

"Talk to you soon."

I switch off the phone, lay it aside, and drop back onto the bed, snuggling closer to Joe. He says, "I take it Ryan managed to get free without any timely intervention from your little band of jail-breakers."

"Yeah. He was left unattended as they prepared to transfer him to the county jail."

"Where do you think he'll go?"

"I don't know. He's got a brother somewhere—Seattle, I think—but they're not close. Has some friends. But surely the cops have frozen his assets. Surely he won't be able to use credit cards or ATM machines. I mean, when he shifts back to human state he won't have *anything*—clothes, wallet, phone, car—I don't know how he'll *get* anywhere. And since his face will be plastered all over the news media as an escaped murderer—" I shake my head, which is just now lying comfortably on Joe's shoulder. "He might not get very far."

"Ryan strikes me as someone who cold-bloodedly plans for contingencies," Joe says. "I wouldn't put it past him to have set up a cache of clothes and money somewhere in case he ever needed it."

"You could be right," I agree. "He won five thousand dollars at the casino a few weeks ago. That could be hiding somewhere in a buried treasure box, just waiting for him."

"So he gets away with murder," Joe says. "Until the next time."

I lift my head and look down at him. I haven't told him about Alonzo's father—not to spare Ryan, but to spare Alonzo. Joe already knows how hideous and mangled somebody's life was. I don't want him to look at Alonzo and know that was Alonzo's life. "Why do you say that?"

"Someone who believes he has the right to kill usually exercises that right more than once," Joe says. "But we'll hope that this time he doesn't."

"Hope hasn't done much for me the past few days," I mutter. "But maybe it'll come through just this once."

There's no chance of falling back to sleep, so we finally drag ourselves up and confront the day. My sleepiness wears off by the time I'm done with breakfast, and I find myself deeply happy to be back in my own world, my own routine, taking responsibility for my own assigned chores instead of relying on the helpfulness of strangers. The puppies and bunnies are fine, but I've sadly neglected the birds under my care, and before the day is out I've released two of them back into the wild.

Jinx follows me from field to barn to enclosure, trotting along self-importantly with his head held high and his tail straight out. He particularly loves our visit to the puppies in the dog run that used to be his, and he prances around on the other side of the chain-link, barking with smug superiority at the lesser creatures still stuck in captivity. I laugh so hard that I can hardly get the gate shut when I finally emerge.

I even have a chance to do a little honest-to-God veterinary work, since two of the clients who left voice mails for me are able to drive out this afternoon with very little notice. It feels good to be productive, to be useful, to be presented with problems that make sense and have simple solutions.

Aurelia was right about the cops, though—shortly before noon, a cruiser pulls onto the property and out of the car steps an officer who looks like she's about seventeen. No wonder Sheriff Wilkerson wants Joe to join the force. She's polite, I'm polite, but we don't have much valuable information to offer each other. I don't know where Ryan is and she can't tell me where they've already searched. But I get the point—and Ryan, if he's lurking out in the fields somewhere nearby, probably gets it, too. I'm under surveillance, and no escaped murderer is safe taking refuge with me.

Joe comes out and exchanges a few words with the officer before she leaves. I hadn't expected it, but apparently Joe has decided to stay out on the property with me all day. I'm not sure if this is because he doesn't have anything pressing to take care of in Quinville or if he's worried about what Terry Foucault might do—murder clearly being something in even more dire need of avenging than a barroom brawl. But Joe makes himself highly useful, fixing broken boards in the barn, rehanging a door in the second trailer, and picking up branches and other debris from the central clearing of the property.

"Trying to earn your keep?" I ask him that evening as I make dinner. He's emptying the dishwasher and setting the table for four.

"Trying to prove my worth," he answers. "I want you to see how valuable I would be to have around for the long haul."

My heart starts pounding madly, but I keep my voice level when I answer. "We have a few more hurdles to cross before we can be sure we're suited for long-term commitments," I say.

"Yep," he says. "You haven't done my laundry yet. Gotta see if you use too much bleach or fabric softener."

"But I thought *you* would do the laundry, dear. And the ironing, of course."

"Do people really iron these days?"

"Well, *I* don't, but I thought maybe you would."

I'm standing at the stove, and he steps up behind me and puts his arms loosely around my waist. "I have to see you through a few trans-formations," he says into my hair. "I have to see what that's like."

I don't twist my head around to look at him. "You'll think it's freaky. You'll think it's weird."

"Maybe. Or I'll think it's cool. Or I'll think it just *is*. But no matter what, I want to be around for the next one."

"Unless you're on the road."

"Okay, then the one after that. I want to be here. I want to share it. I want to put myself at the center of your life."

I don't even bother setting down the spatula; I turn within his arms so I can kiss him. "And I want to be at the center of yours."

"Venn diagram," he whispers against my mouth. "The best part is the part that overlaps."

CHAPTER SEVENTEEN

I'm awake when my cell phone goes off the next morning, but Joe isn't. Or, well, he wasn't. He skids from sleep with a start and a curse.

"Are you fucking *kidding* me?" he demands. "What *time* is it?"

"Six," I say as I dive for the phone. "Celeste, not Aurelia. That might be a good sign. Hey," I say into the mouthpiece.

"He's going to kill Terry," she says.

I sit straight up in bed. "What? He told you that?"

"No. I just figured it out. He's going to shift back sometime today, and he's going to go after Terry."

I put a hand to my forehead. Why am I having so much trouble thinking these days? *Because nothing that's happening is making any sense.*

"Celeste—are you sure?"

"I know how he thinks! Remember? I was just lying here thinking about what assholes the Foucault brothers are and how I still don't feel all that safe with Terry walking around with a gun license, and then I realized—Ryan will think the same thing. He'll decide I'm not safe. And he won't leave Quinville until he makes sure I am."

Every word she says makes me more convinced she's right. "All right. Then we—what do we do? Tell the sheriff?"

"No," she says sharply. "Are you insane? After all the trouble we were gonna have trying to get Ryan out of jail *once*? We have to take care of it."

"Take care of it *how*?"

"It'll be sometime today or early tomorrow that Ryan shifts," she says. She's talking so fast I can tell she's already come up with a plan. "Probably this afternoon—his past few cycles have been about thirty-six hours. We have to go stake out Terry's place and wait for Ryan to show up."

"The junkyard? Where passersby get shot at? I don't think so."

Now Joe pushes himself up on his elbow. "What the hell are you two plotting?"

"Is Joe there?" Celeste demands. "Can he hear you?"

"Yes and yes."

"Then go to another room while we talk this out."

Instead, I put her on speakerphone and lay the cell phone on the pillow between our bodies. "Hi, Celeste," Joe says.

"Dammit, Kara!"

"I'm not hatching up some crazy scheme without telling Joe about it!" I exclaim. "I'm *not*. So either deal with him, too, or count me out."

There's silence for a moment while she fumes. "He can't call the cops," she says.

I glance at Joe and he shrugs his bare shoulders. "Don't need to," he whispers to me. "They're all over you guys."

"He's okay with that," I say aloud. "So go on."

"I don't think we should go to the junkyard. Terry's in-laws own a farm a couple of miles east of Quinville, and Terry and his wife have been spending a lot of time there. Her mom's sick and her dad died last year, so there's a lot of work to do."

"How do you know *that*?"

"I know some people who know them, how do you think? It's a small town."

"Do you have an address for this farm?"

"Oh, I've been there. Ryan and I drove by it last week."

I look at Joe and shake my head. "After the shootout but before the assault in the parking lot?" I say in a dry voice.

"Yeah, something like that. Anyway, I think that's where Ryan will go. He'll expect the cops to be watching the junkyard. And my guess is—well—"

"Well, what?"

"Plenty of places out on the farm he could have stashed Aurelia's gun. For the next time he'd need it."

I groan and sink back against the headboard. But of course! Naturally! If you want to use your firearm again, you don't leave it in your car or your apartment or the scene of your first crime! You plant it on-site where you plan to commit your *next* murder!

"So you want us to go skulk around this farmhouse for the next day or two, waiting for Ryan to show up. And you don't think anyone will notice us. And you think we'll be able to catch Ryan before he sneaks in some back window and puts a bullet in Terry Foucault."

"I didn't say it was a good plan," she retorts. "But yeah. That's what I think we should do."

"And why do you think we'll be able to convince him just to walk away?"

"We'll bring him clothes and money. We'll tell him that we'll only help him if he leaves—otherwise, we'll call the cops. We'll tell him that he's only making life worse for *us*. That we've been repeatedly questioned by the cops, even threatened. That Sheriff Wilkerson said he'd hold me as an accessory to murder."

"He might buy that last one," I admit.

"I think he will," she says. "I think he had no clue how badly this could go and he knows he's not thinking clearly and he might be willing to listen to us. Just this once."

I let out a long sigh of surrender. I'm not happy about it but I simply don't know what else to do. The world has gotten very murky since I started accumulating moral dilemmas.

"All right. When do you want me to be there? Is noon soon enough?"

"Can you make it ten? If he shifts sooner—"

"All right, all right," I grumble. "I'll pack snacks and water bottles and—I guess I'll see you in a few hours."

Joe leans over to make sure the phone picks up his voice. "We'll see you later," he says.

She's silent for a moment. "You're not invited," she says.

"Too bad."

"Kara—!" she whines.

"He wants to come, he can come," I say. "This is a nightmare no matter what."

Now she's the one to sigh in capitulation and frustration. "*Fine*. But don't tell Bonnie and Aurelia."

"Wouldn't dream of it. See you later."

We take Joe's truck but leave the dogs behind. On the one hand, I think Jinx would probably alert us to Ryan's presence before we noticed him on our own. On the other hand, if bullets are going to be flying, Jinx and Jezebel are much safer back at my place.

We arrive at Celeste's right at the appointed time, and she has indeed put together a duffel bag for Ryan filled with food, water, clothes, a burner phone, and about five hundred dollars in cash. I'm assuming she went to Walmart this morning to buy most of the items. I never would have thought of the phone, but I approve. We'll be able to keep in touch with Ryan, at least till the charge runs down or the prepaid account runs out.

She climbs into the back of the extended cab, where I've loaded a couple of coolers and tons of other supplies to make the day pass more comfortably—a few blankets, some pillows, a roll of paper towels, two rolls of toilet paper, and hand sanitizer.

"What the hell, Kara, we're not on a camping trip," she complains as she situates herself among the bags and bundles.

"I didn't bring a tent," I retort. "And I thought about it."

"Someone in the house would probably see a tent," she says.

"Someone in the house will probably see the truck!"

"I don't think so. If I remember the layout, there's a good lookout spot on top of a hill behind some trees. We can hide there."

Joe exits her parking lot and turns onto the main street. "So where are we heading?"

Celeste gives him directions and we follow 159 past the Strip before we turn off on a series of back roads. The last one's so isolated I'm not even sure it's got a name or designation, and though it's paved, the asphalt has degraded so much that you'd be forgiven for thinking the surface is gravel. On both sides of us, the countryside is mile after mile of cornfields, the dry stalks stiff and pale as old lace. Here and there the plowed fields are interrupted by stands of scraggly trees clustering around a shallow pond or a halfhearted stream. Now and then, an architectural feature will rise above the level landscape—a red barn, a white house, a silver silo.

I spend about five miles thinking there will be no place to hide either a truck or a raiding party, but then Celeste directs Joe to turn onto a dirt road that I would have missed completely if I'd been the one driving. About a half mile in, it splits. To the right, it comes almost immediately to an abandoned barn, its front doors hanging loose from the hinges, its paint so weathered you can see the blistering wood beneath it. To the left, the road snakes past a rise in the ground that's dotted with a stand of skinny poplars, probably planted as a windbreak about a million years ago. Beyond the trees we can see that the road leads to a cluster of buildings—house, sheds, another barn—and then the inevitable patchwork of crop fields. Corn and maybe soybeans. Hard to tell, since the harvest is long over.

"See?" says Celeste. "We can leave the truck behind this old place, and creep up the hill to watch the farmhouse. No one will see us from the house *or* the road."

"It *does* look like the perfect spot for surveillance," Joe agrees, guiding the truck to the right. The dirt road is bumpy with rocks and clumps of dried mud, but it feels smoother than the broken asphalt. "So if no one spots us as we're making our campsite, we're probably good for hours."

The doors to the barn aren't quite decrepit enough for Joe to drive the truck straight in, so he pulls off the dirt track and parks behind it. We load ourselves up with comforts and necessities, then hike over to the trees, up the gentle bump in the ground that barely qualifies as a hill. No one comes driving up to catch us in our not-very-stealthy enterprise, and we don't spot anyone crossing the open space between the porch and the outbuildings as we settle ourselves in for a long wait.

Given that it's November, we've got great weather for a stakeout. It's probably close to fifty degrees, and the sun is blasting down on us from a cloudless sky. There isn't even a breeze to whip up a wind chill. I'm wearing enough layers to see me through an Alaskan winter, so I'm pretty toasty, though that might change after a few hours of sitting on the cold ground.

If we were here for any other purpose on God's earth, I might say this was a pleasant outing.

"So where do you think Ryan is hiding?" I ask Celeste once we've taken our spots. She and I are on one of the blankets, lying on our stomachs, watching the compound below. She's actually brought a pair of binoculars, although, after one quick sweep of the property, she lays them aside. "Or do you think he's not here yet?"

"I think he's here, somewhere close to the house. Probably behind one of the buildings."

"Do you think he's seen us?"

"Hard to say."

"Will he come over to us if he has?"

She debates. "I don't think so. Because he'll realize we're here to stop him—and it's going to take some convincing to make him stop."

Joe is stretched out on another blanket, his head resting on a backpack, an open book propped on his stomach. I can't believe anyone could have the concentration to read in such a setting, but maybe he's just pretending, because he looks up at Celeste's comment.

"You're the one who can always figure out what Ryan's thinking," he says. "Where'd he stash the gun? If we can find that, this thing could be over before it started."

I point back toward the truck. "In the old barn? That would make sense."

"Maybe," Celeste says. "But I'm thinking closer to the house. Like, right under the porch or something. Or back behind the air conditioner. *Really* close."

Joe's eyes narrow. "Why do you think that?"

She doesn't look at him, but I'm close enough to see her troubled expression. "Because I think he probably came here straight from the junkyard after he killed Bobby. Hoping to get Terry the same night. But Terry didn't show, or there were too many people around when Terry did drive up, or he couldn't get a clear shot. Whatever. I think he was right there close enough to touch the house, and so that's where he left the gun."

"Makes sense," Joe says, and drops his attention back to his book.

The next two hours creep by more slowly than I thought time could actually pass.

Celeste and I are both on high alert, which makes us edgy, but it's hard to maintain a constant focus on a landscape that shows little movement or change. Now and then we see shadows shuffling behind the windows of the house, and we nudge each other, but whoever is inside doesn't come out. Probably Terry's mother-in-law, I think. Maybe his wife as well. A rooster comes strutting around the side of the barn but disappears again after a few moments. A hawk circles overhead and we both watch it, wondering if it's Ryan and his shifting cycle has been somehow disrupted. But if it is Ryan, he doesn't settle on any of the nearby trees before winging away in silence.

We don't try very hard to make conversation, because there's not much to talk about. We've said everything we can think of about Ryan, and we can't talk about Joe because he's sitting right here. Neither of us brought anything to read, and I don't want to run down the batteries on my phone by playing games on it. Besides, I don't want to be distracted—I don't want to miss seeing Ryan as he slips from the barn to the house, or from the fields to the front lawn.

If Celeste is right. If he actually comes here. The longer the hours stretch out, the more doubtful I am. If he has any sense, he's already a hundred miles away, and we're idiots for spying on some poor old woman and her family out in the middle of an Illinois cornfield.

But Celeste has always been right about Ryan, always been in sync with his moods and his motivations. I was always the one who was just a little out of step.

Around three, Joe makes a cautious trip to the truck to fetch more water and food. Just as he's dropped back to the ground, we hear the low grumble of a car motor drawing nearer. Since we've arrived, we've caught the intermittent sounds of vehicles rattling past on the nearest paved road but none of them have made the turn onto the dirt track—until now. We flatten ourselves on our blankets and try to stop breathing entirely. There's simply nothing else out here. Whoever's arriving has to be headed to this house.

In a moment we spot a rusty blue pickup jouncing down the dirt road; it barely slows as it takes the left turn toward the farmhouse. We can make out two people sitting in the front seat, but we can't tell who they are until the truck stops and they step out.

Terry Foucault and his wife. She heads straight up the steps, a brown paper grocery bag in her arms.

Terry leans against the front fender and pulls a pack of cigarettes out of his pocket.

"Shit," Celeste breathes.

Shit, indeed. Terry has made himself into the perfect target.

Only if Ryan is here, of course, bent on murder.

B ut he is.

CHAPTER EIGHTEEN

There's the faintest movement along the side of the house, hardly more than the shadow of trees brushing along the exterior wall with a shift in the wind. I strain, trying to see more clearly. Is it a black cat—Ryan's typical incarnation? I think so. But it might just be a house pet, or a stray, by happenstance out hunting at this location this very afternoon. But Celeste grabs my arm with a grip tight enough to snap a bone, and I nod. *I see him.*

While we watch, the stalking cat loses its color, loses its shape, turns pale, turns tan, puffs up, stretches out, and resolves itself into a man. He's naked and barefoot and a little battered looking, but none of that makes him seem helpless or vulnerable. Staying down in a low crouch, he inches closer to the front of the house, his left hand trailing along the join between the poured foundation and the weathered siding. Somewhere in that small seam he's found a storage spot, because suddenly he steps away from the house, and he's got a gun in his hand. A sniper might be able to take Terry out from where

Ryan's standing right now, but he's not that accurate of a marksman; he's going to have to step away from the protection of the house to get a clear shot.

Celeste jumps up and screams, *"Terry! Look out!"*

I'm also on my feet and I hear Joe clamber up behind me. Terry's head whips around, but he drops to the ground and rolls under his truck like he's been practicing for duck-and-cover his whole life. I see Ryan's face pull into a scowl. He gestures wildly at Celeste, waving her back, and abandons all caution. He runs forward, still in that half-crouch, now bent over to try to aim low enough to shoot under the truck.

Celeste starts down the hill, waving frantically. "Ryan, no! Wait! Listen to me!"

He actually lifts the pistol as if he's going to shoot her, which surprises her so much she comes to a dead halt. I crash into her, and Joe almost knocks both of us off balance. "Stay back!" Ryan calls. "I'm going to kill him!"

Then another voice says, "I wouldn't do that, son, if I were you."

Everybody freezes.

The world stands so still for so long that I get a perfectly clear, perfectly framed glimpse of everybody gathered at the scene. Terry, rolled into a ball under his truck, hands wrapped protectively over his head.

Two women at the front windows of the house, one my age, one twenty years older, their faces wearing identical looks of fear and horror.

Celeste, a delicate, gorgeous statue of love, pain, and betrayal. Joe, a big, solid sentinel of sanity.

Ryan, poised like an Olympic athlete right before a competition begins. One arm is outstretched and level, pointing the gun toward the truck, one is flung up before him, as if to fend off rivals. He stands on the balls of his feet, ready to leap or run, and every muscle on his naked body stands out in perfect relief.

Sheriff Wilkerson, not twenty yards from Ryan, his own arm out-stretched, his own hand holding a gun.

"Put down your weapon, son," the sheriff says now. His sleepy Southern drawl sounds just as warm, just as soothing, as it always does, but on his face is an unyielding look of absolute conviction. "You don't want to be doing any more killing."

Ryan hesitates for a second, then swings around and points his gun at the sheriff. Celeste screams and starts down the hill again, but Joe grabs her and hauls her back. We don't need anybody else in the line of fire.

"I got nothing to lose by shooting you," Ryan says, his voice so low and guttural I almost don't recognize it.

"Right back at you," the sheriff replies.

For a moment, the tableau holds, no one moving, no one breath-ing, unless you count Celeste whimpering and squirming against Joe's iron hold. Ryan and Wilkerson are so engrossed in each other they don't seem to notice that Terry has cautiously unfolded himself and is now crawling forward on his belly, trying to make it to the safety of the house. The geometry of the gunfight is in his favor, because the truck is between Ryan and the porch. Once Terry's clear of the chassis, he pushes himself to a crouch and starts a quick, crabbed run for the porch.

But Ryan sees him, or hears him, because he whips around. "Fuck!" he cries, and shoots three times. Terry yelps and claps a hand to his shoulder, but he doesn't seem fatally wounded. Within seconds he's dashed inside the front door, which has been flung open by one of the women inside. Ryan fires again in clear frustration.

There's a report from a different gun, and Ryan howls and drops the pistol, cradling his bleeding hand against his chest and staring at Wilkerson.

"I guess you want to do this the hard way," the sheriff says. He lifts his arm and sights down the barrel.

And then finally, finally, Ryan shows some sense. He whirls around and he runs. He runs. He stays on level ground but he heads away from the house, along the dirt road, straight toward the broken-down barn and the open land that will take him to freedom.

"Son of a bitch," the sheriff curses, and takes off after him, holstering his gun.

Ryan's probably ten years younger than Wilkerson, but the sheriff's in good shape and he's not barefoot. There can't be more than fifty feet between them and it's not hard to picture that distance closing fast.

"He's got to change," Celeste mutters as the three of us pivot to watch the chase unfold. We're still on high enough ground that we can see the whole thing with absolute clarity, although within ten seconds, both the runner and the pursuer are out of sight of the house. "He can't outrun Wilkerson on human feet."

"Can he change that quickly again after he just transformed?" Joe asks.

"Yes," we say in unison.

"But it's hard to do in motion," Celeste adds.

"And he's wounded," I remind her.

"It's his only chance."

Do I want him to escape? My longtime friend, my ex-lover, a member of the select secret society that I have belonged to my whole life. I watch him fleeing past the old barn, across the open field, the picture of untamed wild beauty being pursued by implacable civilization. I find my hands clenched and my chest too tight to breathe. *Go, Ryan!* I want to shout. *Go!*

So I guess I do. I want him to escape. I want him to live.

He takes three swift strides, then seems to stumble, seems to trip to his knees, and Celeste can't hold back a cry. She wrenches free from Joe and goes tearing down the hill after them. There is nothing we can do but trail behind.

But Ryan hasn't fallen. He's collapsed in on himself, tucked himself in; he seems to somersault across an old furrow of cropland. When he rights himself, he's a fox, red and slender, built for speed. He stretches out in a graceful sprint almost too quick to follow.

"Yes," Celeste sobs, coming to a halt and burying her face in her hands. "Oh God, we didn't even get to say good-bye to him." She lifts her head and whispers, "Run, Ryan, run."

If Sheriff Wilkerson is dumbfounded at what he just saw, he doesn't stop to bellow out his astonishment. If anything, he seems to pour on the speed until his body is almost a blur. The tan of his uniform glows golden in the sun—but it's not a uniform, it's a coat of fur—and he's doubled over, as if he's fallen to his hands and knees, but he's still running unbelievably fast—

He's changed. The sheriff has shifted shapes.

He's a cheetah, and he is faster than any fox, any animal, any day.

Celeste shrieks and sprints after them, moving in such a pell-mell fashion that she slips and falls, slips and falls, twice before I can catch up with her. I'm terrified she's going to take her own animal shape and go bounding after them, and I grab her arm and start shaking her like a madwoman.

"Don't do it! Don't do it! You can't help him! Stay with me!"

"But he's—but they're— Kara, he'll kill him—"

The sheriff will kill Ryan. The cheetah will kill the fox. I don't know the upper size limit of the kinds of animals cheetahs can bring down, but a fox seems well within their range.

"Maybe you'd better look away," Joe says suddenly from behind us.

But we can't.

The cheetah is five yards behind the fox—two feet—he's sprung onto the back of the fleeing red animal and he rakes the smaller creature to the ground. Celeste wails, breaks free, and starts running again, just as awkwardly, slipping and stumbling as she crosses the dirt road and plunges into the abandoned field. Joe and I lope after her. Just as well, maybe—while we're in motion, our heads bobbing up and down, the scene ahead of us isn't as clear. I see the big cat swipe its paws, once, twice, against the fox's brushy red fur; I see the slim, sinewy legs of the fox scrabble against the air.

But we're still half a field behind by the time the fox stops struggling, all its limbs falling nervelessly to the ground. From this distance, against the green-and-brown of the cropland, the vivid color of the fox's fur, it's impossible to see any blood. But its head is snapped back at an unnatural angle, and its four feet are splayed before it.

And then, while we are still too far away to touch him, the fox begins transmuting into the shape of a man.

Which means that Ryan is dead or dying.

Celeste sobs again and redoubles her pace, but I slack up and finally stop, letting her go to him alone. Despite the fact that Ryan and I had been lovers, in so many ways Celeste was closer to him. They'd always had that supernatural bond, that inexplicable connection, as if they were twins, or soul mates. On the one hand, it seems almost poetic that he died defending her honor.

On the other hand, it seems dreadful beyond description that she is the reason he is dead.

The cheetah has moved off a little distance by the time Celeste falls to her knees at Ryan's side. I see her put one hand on his cheek, one on his heart; I hear her chant his name over and over. In his human state, the fatal wounds are easy to see, most of them centered over his jugulars, but his whole torso is bloody. Celeste doesn't care.

She puts her arms around Ryan's shoulders and pulls him onto her lap, bending down to rest her dark curls against his pale face.

I stand back far enough to let her grieve in private, but close enough that, if she looks around for me, I can be at her side in two seconds. Joe comes up behind me and puts an arm around my shoulders. I lean against him for a moment, drawing in strength, drawing in warmth, trying to regain my balance.

I notice that he's carrying something in his left hand, a bag or a length of fabric, and I squint down to get a better look. That's when I realize he's paused to pick up the uniform the sheriff shed in his mad chase after Ryan.

"Did you know about Wilkerson?" he asks quietly.

I shake my head dumbly. *Janet knew,* I think. It's the only thing that explains how much she trusted him, how much he liked her. He had sworn her to secrecy, though, or so I assume, and being Janet, she was never even tempted to reveal what she knew.

I lift my eyes from the sight of Celeste still on her knees, still holding Ryan's lifeless body, and I look for the cheetah again. Oh, but he's a man now, beefy, confident, naked, striding purposefully in my direction. I can see traces of blood around his mouth, on the backs of his hands, but they're smeared, like he's tried to wipe them off in a patch of grass.

Joe leans forward to hand over his clothes. Wilkerson says, "Thank you, son," and pulls on his pants and shirt and gunbelt. He doesn't look anywhere near his usual trim and professional self, but he looks more normal, more human, more like a lawman. Less like a wild beast.

He angles his head to study Celeste and Ryan for a moment, then turns his attention back to the two of us. His gaze is absolutely steady as he meets Joe's eyes and then mine.

"I'm sorry you folks had to see that," he says in his molasses voice. "Which part?" Joe asks.

Wilkerson's smile acknowledges the hit. "I meant the death. Though I'm not too eager to have people see me changing."

"Woulda been a lot more shocked by that a few months ago," Joe says.

Wilkerson nods. "I figured you were hanging out with enough shape-shifters that you'd already learned the truth."

"How did you know about us?" I demand. "When none of us knew about you? Did Janet tell you?"

He shakes his head. "I just guessed about you, because of where you lived and how you lived, taking on Janet's work. I didn't know about your friends here until that little incident at Arabesque. I mean, obviously Bobby was telling the truth and obviously you both knew it. But there seemed to be no need to say so out loud."

"How'd you find us today?" Joe asks. "Follow us?"

The sheriff nods. "Ahuh. Figured something like this would happen, just didn't know where Mr. Barnes planned to go next."

"You let him go on purpose," I suddenly realize. "At the police station. You didn't pick up the wrong keys—you took him outside and left him alone so he could change. So he could escape."

"Yes, ma'am. I am fully alive to all the disastrous consequences that might ensue if a shifter changes shapes in a public place."

I put a hand to my head. Again, I'm having so much trouble thinking things through. I suppose I haven't quite registered the shock of Ryan's death, which is why I can stand here calmly having this surreal conversation. "But then you—you *wanted* him to be free. You *didn't* think he should be punished. All this time—I've been trying to figure out what I should do—and I couldn't decide. But you made that decision."

"Well, now," he says regretfully. "It's a little more complicated than that. I did let him go, that's a fact. But I kinda thought he'd pull a stupid stunt like this. So you could say I set him up for this very ending."

Now I'm watching him with a cold and accusatory stare. "You murdered him," I say in a hard voice. "Just like he murdered those others. Because you thought you had the right to decide who lives and who dies."

His voice is as hard as mine. "I killed him in the line of duty as he was about to commit a capital offense. I'm paid to make those decisions as I carry out my responsibilities protecting the citizens of this state. If he'd never come here with the intent to commit murder, I never would have caught him. The choices your friend made are the ones that have seen him wind up dead."

I'm too angry and too confused to tell if he's right or not, so I look away. Joe gives my shoulders a squeeze and asks, "What happens now? Gonna be kind of hard to explain away cause of death on this particular body."

Wilkerson sighs and nods. "I know. I think I'm just going to have to say that Ryan Barnes got away and tell my staff to be on the lookout for him. Not a bad thing, maybe—I'll tell Terry he better leave Miss Celeste alone or Mr. Barnes will surely return to finish what he started. After today, I think he'll believe me. That'll be a way to help keep him in line."

I gesture toward Ryan and Celeste. "So then what happens to the—to Ryan?"

"I've got some property over by Springfield—farmland, 'bout as isolated as this. I'll take the body there and bury it."

"No," I say instantly. "We'll bury him on my land. It's where he belongs. Plenty of other dead shape-shifters on those grounds."

Wilkerson gives me a keen look. "Including Janet, I take it?"

"She wasn't a shape-shifter."

"But she's dead, isn't she?" When I nod, he looks sad but unsurprised. "You'll have to tell me all about it someday."

"Maybe," I reply. *Probably not.*

Wilkerson looks around, studies Celeste for a moment, glances back at Joe and me. "Well," he says. "Not much else we can do here. I'll go talk to Terry, see how bad he's hurt, give him some story about what happened. You willing to put Mr. Barnes in your truck and take him back to Miss Karadel's place?"

"Yeah," Joe says. "I've got some tarps in back. Help me carry him to the truck? I'm parked behind the barn there."

"Will do." Wilkerson claps Joe on the shoulder. "Damn, boy. Sure wish you'd reconsider being on the force. It would be right helpful to have someone who *knew* and could watch my back."

Joe glances at me. "Yeah," he says. "Well, maybe. We can talk later."

The men wait while I go talk to Celeste. She's grown calmer but no less despairing. The look she gives me can only be described as heartrending. I bend over and put my hand on her shoulder.

"We're going to take Ryan back to my place," I say gently. "You have to let him go now, so they can carry him to the truck."

Her hands and her cheeks are streaked with blood. Given that she's still got bruises on her face and wrists, she looks ghastly. "I can't stop crying," she whispers.

I change my grip, trying to urge her to her feet. "You don't have to."

"How will I ever get over it? Ever, *ever*?"

"I don't know," I say. "You hope to remember the good and try to forget the bad. But I don't know if that's even possible. Come on, baby, stand up. Put Ryan down and let them take him."

In response, she clings tighter. "I can't—I'm not ready—"

I let go of her shoulder so I can use both hands to try to break her grip on Ryan. "We have to go. Before Terry and his family start getting curious. Before they come out of the house and look for us and try to figure out what happened. We've almost been discovered at every turn, but if we can just get out of here now without being seen—"

She fends me off with an elbow. "Maybe we *should* be seen," she says angrily. "Maybe *none* of this would have happened if shapeshifters could come out of the shadows and just *be*. Maybe it's time for us to step forward and announce who we are and let the world just *deal* with it."

"Maybe," I say, successfully wrapping my fingers around her wrists and pulling her hands away from Ryan's body. "But we can talk about it later. When we're home. When you're calmer. When none of us are quite so sad."

Abruptly, Celeste spins around on her knees to throw her arms around me. I sink to the ground next to her and pull her into an embrace, and feel her whole body shudder as she sobs into my shirt. I pat the wild curls, I whisper reassurance into her ear, I keep her face turned away as Joe and Sheriff Wilkerson slip up next to us and grab hold of Ryan's body and haul it away.

I don't know how to comfort her. I can't possibly make it better, any of it—what happened today, what led up to these disastrous events. All I can do is hold her in my arms and let her cry.

CHAPTER NINETEEN

A couple days later we have a sort of ceremony at my house. Joe's already dug a grave and buried the body; I know Helena and Juliet saw him, but they don't ask any questions. Well. They can figure out part of it on their own. *Shape-shifter dead as a consequence of his precarious life.* They know Juliet and Desi might come to such ignominious ends someday, and they can only hope someone takes care of them.

Celeste has stayed with me since the incident—not so much because she chooses to, but because we brought her back to my place on that awful day and refused to take her back to town and she doesn't have her own car and she hasn't bothered to steal the keys to mine. She's as quiet and defeated as I've ever seen her and I'm not sure how to help her, but I hope she'll eventually work her way through mourning to acceptance.

Which is where I am, I think. I want Ryan back—the Ryan I

thought I knew—the dashing, unpredictable lover, the wayward but stubbornly loyal friend. But that Ryan had a shadow twin, an alter ego more dangerous than any of his wild shapes. And you cannot have one without the other. I miss him so much that there are moments I have to stop whatever I'm doing and wait out a spasm of dizzying grief. But there are moments a small whispering voice in my head expresses relief that Ryan is gone.

Bonnie and Aurelia and Alonzo come out for the memorial service. We've told them everything, of course. I'm guessing Sheriff Wilkerson would prefer that we didn't disclose the truth about him to anybody else, but he's not the only one in this particular drama who doesn't get everything he wants. And if there's anybody I trust with a shape-shifter's secret, it's Aurelia and Bonnie.

"I'm saving this up for someday when I really need leverage against him," Aurelia says. I think she's joking, but with Aurelia, you never know.

The day we've planned for the service is as bright and warm as the day Ryan died. Joe seems to realize that his presence would be awkward, so he stays back at the house making a meal while the five of us tramp out to the freshly dug grave. Celeste immediately sinks down and rests her hands on the churned earth, but the rest of us stand there, looking down, solemn and briefly silent.

Bonnie is the first one to speak. "He was a good man and a terrible man. Like all of us—flawed and striving. Generous and careless. Loving and cruel. Our lives are richer and stranger and sadder for him having passed through." She drops a red rose on the grave.

Aurelia tosses a white rose on top of Bonnie's. "He challenged me, he made me think, he never let me take the easy way or the first answer," she says. "I will have to look a long time before I meet someone like Ryan again."

I've brought a bouquet of five yellow roses, since that's what Ryan gave me on our first date. "I loved him," I say. "Even when I stopped loving him."

Alonzo stoops over and slips something between the flowers. I think it's a rock or a marble—something that has significance for him, but I don't know what it is. "He saved my life," is all he says.

Celeste places a wreath on top of the flowers, something she's woven herself from branches and ivy she's collected from my property over the past few days. "He was my first friend—my best friend—the person who understood me the most," she whispers. "I don't know who I am without him. I will carry him in my heart until I die."

Aurelia falls in beside me as we walk slowly back from the gravesite to the house. Odd—of the two of them, I've always felt closer to Bonnie, but in these past few days it's Aurelia I've relied on more heavily for strength and guidance. Maybe because this whole situation has come close to breaking Bonnie, but nothing could ever break Aurelia, and I've needed to lean against something that wouldn't give way.

"There's been one small bit of good to come out of this tragedy," she says in a low voice.

"Oh, do tell me what. I need to hear something good."

She nods to where Alonzo is ambling alongside Celeste and putting some effort into making conversation with her. Attempting, in his own way, to comfort her. I can tell she realizes how hard he's trying and so she's putting equal effort into responding. Smiling, even. I think they're talking football, but it hardly matters.

"He told us everything. About his dad. About Ryan coming to

take him away. About Ryan killing his father. He said he was never sure if we knew and if we approved. So he never said anything before."

I feel my eyes widen. "That's huge. He's never even talked about his dad before, has he?"

She shakes her head. For a moment, I think I see tears in her big gray eyes. "I think he finally trusts us. I think he finally believes that we're never going to hurt him or let him down."

I see Celeste put a hand on Alonzo's shoulder, then lean in to kiss his cheek. He makes a *yuck!* sound and tries to pull away from the kiss, but he doesn't shrug off her hand. They continue on like that for the rest of the way to the house.

"Never going to let him go," I say softly. "None of us are ever going to let *any* of the others go."

The meal starts out somber, but slowly, insensibly, we begin to cheer up. There are other things to talk about besides murder and betrayal, after all. The world blunders on whether you want it to or not, and sometimes it's a relief to feel it dragging you in its orbital wake. Joe starts joshing Alonzo about something that happened at basketball practice, Aurelia tells Celeste about a case she's working on, and I give Bonnie the skimpy information I have about Helena and her daughters. Now and then I see people smile. Twice I hear someone laugh.

It might take longer than we'd like. But we'll all recover.

Aurelia is the one to push away from the table and say, "I have to go. I've got a client to meet later this afternoon and some paperwork to finish beforehand."

Celeste grabs her arm. "*Please,* for the love of *God,* take me back with you. They've kept me *prisoner* here for the past few days, and I swear to everybody that I'll be fine. Just let me go *home*."

We laugh at her dramatics, but I realize that, between the assault and the calamity, it's been more than a week since Celeste was at her own apartment. No wonder she's going nuts.

"All right, you can go," I say. "But you have to check in with me twice a day, or I'm coming to town and moving in with you."

"Horrors!" she exclaims. "I'll check in every *hour* if that's what it takes to keep you away."

Aurelia snaps her fingers impatiently. "Okay, but you have to go *now*. Come on. Pack up your stuff. We're leaving."

Celeste races upstairs to the guest room to gather her things. I walk the others out to Aurelia's BMW while Joe stays behind to clean up the kitchen. "I know you're in a hurry, but drive carefully," I say as I hug Aurelia good-bye.

She laughs. "I'm the best driver on the road."

I turn to Bonnie and take her in a hard embrace. She feels more fragile to me, as if her bony body has endured more blows this week than she can easily withstand. "You take care of yourself," I whisper in her ear. "You let me know if you need anything."

She doesn't even ask me what I mean. Trust Bonnie not to indulge in pretense. "I'll be fine," she says. "Eventually."

I turn to Alonzo. "You, too," I say. "Let me know if you need anything."

"I will."

"And call Celeste now and then. You know."

"I will," he says again.

I hug him, and for the first time in his life he hugs me back.

I'm still recovering from the shock of that when Celeste comes running out of the house, waving wildly and shouting, "Wait for me!

Wait for me!" It's all for show, and it makes me laugh, and I laugh harder when she slams into me. She squeezes me tight, lets me go, and lunges for the car. "Love you!" she calls, waving from the window. Then she points to the house. "Marry him!"

There's a general chorus of assent from the other occupants of the BMW. Aurelia even rolls her window down to say, "Couldn't agree more!" Then she backs up and takes off down W with barely a spit of gravel.

I trudge back to the house feeling simultaneously lighter and heavier now that all of them are gone.

In the kitchen, Joe has just finished loading the dishwasher and wiping the table. "Are you the *perfect* man?" I inquire.

He smiles and comes over to take me in a loose embrace. I lean against him and feel, for a moment, content and free of worry.

"I am," he says. "'Bout time you noticed."

"My friends love you."

"Better if *you* loved me."

His voice is so casual that it's a moment before what he says has registered. Then I feel my veins prickle with heat and my breath grow shallow in my chest. I lift my head to meet his eyes.

"I *do* love you," I say firmly.

He kisses me swiftly. "See how easy that was? I love you, too."

"You haven't even seen me change yet," I remind him.

"Change? But I like you just the way you are!"

I free a hand to swat him on the shoulder. "You know what I mean."

He grins. "I know what you mean. But I'm not worried about it. After what I've seen and what I know—" He shrugs. "I think I'll take it in stride. I don't think it'll faze me at all."

"And you won't even see it happen very often," I say, "unless you're out here all the time. I mean, like, maybe, if you were living here."

"Living here," he repeats. "Now that's an idea with a lot of merit."

"The dogs like it here."

"They do."

"And you're very handy to have around."

"I'm glad you think so."

"And think of all the money you could save on rent!"

"The primary reason I would consider such an idea."

I look up at him a little anxiously. I can tell he's teasing, but sometimes he uses humor to cover his real feelings. "I mean, no pressure," I add. "It might be too soon to even talk about."

He drops another kiss on my mouth. "I've been trying to figure out how to bring it up," he says. "I didn't want to seem too pushy. Didn't want to overstep my bounds."

I wrap both arms around his neck. "No bounds at all," I whisper. "Let's do this up right."

It's around midnight that night when I think to check e-mail for the first time in days. Joe's sound asleep, but I'm restless, so I prowl through the house double-checking all the doors and windows before I settle in the kitchen and make myself some tea. I've brought in my laptop, so now I set it on the kitchen table and log in to my account. Among the inquiries from clients and the junk mail from advertisers, I find a new message from Janet's mom:

I don't want to alarm you, dear, but it turns out I've been diagnosed with breast cancer. The doctors seem confident that they can treat it with surgery and no radiation, but I have to say it's made me start thinking hard about all the unfinished business in my life. And my daughter is the most unfinished business I have.

I know you're not Janet. I've known for a long time. But it comforted me so much to hear from someone who knew her that I've just let the charade go on. I suppose you could be some kind of shyster, lying to me for no good reason, but I've always thought you must be somebody kind. Somebody who understood how hard it is to maintain relationships with the people we love and who thought it was worth trying anyway.

And now I just thought I'd ask—will you tell me the truth? Will you let me know what happened to Janet, and who you are, and what you're really like? I just want to know. The older I get, the less I care for secrets. And the closer I get to death, the less patience I have for lying.

I hope to hear from you soon.

Love,
Nina Kassebaum

I read this extraordinary letter three times before I take another sip of tea. And then I sit there for another half hour trying to decide how to answer her. How much do I tell her about Cooper? Because Cooper is the heart of Janet's story. Nina might be tired of secrets, but this one has never been up to me to reveal.

I can't tell her the biggest part, the most unbelievable part, I finally decide, but I can give her a version of the truth. I can tell her that Cooper was an artist—I can send her one of his original paintings of Janet, which I think she'll cherish very much. I can tell her that he had a medical condition that kept him mostly confined to the house and took his life too young, and that Janet had let grief send her, too, into an early grave.

I can let her know that despite her short, isolated, eccentric life, Janet experienced deep passion and fierce joy. She had figured out how to wrest happiness from her unconventional existence—she knew what it looked like to her and what she had to do to keep it.

As I intend to do. As I believe I can. I will gather my friends tightly around me and hold on, and never let go, and never give up. I will love without fear and face change without trepidation. I will start celebrating the gifts life brings me, no matter how bitter, on some days, they seem. And I will never, inside the curse, stop searching for the blessing.

ACKNOWLEDGMENTS AND THANKS

To Tami Beckeman, who patiently provided me with insights into being a vet. And cooked the meal!

To Rachel Neumeier, who came up with some cool ideas about shape-shifter science.

(It's not their fault if I didn't always listen to what they said.)

And to Ginjer Buchanan, who was my editor for twenty years. Thanks for the great advice, the wonderful dinners, and the always-entertaining conversation.